Fred's Gospel

(A tale of significant coincidences)

by

Trevor Danby

www.trevordanby.com

**Grosvenor House
Publishing Limited**

This book is published by
Grosvenor House Publishing Ltd
28-30 High Street, Guildford, Surrey, GU1 3HY.
www.grosvenorhousepublishing.co.uk

A CIP record for this book
is available from the British Library

ISBN 978-1-907211-64-5

Acknowledgements

To Kate for her patience while fictional characters monopolized my time.

To Emma for her detailed corrections and to Jan for her encouraging interest and critique.

To the Father of creative instinct, who sent me characters to write about, and cherished friends to shape my own story.... in the hope that the fiction mirrors the real world that mirrors the spiritual.

Cover design by Hilary Perona-Wright

The Last Word. .

Tim, a twenty-seven year old purveyor of art reproductions, and stranger to the north with nowhere to go on a Sunday, strolled in through the municipal park gates, past the small piddling fountain and the curved plots of bare soil confined by hoops of low wire edging, and on towards a bench that faced the duck pond. There were a few remaining leaves on the trees, reminding him of the last remnants at a 'bring-and-buy' sale. The ducks, waddling disconsolately, were not up to strutting before soggy crust throwers; and, anyway, nobody was throwing them today. Neither was the day throwing a celebration. The clouds glowered, the trees scrunched their bark into a wrinkled scowl, and the scruffy lawns cowered back from human contact.

Tim brushed his sleek dark hair out of his eyes and let his gaze travel over the scene in a brooding way. The day had dumped itself on the world, making children keep quiet without being asked. He thought what a gift it was to grave-diggers. His gaze eventually rested on two old veterans sitting on the bench further down on the opposite side of the path. One splayed his legs before him with his eyes closed as if sprawled in front of a party political broadcast on the telly after a Sunday lunch of potatoes, stew and dumplings. His head was propped up by the wooden headrest with a plaque dedicated to some deceased notable that someone thought should be remembered as long as his mouldering remains. His

1

companion was spouting into his ear twenty to the dozen. It was too far for Tim to make out what he said, but, from the frequent expressive movements of his arms and hands, he guessed it was heart-felt and personal. What held Tim's attention was the fact that the receiver of all this unrestrained flow gave no hint of his own feelings. Either he was as bored as he would be in front of a political address in the parlour, or was tacitly resisting his companion's observations. Whichever it was, it had the air of a 'put-off'.

Turning away from his unresponsive friend, the voluble old chap faced out front, slapped his thighs and gave a final assertive nod of the head. Apparently, having suffered enough lack of response, he got up, and with a final glance at his companion, shuffled off towards the gate.

If a twig full of leaves had not chosen that fateful moment to drop full on the nose of the deserted old chap, Tim would have left, feeling he had squeezed the last ounce of questionable appeal from the day. Yet, there it lay, this autumnal offering on a gloomy altar, draped on the nose and cheek, eliciting no response whatever.

Tim crossed over to the old fellow, and, after a diplomatic cough, bent and gently tugged his sleeve. The old man did not twitch, and Tim bent down to see that his eyes were half open. The likelihood of an emergency impressed itself on him, and he looked after his companion, who by this time had gone some distance down the path. Tim hurried to catch him up. As he neared the old fellow, Tim was aware that, since he could not be taller than five foot five, his own six feet one could scare him if he suddenly accosted him. With this in mind he gave a wide berth to the old man before stopping in front of him and saying in a calm, rational tone,

"I say, look, I don't want to alarm you,.."

"Wot's up, then?" Interrupted the old man.

....but I think your friend may have passed away"

"No 'may' abowt it," was the reply. "'E'd snuffed it afore I got 'ere."

He started to circle round Tim to continue on his way to the gate.

Thrown for a second by the old chap's cool acceptance, he hesitated before saying,

"Right. So I take it you're just off to tell the police?"

"Take it 'ow you like. I'll not be goin' there."

"You're not just leaving him there on the bench?"

"I'm not leaving 'im anywhere. E's gone. Passed away, passed on".

"Well, yes...of course. But, nevertheless, well, I mean, his remains are there."

"Aye, 'is remains remain. They'll remind those as come upon 'im 'e were once 'ere, an' now 'e's gone."

The realisation suddenly impressed itself on Tim that it would be down to him to inform the authorities It could only have been curiosity that prompted the next question, and a need to put the incident into some acceptable perspective. He bent down to the old man.

"I expect you were taking your last farewell of your friend on the bench."

"Nay, lad, not at all."

"Well, I couldn't help noticing you were talking to,...um. ." He bent even lower. "... his remains on the bench."

"Oh, aye?. Well, 'appen ye noticed wrong. I'm not in the 'abit of talking to them's as gone. I were chattin' up our good mate, Jesus, who were sittin' t'other side o' Tom."

3

Oh, right."Tim swallowed and straightened up, nodding as he tried to assimilate this last piece of information. *"Yes... Jesus."*

"If ye must sniff yer way into other folk's business, I were remindin' our best friend, Jesus, 'ow Tom 'ad always checked in every day to get an update, so, seein' as 'ow e didn't need to any more, it were time for Jesus to check 'im in fer good."

Tim nodded slightly, as if having some difficulty in ticking this off a list. "Right."

"An' 'what's more', I said, 'seein' as 'ow Tom went so peaceful, I'd look on it as a great favour if he could do t' same fer me when t' time comes'."

He looked at Tim with an unanswerable challenge, but with a moist glaze over his eyes. He gave a sniff.

Tim, decidedly wrong-footed, managed another respectful, "Right."

"So, I'll be comin' back regular ter see if Jesus 'as a mind t' oblige me,.. oh, aye, an' termorrer, special, ter see if anyone's noticed Tom's remains."

Tim thought it would sound indecent to say he was about to go to the nearest police station. A shaft of sunlight pierced the blanket of grey just then, and the old fellow looked up and said, affirmatively,

"There you go, then."

And, with that, he took a handkerchief from his coat pocket, wiped his eye, blew his nose and shuffled out of the park. Unaccountably, the day seemed to have provided a very real purpose for itself and for Tim. He turned on his heel, and after a last look at the peacefully departed, left to sort things out with the authorities.

Down To Earth

In small northern towns, days encircle life in an intimate way, especially when you reach your declining years. The Municipal Park is a good place to meet with those days. Familiar sights, familiar things are friends among friends. They are especially important when your close friend has just passed away on a familiar bench.

For a stranger, however, with nothing much to take his mind off things, any event in this small northern town necessarily has more distractive meaning. It offers the whiff of unfamiliarity and lack of context. Tim remembered vividly the passing away of the old man's companion on the park bench, the previous day, and the remarkable acceptance by his friend of his fate.

Tim decided to revisit the park to see if the old man might be as good as his word, and return to the scene.

The day had not made up its mind what sort it wanted to be yet, but there was an expectant feeling in the air that it was thinking about it. The clouds were a mixture of fair weather cottonwool white and threatening inky dark. The wind seemed not to have settled in its mind to blow in any particular direction, yet. Leaves ran up and down the paths and passed each other on the way back. There was no expression on the day's face that gave anything away. Folk kept lifting their chins in a discerning way to look for signs, but no-one was fooled into believing they knew.

Tim sauntered into the park, looking about him with a nonchalant air, that pretended to care little what he found there. He pushed open the low gate and brought his gaze down from the heavens to the footpath and the bench. Sure enough, the old man was there, and instantly, Tim realised he felt strangely pleased. He sauntered towards the slightly huddled figure who kept his gaze straight ahead, his eyes glinting beneath the peaked cap, seeming to be searching inside himself.

Tim coughed politely to test the waters of receptivity, and the old chap looked up.

"Oh, aye," he said, taking up, without the least formality, where they left off yesterday. "It were you, then?"

"It was me, what?" responded Tim.

"What told 'em about Tom, o' course."

"Er, yes, I suppose so."

The old chap closed his eyes and shook his head in a faintly disparaging way.

"Ee, you Southern folk. Ye can't do nowt wi'out supposing. Either it were you or it weren't."

"Yes it was me, I'm afraid."

"There you go. Now y'er afraid. There's nowt to be afraid of. What next?"

"You've got me there. Sorry to be so southern."

The old man laughed dryly. "Ye suppose y'er afraid y'er sorry, eh?" He laughed again, but not unkindly.

"Do you mind if I sit a moment?" asked Tim.

"It's a free seat in a free town." He continued to stare ahead.

Tim sat and adopted the old man's posture, which seemed strangely appropriate to his mood.

After a couple of minutes silent commune with the bare trees and the soul-less greens, Tim asked with some care, "Did you mean every word you said, yesterday?"

"What? Ev'ry word? Give over!" was the laconic reply. "Did ye 'ave owt partic'lar in mind?"

"About following your friend the same way?"

"Passing on? Oh, aye, all in my mate, Jesus' good time We're in negotiation just now."

Tim smiled. "Forgive me, but you make Jesus sound very down to earth."

The old chap looked suddenly sideways and gave a defiant frown. "That's what he done, en't it? Come down to earth." He looked Tim up and down and with a bemused shake of his head, and added, "What's the problem, then?"

"Oh, no problem at all. It's just that I think I'd find it a bit difficult to call Jesus 'my mate' It seems, well...you know... a little familiar."

"'Appen we are, 'Im an' me."

"But he's supposed to be the Son of God, isn't he?"

"Nowt less. I call 'Im 'Prince Jesus', me. So did Tom, afore he went."

Tim nodded, as if in doubtful assent, and pacing his words with care, said, "But if Jesus is a Prince, how can you call him 'your mate'?"

"Why not, when He made Tom and me princes with 'im? That's what 'e came to do, en't it? Make us all princes in 'is Father's 'ouse?"

The old chap looked ahead of him again and Tim was taken in his mind back to his choir-boy days and to the parson's respectful intonation that relegated God to the amorphous clouds now passing overhead.

"Do you know, I wish I could accept death as easily as you?"

"Give over, will ye? I'm passin' on to life, me. There's no death in't!"

'The old chap was indignant, but not aggressive. 'Forthright' came to mind.

"Please can I know your name?" said Tim.

"Why not? Fred Butterworth. Lancasheer born an' bred."

"And I'm Tim from the South." He took the old man's hand in his and shook it with unsolicited warmth. "I doubt if our paths will cross again, Mr. Butterworth, but, thank you."

He stood up and smiled down at him. Fred looked a little puzzled and said, "Oh, aye? Wot fer?"

Tim just shrugged, shook his head slightly, and walked away down the path under Fred's quiet, bemused gaze, and passed out of the park gate. He did not look back; the moment to carry away had already passed.

Yuletide Message

Tim had never expected to meet Fred Butterworth again, but, as things would have it, he found himself in the same unpretentious northern town as Christmas was coming up. It had been two months since he had last been there, but now he was there to re-establish contact with his business connections. With some time on his hands he decided, without being able to explain it, to revisit the same municipal park, where he had last seen Fred Butterworth. Whenever he remembered the incident in the park, it always seemed to suggest itself as a kind of haven, where you could sit without anyone requiring you to come to a conclusion about anything.

This particular day, covered by a battleship grey sky, belonged to Grimm's fairy tales. A cutting east wind interfered with your person in an unacceptable way, tracing its icy fingers round your ears, blowing up your trouser leg, and indecently assaulted all parts not covered by at least three substantial layers.

Tim was greatly surprised when, peering out from behind his scarf beneath the peek of his cap, he saw the figure of the old man sitting on the now familiar bench, wrapped in a heavy coat and muffler, and confronting the excesses of the day. Tim sauntered up and stopped just short of the old chap. He waited a second while Fred looked up.

"Oh, aye," said Fred, in recognition of the young man from the South.

"I'm up again", said Tim, for want of anything better to say.

"Don't ye like it down there, then?"

"I'm up for the Christmas trade."

Fred screwed up his face. "All the worse," he growled. "Ev'rywun rushin' to get ready fer it, flaked out during it, and regrettin' it ever 'appened, till it comes round agin."

"You're not keen on Christmas, then?" Tim sat next to him and stretched his legs out, carefully tucking his coat over them.

"'Appen I might be, if it ever came". Fred scowled. "These days it's nowt but a diabolic pagan excess," he added, half under his breath.

"What have you got against Christmas, then, Mr. Butterworth?"

Fred looked surprised at hearing his name. "Oh, ye remember me name, then?"

Tim nodded and adopted a careful tone.

"I'm sorry you don't like Christmas."

"Give over! It's nowt o't sort! It's s'pposed ter be Prince Jesus' birthday! It's jus' a flamin' excuse fer a blow out! Any road, who knows wot date 'E were born?"

"That's true," Tim conceded, "but we had to choose some date to mark the celebration."

"Why?" Fred challenged. "Who said we 'ad ter?"

"Well, the church, I suppose." Tim shrugged, uncertainly.

"Jesus never mentioned it. Never once said anythin' about stuffin' oursels wi' vitt'ls an' booze on twenty fith o' December. Weddin's and takin' yer leave o' yer mates is diff'rent. He weren't agin drinkin' a glass o' wine to the newly weds, or 'e'd never o' changed the water into it. But t' only time 'E said we wus ter drink to 'Im wus when we thowt on 'Is end, - an' what 'E done fer us."

Tim nodded, and found himself adopting a rueful expression, followed by an apologetic shrug.

"You in trade, then?" Fred suddenly shot the question at Tim with a searching look.

"I'm Retail Manager for an art printing firm."

"Oh, aye." Fred shook his head with deep misgiving. "Sellin' things," he added, as if such activity was a danger to health. "What're ye sellin', then?"

"Well, just now we're in the Christmas card market."

" 'Eaven preserve us!" Fred exclaimed.

"We stand to make a killing in art reproduction at this time of the year," Tim declared with a confident smile. "You can see our work on all the Christmas cards."

The smile slowly faded as the old chap turned a look of deep disdain on him. The hollowed cheeks and sober expression of his eyes above the pinched, rose coloured nose, made him look like a judge about to pronounce the death sentence.

"Ee, lad," he said with profound sadness. "what ye've t'account fer!"

"What do you mean?" said Tim ,drawing his legs in and sitting up to attention.

"The burden o' guilt!" Fred intoned the phrase as if the sin weighed heavily on the whole world.

"Guilt for what?" asked Tim, who was now feeling strangely uncomfortable for no reason he could think of.

"T' trials, decisions, t' broken friendship,..."Fred went on to declaim, shaking his head with deep sadness, and adding finally, "not t' mention t' financial cost."

Tim smiled confusedly. "How can I be accountable for all this?"

Fred rose slowly and deliberately to his feet, and stood, looking down on Tim.

"Ee, lad, the trouble folk 'ave makin' t' Christmas card list! T' jottin' down an' scratchin' out that goes on..t' guilt getting' cards from folk ye forgot, 'who stop givin' yer the time o'day 'cos they reckon yer've cut 'em out! An' the flamin' price of the ruddy things, an' all!"

"I'm sorry Christmas cards give you all this trouble."

"Me? Trouble? Not on yer nelly. I don't 'ave owt ter do wi' 'em. Any road, I'm off to meet Elsie in 'The Dragon's Arms' for a glass of ale an' t' work out 'ow we're to get through all this festivity. You'd think it were Father Christmas's birthday t' way folk go on. Just think on, lad, just think on." He jerked his thumb up to the grey sky, and added, in a tone that challenged any further dispute, "E's not impressed, an' that's t' truth."

With that, he stood and left without ceremony or another look, and wandered out through the park gate, leaving Tim to feel convicted of a cosmic misjudgement. He was unsure of the personage to whom he was to be accountable, but felt obligsted to 'think on'. As was usually the case, he came to no clear resolution in the matter. He thought of Fred sipping ale in the pub and decided that, if he was to reach any clarification, it would be greatly aided by some liquid refreshment he had stowed in the wardrobe in his lodgings.

Getting 'Em In

Tim could not explain it, but Fred's abrupt, unceremoni-ous departure the previous day left him with the impres-sion that his life might gain some advantage from some revision. Heaven knows why but it seemed to matter what Fred thought of the whole business of Christmas. He decided to walk back to the park, just for some fresh air and exercise and having arrived to an empty park, felt Fred's absence strikingly evident, as if his presence had become part of the essential ambience. He recalled the old fellow's intention to share a jar of ale with a certain Elsie in the Dragon's Arms. It was coming up to lunchtime, and he winced at the thought of a lacklustre, pre-Christmas lunch at his characterless bed and break-fast pension The drizzly day draped itself round him and misted up his glasses. The best way to uncoil it was to find some interior filled with convivial chatter.

He decided to seek out this Dragon's Arms that Fred had referred to, and approached passers-by for direc-tions. They took in his relatively smart appearance and, with a quizzical expression, pointed him to the less salu-brious quarter of the town, where, having left all fash-ionable pretence behind, he stood before a dingy white tiled public house. He nudged open the unvarnished doors, and was gathered in by a dull but unthreatening atmosphere of faded Windsor chairs and well worn brown leatherette benches, somehow the cosier for having seen better days. A million propping elbows had polished the dark brown counter, and the generously proportioned seats that circled the room bulged in directions only years of sprawling bodies could have shaped. The room smelt of spilt ale, stale perspiration and a waft of cheap air spray. No-one could enter here with any pretension to style; only a preference to avoid it.

There, seated in a circle round a living fire in a wide grate, sat Fred with a thin, wiry woman of advanced age in a tight beret and a misshapen woollen coat and three other dishevelled men with dank hair of varying length and un-engaging expressions on their unshaven, weather-worn faces. They were dressed in grubby, stained mackintoshes, tied round with stringy belts. As Tim took in the scene, Fred looked up at him and said in a loud voice,

"Aye-oop! Look what's turned up!"

Tim felt as though an alien entering another world. He tried to think of a fitting response, and, acutely aware of five pairs of eyes fixed on him, failed miserably to come up with one. He nodded. Nobody nodded back and there was silence. He nodded again, as if this might miraculously set some social clockwork going. They might have entered a time warp if Fred had not broken the silence with, "Well, since ye're 'ere, sit yer down, if ye've a mind. Will an ale do ye?"

Jerked out of his gauche pose, Tim replied, with over-emphatic enthusiasm, "I'd be delighted."

He squeezed past the man at the end and made as if to sit in an empty chair in the middle of the group. Fred instantly got to his feet and barred his way. He cocked his head slightly to one side and with a defiant smile said,

"Well deelited or not, ye'll NOT be sittin' in the throne o' grace."

"I beg your pardon," said Tim.

"Granted. That seat's reserved fer Prince Jesus. Plonk another chair next t' Elsie." He pointed at the next table, and Tim obediently backed away, while Fred went to the bar and ordered him a glass of beer. Tim lifted the chair over the heads of the group and set it down between Elsie and the hearth. She turned to him with a thin smile, said, "You'll be t' picture fella, eh?"

"Um, yes, I suppose I am," responded Tim, with a hint of a shrug and apologetic smile, adding, with a slight grimace, "I'm afraid."

"Fred said ye wus fearful," she continued confidently, as if she were settled in her mind to have it confirmed. Before Tim was called on to make further response, Fred put a glass of beer in his hand, and lowered himself in his seat again.

"So, 'ave yer thowt on, then?" asked Fred. He turned to the company and added, "This 'ere's t' young fella as I were tellin' ye about, retailin' Christmas cards." Turning back to Tim, he continued, "They'd be a fat lot o' good t' these mates 'o mine. They don't 'ave post boxes to put 'em in, eh?" He nudged his neighbour gently with his elbow, and gave a wry chuckle. All three companions of the mackintosh brigade corroborated with nods and gap-toothed smiles.

"Unless ye marked 'em clearly 'Third cardboard box on the 'igh Street'," returned the tallest fellow, whereupon they all nudged each other again and smirked like accomplices to some crime on society, and drank heartily.

Tim suddenly felt over-dressed, over-polite, and over-exposed.

Fred indicated Elsie, as he said, proudly, "Her an' me, we send nowt to nobody", and nodding to the three vagrants, added, "It's much better bringin' us mates in 'ere to meet the Prince with a pint o' cheer, en't it, Elsie?"

"Aye, lad, it is, an' all," she agreed heartily. "Worth a mantelpiece o' Christmas greetin's."

Fred lifted his glass towards the empty chair and said, "Now, lads, a toast ter t' Birthday Prince. Good on yer, Jesus!" They all raised their glasses and repeated, "Good on yer, Jesus!" Tim surprised himself by muttering the same.

Fred turned to him. "Now ye're talkin'," he said in a loud voice. "God bless us all! An' ter show 'e means it, this young fella from the South's goin' ter get us in another round!"

Tim took his prompt and did precisely that. They all gave a cheerful smile, and thoughts of Christmas cards went out of the window, as the flames from the hearth cast their light on the assembled group, filling them all with a flickering glow of irrational hope as they huddled round the chair of honour.

They jested and laughed, mainly on the topic of how hard life was to those who were not favoured by the right background, but it was all done in the right spirit. They vied with each other to tell the worst tales of early childhood memories of Christmas, mostly of how they received nowt but a thick ear if they made too much noise and woke up an inebriated father, or of how they never knew where most of the festive fare had been stolen from. Strangely, Tim somehow did not feel at all shocked to hear this, because it seemed to be recalled in the vein of history seen from a moral perspective.

There were moments of reflective silence as they all stared into the fire and put their memories into some kind of personal order.

In one of these moments, Fred turned to Tim and enquired whether he had any memories. Tim was suddenly confronted by what a protected and privileged background he came from by comparison with anyone there..

"I'm afraid I had it very easy," he said, apologetically.

"We could've guessed that wi'out too much strain," said Fred.

"And nowt wrong wi' it, either," added Elsie. "I 'ad mostly 'appy days as a kid, though we found it tough to make ends meet. Was ye alus 'appy as a child, then," she asked, addressing herself to Tim.

"I think so," he reflected. "I was the only one."

Everyone concentrated on the idea of being the only child in the family and found it strange and almost unimaginable. One of the mackintosh brigade asked, in an earnest way, if that meant Tim got it 'all 'is own way'. He hesitated before replying that he was aware that he never went without things.

"That's not the same thing," offered Fred. "Ye often get one instead o' t'other."

"Aye, well, ye don't know if that's true in Tim's case," said Elsie in a reproving tone, "so ye've no call to say it."

"I was nowt but sayin'," Fred said, defensively.

"An' if I were Tim, I'd be sayin' nowt an' all, jes' ter keep ye guessin'."

Tim felt grateful to Elsie, and shortly they all decided they would call it a day and go their separate ways. They all made a point of shaking hands with Tim, which somehow told him they had accepted him. He found himself rather touched and proud to have been thus taken into their social group, as if his background had been unimportant, and class difference insignificant. Tim stayed behind staring into the fire for some minutes, his mind filled with questions about how the group must have been formed, and what they meant to each other.

Greetings

Business kept Tim away for several weeks after that, and it was Easter Day when he next found himself in the town. It was bright and sunny enough for all the optimists to wave cheerfully and confidently at each other, with just the amount of chill in the air to satisfy all the pessimists in their predictions that this year was 'not up to much so far' and promised ill for the rest of it. As Tim strolled to the municipal park, he reflected how some people always needed overcoats, while others seemed protected by warmth carried about with them. He reflected briefly that he might not have reflected like this the same time last year.

He more than half expected to find Fred taking his constitutional perambulation in the park, drawn, by the power of the safe place from which to review the future.

He entered the gate to find the local council had not yet activated the piddling fountain. However, the grass had been given its first 'going over', so things were definitely happening. Sure enough, Fred was standing gazing down on a small flower bed imprisoned by low rusty iron paling. Tim sidled up to him, and stood for a moment to ascertain the focus of his attention.

"Oh, aye," said Fred, with the briefest sidelong glance at him.

Tim, acclimatized by now to the language of Northern brevity, announced himself with a' Yes'.

They stood side by side gazing down at two undernourished cowslips that rather wearily rang their silent jaundiced bells in the light breeze. Behind them two chorus rows of irresolute primroses and miniature hyacinths cowered, holding their leaves in front of their faces. Altogether, it was a pretty second rate show, but someone seemed to have advanced the cowslips front of stage to do their turn before the interval.

"An' the daft thing abowt it," Fred declared without preamble, "is I doubt they wus planted. They jus' come up."

"Well, anyway, Fred, - 'Happy Easter'!" said Tim, punctuating his greeting with a smile and a nod.

Fred turned his head to look at him. "Ee, yer wud 'ave ter say that."

Tim gave a half apologetic shrug. "It *is* Easter Day".

"Oh, aye, an' all that 'ow d'yer do." He shook his head sadly. "An' wot d' yer mean by it?"

"Mean?"

"Aye. Wot's this ''appy' yer on abowt?"

"Aren't we supposed to be happy at Easter?"

Fred turned abruptly away down the path towards his usual seat. Tim followed a second later, like a puppy to heel on its walk. Fred sank down on the bench with a sigh. Tim joined him. They sat shoulder to shoulder gazing into the middle distance at nothing in particular.

"Aye," Fred muttered. After nodding thoughtfully several times, he scrutinized Tim and added, "'Appen it's a reminder o' wot we've all been told, or ye'r tellin' me what I'm suppos'd ter feel 'bowt Easter."

Tim, feeling slightly affronted, said, "I was just hoping you'd have a happy Easter, that's all."

"Aye well, I wonder why you didn't say, 'Hullo Fred, Happy Sunday!' last time we met?"

"Well, it wasn't Easter, was it?"

"So yer want me to be happy but once a year, is that it?"

"Not at all!"

"Then wot's special abowt today?"

Tim decided Fred was nit-picking and looking for disagreement at any price. It looked as if he'd be found wanting, whatever he said.

"I'm beginning to wish I hadn't mentioned it," he said, a shade peevishly.

"Aye, well, that's a start, lad." He was silent for a moment and then he spoke with the full weight of his years.

"Today is a day of joy, not one of your middlin' 'happy' ones. 'Happy' is fer bunny rabbits and chicks burstin' out'o' eggs, an' pretty posies an' such like. T'day's t' day…" he said with emphasis, bringing the full import of his speech round to Tim, "…Jesus, Prince of Peace, were brought back to life wi' the best gift he could ever give ye - a second go at gettin' it right wi' 'is Father. Tha's worth dancin' in the streets fer, is that. It's worth hollerin' 'This is yer big chance! Don't mess it up!' It's not fer sidlin' up ter someone and sayin', 'Appy Easter', like it were yer birthday."

Here, Fred adopted a more sober and reflective tone.

"D'yer know, lad, I think it 'ud be right gradely ter go round wishin' shame and woe on folk on Good Friday, seein' as there's nowt fer 'em ter be proud of, t' way they be' ave. It were on our account that the Prince had ter give hisself up ter terrible sufferin'. Gettin' a proper notion o' that might jus' get it in ter folk's 'eads that t'-day's a day ter shout abowt, or it's fer shuttin' us traps."

Tim reflected on this and after a pause offered the careful observation, "Well I suppose that might be one Christian point of view.

Fred gave a fatalistic shake of the head before replying with a calm and measured tone,

"Leavin' aside yer 'supposing', which never did no-one any good at best o' times, the truth on't don't rely on being a Christian. The truth's the truth fer all that. Jus' think on, lad, either ye reco'nise what Jesus done fer ye, or ye've ter do it fer yersel'. An', from what I know, that's not on. The whole world thinks it's no better nor it should be. But that's a powerful lot less than Jesus's Dad thinks is awright. So jus' think on."

He underlined the message with raised forefinger and staccato head movements, and by the end of it he wore the look of an irate headmaster reading the riot act at school assembly.

Just then Fred's friend, Elsie, came through the gate, and his eyes lit up with pleasure. He gave a wave of his gnarled hand and she returned a beaming wrinkled smile. While she was yet twenty yards up the path, he shouted, "Are ye joyful then, Elsie, lass?!"

"I am that, Fred, lad!" she shouted back. "So 'e's back wi'us?" she added, referring to Tim.

"Aye, but he's a ways ter go, afore he arrives yet."

"Aye, well, never mind, eh," she panted as she drew level with them. "Time waits fer no man, but God does, so tha's awright, eh? Tell ye what, let's go and 'ave a jar int' Dragon's Arms, an' celebrate.

Fred turned to Tim. "Are yer comin', then?"

Tim nodded, somewhat surprised to see how Fred's mood had suddenly lightened, and thought how welcome a pint of ale would be. It would be good to get in out of the cold and have some life put back into him. As if Fred had overheard his thoughts, said,

"We'll toast the Prince fer the life 'E's give us."

Fred took Elsie's arm and all three stepped, as jauntily as the years would permit the old'uns, out of the park to celebrate whatever each had in his or her heart that Easter Day....

Shape of Things to Come

It was a few days later. The fire crackled in the hearth at the Dragon's Arms. As had become their wont now that Tim had taken up with Fred, they were sipping beers in silent contemplation, their legs extended obliquely towards the warmth. Fred's legs were sprawled apart and Tim's were neatly crossed at the ankles, their respective shapes somehow emblematic of the way they each confronted life.

Tim feared to break the silence just then, from a conviction that Fred's quiet brooding face spoke of reminiscence. He had learned, very soon, not to intrude on the old man's thoughts with unsolicited comments, and sensed the sequential nature of Fred's life. Fred's decisions derived from his experiences, and he never thought twice before acting on feelings or voicing his convictions or memories to surrounding company. Tim was well aware of the anomaly of a middle-class thirty-something Southerner being drawn into the circle of a seventy-going-on-eighty-year-old Northerner with the social aplomb of a traffic warden.

An inclement bout of late Spring weather had driven them into the familiar white-tiled retreat. It was one of those days that dare you to cross the threshold at your own risk. Wind hurled buckets of horizontal rain as if it were creating an advert for the durability of the human frame; conditions for which meteorologists have no effective language. It was the kind of weather for hibernating, or to provide a background to stories that ended badly, as you listened in the comfort of your parlour or in front of the hearth of a chosen asylum such as The Dragon's Arms.

Fred sighed and, stirred himself to slowly sip the last dregs of his pint. "It's a blessin," he said "'e wusn' taken on a day like this'un." He gazed into the flames that danced in his unblinking eyes. Tim waited for something expositional to follow, but when not forthcoming, felt he was called on to nod slowly without understanding. After another moment's silence Fred added, "Tom could never a' gone peaceful in this wind, that's fer sure. 'Is spirit 'ud never a' left his body. "Tim nodded again, and was able, this time, to give a non-committal mutter of recognition. He took a slow draught of his stout ale, passed the back of his hand across his lips before finding the courage to ask,

"Is that how you see it, then? Your spirit just slips away and leaves it all behind?"

Fred focused on Tim for a second before shaking his head and sighing at the obtuseness of his younger drinking companion.

"Well, 'e didn't take it with 'im, did 'e?"

"No, maybe not."

"There's no 'maybe not' about it. 'E left 'is remains on't bench. 'E 'd no further use fer it."

"Right. So his spirit went to... a better place, then?"

"Ee, lad, don't be afeared ter say it. 'E went ter 'eaven."

"Right, urm...to heaven, then."

"'Course 'e did."

Tim had a compulsion to follow his nose on this question. He took a breath. "So what does he look like now?"

Fred frowned and Tim thought he might be irritated. However, far from becoming 'crochety', he turned to him and said with an earnest gleam in his eye, "That's a grand thought, is that." He reflected a moment or two before adding , "D'yer know, I alus think better wi' a pint in me 'and." It took Tim but a second for the non-sequitur to sink in, but when it did, he downed the last half inch in his glass, rose straightaway,and made for the bar.

I'll be right back," he said.

He returned shortly with an amber bitter for Fred and a froth-topped Guinness stout for himself. "Ta," said Fred. "This is t' stuff ter stir yer grey matter, is this."

"So?" prompted Tim, having learned that a succinct approach worked best.

"My mate, Tom," began Fred, "were a fine upstandin' lad in 'is day. I reckon that's 'ow it'll be fer 'im now."

"How do you explain that?" insisted Tim.

"Hold up!" Fred parried. "I'm not explainin' owt." He sipped his beer and said in a calmer tone, "I'm jus' reflectin', tha's all"

"You mean, your friend just gets younger again," - Tim flicked his fingers - "just like that?"

"'Appen he will, if that's t' Father's way o' things. All I know is 'e 'll 've been renovated fer sure."

"Right," said Tim, circumspectly. "but what does 'renovated' mean?"

"Well, 'ed 'ave ter be, wouldn' 'e? 'E were no flippin good as 'e wus, poor ol' bloke. 'E weren't even up ter thinkin' too straight at t' end. No," Fred continued with firm conviction, "'e'll 'ave 'ad a complete refit, an' MOT service, like". He took a long satisfied swallow of his beer to underline his assertion.

"And what will the refit fit him for, up there in heaven?" asked Tim, aware, as soon as he said it, of being dangerously provocative. But Fred rarely, if ever, took notice of irony.

"Fer dancin' and singin' an' fer the joy of bein' wi' our mate, Prince Jesus."

"But he won't be doing that all the time, will he? I mean just dancing about and singing songs. You can only do that for a certain length before it begins to lose its attraction. What else will he be doing?"

"I don't know, do I? Whatever 'e's a mind ter, while 'e's dancin' an singin'. Your guess is as good as mine."

Tim smiled as he contemplated the scene.

"That does limit the options if you have to be dancing and singing in unison with whatever else you're doing."

Fred eyed Tim long enough to make him feel uncomfortable, and then, in an uncritical tone, said, "Ye've ter let go o' some things, lad, an' let 'em be. Ye can pin down some things o' this world, but there's no way 'o knowin' abowt t' next, 'cept what the good book says."

"What *does* it say? asked Tim.

"There's a grand place waitin for us, we'll all be renovated, an' be glad ter live forever wi' Jesus and 'is Dad."

"With non-stop dancing and singing," added Tim, obdurately.

"In our 'earts, aye. That's the thing about joy, see. Yer don't 'ave ter be flappin' yer arms abowt, or makin' a ruckus every second o' the day. That's where folk get it wrong. There's them that think ye've always ter be solemn and poe-faced to respect 'our Father in 'eaven', an' there's some what think, if ye're not jiggin' up an' down, thrashin' yer limbs abowt, ye're not filled wi' 'Is spirit."

"So neither of them have got it right, then?"

"Nay, they're both right, - some o' t' time. Its grand ter be solemn when ye think on how ye've made a fool o' yersel' takin' the wrong turnin', an' it's a serious thing ter admit what a good job it were Jesus came an' sorted things out. The time fer shoutin' is when yer know what Jesus 'as in store fer yer, when yer do admit it."

Tim shifted in his chair and stared into the flames for some seconds, and they supped their ales as the silence crept back to fill the space between them. From the unfocussed view he held that moment, Tim was suddenly aware of a vacuum. When he spoke it was from the need to express himself in the simplest manner.

"I don't know how to do that."

"Do wot?"

"Admit all that about Jesus."

"You an' the rest. That's 'cos ye're all tryin' ter work it out fer yersel' most o' time."

"But *you* are *certain*, aren't you?"

"Aye. But tha's not 'cos I know 'ow to be. I jus read the story an' it told the truth itself."

"How did it do that?"

"Because I wanted it ter."

"But children do that with make-believe."

"Aye. That's the special thing 'bout children".

"Then later they learn that fairy stories aren't true."

"'Cept the parts that stay with yer."

"That's just giving up your reason in exchange for imagination."

"Oh, aye!" Fred chuckled enthusiastically. "I'm ready ter do that any day." The argument was suspended in the air. Fred swallowed half his beer and then took in a long breath before squaring up to his thought.

"Before 'e got real poorly, Tom asked me how ye can believe in Jesus wi'out proof. I knew t'answer soon as 'e asked it. Yer can't believe in Jesus if yer can explain 'im. Soon as ye start explainin, it's not 'Im at all. So I said ter Tom,'proof's the thing what gets in t'way o' knowin', I said. 'Gerraway with yer', he said. An' I said, 'No, think on, Tom', I said, 'if ye can explain Jesus, then he could'a bin invented by anyone. But, because ye can't explain 'Im, he can't a been invented at all'. An' that's where I rest me case. I'll tell yer somethin' else, though, young Tim. I 'aven't a clue what shape I'll be in, when I pop off, and I don't give a monkey what 'appens ter me body, neither,.. jus' so long as I know I'll be meeting my mate, Prince Jesus on the front door step of me new mansion."

With that he downed the second half of his pint, and said, "I'm about ter get the last pint in, an' that means I'll be past me best. Will yer join me?"

"Thanks," said Tim, knowing he had been given formal notice of termination of this particular exchange. As Fred stood at the bar, Tim re-crossed his ankles and listened to the wind howling outside, as he let his thoughts slide into the embers of the fire. There seemed to be just the possibility of a good ending to the story if only he could wrestle with the clues. But he wasn't sure it was going to be worth his while.

The Right Tie

A few days on, Tim happened to find himself making for the menswear department of Harvey and Bagnold in the High Street to buy himself a new tie. The last time he had looked in the mirror before setting off for his meeting with the Chairman of the Local Trade and Industry Committee, he was aware that the tight-knotted version he was wearing gave him a desperate strangled look; made him look out of sorts with life and ready to do away with himself. He needed something more substantial, something with a Windsor knot to make a bold, calm statement.

No sooner had he turned into the entrance and pushed open the double doors with their long vertical brass handles, than he almost collided with Fred and Elsie. They were looking smarter than usual, and Elsie had her arm in Fred's.

He had on a light grey jacket over a summery shirt open at the neck and a pair of corduroy trousers with the definite makings of a crease in them. Unfortunately, he had not abandoned the mackintosh. Elsie sported a floral two piece outfit with a straight neck simple blouse and carried a long handled cream handbag with a large clasp.

They took their time to look Tim over, as if he owed them some kind of explanation for his sudden appearance on the scene. Tim found himself giving one.

"I'm just about to get myself a new tie. The one I'm wearing has seen better days."

"I doubt it were up t' much ter start wi'," said Fred. "What do ye say, Elsie?"

"My family never wore a tie if they could 'elp it," replied Elsie, "so I can't say as I'm the one t'ask."

"Only time I ever wore one," said Fred, " were when I were up fer a job. I packed it away in't drawer soon as they 'ired me," he added airily. Then he turned to Tim and said, "Are ye lookin' fer a job, then?"

"No. I'm still with the same firm."

"Then why d'yer need a new tie?"

"This one's past It," said Tim, almost apologetically. "I've got to keep up appearances."

"Oh, aye? Appearances, is it?" Fred grimaced and looked away as if the very thought offended. Just then a small boy half dragged along by his mother looked at Fred and stuck out his tongue at him.

"D'ye see that, Elsie? I may need a witness." With that he trotted off to catch the mother up and tapped her on the shoulder. She turned on him with a scowl.

"Yes? What is it?" she barked.

Instead of addressing himself to her, he looked down at the boy, who wore an expression of wide-eyed innocence mixed with a touch of apprehension.

"'Scuse me, young fella me lad, 'ave we ever met afore?"

The boy shook his head, and looked at his mother, who was temporarily taken off guard enough to be rendered mute.

"So," went on Fred, "since us paths never crossed afore, it's safe to say I never done owt to put ye out?"

The boy remained silent, nodded first, then shook his head. The woman recovered her voice. "What *is* all this?" She glared at Fred.

"I were just wonderin' why yer young chap put his tongue out at me."

"Put his tongue out at yer? Is that what this is all abowt? Have yer got nothin' worse to fret about? What 'arm's 'e done yer?"

"None at all, missus. I'm not worrited fer meself. It's 'im I'm thinking on."

"Then, that's my concern, ent it?" she retorted and made to move off, towing her boy behind her.

Fred kept pace with her, like a Welsh Colley dog, and began a discussion. Elsie trotted behind, nodding agreement with Fred's comments. Tim was drawn into the slipstream by a consuming curiosity.

Fred began with a plain statement. "Trouble is, madam, I doubt ye're concerned at all. Yer young lad's got a problem plain fer all ter see."

The mother stopped in her tracks, turned on Fred, her free hand on her hip, and in measured scorn, said, "If anyone's got a problem, it's someone what harasses someone minding her own business just because a small boy does what small boys do."

Fred turned to Elsie, and with a sad shake of his head, said,

"Did ye' 'ear that, Elsie? This guardian of tomorrer's 'ope wants us to believe that stickin' yer tongue out is normal behaviour."

"Aye, I 'eard, Fred," she replied, joining him in shaking her head.

" Sad, en't it?" she said with a grimace, addressing herself to Tim and one or two customers who had stopped to listen. Tim dissociated himself by looking at nothing in particular, and felt cowardly.

The mother was turning florid, as more shoppers began to form a group and incline their heads towards a free cabaret. Her voice reached a higher octave and rose several decibels, as she adopted an offended middle class attitude with increased blink rate.

"If you don't leave us alone, I'll call the manager and make a complaint."

"Complaint?!" Fred said in a tone of utter astonishment. He reflected on the word for a moment, and felt obliged to repeat it to make sure he had heard aright. "Complaint, Missus? What abowt?"

"Causing a public nuisance!" she threw at him.

"I'm fair flummoxed to know 'ow me concern fer yer boy can be taken as bein' a nuisance." Here Fred spread out his arms to appeal to the surrounding crowd who were fast gathering for the entertainment. "The poor lad needs 'elp. 'E's in a bad way."

"Tommy rot!" shouted the woman, who by now was losing self control.

" 'Tommy rot', you may call it, lady, but that lad o' yours 'as a very poor image of hisself."

He has a poor image of you, more like it!" she retorted, looking round the crowd for support. The crowd looked towards Fred for his next riposte.

"No-one insults a passing stranger if 'e's happy with hisself," Fred insisted.

"Fer cryin' out loud!" the woman burst out, "'E's eight years old! An' ye want 'im t' be 'appy with himself?! 'Ow's 'e goin' ter do that?!"

"By bein' told that his heavenly Father loves 'im, and making clear where ter draw t' line," Fred persisted, emphatically. "When t' only way ter get noticed is by stickin' yer tongue out at someone," he continued, "then ye must be right confused as ter who y'are." Looking round at the shoppers, like a Weslyan preacher, he launched himself. "Tha' boy," he pronounced, pointing his finger at him, "needs ter be affirmed, that 'e does!"

E's right, ye know!" said Elsie, addressing herself to the crowd.

"An' wi' t 'elp of Prince Jesus, I'm yer man ter do it,"

"Don't be ridiculous!" shouted the mother.

The boy had fixed Fred with a mesmerised stare, partly in apprehension, but also admiration; no-one had ever talked to his mother in this way. Tim had completely forgotten about ties; appearances were no longer on the agenda.

The assembled crowd stood on all sides by now and the sales attendants were standing on tip-toe to catch a glimpse of the action over their heads.

"Beware 'e who calls into question t' name o' Prince Jesus," proclaimed Fred, with stern command. There were murmurs among the onlookers.

"I never did any such thing!" the woman objected.

Fred took hold of the moment.

"In that case, I can tell this young lad o' yours that Jesus knows who 'e is, and thinks the world o' 'im. E'd also be grateful if the boy's mother could confirm this by givin' her lad a big 'ug. That way 'e'd feel good abowt hisself and wouldn't go round stickin' 'is tongue out at people."

One or two among the audience nodded to each other.

The mother was bereft of words, but struggling to come up with some response to reinstate her authority. She stood with arms akimbo, opened her mouth once or twice as if to remonstrate, and began to deflate, as the words refused to come to her. A fifteen year old boy near the front suddenly raised his voice. "Give 'im a 'ug, missus!" and was promptly clouted on the back of his head by his mother, with a "You keep out of it, you!"

"It's all 'e needs," said Elsie to the congregation.

"Aye," added Fred, "but it's got t' be meant."

The woman was starting to feel hemmed in, surrounded by the crowd, who were breathlessly waiting for some reaction.

"It on'y takes a second," said Elsie.

"An' t' result's miraculous," Fred emphasised.

The mother now resembled a startled deer looking for the nearest undergrowth.

"Tell yer what," said Fred, "I'll start things off." He bent down to the lad and clasped him to himself saying, "Yer Father in Heaven made yer as y'are, an' don't you forget it, young fella me lad."

The lad looked astonished, but unable to resist. Fred turned back to the mother and more discreetly this time, said,

"It's a mother's 'ug that does the trick, yer know. Go on, missus, give it a go."

The mother looked first at the crowd, whose eyebrows were all raised in suspended animation, then down at her lad, who seemed none the worse for having been hugged by Fred, and then pulled him in close to her and cupped his head with her hand. The eyebrows descended in unison and a general murmur of approval floated round.

"Right, missus, ye done good there," said Fred. Then turning to the crowd, he said, "Right! Now ye can all get on with yer own business. Praise The Lord !"

As if suddenly coming to their senses, and given a sense of sudden urgency, they all dissipated into the various shopping aisles. Fred and Elsie closely followed by Tim, walked away, too, leaving mother and son in the middle of the floor, like a study for a Rodin statue, until suddenly she turned to her lad and said,

"Just you dare breathe a word about this t' yer father, when we get 'ome! An' ye can take that smile off yer face, an 'all!"

"What 're you in 'ere fer?" Fred asked Tim.

"Urm, .. a tie," Tim recalled.

"I wouldn' waste me money." What d'y' think, Elsie?"

"A tie's nowt but a tie. Best choose one to please yerself, tho', if ye 'ave ter," added Elsie, wisely, "'cos it never looks right if it's ter please someone else."

"Better still, come and join us in t' tea room for a cuppa," said Fred.

"Right. Thanks. I will," said Tim.

And that's what they did.

At The Hustings

Bruised yellow clouds scowled and glowered, and a
threatening storm cleared its throat in guttural growls, as
Tim left the bar of his small licensed hotel, to get some
air. He had been sitting listening to semi-inebriated residents exchanging increasingly clamorous 'wisdom' on
the subject of the imminent election occasioned by the
recent demise of the local member of parliament. The
last thing he was seeking, then, was an address by the
candidate for the National Democrat Liberal Green
Party from the platform of the disused bandstand of the
municipal park. But life being full of harsh predictability,
that, as he entered the park, was precisely the situation
that confronted him. He accepted his fate with a shrug
that expressed neither dismay nor amazement, and set
out to complete the full circumference of the park, being
the minimum required for a comprehensive lung-clear-
ing exercise.

The bandstand stood dejectedly at the far side of the
park beyond the ornamental pond that had been
untenanted by goldfish ever since the last shoal had been
dredged out by a party of indigent fairground travellers
in search of a free supper.

Tim came level with the group of aimless loiterers,
who had collected at the base of the stand faintly hoping
for a modicum of free entertainment, but who exhibited

little appreciation, as they tilted their heads back, lending a listless ear and dull eye to the voluble delivery of the prospective local counselor. For his part, and maybe to his credit, he appeared not in the least discouraged by the paucity of numbers or rows of glazed eyes in front of him, but held forth with the tenacity of a cross channel swimmer.

As Tim was about to make his way past the group, he suddenly caught sight of Fred's unmistakable slightly stooped, cloth-capped figure, ensconced front row centre with firmly folded arms. His whole stance and demeanor expressed adamant resistance to all persuasion and Tim immediately felt an optimistic wave of expectation come over him. For someone as poor a listener as Fred, it would be only a matter of time, - and not too much of that, either, - before he would pipe up. Tim slid behind the back row of this apathetic band, hoping to remain un- detected, and held his breath like a schoolboy waiting in eager anticipation for someone to tread on a banana skin.

The candidate was well primed with electoral issues and determined to cover them all. His voice had that recognisable measured rhythm, full of energetic emphasis that belongs to the aspiring politician. He beamed his intimate acquaintance with the deep-rooted needs and yearnings of the local population, and was ready to fall over himself to supply those needs with incomparable devotion.

"I know what you're saying to yourselves!" he proclaimed. "You're asking, 'What happened to all those promises this government made at the last election?! Why are they allowing the north-south gulf to get ever wider? Why are they doing nothing to alleviate the

unemployment or to re-allocate industry to this area'?!'"
His studied gaze raked the collective apathy, and after a
prolonged dramatic pause, he raised his fist and shouted,
"You're right to demand an answer! Where is the education to equip the next generation to meet the future?!
Where will they find jobs?!" Another pregnant pause.
"'What', you will ask me, 'are *you* going to do when you
come to power? How will *you* bring life back to this
town?' you ask?!"

"Not me!" Fred suddenly shouted in scorn.

"You want substantial evidence of our ability to
solve the social problems," continued the prospective
representative, ignoring Fred's outburst. "You expect
me to speak plainly and provide you with the blue-
print!"

"Don't e'spect nowt o' t' sort!" shouted Fred.

"You want the i's dotted and the t's crossed," continued the candidate, emphatically blocking out the interruption.

"That'll be t'day!" retorted Fred. "Politicians are
awready dotty and their eyes are so crossed they can't see
owt straight!"

"Ah! A waggish heckler among us!" retorted
the candidate, finally.

"Funny how such folk never want a constructive answer!" He was about to dismiss the interruption with
a wave of his arm, when Fred shouted, "Never mind
the answer! Ask the right question!"

"Very well," said the candidate delivering a superior
smile with cool detachment, "Perhaps *you* would like to
inform us all of the pressing question of the day? We
await your wisdom." The whole harangued body turned
to focus on Fred.

"Right!" said Fred. "What we 'ave ter know is, where do you stand wi' Jesus?"

Everyone looked at Fred with raised eyebrows, and then turned back towards the candidate. He stood as if riveted to the platform, shaking his head like someone who has just remembered he left the gas oven on. When he recovered sufficiently, he coughed and affected a self-conscious comic expression, saying with heavy irony, "Well, I'm sure we all see the relevance of that question!" Smiling like an assistant in the men's department, he was about to take up where he left off when Fred cut in with, "That bein' so, we'd like an answer."

Attempting to maintain a confident air, the candidate gave a staccato humourless laugh, and said, "I think you'll find you're alone in that!"

"Shall us 'ave a show of 'ands, then?" continued Fred, and before the candidate could reply, he turned round to the assembly and said, "Oo's fer getting a straight answer to where he is wi' Jesus?" This prompted a general murmur, from which it was agreed that, considering how unchallenging the candidate's delivery had been so far, it might liven things up a bit and, anyway, couldn't make it any worse.

"Show of 'ands, then," said Fred.

Without being able to explain to themselves why, they slowly raised their hands in the air, murmuring lukewarm approval, one by one.

Somewhat disconcerted to find himself diverted from his agenda, the candidate adopted the stern attitude of a schoolmaster rebuking pupils caught in some foolish prank.

"Look here!" he began. "What have my religious affiliations got to do with political decisions?"

"Everything!" shouted back Fred.

"How ridiculous! Maybe you'd like to tell us which party He belonged to?" sneered the candidate, pointing up to the sky. "Then we could all vote for it." He laughed at the comic potential of his own joke, and with raised eyebrows, invited the small crowd to join him.

"'E don't vote others into power wot belongs to 'Im."

Everyone looked at Fred and somehow seemed hesitant to accept the candidate's invitation to vote at all..

"Ee, but ye've got 'eckuvashock comin' ter you, lad," continued Fred jabbing his finger at the politician with a sad shake of the head. "Praise be, Jesus don't belong to a party. We all belong to 'Im!"

Everyone present was, by now, eagerly following the exchange between Fred and the candidate like a Wimbledon final. One chap with a hat too big for his head turned to his neighbour and said, "E's got 'im there!" "Wot d'you know abowt it, then?" replied the neighbour. "Nuthin', said the poor chap, deflated. "Then shut it!" retorted the neighbour, "an' leave the argufyin' ter them as knows."

The candidate was wholly uncertain where this exchange was taking them, and a tone of desperate reasonableness entered his voice. "You cannot seriously suggest that my religious affiliation has anything to do with my politics!"

"Yes I can," was Fred's immediate retort.

"You don't mix politics and religion," insisted the candidate.

"It's not abowt mixin' 'em. I'm talking 'bowt the company yer keep.

Oo's leadin' yer?"

"Jonathan Standing is a fine leader with a clear vision for a brighter future."

"Oh, aye?" Fred turned his head both sides to gather in attention before adding, "An' who, may I ask, does 'e follow?"

"He's the leader! He doesn't follow!"

Fred waved the thought of this leader away with his arm. "There y'are then. The blind leadin' the blind!"

"His policies are radical and inspired!"

"Inspired by who?"

"By... by... himself,... his reflections on the state of things," persisted the candidate.

A grimace of disgust overtook Fred's whole visage and he raised his eyes to heaven. Just at that moment the clouds emitted a menacing growl.

"You mean ter tell me, this so called leader of yours, is tryin' ter do it on 'is own?"

"He's done a damn fine job of getting the party together, so far!" shouted the candidate with a rising note of desperation. "Which is more than can be said for any of the other parties!" he added quasi-triumphantly.

I wouldn' give ye tuppence for any of 'em!" Fred shouted back. "I want ter know when ye're goin' ter 'and over the country to Jesus. 'Cos 'E's the only one with the proper credentials to lead us! You get 'Im on yer side, an' yer'll 'ave a lan'slide victory."

At this point Fred stepped forward to address the whole company from the front, and ignoring the candidate, he proceeded to assert that their future would only be assured if they turned to the Prince of Peace and the

Saviour of Souls. He did it with such gusto that everyone immediately swept from their thoughts the predictable and un-inspiring previous speech of the candidate, who, having accepted that the meeting had been usurped, ambled slowly to the rear of the bandstand and sloped off across the park with a slack jaw, muttering quiet obscenities.

Fred took the opportunity to elicit from the whole assembly the promise they would vote only for candidates who confessed the need to share government with Jesus, and then pulling the peak of his cap firmly down, glanced swiftly at the sky and advised everyone to get off home before the heavens opened up and doused them all to the skin. Without any further formalities he strode off towards the town. Tim left the group and trotted after Fred on the narrow footpath. When he came alongside, Fred did not even bother to recognise him.

"That was something to take back home with me, Fred."

"Aye. I saw you was hangin' round the back," returned Fred.

"You certainly saw that poor chap off."

"I 'ope as 'ow it went home with you, an' all," said Fred, without interrupting his stride. "I don't know 'ow they vote where you come fro', but ye'd best keep in mind that a man who thinks 'e's got the answer wi'out checkin' it out with Jesus is like a lighthouse keeper who don't pay his electric bill. If the supply gets cut off, it don't work."

"On Ilkley Moor without a hat, eh?" suggested Tim, attempting to provide local colour with his allusion to the famous song.

"If yer goin' ter say daft things like that, young Tim, ye better get off 'ome before ye get struck by lightnin'."

With that, Fred suddenly veered away. Tim, warmed by Fred's mention of his name, shouted after him, "Tonight at the dragon's arms?!" Fred waved his hand above his head without turning, which Tim took to be the affirmative. Just then the first drop of rain landed on his nose and immediately his hotel, leaving aside the political warts, seemed a more appropriate place to seek in the immediate future.

Because She's Worth It

Now, although he would not have admitted it to anyone else to this point, Tim had for some time believed he could be in love; but, whatever it might be, it was a feeling that completely pervaded him. He had, over a long period, searched the faces of his female colleagues in a half-hearted way, and, although occasionally appreciating the beauty, shape or style of this or that young woman, he did not feel the passion that demanded the kind of commitment he sought in himself before he could make any overtures. If he were honest, with himself, he was a bit short of real confidence in approaching the opposite sex, but, in any case, his frequent travels back and forth between the north and south gave him little chance to develop relationships, and the brevity of his social exchanges had not provided him with the sort of script that most fellows of his age seemed to have at their fingertips. He had tried rehearsing cool small talk in front of the mirror, but words dried up after the first two or three practised sentences and he soon lost heart. Those Hollywood films, in which matinee idols referred to women casually as 'baby', depressed him with their frightening arrogance in the face of a mystery that was totally insoluble to him. He decided he was just not up to it. He found his reflection not unappealing; after all his eyes were wide and well placed, his jaw had a firm line to it, and his mouth was not too serious, yet, sadly, he accepted that he was not your typical ladies' man, especially when he had to wear glasses.

One can imagine, then, what effect a pert and attentive young lady called Lydia, with a gleaming smile, long curled eyelashes, wearing a pretty blouse and a shape that filled it, when she appeared to 'come on to him', as modern parlance had it.

It occurred on a visit to a firm of agents selling holiday homes in warm climes, with whom he had been in communication for some time. He had, in fact, devised what he thought was an effective advertising campaign based on French Impressionist paintings, with the slogan, *"Invest in your future and step into the past"*. It was intended to convey that the less hectic world of yesteryear awaited the client in a world of rural simplicity.

Lydia, a junior member of the board of the firm, who was responsible for short-listing advertising ideas, had already spoken with Tim on the phone and they had had an amicable exchange. At this inaugural meeting she had focused her smile on him as soon as he entered the office and invited him to sit at her desk to display his latest range of artwork suitable for the publicity campaign. From the beginning, she had shown an enthusiasm beyond what he could normally expect, and significantly, at one moment, as he was turning the pages of the picture files, she leant in towards him with an unexpected familiarity, resting her hand on his, ostensibly by accident, but certainly a delicate moment longer than seemed necessary. Her attendant smile seemed to speak mountains, and when she had promised to convey a glowing report of his ideas to the board of directors, his impression was that she felt an indisputable attraction towards him. When he came to leave, her lowered voice suggested an intimate understanding. She looked forward, she said, to his next visit and who knows what good news she might have for him. She insisted that from now on he should call her by her first name. The way she obliquely lowered her eyes beneath those lashes and raised them at the last moment insinuated something impossible for his heart to repudiate.

He carried this indelible moment away with him and marked its effect on his mental stability. His thoughts were confusing enough in themselves, but deciding what to do about them completely overtook him. He became wholly pre-occupied with how he could prepare for his next meeting with Lydia. Surely, he had to provide some palpable hint of his reciprocation, but, since no immediate solution offered itself, he decided to further reflect on the matter in the open air.

Ever since the first encounter with Fred, the municipal park had seemed a place of pilgrimage, and whenever he visited the town, he never failed to orientate to it. On this occasion it seemed more appropriately spacious than ever to allow him to expand his thoughts. As he strolled through the down-at-heel, rusty iron gates, it seemed, for some reason he could not explain to himself, that he should confess his present condition to his aged friend, whom he had somehow permitted to infiltrate his life as an undeclared mentor. Yet, the more he reflected on his intention, the more he felt apprehension of what his reaction might be. Losing one's heart to a lady had nothing logical about it, and Fred had always seemed a pretty practical fellow, who, even with Elsie, showed a caring but less than romantic attachment. Tim, on the other hand, was immersed in romance of the most rose-spectacled kind.

As he walked round this scruffy municipal apology for a recreation area, he looked up and saw how clouds were magnificently arrayed across an opalescent space that, until then, he had previously merely regarded as sky. He felt he could wrap himself round with those serenely draped white velvet shapes and sail away in them. From another perspective, he imagined sprouting wings and gliding round them on a crystal dance-floor with his Lady Lydia in his arms, dressed in flowing silks. When his immediate surroundings dragged his feet back down to the scuffed and generally unkempt park surface, the confession of such flights of fancy to Fred seemed suddenly daunting. And yet the need to give some perspective to his feelings persisted, and he knew that his old friend's mature vision of life's practicalities might well be indispensable.

As he breathed in the relatively fresh air and contemplated Lydia's allure, he was inspired by the idea of buying a small gift as a token of his feelings. He was not confident enough to believe he could be absolutely sure of her amorous interest in him, but knew he had no option but to follow his hopes in that respect. He decided that he would offer her some perfume. Yes, he would pay a visit to the perfume department of the House of Harvey and Bagnold, make his purchase, and then put his intentions before Fred.

It was a blessing he did not foresee the stress that the purchase was to cause him. Of course, he was always conscious of an intimidating feminine aura that surrounds a perfume counter. It felt as if you should carry your passport to gain entrance, and, at the prices listed, dress smartly enough to suggest a substantial cheque account. Whenever he bought toilet water for his aunt Augusta down in Surrey, he found the sales assistant overbearingly helpful, like someone making a particular effort with a non-Anglophone. And buying perfume seemed to invite the shop assistant's intrusion on an undeclared intimacy. However, it was one thing to buy 'Autumn Bouquet' for a middle-aged aunt, but buying a perfume for a pert and pretty junior member of a management board, who had hinted at intimacy, was quite another. He found it difficult to imagine what any shop assistant might think when men bought bottles carrying names like "Desire" "Bliss" or, something dangerously explicit like, "Nights of Passion". The only way he could survive the experience, without exposing himself to conjecture, was to adopt a nonchalant attitude and pretend he was buying perfume as an afterthought.

"May I help you?" asked the assistant, wearing the deep concern of a nurse preparing to bandage a life-threatening wound. She was middle-aged, with hair combed straight back off the forehead, and an impeccable 'maquillage' ; lips outlined, eyelids penciled and eyebrows persuaded upwards to complement the wide expression given by the subtle shade of brown shadow. She was a mature version of the manicured, professional exponent of 'chic'.

"Er,.. yes, I thought maybe,.. well it occurred to me,.. it might be a good idea to buy something as a.. ' thank you'.. for a... friend."

Oh, dear! He had hesitated slightly before the word 'friend'. Would she notice the 'giveaway'.

"Oh, yes? Can one know what kind of thing one is thanking the person for?" returned the assistant, in a tone that somehow managed to suggest it could range from a mother's lifetime devotion to a passionate week-end in Paris. He hesitated, desperately trying to come up with something non-committal. "Perhaps," she contin-ued, in a helpful tone, conspicuously loaded with infer-ence, "you just wish to thank her for being who she is?"

"Er, well,.. yes, you could say that."

"I see," she said in lowered tone, that recognised his motive for reticence. "And is the person you wish to thank young, middle aged or, may we say, more mature?"

This was the most helpful person he had ever met in his life. He began to feel overloaded with her surreal assistance. He became increasingly guarded.

"I think you would say, on the younger side," he said.

"Right. 'On the 'younger side'," she repeated, smil-ing, as she assumed an attitude of reflection. "May one ask, 'on the younger side of what age'?"

"Yes, of course." He responded, attempting a careless shrug of agreement, and thereafter, hung helplessly on to silence.

"It does help to home in on an appropriate choice," she urged.

"Of course," he responded rather too swiftly.

"So?.."

"Well,.." he pondered studiously, "let me see,.. I suppose... less than thirty."

She lowered her voice, like a mother drawing the truth out of a child arriving home late from school to utter, "Ah,ha", which might be translated, "Well, that wasn't so difficult, was it?"

She now moved seamlessly on to psychological insights into the lady 'on the Younger side of thirty'.

"Before making a proper choice of perfume, one needs to consider how well one knows the lady. And, of course, it is important to have some idea whether she is outgoing or more introvert in her personality."

"Really?" Tim said, nodding, aware that he hadn't the slightest idea how to judge such a thing, especially in the case of a wholly fabricated character.

"What would you say?" The assistant's smile demanded the key to gain access through the doors of perception. Tim was conscious of the depth of the hole into which he was digging himself, and realized he would have to be creatively imaginative, if he was not to expose himself to ridicule.

"Urm, it's difficult to say. She's a cousin returning from a long stay abroad. We haven't met for ages."

"Really? But perhaps you've written to each other?"

"Oh, yes, of course," he decided

"Then perhaps we can tell from the kind of things she wrote about?"

Oh, dear, the inquisitor had formed a partnership with him to elicit clues from non-existent letters! She was out for a full confession now; her eyebrows were half way up her forehead in expectation. It was like creating a missing person's identi-kit.

He swallowed hard before inventing the next fabrication.

"We-ell,…" - He struggled to create imaginatively - "she was touring…the museums of Europe,.." - adding, staccato - "studying art." Inwardly, he sighed with relief at having had the presence of mind to come up with a subject in which he was well informed.

"A studious type, then, would you say?" she probed, fixing him with her gaze.

"Yes, I suppose so," he stammered.

"Hmm." She mused, like a literary critic reflecting on the character. "Such ladies are more difficult to cater for than most. Has she any other attributes? Is she a social animal? Did she mention dances or sizeable gatherings of young people?"

"Er,...yes," he decided. He was becoming as inventive as an interviewed politician. "She likes to be among people and enjoys dancing and ...things."

"Good. That's helpful. Does she play sport?" she suggested.

He filled his hesitation with affirmative nods until he could come out with the unsolicited word, 'Tennis'."

"Splendid!" The assistant was getting quite excited, and Tim began to feel almost pleased at his success in keeping up with his own invention.

Her whole demeanour expressed victory. Her lips were compressed in purpose and her eyes narrowed in meaningful focus. "I think we can now consider some selections," she declared, nodding confidently at Tim. He managed to hide his relief.

She took him through several tester sprays on strips of absorbent paper, on wrists and lower palms. He was invited to imagine each one worn by his sporty, artistic, social, trendy, studious 'cousin'. Some bore jolly sportive names, some wistful, some heady. Others suggested the life of an ardent go-getting female, a languorous sophisticate, or a lighthearted free spirit who made a party bubble round her. It was, all-in-all, a journey through the whole feminine gamut. In the end, it proved so confusing that Tim was forced to choose 'Mystique' from the House of Choufleur, simply on the grounds that it expressed his own total lack of comprehension.

Whether or not the assistant was impressed by his selection he would never know, and, by this time, did not greatly care, but she said, "A wise choice," as he wrote the cheque, "I'm sure she'll adore it," as she gift-wrapped it, and gave an inscrutable smile of what he took to be encouraging innuendo as he turned from the counter.

As he emerged, he felt the cool air strike the perspiration on his brow. It was now past one o'clock and he felt sure that Fred would be found in the Dragon's Arms. He hoped Elsie was not with him; the subject he was to broach was exclusively male.

Sure enough, Fred was there, lounging back with splayed legs in the chair nearest the fire. Thankfully, he was alone. He looked up and greeted Tim with, "Ey-oop', patting the chair next to him.

"Be with you, when I get a pint in my hand. Are you all right there, Fred?"

"Aye, but, I'll not say no, if yer askin'."

"Right," Tim said, as he marched over to the counter. The pint placed before Fred, Tim settled in his seat and dived straight in with, "I've something on my mind."

"Oh, aye?" Fred muttered into his glass. "The wheels are turnin' in the top storey, then. Keepin' ye busy?"

"Busy? Yes," Tim said dismissively. "But I want your opinion about something."

"That could cost ye another round." Fred tapped Tim's knee and winked.

"Cheap at the price," said Tim, smiling uncertainly. He hesitated and looked sideways at him several times before Fred said, "Let's be 'avin' it before yer 'ead drops off yer shoulders."

"Right," Tim responded with a determined nod, swallowing hard. "Straight into it, then. I've met a girl down South I want to know better."

"Aye, well, yer first mistake is choosin' a southern girl, en't it?" he chuckled.

"All joking aside, Fred, I think I've been smitten, if you must know".

"I don't 'ave ter know owt, 'cept if ye want ter tell us."

"I thought I'd ask you what you think."

Fred appeared to preen himself slightly. "I'm yer man. Is she a child'ood sweat'eart, then?"

"No, not at all."

"But ye've knowed her a fair time," he said, with assumption.

"Not really."

"No?!" Fred turned to Tim and placed his glass on the low table in front of him. He scrutinised Tim with new interest, and wrinkled his brow with concern.

"Where did ye meet' er? 'Ow long 'ave ye 'ad these feelin's?"

"Since last Wednesday," replied Tim in a subdued tone, suddenly acutely aware of Fred's gaze.

"Last Wednesday?!" Fred's voice rose an octave. Three heads at the table the other end of the bar turned towards them. "Three days ago, and ye call yersel' 'smitten'? There's summat daft 'ere, an' no mistake! By 'eck, ye better come clean, lad."

Tim waited for the heads to turn away again before he continued. "There was... a moment..." - Tim paused and searched for the word till finally managing to breathe out the meaningless phrase, "...of unspoken recognition."

Fred's face expressed incredulity. "Un - - spoken... re – cog - nition?" Deep concern and distaste elongated his words. "I can't take in wot I'm 'earin'." Suddenly with a missionary look in his eye, he said abruptly, "Right! Let's be knowin' wot 'appened! Give it us straight!"

Tim stammered his way through a description of two people touching each other's sensibilities with hands, smiles and eyes, all playing their part in the magic encounter he had had with his lady Lydia. Fred listened with an intensely baleful glare until Tim gradually faltered and came to a halt.

"So, there it is, Fred. That's where I am just now," he concluded.

"Eee, lad," Fred almost moaned, "don't go down that road, fer 'eaven's sake, or ye'll give yersen over ter perdition."

"But you don't know the lady, Fred," Tim persisted.

"Don't 'ave ter," retorted Fred. "Ye've just not ter do it. Simple as that."

"Whyever not?" asked Tim, resentfully.

"I'll tell yer why not, lad. List'n careful." Fred's expression was severe. "Ye're on the inside looking out instead o' outside lookin' in."

"What d'you mean?" asked Tim, shaking his head.

"Ter speak plain, ye take one look at this young woman, - she gives you a bit o' glad eye an' a touch of 'er 'and, an' that's enough ter set ye off? It's daft, is that. Ye don't 'ave the faintest inklin' o' wot she's abowt!"

"But I'm sure she likes me."

"There's nowt to being liked! If yer goin' ter fall in luv, ye'd better know wot with. It's best ter see 'ow she is at sweeping t' steps, scrubbin the clothes an' bakin' pies galore 'afore ye take t' plunge! Wot 's this Lydia done ter make her so special?"

Tim was lost for words and Fred, now in full spate, continued, "There was many a lass I could 'a took to if I'd been led by 'er looks an 'er winsome ways. It would-n'a done at all!"

"But I don't want Lydia to cook and scrub."

"A lass oo's afear'd o' scrubbin' an' cookin' won't make a 'ome," persisted Fred.

Tim felt aggrieved and became defensive. "She's not that sort of girl," he retorted.

"Ey-oop!" interjected Fred. "There y'are! Ye'r stuck into lookin' out on't world in place o' lookin' inside."

"That doesn't make any sense," said Tim, petulantly.

"It makes sense ter know wot ye'r lookin' fer afore yer see it."

"Really?" returned Tim with a touch of sarcasm. "And how do you know what you want before you see it?"

Fred rolled up his metaphorical sleeves. "Well, fer a start, ye ask Jesus to tell ye wot 'E's got in mind fer ye. Then ye can know what ye want yersen."

"Even though He's not the one falling in love, I suppose," Tim replied with a sharp edge.

"Aye,well," Fred grunted, eyeing Tim with something akin to disdain, "Jesus 'as more sense than ter fall in luv wi individuals. 'E luvs us all'- even if, 'appen, 'E 'as a few favrits. Them's the one's as listens to 'Im and takes note an' all. They do that by goin inside their own 'earts, 'cos that's where they 'ear 'im proper."

Tim, by now hot under the collar, burst out with, "For Pete's sake, you don't go round asking permission to fall in love! It just happens…whether Jesus or anyone else, approves or not!"

The heads at the other end of the bar turned towards them again. Tim took hold of himself and drank down a long draught of beer. Silence reigned for some seconds. When Tim next sneaked a glance at Fred, he was stroking his chin eyeing him with a pensive scowl.

"What?" asked Tim.

"Nowt but this, lad," said Fred as he picked up his glass and, as if purposely keeping Tim hanging on, downed the contents in one draught. He wiped his mouth with the back of his hand before adding, "Fallin' fer a lass can be a trap set fer ye by the world when ye're on yer own. Yer eyes drink it up an' get infected wi' madness. Tha's the moment ye need Jesus' 'elp. An' that's wot I'm in t'process o' prayin' 'E'll give ye.

Tim sighed impatiently and let out a subdued "humph."

Fred shook his head. "Aye, well, be that as it may, if ye'll not take my word fer it, I'll leave ye t'mull it over." He suddenly got up and stood over Tim. "Jus' one word o' caution. Don't do owt 'asty till ye've 'ad a word wi' the Prince o' Peace. 'E's the only one ter put ye right."

He walked over to the door, stopped, looked round and said, by way of challenge more than invitation, "Ye can tell me wot 'E says next time I see yer." Then he was gone, leaving Tim to reflect on the 'advice' he had least expected to hear. The challenge however, continued to ring in his ears; something outside himself that nevertheless compelled him beyond his understanding to seriously contemplate,.. well,... consulting something or someone inside himself, whatever or whoever that might be.

The Filtering Truth

The following day, Tim was conscious of having been left with something of a dilemma. Fred had confronted him, rather aggressively if the truth were admitted, with doubts concerning the motives behind his amorous interest in Lydia. Instead of offering any practical advice, he had handed him a brief which, on reflection, suggested a serious challenge to his emotional state. The idea that you could consult someone else inside you challenged your reason and seemed to call emotions into question. In addition, it inferred some kind of embarrassing ritual. Just what might it entail? Tim tried to remember any other of his peers having problems with the opposite sex, and could only think of some whose problems arose out of being found out in double-dealing or having to withdraw from relationships when interest faded. Fellows back home never seemed to question what they did when they went out searching for experience with girls. They just seemed to follow their predatory noses where their advanced were welcomed. Neither had Tim really got into deep conversations with his own subconscious, but was vaguely conscious of it, having read up a bit on Freudian psychology. He had learned about something called 'the child' and 'the parent' who were supposed to be part of one's psychological make up, but had never really consulted them to keep his emotions in control. In fact, if the truth were known, he had suspected that having a 'child' to blame was a kind of cop-out that encouraged him to surrender to the invention of romantic fantasies. But now, he was firmly convinced he was in love. If he were honest, he might have to admit he had become a mite too vulnerable to female charms and subtleties. He reflected on this, and decided it might be put down to his 'child' seeking to retain his (or was it 'its', he was never quite sure) mother, as Freud had suggested. And what if, on the other hand, the very thoughts he was having were prompted by his 'parent' alerting him to dangers of his 'child'? Such speculation only took his mind round in a whirl, like the proverbial chicken and egg. There was no alternative to thinking his way through all this in the open air, and so decided to make his way once again to the dingy neutrality of the municipal park.

As soon as he descended the area steps outside the small pension, the day seemed to hover over him. The clouds posed motionless, like half-dressed models waiting in the wings at a fashion parade. The sky was an indeterminate shade of blue, the subtle kind that artists find difficult to blend, and the sun, surrounded with a halo of haze, peeped through a motionless lace curtain. The whole day gave the impression of unresolved deliberation in halted time. The clouds were certainly not of the kind to dance around; vanished was the crystal floor of romantic abandon; the day seemed to entertain no idea of movement at all.

As he pushed open the thin rusty gate, he hoped, on this occasion, not to find Fred seated on the bench. He had to reinforce something in himself before he could return an eye to eye regard with the old man; he was, therefore, relieved to see the bench empty of the familiar lounging figure.

He started round the circumference of the recreation green and set himself to reflect on his predicament.

Leaving aside all those concerns about child and parent, what exactly did he feel about Lydia, junior advertising executive for purveyors of holiday dreams in far-off places? In the notably unromantic environment of the park, he found it easier to confront the emotional issues. Lydia was decidedly attractive, had a welcoming smile, and was a woman of some influence, but, above all, she had focused her attentions undividedly on him for several minutes. He accepted that her physical attraction accounted to no small degree for his feelings, but surely this was not the only reason for them? Since her attentions to him had resulted in such a sudden emotional release, he had to ask whether she habitually focused her attention on other men as she had with him? She wasn't the motherly type that would appeal to his 'child', so to which part of him did she appeal? What had Fred said?.. 'Infected with madness'? Oh, dear, it was back to the memory of Fred insisting he should ask help from ... he balked at the name ... Jesus. Where was Jesus supposed to be in all this? Somewhere in the middle of what? Between his 'child' and 'parent', perhaps.

He stopped in front of the dilapidated bandstand, scratched his head and fondled his chin in perplexity. He recalled how Fred had invaded and occupied the political meeting and how the candidate had slunk away when Jesus' name had been thrown at him. None of the gathering had objected to Fred, and, in fact, had seemed to prefer him to the rather predictable delivery they had received to that point. What was it about Fred that gave him such extraordinary aggressive confidence? Why did he never act his age? And what was Tim doing, at a bit over thirty, knocking about with this eighty year old, anyway?

Tim sank down on the bandstand steps and let his gaze fall on the scuffed green that served just then as a pitch for two three-a-side ten year old football teams. His gaze wandered from them to a young woman in a tweed coat and a hood pushing a pram and dragging a young toddler by the hand along the far path leading to the swings and roundabout. Had **she** been in love? Was she still in love? How did she know if she was? How had she reached the decisive moment to begin the life of her child, he wondered? How long before that child would play three-a-side football on the same pitch? Tim was suddenly confronted by a sense of racing time and a feeling that being alone was decidedly second best. Could this be what his preoccupation with Lydia was all about? Did he just want not to be alone, and was snatching at the first apparent encouragement that had come his way from an attractive woman. No, he could not entertain the possibility of that, but he had, at least, logged the thought into the equation. It was at this moment that he became conscious of having had a real conversation with himself, a self that was involved in a debate allowing for the possibility of more than one answer. Not exactly firm doubt, but a state of being called into question, nevertheless. The trouble was, being smitten was not something you reasoned yourself into or out of. Reason might well do battle with feelings, but, at present, his feelings were pretty dominant.

Fred had cautioned him not to do anything till he had a word with, - what did he call Him? - 'The Prince of Peace'. Well, peace was something he was not feeling at present. He was not sure whether he wanted it, for with it might be lost the pleasure of his painful involvement. Anyway, what did he know about this Jesus? Not a lot. Did he believe in Him? Well, he had been called into the equation, too. But, how could he have a conversation with somebody he wasn't sure existed. Well, he supposed he could start with 'Is there anybody there?', and see what happened. He looked at the uninspiring sky and silently mouthed the words, "If you're there, as I don't suppose you are, then perhaps you'd do me the kindness to let yourself be known by saying something. Anything will do for a start." A crescendo of silence followed, until just as he took his gaze away from the sky and closed his eyes, he recalled Fred saying that he had to be on the outside looking in. With minimal expectation of any answers, he tried to weigh up where his thoughts had taken him thus far.

Whether he was creating a script or whether thoughts came to him unbidden, he was not too sure, but the following conversation ensued.

"The truth is I don't know whether you exist or whether I'm trying to fabricate you," he thought.

"I can see your difficulty. But do you want me to exist?" came the reply.

"I suppose I'd quite like you to. It would be company. But it might be for the same reasons I want to know Lydia. Perhaps it only comes from a need to fill a vacuum."

"And what is wrong with that, Tim?"

Now the thought might have remained nothing more than an imaginative creation of his own, except that he was startled into the consciousness of having been addressed by name. He seemed to have physically heard it; a decidedly audible sensation was involved. At the same time he knew intuitively that there was no point in searching for its origin; it had entered his mind.

Tim was drawn to proceed further. "Well," he persevered, "I might be inventing you to meet that need, mightn't I?"

"Is that a real question, Tim?"

"I think so," he half muttered.

"Do you think I am someone you can invent, Tim? Am I within anyone's worldly power to create in the imagination? Nevertheless, you can still refuse to believe in me, or even reject me, if you want."

"I'm not refusing or rejecting," thought Tim, "I'm just wondering how I can know if I am really talking to you."

"What else do you think you're doing? How do you think you can know me unless you decide to invite me in."

"In where?"

"Into your life."

"Aren't you already here?" he wondered.

"To a point. You've invited me into this moment just by talking to me."

"Invite? What do you mean?"

"Just allowing for the possibility of my reality is an invitation."

The conversation stopped as he opened his eyes. It felt like laying one book aside to open another.

Tim did not know whether he was ready to make the invitation. This Jesus seemed to be asking him to dispense with reason, and yet he might just be a figment of his imagination. On the other hand, if Jesus was as preoccupying as Fred made Him out to be, then it was crucial to consider the price of committing himself. Who knew what would be demanded of him? And yet, Tim could not get rid of the awareness of having been addressed by name, and neither, for some irrational reason, could he rid himself of its implication. But, at the end of the day, how did this solve the problem of his feelings for Lydia? Though he had come into the park to inspect his emotional involvement, he had temporarily forgotten to introduce the subject. Instead, he sensed he had been trying to discover a means of being in control of himself before he confronted Fred next time they met. Since Lydia had not dominated his thought for, at least, the last ten minutes, it suggested that he had been released from total enslavement to his emotions. He had the impression that he had stepped sideways from one self into another, and this being possible, he reflected that it might be time to collect this new self together, make his way out of the park, eat a good meal in a small restaurant he had found in a little backstreet and get an early night in, leaving his 'child' and 'parent' and anyone else, to resolve something between them, while he had a good night's sleep. Tomorrow, refreshed, he would seek Fred out and take up the subject of Lydia but hopefully by that time, with a more balanced viewpoint. As he passed through the small rusty park gate, he felt things were on the move again, and noticed that the clouds were being gently nudged across the sky.

A Testing Time

Tim, lying under the bedcovers, stretched the stiffness out of his limbs and looked up at the ceiling. Recumbent and somewhat rejuvenated by a sound sleep, he began to comb out irrelevant dream sequences from his waking thoughts. He needed to separate his preoccupation with Lydia from thoughts that centred on what he understood about himself. He had the impression that they were braided together too tightly, and, in the middle, still stalking through his thoughts, was the figure of Fred. The moment Tim recalled him, the old man walked down to the apron stage and invaded his rumination. There he stood, framed by the plaster coving of the ceiling with that familiar expectant expression that dared Tim to deny his responsibilities. Then Tim recalled Lydia and she smiled down at him standing to the left of the ceiling rose. Notable was the fact that Fred immediately turned his head towards her with a quizzical expression as though sizing her up, while she seemed to actively resist all eye contact with him. She smiled at Tim in a way that suggested not only a focussed interest, but also a brazen conviction that she had captivated him. It occurred to Tim that the strangest aspect of this whole imaginative exercise was that he had somehow assigned Fred and Lydia roles in the same piece of theatre. Well, however, improbable it might be, Tim thought, as he forced himself into a sitting posture, his next move would be to meet Fred in the Dragon's Arms. There was no point in deliberating with himself as why this should be so; it simply had to be done. The afternoon would be taken up by a visit to the local branch of the Michelangelo Repro. Art Printers, so he would have to catch Fred over a liquid lunch.

It was almost a relief to have the morning taken up by phone calls to prospective customers in the neighbouring towns, requiring dedication to the mundane matter of earning a living.

Towards twelve o'clock he had completed all arrangements to meet with his clients, and was free to return to affairs of the heart and the prospect of meeting Fred. 'Free', however was not a word that offered itself as an appropriate description of any choice he might have. He was driven by a compulsion, which induced a hard knot in his stomach.

He found himself dragging his feet, and lagging behind his intention, as he made his way to The Dragon's Arms. Occasional gusts lifted and carried scraps of litter along the gutters, providing a brief mindless distraction. There were a few breaks in the clouds, which constantly reshaped themselves, as they crossed the urban landscape of serried roofs. At his feet, sudden wind currents tossed up cigarette packets and small paper bags in all directions, depositing them, among other places, over drain covers. Maybe the next rainfall would see them all disappear into the depths. Who could tell what the future held for anything; for anyone? Who knew what the future had in store for him? What would he say to Fred when he met him? What would they actually talk about? Would he be able to return smoothly to the subject of his infatuation with Lydia or would the meeting entail providing Fred with a progress report on his search for Jesus? He ruminated a moment as he stood outside The Dragon's Arms and, without knowing why, felt obliged to reassure himself that he could, if pressed, give a reasonable account of his initial move in that direction. Why he should feel in any way accountable to the old man was not something he could conjecture over just then. He swallowed hard and set his body and face to express a composed autonomy before he brought himself to push open the doors of the pub.

There were several relaxed and jolly 'regulars' gathered at the bar, lounging and leaning towards each other, some grinning, some making gargoyle faces. One of the things Tim had come to appreciate about this pub was the way everyone assembled to disagree with everyone else in the most agreeable way. Whenever someone said 'owt' political or religious, or commented on the fortunes of the local football club or the status of the trainer, someone always shouted "rubbish!" in a jocular way to be followed by raucous laughter and much emphatic jabbing of fingers. Everyone was allowed to voice his opinion and be ridiculed, but no-one was ever shouted down. They were proof that total consensus of opinion on anything is impossible, and, at the end of the day, undesirable. They proved also that politicians are merely voted in to continue the dispute by agreeing to disagree on principle. And yet Tim was aware that, whatever disagreement Fred might have with anyone, he would on no account agree to debate the validity of his faith. He would stand toe to toe with anyone on questions of politics, society, philosophy and where the local team ranked in the league, but where his religious faith was concerned he merely stated his belief and left others to refute it as they wished. Quite literally, when anyone attempted to ridicule his convictions, he would leave. His parting shot was always to the effect, "Nowt's decided by arg'-ment where Jesus is concerned." or "Ye can tell me when ye come up wi' owt better."

There were quite a few who thought it unfair of him not to stay and be baited, and that was something else he "didn't give a fig about."

As soon as Tim walked towards the counter, he was aware of Fred sitting the other side of the fire. If he had seen Tim enter, he gave no sign of it, and Tim was too uncertain of the present state of their relationship to be able to sail up to him before he had armed himself with a pint of ale in his hand. One or two of the regulars nodded and grunted their recognition of Tim's presence, but beyond that they were too involved in ribbing each other to take any further notice. He paid for his drink and took a sizeable draught before making his way towards the hearth. He arrived at the seat the other side of the fire from Fred and sat down.

"So," muttered Tim

"Aye," responded Fred, without turning his head.

"You all right, then?" asked Tim.

"Fair enough, as t' world goes," offered Fred.

They raised their glasses simultaneously to their lips and placed them back on the low table before them. It was a signal. With nothing in their hands they were both forced to recognise the unspoken subtext. Feeling the pressure of the silence, they simultaneously launched into breaking it.

"I've been giving it a lot,..." began Tim

"Appen I've been a mite too,..." muttered Fred.

"Sorry? said Tim.

"Come agin," said Fred.

Tim shrugged and ineffectually waved his hands about. "I was just going to say...." - Tim prompted himself with more hand wagging. "...I've been thinking ... about what you said."

Fred looked at Tim from under his bushy eyebrows, with an uncertainty unfamiliar to him. He nodded silently for quite some time before briefly shaking his head and saying, "Aye, well, be that as it may, I've had it put ter me that I went beyond the bounds." Fred looked away again. There was more silence. Tim looked back and forth between Fred and the hearth, expecting some further expansion. When none came, Tim felt compelled to take up the initiative again. "I'm not sure I understand what you mean".

"No, well, that's yer way, en't it? As I see it, either ye do or ye don't understand."

Tim was confused. A deep furrow creased his brow. "Sorry, but I'm not sure what I do or don't understand, here."

"Strewth!" exclaimed Fred. "We're on abowt not understandin' understandin', now! By 'eck, yer don't make it easy, an' that's t' livin' truth!"

"I suppose it's this North-South problem we have, isn't it?" Tim proposed with some attempt at appeasement.

Fred turned to look Tim squarely in the face. "Wot I'm sayin' is, 'appen I went too far wi' me advice, las' time we wus 'ere. It were not my place ter read the riot act like that. I'm jus' admittin' that 'afore we go further for'ard, see."

Tim was quite taken off his preconceived agenda, as he realised that this was Fred's way of apologising. It was a whole new kettle of fish, which released in him a feeling of wholly unexpected gratitude and warmth towards Fred that made him laugh out loud.

"Wot's so funny, then?" asked Fred in an injured tone.

"No," responded Tim, instantly, "not funny. I was just,… well, you know,.. taken by surprise. As a matter of fact," he added, to prevent any further misunderstanding, "I was about to say that what you said last time made me think."

"Oh, aye?" Fred eyed him with what looked like suspicion, but was probably guarded interest.

"Yes, I know you're right. . I needed to ask myself what my feelings really mean."

Fred turned away with a shrug, and lifted his glass up again. "I never said owt such thing," he mumbled as he downed another hefty draught.

"Well, that's how it appeared to me, Fred," Tim insisted.

"Aye, well,…" - Here Fred appeared to be somewhat defensive.- "I 'ad a word with Jesus abowt that, an' 'E made it plain as 'ow it weren't my place ter turn ye agin yer own amorous inclinations wi' a barbed tongue. So there! I've put it to ye simple." He raised his first finger and pointed it directly at Tim. "But I never said owt abowt asking **yersel'** anythin'. I put ye on ter askin' Jesus to show ye yer next move, an' I'd be greatly cheered ter 'ear that's wot ye did!"

Fred stared into the fire, slumped in his chair like a venerable priest waiting to hear one of his flock petition for forgiveness. Tim looked at his obdurate, motionless form and focussed his mind to answer. "Well," he said carefully, "I'm not sure who I was asking." Fred shot him a quick glance. "But," he hastily added, "I did try to make contact with…"- Tim tried to find the tone that avoided making it sound ridiculous, - "er, … Jesus."

"And?" interjected Fred, now like a headmaster prising the truth from an errant schoolboy.

"And," repeated Tim, sounding as if he were searching for his alibi, "I have the impression that it's possible I may have made the first step."

Fred's face broke into an expression of total incredulity. The errant schoolboy had failed to provide him with the required answer. He stared at the hearth, took another draught of ale and frowned at the smoky flames of an uninspiring fire. He sighed, and with heavy emphasis, asked, "And wot impression wus it that made ye think ye may 've got through? Wus it a bad line, or summat?" Tim was determined to ignore the irony, and keep it direct and simple. It was a decided challenge, but he continued. "I simply asked if there was anyone there to speak to?" Fred eyed him again and signalled his acceptance of this confession by the slightest nod and the raising of an eyebrow. "Right," he muttered in a low, half committed tone. "And…?"

"Well,… it did seem to me that I managed to… see things from a clearer perspective."

The Father Confessor introduced into his questions a tone of qualified patience and forbearance that one who understands hidden truths lends to one who does not.

"An' where d'ye think this perspective come fro?"

"I'm not sure?"

"An' wot made ye not sure?"

Tim shrugged helplessly before offering, "I.. wasn't sure if I was talking to myself or to someone else."

Fred nodded slowly as though willing something to develop in a photographer's dark room.

"Wot.. made ye... not sure?"

Tim returned to the memory of his conversation in the park and then said, "It wasn't so much what I was thinking,..." - and here Tim surrendered to his own uncertain memory – "well, if you must know, I felt as if someone addressed me by name."

Fred sank into his chair and whispered, almost inaudibly, the softest "Hallelujah!". A blissful smile spread over his face, the like of which was beyond Tim's metaphorical powers to describe, and then he suddenly turned and leant over to slap Tim's knee. "There you go, then!" he burst out. "'E's got yer number, 'as Jesus! Ye contacted 'im , an' now 'E's got yer in 'Is book!"

To Tim this bizarre idea of having had one's name placed on some kind of heavenly organiser seemed overstated and premature. The group at the other end of the bar had stopped to observe what the excitement was, and Tim suddenly felt exposed. He dropped his voice almost to a whisper to say, "Perhaps we could keep our voices down a bit, Fred. It's a touch loud."

"By 'eck, I should think it were deserving a bit o' noise, an' all! It's not ev'ry day ye get called! 'Ere! That's worth another glass, is that!" With that he swallowed the remainder of his drink in one go, and was on his feet, practically skipping over to the bar. He ordered two pints of ale and proceeded, straightaway, to relay his good news to the assembled company in voluble but indistinct terms. As if on cue, they all looked over at Tim, turned full frontal and gave him the 'thumbs up'. With the thinnest smile, he reluctantly returned his own raised thumb. They all broke into grins. It was not within Tim's experience to know whether this was a sign of congratulation or jocularity. But Fred seemed greatly satisfied and returned to the hearth like a spaniel fresh from the cull.

"There ye go, then!" said Fred, planting a full pint glass in front of Tim. "Now we can start plannin' things."

"What things?" Tim asked, alarmed and feeling left in the dark.

"Why! Yer amorous persuasions, o' course!" Fred beamed over the rim of his glass at Tim as he took another long draught of ale. He sighed with satisfaction as he put the glass down again on the low table. "Right! Let's be 'avin' it, then. Wot did Jesus tell ye ter do?"

The question had been thrown at Tim, and he was swept aside from his own thoughts into a place of total indecision. He shook his head, possibly with the subconscious intention of clearing his mind, and made indecipherable breathy noises, before managing to stammer out, "Well, er,...I'm not sure that anyone told me to do anything at all,...actually."

"Ye don't get ter speak ter the Prince o' Peace wi'out E' lights yer way. Come on, now. What thoughts did 'E bring ter mind?"

As Tim struggled to imagine what thoughts would satisfy Fred as being authentic words from Jesus, the door of the pub opened and Elsie entered, and straightway seeing them both, made a bee-line. She focussed a rather stern expression on Fred, before saying in a clipped and accusative tone, "I 'ope ye 'aven't bin givin' this young lad from the South a rough time, Fred. An' I 'ope ye'll be gettin' me in a half o' guiness fer the good o' me 'ealth."

Fred smiled rather sheepishly back at her and got up to comply with her request. As he strode up to the bar, Elsie sat next to Tim and put her hand on his arm. "'E means well by it all. But, as I say to 'im sometimes, 'A sharin' heart comes afore the best advice'." She lowered her voice to an intimate level. "I said to 'im, I said, 'Fred, a young man's 'eart will lose its way afore it finds it'. It's the natur'l way o' things."

Elsie's affectionate smile disconcerted him, as if she was seeing him in a new light for the first time. "Ee, wot it is ter be young, eh?" Tim thought that he was not as young as all that; in fact he was the right age to be thinking seriously of settling down, which he had always taken to be the mark of a mature intention not to enjoy oneself with abandon . On the other hand, he didn't think he could be accused of having done anything to excess in his life, and as for being 'abandoned' in his pursuits, well, that was out of the question. He nodded, "Well, I suppose so."

"But it has its drawbacks, eh?" Elsie prompted with a wink, clearly implying that she had been through it all, in her day. "At best, it's a confusin' time, an', at worst, a time fer makin' mistakes as can last a lifetime."

Fred saved Tim from having to reply to this, by arriving back with the glass of Guinness for Elsie, which he placed in front of her with something akin to respect. "There you go, Elsie. Yer constitutional medicine."

"Give over, Fred. I drink fer pleasure. Ye know that," she retorted, as she lifted the glass and downed half its contents in one swallow, something Tim thought quite a feat for someone so slight of frame.

"An' now, let's be hearin' from the lad 'ere," she said with a confidence that promised itself an optimistic outcome. "What ye need is the insight of a mature woman t'elp ye get a fix on this lass as ye've got an inclination t'ward."

Tim, hemmed in between them both, felt that he was about to be given a third degree.

"Trouble is", interrupted Fred, "the lad don't know 'er at all."

"Now jes' ye 'ush yersel', Fred," retorted Elsie. "Jumpin' on a body's no way ter get 'im te see 'is way for'ard." Amazingly, Fred appeared to recede under Elsie's chastisement. She turned to nod indulgently at Tim, folded her arms and settled into her chair. "Now, lad, first we need ter know what 'exactly took yer fancy with this lass?"

Tim stared into the cheerless fire and sought some means of halting this interrogation. Could he, he wondered briefly, be taken suddenly with an attack of colic or a migraine? He looked at Elsie, who gave him her indulgently patient smile, and he suspected he would need to muster up some kind of convincing performance. "Take yer time, Tim, lad," she murmured, "It en't alus easy to find the words." Since he had not explained his infatuation to himself, he felt himself in imminent danger of coming over as simple-minded. He tried out several phrases in his mind, before he settled on what he hoped was the least open to dispute. "In a relatively short encounter, I think she showed warm feelings towards me."

"Aye, well, but," she said, with emphatic dismissal, "what's it abowt 'er that draws you? Is it 'er looks, 'er per's'nality, 'er voice, or wot?"

Here Fred, unable to contain himself, interjected, "'E don't know owt. 'E 'an't asked 'er owt abowt 'erself."

"That true, lad?" asked Elsie, peering directly into his eyes. Tim shrugged in a hopeless fashion, and Fred took the opportunity to reinforce his opinion. "A lamb to the slaughter, that's 'im."

"Nay, Fred, there's a way for'ard," she insisted. Fixing on Tim, she said, purposely, "It do seem ye've based yer feelin's on a scarsity o' facts. So, as I see it, ye"ve ter ask 'er out ter winkle them out."

"Winkle?" echoed Tim.

"Aye," she persisted. "It's not as tho' ye'r alone. You take Jesus along wi' ye an' 'E'll prompt ye." She turned to Fred, "That's right, eh, Fred?"

"It is an' all!" exclaimed Fred, glad to be consulted in the matter. Tim tried to imagine sitting at a restaurant table ready to tuck into a meal with Lydia on one side and Jesus on the other, and found it quite beyond him.

"Yer name's in 'Is book!" insisted Fred.

"All ye've ter do is ask 'Im ter light yer path," added Elsie.

" 'E'll make it clear ter ye if she's the wun wot 'E's cut out o' the 'erd fer ye," said Fred, drawing a censorious glance from Elsie at the implication that she was to be lassoed.

Tim suddenly felt like a cat that had been stroked too much and decided he had to draw this advisory session to a close.

"Yes, yes, I'm sure you're right, both of you. Indeed, that's what I'll do. Look,.." - and here he took a quick gulp from his glass, and glanced quasi-anxious, at his wrist watch, - "I've just remembered I've got to meet some people on business. I must run, now."

Fred and Elsie appeared completely flummoxed by Tim's unexpected closure, And, as he stepped hastily towards the door, hoping to prevent any further advice on his amorous prospects, he added, "See you next week, when I get back from the South." The vision he took away with him as he waved a cursory goodbye was of two open mouths and two chins dropped to the floor.

What he didn't stay to see was the wise wagging of heads that the aged use to pronounce their verdict on youth.

The Resolution

Tim inspected himself in the bathroom mirror and willed himself to retain a smile of unselfconscious confidence. His teeth gleamed, his cheeks had a healthy glow brought on by liberally applied after-shave lotion, and his hair was moisturised to tame the quiff into falling back from his forehead. He pressed it into a wave and turned his head both ways to glimpse the sides. As far as he could see that was the best he was going to accomplish with himself before he set off to the property agent's office and the all important rendez-vous.

He muttered to himself that life would, one way or another, take a new turning from the moment his eyes met those of Lydia, and the door to joy unbounded might well be opened to him thereon. He vowed to be assertive and cool and to conduct himself, as if he found this young woman's attraction to him wholly unsurprising, and, in some measure, merited. He would smile and look self-contained; he would encourage her opinion that women's interest in him was completely expected, and born of experience. He would, in a word, take upon himself the mantle of a man of the world.

As he descended the steps from his lodging, he glanced at the sky between the roofs of the town, and registered the mixture of optimistic blue and glowering grey. There was a breathless atmosphere, and it was difficult to sense the direction of the clouds, or whether they intended to divest themselves of their contents. He carried his mackintosh over his arm with a cap folded in the pocket, just in case. He did not take his umbrella, believing it would detract from the image he had calculated to project. As he marched along the pavement, his adopted jaunty gait was gradually tempered by a sense of indeterminate purpose. He suddenly remembered a superstition he had as a child, which forbade him to tread on the joints of the pavement slabs in case it brought ill fortune, and just as swiftly, dispensed with the thought as an immature detraction from the debonair role in which he had cast himself. He adopted a studied gaze into the distance, as if in a self-contained and focused world, engrossed in matters beyond the reach of others. And, as he played with this thought, he realized that he was, indeed, in a world of his own. All at once, Fred's face, full of disbelief and indignation, projected itself on the screen of his mind, and he had to shake his head to rid himself of his presence.

As he approached the property agent's office door, he fingered the Windsor knot of his tie, eased the collar away from his Adam's apple and took a deep breath. He took a firm grip of the handle and entered the vestibule. There she was, smiling broadly with an air of eager welcome wholly focused on him. Such a smile, so obviously dedicated to him, rested comfortably on her face and stayed there to ensure his full appreciation of the sincerity and intensity of her feelings. He imbibed the smile and almost entirely forgot to hold on to his adopted image. He smiled back in what he hoped was a confident and openly expressive manner. She came from behind her desk and said, with words that fell sweetly from her lips,

"Oh, I have been so looking forward to seeing you back again."

Involuntarily, his breath left him in a gasp of pleasure, which he translated into a laugh and a staccato, "Me, too." She took his arm and pulled him gently towards the front of the desk. There she took his mackintosh and draped it over another chair at the side, before gently pushing him down on the one in front of the desk. She relinquished him and returned to her own chair the other side, smiling all the time. Tim grew tall and smiled back with the confidence that only deeply recognized mutual feelings can elicit. She took her time looking him over in a way he took to be almost a possessive appraisal. He found her adorable, and thought how delightful it would be to lean over and kiss that smile, then breathe on that slender curved neck with a slow, assured and delicate passion. He sat erect and alert for her next words, completely forgetting that she might be waiting for his.

After some silence, she said, "I have some wonderful news for you and a proposition that I hope you can consider. It could well mean.." – and here she blinked, lowering her gaze a fraction to emphasize the implication, - "that we may see a great deal more of each other." The words carried so much import that Tim could hardly find the breath to reply. "Really?"

She shrugged and looked faintly coy as she lowered her voice, "I hope that might appeal to you." "Oh, yes, of course!" he blurted out, and then in order to maintain some semblance of self-containment, added, "All things being equal". He had not the faintest idea what he meant and wished to heaven he had not said it. However, it did not appear to faze her, and the moment passed. Suddenly he remembered the perfume in his mackintosh pocket, and startling her by the abruptness with which he got up, he strode over to the coat, fished within its folds, and extracted the small, neatly gift-wrapped package. He stood over Lydia and extended the gift, saying, "For you."

She seemed overcome with unexpected pleasure, and parted her lips, bereft of words. Tim nodded as she slowly reached out for his gift, and said, "I hope you like it." Lydia looked back and forth between him and the package. Slowly she peeled the wrapping off, as if engrossed in an awesome ritual. When she came upon the bottle itself, she emitted a gasp of undisguised pleasure. "Oh, how wonderful!" she whispered. "I love this one."

"It was carefully chosen," he said in a modest tone, remembering his experience with the assistant in the department store.

"But how did you know?" she asked, after a moment's silent reflection.

"Oh, I had an insight into your character," he said with devil may care confidence. She shook her head in uncertainty. "No," she replied, "I mean, how did you hear about it? We only let it out of the bag a week ago."

Tim shook his head slightly, bemused. Mercurial adjustments registered on his face. 'Out of the bag' He had heard nothing. What could she mean?

"Did someone from the office telephone you?" she pursued. "I mean, how else could you have known?"

"Er,.. no-one phoned," he said expressionlessly.

"Then how did you come to hear about?" She paused to think. There was silence for a few seconds, before she said slowly and knowingly, "Someone let you know, didn't they?"

His thought was suspended, and, without an inkling of her meaning, he murmured, "Know what?"

"Of our engagement." Her smile had an air of apology as well as self congratulation about it. She extended her hand to show him the ring on her fourth finger. "James said it was time we made it permanent before everyone started talking. You know how things get around."

Tim's head swam and his thoughts revolved in a vortex that threatened to swallow his composure and release a scream. Oh, God, no! She was engaged to….. 'James'?! his face was a blank.

"You know," she promoted, "the director's son. He's in charge of publicity. It was James who took such a shine to your ideas in the first place. That's what I was going to tell you about. I hope you'll be pleased." She began to bubble with enthusiasm again, and all Tim could do was stare vacantly at her as if he had been betrayed. She could not read his expression, but obviously took it to be one of astonishment. "Oh, bless you for thinking of me," she said effusively. "I've just got to give you a kiss for that!" Here she got up and racing round the desk planted her lips on his cheek, emitting a theatrical "Mwah!" as she did.

"Did her cruelty know no bounds?" thought Tim, as his head began to whirl round in the confusion that emotional pain and a search for reason created.

"Thank you, thank you, thank you," she repeated. "I'll treasure your lovely gift for ever."

"I doubt you will," he thought in a sudden wave of bitterness. "You'll make extravagant use of it for smart social gatherings, and it will be forgotten as soon as I am." But he said, airily and without a hint of irony, "Oh, it's a pleasure. Just a small token, you know."

"Well, now let us see what I can do for you, dear boy." She leant over the desk tilting her adorable chin towards him as if taunting him with its proximity. "I spoke to James about your ideas for using Monet. James liked your draft ideas for the script very much indeed. In fact,"- and here she reached out and gripped his arm to stress the fact,- "James liked it so much, he asked me to put a proposition to you. He is so much a man of impulse is James, but it usually comes from the right place and works, which is what we want, isn't it. I said to James, I said, 'James, are you quite sure? And, straight back, James says without blinking, 'Lydia, trust me'."

She smiled the smile of a benefactor about to bestow an inheritance, as Tim wondered how many times she needed to pronounce James's name in one paragraph. It was not a name he had ever particularly taken to, and now it had such an odious connotation, that he could hardly prevent himself from shouting his objection every time she uttered it. As she continued speaking, he pondered on the possibility of suddenly shouting, "It isn't fair! You can't know what being loved is, if you give yourself to a man, who calls himself James!" He began to wear the expression of a criminal under investigation at a police station, and he cast his eyes to both sides of Lydia, vaguely hoping that she would take this as a sign that he was reflecting on what she was saying. Occasionally, he flicked his eyes across her to establish that she was still in full flow. His gaze once more fell on her face, and suddenly he realized she was silent. Tim cleared his throat, and they stared at each other in silence.

Lydia broke the silence with a broad smile. "So, what do you think, Tim?"

Tim had not the slightest idea what he was supposed to respond to, and said, "Ah, well,.. er... I suppose that, er... I need to think about it."

"Really?" She seemed quite astonished that he should have any reservations. "Why so?"

"Ah, well, sometimes these things take time," he offered lamely.

"James and I don't expect you to do it in a rush. But, in principle, we can agree, can't we?"

"Look," he said, trying to walk on the thin ice of his total ignorance, "I think the best thing would be to put it down on paper."

Again, the look of incredulity appeared on her face. "But I would have thought the opportunity would be irresistible. What can possibly hold you back from accepting it?"

Tim stood at this point and, searching around for some kind of alibi for his obtuseness, said, in a tremulous tone, which arose out of his emotion, "To tell you the truth I've just received some very bad news."

Lydia stood and slowly came round from her side of the table her face full of concern. "Oh, Tim, I'm so sorry. What on earth has happened?"

"I just learned of the end of..." - he sought desperately for a word to present itself and came out with - "a friend."

She came right up to him and took both his hands in hers and stared into his eyes. He stared back wearing an expression of burdensome sorrow, which, considering his feelings, was not at all difficult. Her hands went up to his arms, and she stroked them as a mother might a child.

"A close friend?" she asked.

"I thought so," he muttered.

"I'm so sorry. Was he one of the family?"

"She," he corrected her, miserably.

"Oh, I see," she said lowering her voice with the implication that this was, maybe, the love of Tim's life. She lifted her hand to his cheek and stroked it. The compassionate expression of her face, the touch of her hand and the tone of her voice, that so fell short of the truth, was too much for him, and leaving behind all rational consideration, he grabbed her waist and kissed her full on the lips in an abrupt, clumsy movement that almost made him lose his balance. He tried to maintain the conjoining of their lips, but she suddenly pushed him away from her, and they stood a yard apart, both slightly breathless, he from the realization of his boldness and she from a growing sense of outrage.

Tim saw her wipe her mouth with the back of her hand, which somehow left no room for doubt, and he drooped with the shame of having gone beyond the bounds of decorum and made an absolute ass of himself.

"What on earth got into you?!" she finally managed to say. "And you say you just lost your close friend?!" She seemed to be implying that he was absolutely fickle and undependable to have so easily let feelings of personal loss turn to passionate interest in someone else, and especially her. She returned to behind the desk, and suddenly resembling a primary school teacher, turned to him and primly lectured him, saying, "After I told you that I am engaged to James."

As he took her accusation in, the hopelessness of his position and the tension that her reference to her fiancé created in him, made him throw all caution to the wind and he blurted out, "Oh, to hell with James! May you be very happy together!" She glared at him with a mixture of scorn and anger, which stoked his embarrassment into saying, "And what's more, you should be more careful about the way you throw yourself about. It gives people the wrong idea."

"Throw myself about?!" she almost shouted. "How dare you!"

Tim went over to the chair where his coat was draped and gathered it up. "Oh, what's the point?!" As he moved to the door, she picked up the bottle of perfume, extending it out to him. "You'd better have this back. It obviously didn't get what you were after."

It was his turn to express his anger and frustration, and he shouted out, "You can keep it and have the satisfaction of remembering my stupidity every time you wear it." With that he swept out of the office and into the street without waiting another moment to see what effect his words had.

Outside the weather had somewhat changed. The steely grey was definitely being moved away to the east and clear skies were coming up behind it. Dim shadows of the buildings became clearer as the sun began to peep from behind a bank of thinning clouds. Tim inhaled deeply and shook his head. He found it difficult to imagine how he could have behaved so rashly, and yet, at the same time, he felt a growing sense of entitlement. Lydia's prim response to his - well, yes, admittedly – outrageous action, was less than he would have hoped from a truly compassionate woman; one who would ask for a proper explanation of his motives. She had assumed the worst of him, and never showed any desire to understand his emotional state. He had been mistaken, not only about his hopes of being involved with her, but also about her capacity to have feelings of real depth. He was not able to banish all his amorous feeling in one fell swoop, but he felt some slight compensatory encouragement in being able to find the first qualifications in them. As he looked up at the opening sky, he agreed with himself that he must seek every chance of surviving his pain and disappointment, and must not sink into depression. He would, - well what would he do? – yes, he would start looking for something he had been thinking about for some time. He would look out for a small car.

Taking a New Road

A sensible car for someone in Tim's position would have been an inexpensive one, reliable, with low fuel consumption and maintenance. Having considered this, he asked himself what kind of an image that would create for a fellow in need of a boost to his ego. After a brief internal debate, in which common sense battled with status image, he decided he needed something with flair that would show a careless defiance of life's setbacks.

It would have to be second hand; his finances did not stretch to a new one. 'Retail manager' was his job description, but, in reality this was another way of describing a glorified 'traveling salesman'. But, he had heard that you could snap up a pretty good bargain among prestigious cars that dropped dramatically in price from their initial value, so long as you did not mind them having eaten up a fair number of miles. Also someone said that the more powerful the car, the longer you could rely upon the engine. In this way he encouraged himself to think big, to lash out on a vehicle that would take him down a more adventurous road. He wanted to give off a nonchalant air, especially when he returned to the north. He wanted to fend Fred off with as careless an attitude as possible, as if Lydia had been a passing and unimportant affair, which he had now left behind him. Above all, he was determined to nip all gra-

tuitous advice and folk wisdom in the bud. Tim sometimes asked himself why he tolerated Fred's intrusive
and dogmatic advice, and yet he was aware that Fred
somehow showed more interest in his welfare that anyone else he had known. Although Fred was blatantly
judgmental, Tim felt it all came from a genuine personal
concern. In fact, he had begun to feel a real warmth towards the old man, and was conscious of being surprised at just how entertaining it was to be in his company. Nor was he sure it was just entertainment; Fred
had opened a door to new perspectives on life, perspectives he might never have explored had he not been
given a push. He had only put his toe in the shallows,
but he was intrigued by Fred's conviction of the presence of his mate, Jesus, always at his side - or was it inside? Anyway, Tim had reached an agnostic rather than
resistant state of mind, and, at a time when his emotions
were sorely tested, had been drawn into a more focused
self-inspection. Tim was not ready to place his confidence in this presence about which he knew so little, but
he had been conscious of a sense of a vacuum that invited him to test out new territory.

However, presence or not, right now, he was determined to shape a new life for himself and compensate for
his recent sense of loss and hurt pride. Accordingly, he
delved into the magazines advertising cars for sale and
picked out several models offered as 'genuine bargains'.
In fact it was difficult to find any adverts that did not offer
them. There was a plethora of 'careful owners' practically
weeping at the thought of having to relinquish their faithful treasures, whom they had cosseted with unmitigated
devotion and which had served them unstintingly and
without fail at all times. It was with passionate reluctance

that they had to release their four wheeled friend to someone who would hopefully bestow on her the tender loving care to which she was accustomed, and to whom she would render impeccable service.

Tim homed in on two that particularly captured his fancy. One was a Japanese four wheel drive model, with the distinction of a snazzy spare wheel suspended below the back window and an elevated driving seat affording an imposing view of the road; the other was a drop-head coupe with twin exhaust system, armchair seats, and dinky convertible roof that folded back over the boot. He had visions of driving with a smile of cool aplomb, hair swept back by the wind, his arm, bronzed by the sun, carelessly resting on the window.

In the case of the Japanese model, he could imagine the effect of the elevated seating and the high-tech dashboard with electronic read-out. It would demand a strong masculine hand to govern it, and any female passenger would have to be impressed, always supposing one was to be found.

He inspected them both and mused. He listened to their owners' woeful tales of enforced sacrifice and the need to sell at the ridiculously low prices for a quick sale. Apparently, there had already been incredible interest in both the cars, and anyone intent on obtaining the bargain of the century was strongly advised not to lose any time in making his decision. After earnest deliberation, and finally deciding that the drop head coupe provided a greater opportunity to flaunt an adventurous image, he went straight round and declared his interest to the owner.

"You recognise a bargain, when you see one," said the owner, confidently.

"It certainly looks good. I expect you have a service record I can see?" said Tim.

"Oh, dear," replied th owner, with a laugh that turned into a superior smile, "I never cease to be amazed at the need for bits of paper. Matter o' fact, I've never allowed this beauty to leave my sight. Heaven knows what a garage mechanic could do to her. I let them do the MOT. The rest I do myself. It's the only way to be sure she gets the proper care and attention she needs."

"Well," said Tim, with a hint of reserve, "I know nothing about cars, so I'd have to put it into be serviced." The owner immediately picked up on this reservation and hastily assured him that there was nothing to really worry about.

"With me, it's just I'm a perfectionist," he insisted. "I like a hands on relationship with my car. But if you're not up on them, you have to leave it to the experts."

Tim thought there was some inconsistency, if he was prepared to call mechanics 'experts', but when the car burst into life when the key was turned and the lights and electrical equipment seemed to be in good working order, the tyres had some good tread on them, he capitulated to what he regarded as 'a bit of a dream'. Any doubts he may have had about the owner's claims were over-ridden by his growing passionate desire for this car. He sat in the armchair comfort of the driving seat, surrendering to the visions that rose up before him, and convinced himself that he had read somewhere that someone had said that the reliability of a car could be judged by its appearance. This was one very smart model indeed. He got out of the car, stroked the bonnet and, swallowing hard, offered the owner two hundred pounds less than his asking price. To his surprise and gratification, the owner accepted the offer with minimal hesitation.

"You're a canny businessman, you are," the owner said, with a rueful shake of the head, "but I want the car to go to a good home and I think you're the man to fit the bill. OK she's yours. I'd like cash, if it's all the same to you."

"Right," replied Tim. "If you can drive it over to my place, I'll have the money ready and I can arrange for insurance cover. When can you do it?"

"Soon as you like," returned the owner with obliging alacrity.

That same afternoon the owner drove over accompanied by an obliging mate with his car in convoy. Tim, having drawn the cash from his bank, handed it over in exchange for the MOT and the proof of ownership documents, and before he could blink, found himself the proud owner of a sports-car and raring to cut a dash. As the previous owner left with a mate, his parting remark was "You buy as you see, as they say. Good luck with it."

What he saw was good enough for him. He intended to put it through its paces by driving north the very next day. It would be a test for himself, as well, being over three hundred miles.

As he set off from Surrey suburbia rather late the following afternoon, he felt the exhilaration of the challenge, and was determined to pass it with flying colours. A bank of thin grey cloud strung itself thinly across the pale salmon sky to the North. Immediately overhead thicker cloud glided almost impercptively by, as if propelled by the gentle breath of invisible mouths. He felt as if his way ahead was being cleared of all obstruction.

As soon as the engine roared into life and his foot pressed down on the accelerator he was dramatically conscious of the response. It took some time before he could control the car's desire to leap ahead by remembering to apply minimum pressure. The car's aggressive growl, as it accelerated, was a warning to other traffic to give it plenty of space. Feelings of power mixed with a sense of danger overcame him, as if he had just shouted at a crowd of street louts to keep the noise down. As he opened the throttle up on the motorway, he took courage. and sank into the comfort of his seat, relaxing into an increasingly bold belief in car's ability to eat up the miles. This was a beast you had to treat with respect, a very different kettle of fish from the small about-town model his mother lent him from time to time. He could feel the powerful thrust of the engine pushing into his back, telling himself that he would soon take the present elation for granted and display a nonchalant face to the world. He inspected the dashboard, with its plethora of dials, clear proof of technical excellence, and he noticed that the needle of the fuel indicator had dropped down rather quickly. He was sure it had registered 'half full' as he left home, but now, it seemed, he would have to look for the nearest motorway garage. He was relieved to find a service station just north of Northampton, when he saw the needle had begun to touch the empty mark. He decided to half fill the tank, since fuel on the motorway was more expensive; he could, after all, refill again when he reached the other end. When he discovered how much it cost to make the indicator register half full, he decided that the tank must be larger than he'd been led to believe. Having stopped, he decided he would take the opportunity to have a coffee at the café. The engine's roar as he parked and revved up prior to turning off the engine, caused people's heads to swing round. He was the centre of attention as he climbed out of the car and strolled nonchalently into the café, whistling tunelessly under his breath. He ordered a cappuccino, topped with chocolate, and sat near the window to survey his possession. He thought he had acquitted himself pretty well, and felt a new entitlement to be called the 'rightful' owner of this impressive status symbol. Adopting a careless attitude and studiously gazing into the distance, he became aware of passers-by slowing down to crane their necks over the driver's seat and inspect the dashboard. It occurred to him he ought to buy a pair of driving gloves at Harvey and Bagnold as soon as he got up north, - the ones with the backs cut away and a thin strap to bind them to the wrist, unless, of course, such things were too cosmopolitan for such a small town. He sipped the last of his drink, sauntered back to the car and stood over it long enough for passers-by to log in his ownership. He opened the door and slid into his seat like a fighter pilot in a war film, and turned the ignition key. At first attempt it only half fired and then iccupped out again. He turned the key a second time and, after a few reluctant staccato coughs, finally emitted a sustained growl and then roared into life. A passing elderly lady started and her husband had to take her arm. Everyone within a radius of thirty yards turned in a sudden defensive move, and several people directed purple- faced disgust towards him, before seeking sanctuary inside the café. Tim pushed the gear lever into reverse but felt the gearbox resist him. He pushed harder and it made a grinding noise like a sudden burst on a washboard. Two young men stopped to contemplate the car's performance, and one jerked his head towards it with a grimace, making some remark to his companion with a sardonic smile. This elicited a superior smirk and a dismissive shrug, as they waved their arms to waft away the fumes that had suddenly been kicked out. Tim studiously adopted an unconcerned expression and reached into the glove compartment for his sunglasses, which always aided inscrutability.

He had parked on a slight incline with some space in front of his bonnet, and so, a little nervously, he took off the brake and allowed the wheels to inch forward while he eased the gears into reverse. He was greatly relieved to feel the gear engage, enabling him to back up into the passageway leading to the exit. He shot the bystanders a glance of studied indifference before revving up and pulling away at twice the speed necessary. As he re-entered the mainstream traffic on the motorway, he suddenly felt a wave of intense relief at not having had to get out of the car before his spectators, and was aware of beads of sweat on his brow. He would certainly have to have the garage look at the gears when he got up north. As the wind cooled his forehead, he settled down, once again, to enjoy the sensation of comfortable and effort-less speed and a sense of pride at such power under finger-tip control.

As Manchester drew near the light began to fade and he switched on his headlamps. Some gathering clouds were fringed with threatening edges, and he looked for the next service station to pull-in. Just short of the petrol pumps, he got out and, leaving the car ticking over, smoothly and effortlessly pulled the roof over the body. At once it was transformed into a protective interior, with womb-like comfort and warmth, almost the reverse of the bold image he aspired to. A few spots of rain fell as he ducked back into his seat and sat for a few moments inspecting the dashboard with satisfying sense of security. As his gaze swept over the dials, it fell on the fuel indicator, and he was surprised to find that, once again, the needle had almost dropped to register 'empty'. This was disturbing since it was only ninety miles or so since he had put petrol in, believing that it was sufficient to complete the journey. For the first time, he was conscious of grounds for real misgivings. In the circumstances he had no alternative but to drive up to the pumps again, only this time he would have to fill her up, if he was to be sure to reach his destination. He could not afford to find himself stranded, and he had to bear in mind that, once off the motorway, he might not find a station so easily before he got to the town.

Evening was drawing in and he was still at least a hundred miles away. He was suddenly aware that he might not reach his lodgings before the little restaurant round the corner closed for the night. Perhaps, he thought, he had better catch a quick bite at this motorway café. .

As he sat at his table with burger and chips and a bowl of pink gooey substance that called itself something 'delight', he mused on the car's performance. Leaving aside the swift, smooth ride and the classy appearance, there was that irksome question lodged in his mind concerning its apparent thirst for fuel. Maybe there was a leak in the tank to account for the need to refill. He would have to have that seen to as soon as he could, and, certainly, before he could show off his new acquisition. For a vehicle that had been given such tender loving attention, it was showing itself singularly ungrateful.

Casting aside doubts, he rose and went to the car with a renewed and vigorous desire to get to his lodgings. Turning on the ignition, he was met with the same initial reluctance to burst into life, and it was only on the third attempt that it condescended, with a consumptive cough, to fire into action. Having parked with space before him, he was able to put the gear into forward and pull away with a purposeful roar. As he got under way, he began to dwell, with growing concern, on the car's temperamental moods. These would also have to be taken in hand, but - hey-ho! - , he would meet the challenge and overcome any obstacle that confronted the new way of life he was designing for himself, freed from timid choices and frustrated hopes. .

Soon the sign for the town came towards him and he turned off the motorway on the winding roads taking him from those endless files of traffic, everyone competing with the car ahead for the empty open road that remained obdurately filled with traffic. There was something more demanding, more meaningful in tracing the bends and undulations of the country roads instead of merely pointing the bonnet into the far distance. The steering was easy and finger-touch light, allowing him full concentration on the variables of the road. This was new freedom that called on precision and initiative. He felt tall.

The light began to fail as he turned his lights full ahead. He enjoyed the sensation again of the powerful engine eating up the miles, as he sat cocooned in his 'pilot' seat, until, reaching the brow of a hill, the town revealed itself spread out in rows of amber lights in the valley below.

He let the car cruise down the slight hill, as he anticipated the reaction he would elicit when, tomorrow, he was seen driving this wicked beast.

As he brought the car to a halt in front of the small lodging house, he lightly revved the accelerator as he switched the engine off. It was now eight o'clock and nobody was walking around under the ill-lit streets. He got out, took his bags from the boot and climbed the short flight of steps to the door without anyone noticing his arrival. The door was locked. He tapped on it and pressed the bell under which was written, 'press for attention after seven o'clock'. Shortly, he heard a door at the end of the passageway open and the proprietress, Mrs. Gertrude Delaney, shuffled her shapeless form forward in her fluffy slippers.

Tim recognized that tight-lipped look that betokened an unspoken censure of those who, in the slightest way, inconvenienced her. She had always given the impression she had taken on the lodging house as a form of self punishment. The only time she relinquished this severe expression was at settling up time when she would look alertly at the client with raised eyebrows as he extracted money from his pocket.

She pulled back the bolt of the door and drew it open.

"Ah, thank you, Mrs. Delaney. A little after hours I'm afraid," he murmured.

"Aye, well, there'll be nuthing open now, an' the kitchen staff 've gone."

"Oh that's fine," Tim said brightly, as he gained entrance past her bulky frame, "I had a bite on the way."

"Just as well," she retorted, as he pushed home the bolt again.

"Breakfast at eight, I take it," she added, padding back down the passage without waiting for his reply. She disappeared round the corner, and he was left to climb the stairs unattended. He reached his room, deflated by the contrast between the ambience of the car and the cold impersonal quality of the minimal furniture that stared back at him. A sudden vision of Lydia's face expressing outrage burst on to the retina of his mind and a feeling of rejection suddenly overcame him. It was a mixture of loss, self-delusion and betrayal; he knew that his loss came from deluding himself into believing what mere appearances had hinted at. But there was also a conviction that she had somehow led him on by over-familiarity. He wanted to hold on to that last belief, for it fed him a kind of anger that held her at arm's length. He wanted to push it away. He wiped a cold flannel over his face, got undressed and closed the bed sheets over the day.

Infernal Combustion

Tim awoke to a cunning kind of day that casts shafts of sunlight in through the net curtains to lure you out without an umbrella, while it lines up weather to fling at you as soon as you reach the point of no return. It was the kind of day that can blow up a storm in less time than it takes a conjurer to pull a rabbit from a hat, the kind that opts for perversity. The fact that the landlady's eggs were overcooked, the toast underdone and the coffee lukewarm was as nothing to the catastrophic sequel; the fact that his lovely new car obdurately refused to show the least inclination to recognize its vehicular purpose; in short, to start. For a machine that had had so much tender loving care devoted to it, it was not adopting the right kind of grateful attitude at all. Several turns of the key and firm pressure on the accelerator pedal were of no avail. Tim opened up the bonnet and gave stern looks to the engine, demanding that it pull itself together and meet its obligations. It was not impressed. It remained stubbornly resistant to every facial expression he chose to wear. It teased him into entertaining a flicker of hope with whirring and clicking noises when he turned the key, but refused to muster even a cough. Tim was not fooled by its pretence to be pining for its previous owner; it was out to be perversely uncooperative. He eyed the exterior with disdain, kicked the tyres with his shoes, banged on the dashboard with his knuckles and mouthed unrepeatable words at it.. Nothing was less likely to create a cool image than a car that did not start; it was letting him down badly. Since he obviously knew nothing about cajoling a reluctant car into action he would have to visit the nearest garage to have it looked at immediately.

He set out on this mission just as the day was pulling a grey curtain across the sun and by the time he was three blocks away it had begun to turn on the shower. If his mind had not been so taken up with the injustice of the car's bad behaviour, he might have taken more notice of the sky and observed the signs of the day's intention to enact gross hostility. In very few moments the clouds began to open up and throw their contents down in earnest, forcing him to break into a run. Seconds later, he was staggering, breathless, through the sliding double doors of the garage workshop, just before the very worst effects of the cloudburst held sway. He was, nevertheless, soaked, to say the least. He felt great relief when he recalled that he had, at least, closed the car roof over .

He turned to meet the gaze of two young fellows in greasy blue overalls, who looked him up and down like schoolboys whose game had been gate-crashed. One of them ambled over with a tight-lipped grimace, wiping, his hands on a cloth that conferred more oil on them than it could possibly remove.

"Yeah?" he grunted. "Summat you want?"

"Yes," said Tim, out of breath, but in a defensive tone that suggested he could kick a ball as hard as the next boy. "As a matter of fact, I do. I've got a problem."

"Oh, yeah?" answered the fellow, looking behind him at his mate with a laconic stare that suggested that there was a witty response if he could think of it.

"I've just driven up from Surrey," began Tim.

"Oh, Surrey, is it?" interrupted the mechanic, with the implication that this could be the cause of the problem.

"I began to notice something not quite right on the motorway," Tim added.

The mechanic nodded and raising his eyebrows in feigned wonderment with a distortion of his mouth, said, "Something not quite right, eh?" With the smirk of a music hall comic, he turned again to his mate and added, "Sounds to me like something's wrong, then."

"Er, yes," muttered Tim, manufacturing a patient tone. "Whatever it is, I began to suspect something when the car started coughing."

"Sounds like a heavy smoker to me," said the other youth, and they both chortled in a mindless way.

"Well, since you mention it, black smoke was emitted from the exhaust when it started," Tim offered, studiously ignoring the levity and raising his voice in the hope of instilling some urgency into the situation. "And this morning it refused to start at all."

"Where's it parked?" asked the mechanic, throwing the rag into a bin at his side, and fixing his narrowed eyes suspiciously on Tim. "That'll be a call-out charge," he said, shrugging.

"It's only five minutes away," suggested Tim.

"We've still ter drive the van round, right?"

"Just to inspect it?" objected Tim in as reasonable a tone as he could muster.

"Could be anything. Valves, pistons, electrics. Need the whole bag of tricks to make an inspection." He delivered this as a clear take-it-or-leave-it offer. Tim hesitated long enough to recollect that this was othe only garage for miles, and suppressed a desire to argue. "When can you take a look at it?" he asked with a shrug.

"Aye, well, that's just it, en't it?" replied the mechanic, turning to his mate, pulling a wry face. "There's the Mapleton's Ford, the Clarkson's van an' Mrs. Riley's Bentley ter sort out, like. You don't mess abowt wi' that lady, eh?!"

"Not unless yer up fer an ear drummin'!" agreed his partner. They played at being terrified for a second or two and turned to looked at Tim with pseudo rueful expressions. Silence followed, during which they looked as if they had fallen into reverie. Tim, held his ground in as cool a way as possible, until the first mechanic turned to his mate and said, "This looks like one of yer out of hours jobs, Bobby lad." Bobby drew his breath through his teeth and leant on the wheel arch of the car he was working on. "Could be, Ron," Bobby returned, ruefully. Having introduced the question, they returned to silent musing. Ron ran his tongue over his lips and nodded slowly as if reflecting, while Bobby drummed his fingers on the wheel arch. Tim was reminded of Tweedledum and Tweedledee, and felt anything he said now would break a spell and prompt even worse nonsense. At last Ron raised his eyebrows, made a constipated face, and in a measured tone that suggested a great mystery had been solved, said, "Well, - I suppose it could be done after hours. Time an' a half, o'course. What d'yer think Bobby, lad?" Bobby blew out his cheeks and then made contemplative noises with his tongue, like a punter wondering which horse to put his money on. "Takin' time an' a half as read, I reckon I could square it wi' my doll. She'd not be best pleased fer less than time an' a half, that's fer sure."

"Look," said Tim in some exasperation, "if that's what I've got to pay, then fine. Can you make it this evening?"

"Righto. Yer on!" said Ron, as if it could have been solved ages ago. "Be there at six o'clock." He turned abruptly away, went over to a van, spread his frame on a sliding trolley and disappeared under the chassis.

Tim felt like a small schoolboy dismissed by two surly prefects, though personally he doubted they would be given a position of authority in an abattoir. Well, maybe they would show a little more respect when they saw the car they were going to inspect.

Having hopefully sorted out the means of getting the car running again, he was now faced with keeping from being water-logging. The rain was bucketing down, and he was without the least means of fending it off. He peered out from beneath the canopy that jutted out from the workshop doors, searching, without success, for the least break on the clouds. He was contemplating the inevitable consequences of making a dash for the shops up the road when suddenly he saw Fred's familiar figure proceeding towards him. He was instantly recognizable by that characteristic gait that suggested he had no destination and was out and about for no other reason than to take in the world about him. Dressed in the same cap and gabardine mackintosh he always wore except on very warm days, he held his umbrella aloft, impervious to the weather. Fred caught sight of him, and Tim converted a frown into a pale smile as he contemplated Fred's curiosity at finding him in the garage. Tim presented a pathetic figure holding the lapels of his coat together to close himself against the spray. Fred came abreast and drew up with a rallentando. He gazed at

Tim from beneath his umbrella, as if assessing the mood, before saying, "Aye up, then. A bit of a predic'-ment, eh?"

"You could say that, Fred," muttered Tim, with a self-conscious shrug.

"Well, then, it must'a bin providence what brung me along here at this time," Fred offered with a nod. "Specially since we 'aven't seen 'air or 'ide o' ye fer nigh on two weeks," he added raising his eyebrows to elicit a response.

"Yes, I've been pretty occupied," Tim responded lamely, aware that the rain he was sheltered from was turning Fred's umbrella into a waterfall. "Hadn't you better step under cover?" said Tim.

"Elsie and me thought ye might 've got yerself 'itched by now," Fred said, ignoring the invitation, and raising his eyebrows, added, "seein' as 'ow ye were so keen."

"Was I?" Tim recognised Fred's attempt at irony, but had already made up his mind to sound as if the episode with Lydia was left behind. "Heavens, that's water under the bridge!" he retorted expansively. "Oh, aye?" muttered Fred, and then, after a pause, added, "So this water we're getting's nowt ter do wi' you, then?" The riposte was delivered in a tone that made it impossible to decide his mood. Tim nodded and compressed his lips to simulate a smile of mild regret. He would be certain to conceal any hurt he felt from Fred, for sure.

"Well, Tim lad, as I'm on me way ter join Elsie at the refreshment area of 'Arvey an' Bagnold, maybe you'd be of a mind ter join me. Come ter think on it, what alter-native d'ye 'ave when there's an umbrella on offer?"

The way he said this made Tim aware of an immedi-ate change in Fred's attitude, which seemed to express subdued relief and optimism that was best ignored. As Fred had implied, the chance of being rescued from his present plight any other way seemed balefully unlikely. Tim engineered a smile as he said, "Right you are, Fred. Thanks."

Fred took this as a signal to pull Tim under the umbrella by his arm. Tim had to duck down and bend his knees to remain under cover, and was forced to proceed along the pavement like Groucho Marx arm in arm with Charlie Chaplin. There was something grotesquely embarrassing and rather too intimate about it, and Tim was very relieved when they reached the revolving doors of Harvey and Bagnold, and he could be released from Fred's clutches, like a puppy let off the leash.

Straightaway, they made their way up the centre stairway, leaving a trail of wet footprints on the parquet floor, through the gentlemen's outfitters department and thence up to the second floor given over to curtains, carpets and small furniture. To one side of this was the café, which, apart from the three or four posh restaurants in town, was the only one that offered table service. The round tables with embroidered tablecloths and the small white aprons and hair bands worn by the waitresses contributed to a nostalgic flavour recognizable only by those increasingly few old enough to remember. Even so, it was seldom less than half full, and it was a comfortable, not to say comforting, place to rest one's shopper's legs, when recovering from having spent far more than one should.

Elsie was sitting in the corner, demure and slightly prim, with a featureless hat fitting close to the head that spoke of an ignorance of fashion. However, she looked twice as bright and pleased with life than the fashionably dressed around her, and her eyes scintillated with pleasure as she caught sight of Fred. When she realised who accompanied him her mouth opened, first in mild astonishment, and then into a smile of welcome with just a hint of curiosity.

"Look oo the wind's blown in, then, eh," said Fred with a confident nod.

"Aye I can see, who it is. Wot's the story, then?"

Before Tim could greet her, Fred cut in with, "It's all right, after all, Elsie, - leastways, as far's I can tell."

"Thank the Lord fer that!" she exclaimed, pointing to the chair next to her.

"Come on then. Let's be 'avin' yer. I bin waitin' til me tongue's 'angin' out fer a cuppa."

"Right. I'll give 'er the nod next time she looks this way," he muttered as he sat down. "Come on lad. Don't make us all look like midgets. Sit yer down." Tim took the chair next to Fred and opposite Elsie, feeling like a case study, with the third person references to him.

"Well, now," began Elsie, without losing a second in directing the conversation where she intended it to go, "where 'ave things got to, then?"

"Aye, let's be knowin'," added Fred, pushing himself back in the chair and interlocking his hands. Tim had made no real preparation for this direct approach, and was glad when the next moment Fred suddenly raised his arm to beckon one of the waitresses over. As she took their order for a pot of tea for three and two custard slices, he had time to shape some kind of a internal script that he hoped would satisfy their curiosity.

"So, then?" said Fred. "Aye," added Elsie, as they both settled back expectantly, their attention wholly focused on him.

"Well, things haven't got to anywhere,.. actually," Tim said, knowing he shouldn't have added 'actually' the moment Fred gave his wry face. The word was likely to render any statement entirely unconvincing to Fred's ears. "I mean," he went on, aware that any faltering understatement on his part could further discredit his story. "I mean that I revised my feelings for Lydia and had to find a way of rejecting her advances as gently as possible."

"Very proper," affirmed Elsie, turning to nod at Fred. "Aye. Does yer credit, does that," pronounced Fred, "'cos it's not easy, that sorta thing, eh lad?"

"No, I suppose it wasn't,… considering."

"Considerin' what?" asked Elsie, suddenly boring into him with an expression that detective sergeants reserve for criminal investigations.

Just then the waitress came with their order and placed the pot and so forth on the table, which gave Time a few moments respite to gather himself together. Why, he asked himself, did he always go one stage too far and then have to explain himself? He swallowed hard. The waitress left and two pairs of eyes focused on him again. "Considerin' what?" repeated Elsie. Tim hesitated before saying, "Well, I mean,..you know,.. letting some-one down lightly...without hurting their feelings." He hoped they would take his halting delivery as a sign of sensitivity on his part. They nodded slowly as they sipped their tea, still focusing on him over the rims of their cups.

"What d'ye think 'appened ter change yer mind?" asked Fred, pressing in with a sudden unrelenting gaze.

Tim opened and closed his mouth several times before stammering, "To tell the truth, I don't really know. I mean,..well,..it just didn't seem right,..you know,..to go on with it." He tailed away and looked down at his feet.

"There y'are, Elsie," said Fred triumphantly, casting a confident smile at Elsie before adding, "I said as 'ow us prayers'd be answered, if we kept at it." He jerked his head towards Tim, as if to confirm his opinion. "I reckon you was visited," he went on. "I'll go so far as ter say ye was diverted fro' certain disaster. Elsie and me"ve bin prayin that ye'd not be led down the path of desolation."

"Ee, Tim, lad," added Elsie, "we're ever so glad ye've not give in te yer instincts." She turned to Fred and frowning severely said, "Though I must say I doubt there's a need ter be so dramatic about it."

"Aye oop, Elsie, luv, I was only sayin'," he replied, rather lamely.

"Aye, well," she muttered, "but we 'ave ter think on."

"Oh, aye," he restricted himself to muttering.

There was a moment's silence, and they drank their tea as Tim inwardly sighed with relief and Fred and Elsie appeared to reflect on a situation redeemed from disaster. At length, Elsie broke in with a polite smile. "So, Tim, what've ye been doin' with yerself, now ye're liberated, so ter speak?"

"Urm, this and that," he said with a dismissive shrug.

"Oh, aye?" Fred interjected. "What was ye doin' at the garage?"

"Oh, er..oh,ho,.. that?" Tim stammered, attempting a nonchalance that could not be further from him . "It's nothing really."

"It were never nothin' whenever I 'ad ter go t' garage. It must a bin summat. So what's up?" persisted Fred.

Tim decided he had better come clean and get it over with. "Well, if you must know, I've just bought a car."

"Well, I never!" let out Elsie.

"An' it's givin' ye a bit o' bother?" suggested Fred with alarming percipience. "Well, actually, yes,... a bit," Tim unwillingly confessed.

"What sort'a trouble?"

"This morning, it just wouldn't start."

"An' ye went round there t'ave it fixed?!" Fred continued, raising his eyebrows and his voice in disbelief and shaking his head. "By all that's holy, it's divine providence!" he exclaimed. "They're a couple o' cut purses, them! I were sent ter save ye in the nick o' time!"

"What do you mean?" asked Tim, suddenly alarmed by Fred's passionate outburst.

"They don't know a big end from a crankshaft, them two. An' they charge twice as much as anyone else fer the privilege of lousin'up yer car."

"But, I've told them to come round and inspect it this evening," Tim said in some alarm

"Then that's ter be stopped!" said Fred. "An' I'm the man ter do it, an' all!"

"You can't! They're the only garage for miles, and they agreed to come round this evening!" objected Tim, suddenly alarmed to have his chance of repairing the car jeopardised.

"Look 'ere, young Tim lad, it's either got to be put a stop to, or the car's a write-off!" insisted Fred. "You ask Elsie if that's not gospel."

"Oh, aye, if 'e says it's true, 'e should know," obliged Elsie, with an old fashioned look that promised a tale, if the need arose. "You listen to 'im. 'E's a canny lad is Fred."

"'An wot 's more," Fred went on, with a suitable look of disgust, "ye don't need *that lot* to give yer car a doin' over." He prodded his own chest with a cock of his eye, adding,." 'cos, I'm yer man fer that."

"You?!" Tim exclaimed. "What do you know about cars?"

"Me! Know about cars!" exploded Fred "What *don't* I know, more like it! I've been under more car bonnets than ye've 'ad hot dinners. Ask Elsie."

"Right enough," said Elsie on cue. "You tell 'im, Fred, luv."

"I wus in the Royal Engineers secunded t' Ambulance Core in t' war," he asserted, sticking his chin out. "An' it was me what kept them wheels turnin', hail, rain, snow, blow, an' all."

"But surely that was some time ago?" Tim suggested, treading carefully for fear of wounding the old man's pride. .

"Get away wi' yer! I've kept me 'and in, don't you worry! It's like swimmin' – ye never fergit. An' I work wi a mate o'm ine who's a right genius an' all. Come on, let's sup up and get round there. Hey oop, it's stopped rainin'!" He pointed towards the window, and as they followed the direction of his finger, he waved the waitress over with his other hand.

When they left Harvey and Bagnold's, they found that, although light rain still hung in the air, it had, indeed, stopped throwing it down, and the sky smiled in optimistic patches through frowning clouds as if it would soon relent and sidle away to the east to cry on someone else's shoulder. As they moved down the street, Fred gripped Tim's elbow from time to time as if he might make a sudden break for it, while Elsie, with one arm through Fred's, held aloft the umbrella with the other. Tim could imagine what a sentient hand puppet might feel and became increasingly uncomfortable with Fred's alarming confidence. It was unreasonable to expect him, at his age, to be '*au fait*' with the latest developments in mechanics, and yet, as they went along, he continued to insist on the providential guiding hand that had led him to rescue Tim from the miserable consequences of giving his car over to those two garage mechanics. Whatever their lack of social skills, thought Tim, surely they were bound to be more versed in the inner workings of cars than an aged maintenance engineer of world war two ambulances. Yet here he was being swept along by his sheer ebullience and Elsie's complicity.

As soon as they reached the garage, Fred left Tim and Elsie to dive in to the workshop and got straight to the point. He strode up to the nearest car and coughed very loudly at the mechanic half submerged on the trolley. As soon as a face appeared from beneath the car, he said, "No need ter put yerself out, t'night. The young feller here's suitably catered fer." He jerked his thumb towards the door. "So we'll not be needin' yer services, ta very much, and a good afternoon to yer." A second face rolled from under another car and joined the first to exchange open-mouthed frowns as they saw an old man stride purposefully out of the double doors out of sight. Tim was just able to hear one say "Well, bugger me!" before Fred swept him and Elsie down the street, thankfully out of earshot. Tim was glad to be away down the road as fast as was possible, but Elsie began to puff and pant as Fred chivvied her along by her elbow.

"Ey-oop, Fred, easy does it, if yer don't mind!" she exclaimed. "Can we 'old up a bit. We're not on the way t' sales! The car's not goin' anywhere is it? It's incapacitated."

Fred nodded assent and slowed his step. "Is it much further, then?" he asked. Tim pointed ahead and muttered, "The second turning on the right and half way down the road. It's parked just outside the Fairview Guest House."

When they turned the corner of the road of Tim's lodgings, they were met with vehicles ranged the whole length, and Fred began to peer earnestly ahead, anticipating the model he imagined Tim had chosen for himself. He judged a small white saloon to be appropriate and as they came towards it, pointed and asked, "Is that it, then?" Tim shook his head and brought them to a halt abreast of his drop-head coupe. "This is the one," he said with a touch of pride, patting the top of the hood.

Fred and Elsie went suddenly very quiet and appeared to go immediately into a trance as they slowly surveyed the car from bonnet to tail. A frown of total incomprehension spread slowly over their features, and they slowly turned to each other in utter disbelief. Fred shook his head and Elsie pressed her lips together and looked heavenwards as if she could perhaps seize an explanation from the clouds. They fell into a contemplative pose, while Tim waited for them to express some kind of appreciation of what they were privileged to see. So engrossed were they in coming to terms with the grandeur of the vehicle that they seemed unable to find the words to express admiration. When words came, they were clutched at, one at a time and delivered haltingly implying, as Tim would prefer, awe and reverence. But reverence, as it turned out, it was not.

"What?!.." whispered Fred, looking with open mouth at Elsie.

"...could 've brought 'im?...." added Elsie, sotto voce.

"..ter such a pass?" concluded Fred with a final exhalation of his breath.

Elsie shook her head like a woeful philosopher, and, with the look of a messenger in a Greek tragedy, turned to Tim and said, "Ee, lad, wot in 'eaven's name possessed ye t' go down this road? It must'a bin summat dire ter get ye ter do such a thing."

"What d'you mean?" asked Tim, querulously. "I didn't steal it or anything. It's legally mine."

" 'Legal', he says," murmured Fred mournfully.

"Well, o'course, it must'a bin unrequited love that did it," pronounced Elsie, suddenly visited by this obvious explanation.

"'Appen yer right, Elsie," said Fred. "Strange 'ow it takes some folk."

Tim looked from one to the other feeling like a sick patient being talked over by two nurses.

"Look here!" he exclaimed. "I've no idea what you're on about. I need a car to get about in my job." He swallowed hard before adding, "This one's ideal for long journeys." It somehow lacked the air of authenticity to convince Fred and Elsie, who shook their heads in slow unison.

At last she looked at him like an indulgent nanny and murmured gently, "It's not your fault, lad. These things can take ye queerly."

"What things?" demanded Tim.

"Best not dwell on 'em," broke in Fred. "Least said, soonest mended, my grandad used ter say."

For a brief second, Tim reflected how long ago that must have been, before he blurted out, "Well, if a chap can't buy himself a car for the purpose of furthering his career, without being suspected of...heaven knows what, ... well, ..." — pausing again before petering out with, - "I just don't know."

They said no more, but stared at him fixedly with the deepest sympathy.

He tried to stare back but could not sustain the effort to confront their undeclared accusation of his evasion. He turned away to the car and changed the subject by observing, "And now I have the problem of getting it up and going again, with no mechanic to do it."

"Nay," returned Fred, "that's the easy bit."

"Oh. Aye," added Elsie. "'E's a dab 'and at these contraptions, is Fred. So all's well that end's well." She seemed suddenly to have become cheerfully reconciled to the situation, while retaining the right to regard it as a forgivable aberration on Tim's part.

"Aye, well," said Fred, "be that as it may, it's not a model I'm overly acquainted with, so maybe I've ter do some consultin' an' come back t'morrer." Continuing to shake his head, he looked the car over with a mixture of disdain and reluctant awe, before suddenly breaking out with, "Well, there ye go, then. No point in cryin' over spilt milk. we'll be round t'morrer with me tools t' sort yer out."

He turned to Elsie with an affirmative nod and took her arm. "Let's be off then, Elsie. 'E'll no doubt 'ave things ter do, and I've ter ruminate awhile."

He gave a dismissive wave of his hand and added, "Don't fret yersen'. It'll all get sorted."

With that, they walked arm in arm back up the street, with a supremely confident air, while Tim was left on the steps of his lodgings to conjecture on the unlikelihood of Fred's confidence being translated into any practical solution for his precious new status symbol.

Skeletons Under The Bonnet

The following day, as Tim awoke and stretched himself into consciousness, his mind leaped immediately to the moribund vehicle parked outside that had fallen so abysmally below his expectations. The next second saw him involuntarily cover his eyes with his arms, attempting to shield his mind from the memory of it.

He had sunk into a morass of despondency ever since he had watched Fred and Elsie disappear up the road. The incapacity of the car was expressed in his whole body and facial language and took over his whole personality. The rest of that day had seen him tentatively telephoning to arranged mediocre meetings with disinterested clients, who were totally uninspired by this distracted salesman's lack-lustre presentation of his exhibits. They detected that his heart was not in it and that his mind was elsewhere, which was, indeed, the truth of the matter. By the end of the day, he had reconciled himself to the painful prospect of crawling back to the garage mechanics, cramming his mouth with very humble pie, and inducing them with grossly inflated remuneration to bring his car back to life. He retired that evening extremely dispirited, and he was still dispirited as he descended the stairs the next morning, with no appetite for his landlady's less than savoury offerings. As he was about to enter the parlour-cum-breakfast room, he met a decidedly disgruntled Mrs. Delaney, who made a particular point of flouncing past him with a platter of burnt toast and rubbery fried eggs. She cast him a withering glance as she brushed him with her tray, allowing her elbow to come into abrupt contact with his solar plexus.

"Good morning, Mrs Delaney. I hope I find you well," he attempted, as a means of thawing the frost.

The pointed way in which she placed the tray on the sideboard made a clear statement of her feelings. She turned towards him with a determined look.

"There is little to worry about concerning my health, Mr. Carter. Health is not one of my worries, I am glad to say. It is the good name of my residence that I have to be concerned about."

"Oh, I'm sure you have little to be worried about there, Mrs. Delaney," he said with an ingratiating smile as he made his way to his corner table.

"Is that so? Then perhaps you would take a look out of the window and tell me if you think I should continue to be optimistic in that respect," she retorted tartly with a curl of her lip.

Tim crossed to the window and looked out. Below him stood his inoperative car, as glaringly stationary as he had last left her, but now with a large striped bed sheet draped over the bonnet. At the kerbside, in front of the car stood a dingy pram with a torn hood full of jacks, tools and spanners, and at the bottom of the steps to the front door, two ill-dressed figures sat disconsolately. One was Fred and the other a complete stranger, a giant of a man, unshaven, unkempt, and, judging by the state of his shabby mackintosh and unwashed shoulder length hair, a person of indeterminate age with limited means. Tim shuddered internally and turned to confront his glaring landlady with the misgivings one might associate with a gum extraction at a National Health Dentist's. From the expression on her face, he knew he had some painful explaining to do.

"Well, yes,.. I am acquainted with one of the gentlemen sitting on the steps, Mrs Delaney."

She raised her eyebrows at the word 'gentlemen' and cut in with, "Oh, I am well aware you have taken up with the 'gentlemen' as you call them. They made it very clear you invited them round."

"Oh, not exactly 'invited'," Tim returned hastily. " I mean, I had a kind of understanding with one of the gentlemen, but er...nothing definite, you see."

"No, I do not understand, Mr. Carter," she said emphatically. "All I know is they must remove themselves from the entrance to this residence."

"Yes, of course. I'll go and tell them right now."

He slid past Mrs. Delaney and went down the hall door, stopping briefly to mentally rehearse a script with which to approach Fred. Before he opened the door he had reached the conclusion that no such script existed. He walked down the steps with the appearance of confidence he was far from feeling. Fred and his companion got to their feet straight away.

"Fred," said Tim in acknowledgement.

"Aye, 'appen it's me. This 'ere's Monty, who's keen ter give an 'and."

Tim turned to Monty, whose face suddenly cracked open into a smile, revealing a row of tobacco-stained irregular teeth.

"Right," muttered Tim uncertainly. "Actually, to tell the truth, the landlady is not too pleased," he continued, delivering the message as if he was musing upon a mystery. "I think that she would feel better if we all got off the steps," Tim urged, as he strolled across the pavement in the general direction of his car, hoping that this would encourage Fred and his companion to follow.

Follow they did, and all three stood in a row in front of the bonnet.

"Right," proceeded Fred, "we can git started soon as we open 'er and get the bonnet up." He rubbed his hands in anticipation and nodded reassuringly towards Monty, who continued to smile without saying a word and stared at Tim with a disquieting fixity.

"I've been thinking, Fred. Maybe I ought to get the garage to look her over, before we go any further." Tim simulated an agonised expression, as if he had reached the thought only with the deepest soul-searching difficulty. The agony arose from the thought of delivering his lovely new car into the hands of two amateurs, one of whom seemed mentally stray.

Fred turned to Tim with slow deliberation and eyed him with a magisterial sternness before saying with the full weight of his conviction, "Ee, lad, ye of little faith! Will ye give yerself over ter the unscrupelous world cos ye can't trust yer fellers with yer best interests at 'eart?" He shook his head sadly as he continued. "Are ye tellin' *me* that ye'll not place the keys o' this car in ter me 'ands, when me an' Monty, an' my mate Jesus 'as put oursel's out fer ye? Nay, lad, let that never be the case. Let's be 'avin' them keys, then we can 'ave a quick prayer afore gettin' on wi' task 'in 'and!" Fred held out his hand, and looked at Tim with a pitying stare.

Tim, with every breath of resistant wind driven from his sails, drew the keys of the car out of his pocket and handed them meekly over like a small boy discovered with a purloined bag of sweets by an admonishing shop keeper.

"Tha's the ticket," said Fred, as he moved round Tim to show the keys to Monty, who instantly broke into an even broader smile. The next moment Fred imperiously waved his two fore fingers at the other two either side of him and said, "Time ter bring our mate, Jesus, in ter t' situation. Eyes closed and heads bowed if ye please." Tim found himself following Monty's immediate obedient response, and an elderly lady passing at that moment looked at the three figures and then at the hotel entrance to see if a coffin was about to be brought out. Oblivious to the world around him, Fred lifted his voice in prayer. To say lifted is to say less than justice; he gave forth as if he were speaking above a howling gale at sea. Several passers-by were stopped in their tracks as his voice broke out with megaphonic clarity. "Righto, Jesus, as yer can very well see, we've got a fair bit on us plates, so we're going' ter need evry bit 'o 'elp Ye can gi'us. An' I know there's them as needs t' increase their belief in Ye, an' all. Any road, I ask Ye ter overlook this jus' now in the interests o' makin' it clear 'ow things work out when we 'and 'em over ter You. Thank ye, Jesus, in anticipation of yer special corp'ration. Amen." Fred prodded Monty who straightaway bellowed an "Amen", all the more dramatic from being the first word he had uttered in Tim's presence to that moment. Fred turned his eyes on Tim, who obediently echoed the response. "Right, Tim lad, ye can get off about yer business now, an' leave it t'us," said Fred dismissively

Tim was aware of several passers by who had briefly halted, like an arrested single frame in a film, to take in the sight of this little group. With a brief nod and a pale smile, he retreated back up the steps into the hotel as the potential crowd of onlookers, having decided the show was over, broke into action again. As Tim closed the door behind him he glimpsed Fred whipping the bed sheet off the bonnet, laying it on the road in front of the car, and then inserting the key in the door. Tim averted his eyes and decided that the only thing to do was to immerse himself in his schedule for the day. The last thing he could countenance was taking the least interest in watching the innards of his precious car being surgically operated on by the auto-mechanical equivalent of Burke and Hare. He concentrated his mind on the programme he had devised for visiting the local firms, but was inevitably drawn back frequently to thoughts of how much it was going to cost to have the car rescued from the consequences of having been interfered with by two over-confident amateurs.

After a quarter of an hour, he decided that being in such proximity to the assault on his car was too much for him; he would have to take himself away completely from the scene. Packing some samples of artwork in his brief case, he sped downstairs, along the hall, through the front door, and slid covertly down the steps, averting his eyes from the kerb side, like a thief running off with the silver. Fortunately, Fred and his cohort were too involved in prodding and tapping under the bonnet to even notice him, and so Tim was able to reach the end of the road, undetected.

As he turned the corner, the last fleeting glimpse was of Monty getting down on his back and beginning to crawl, in his lumbering way, under the car.

He called himself to order and steeled himself to remember that the first port of call was the offices of the

Local Council, whose Chairman had, in the bizarre way that fate sometimes thrown up, shown himself open to the idea of an artistic cover for the latest annual financial statement as a strategic cover-up of the local authority's parlous state. The Chairman having managed to bulldoze through the plans for the erection of new Council Offices, assuring its members that, although seemingly expensive, he could divert the public from concern about rising Council Tax with some pleasing presentation. He told the executive committee at the last meeting that something scenic on the cover would instill confidence in the idea that the town was about to be given a transforming face-lift. He regarded it as a politically sound move and had stressed that the three things to concentrate on were, "presentation, presentation and presentation". When the Borough Surveyor suggested that content might be just as important, and favoured some reference to the amount of work he had personally put in, the Chairman pointed out that the present over-riding need was to prevent the public from understanding the full implication of the information provided. Everything should be done to provide the 'feel good factor' that by-passed the need for awkward questions. "If the papers get hold of the figures, they'll make a bloody great fuss and stir up the populous in no time," he stressed.

He put it to Tim slightly differently, explaining that they were ready to patronize art by putting it to work for commerce, It somewhat cut across Tim's perception of what art was about; it was, indeed, patronising, - but, at the end of the day, he remembered that, whatever art was for, he had to make a commercial living. Accordingly Tim set his mind to find something to serve the purpose.

He wondered if the chairman would buy Canaletto's grand preoccupation with stately buildings, but reminded of the polluted stretch of the local canal thought it was hardly compatible with the Adriatic coast or Canaletto's pillared confectionary. He turned his mind to the twentieth century painters for something symbolic. The Chairman's plans for the proposed administration buildings were flauntingly minimalist, with glass panes set at angles that recoiled from the world with disdain. Tim had tried to imagine what kind of art could prepare the public for such an implied respectful dread of authority. He imagined serried ranks of workers hidden behind opaquely reflective glass tapping away at keyboards, or letting their sad wandering minds gaze out like Edward Hopper's motionless characters. It recalled Huxley's 'Brave New World', maybe inhabited by Lowry's anonymous matchstick figures. Perhaps the Chairman would accept Lowry for his essential northern character. 'Coming From The Mill' came to mind, filled with cloth-capped figures all bent slightly forward, weighed down by their towering surroundings. No, the Chairman might detect the irony. Tim felt the appropriateness of Chiroco's 'Melancholia; Mystery of a Street', but knew that that was entirely out of the question. The Chairman had stipulated the painting should, at this stage, not preempt the building in a representational way, but should simply make an optimistic statement. Tim listened to the Chairman's requirements, and though outraged by such banality, nodded while inwardly imploding. He recalled Corbusier's definition of a house as, 'a machine for living in', and decided that the Chairman was obviously constructing a 'machine to work in'. The Chairman's demands elicited the image of Leger's, **'The Builders'**, and recalled what the artist had said of his picture of builders working up in the girders of a constructed factory; *'I saw man as if he were a flea- he seemed lost in his own invention, with the sky above him. I wanted to show this contrast between man and his inventions, between the worker and that metal architecture, that hardness, that ironwork, those bolts and rivets.'* And, yet, thought Tim, the subjects looked at home among the girders, wearing their caps at a jaunty angle. There was something beguiling about them, working in unison to a confident rhythm. There was enough ambiguity to express his own feelings and, at the same time, satisfy the Chairman.

"Not very picturesque, is it?" retorted the Chairman as soon as it was shown him.

"True," said Tim, carefully. "But it speaks of things getting done, and the blue sky is so optimistic, don't you think?"

"Aye, but the workmen aren't very smiley, are they?" pressed the Chairman.

"That's because they're so focused on their work," said Tim with the confidence that came from having spoken so many times to the uninitiated. He had become very proficient at spouting nonsense.

"You will notice," he added with a reassuring smile, "the way the four central figures are all lifting the same girder. There is a fundamental togetherness that projects us into a promising future."

"Well, maybe you're right," conceded the Chairman, with a shrug.

"You're the expert, so I suppose that's how it will come over to the populace at large. Better had, anyway."

The Chairman seemed happy enough at the choice, and Tim felt he had preserved a modicum of integrity, while accomplishing a commercially successful meeting. Hands were shaken on the dates for the printing and the price to be paid, and he was free again - to worry about his car, which had been lurking just below consciousness, throughout.

As he made his way back to his lodgings, he alternated between trotting when he was overtaken by his concern to see the car again, and slowing to a crawl when confronted by the thought of the consequences of Fred's and the burly, taciturn Monty's attentions on his precious new acquisition. The tension increased as he neared the final corner, and he almost had to reverse into it, metaphorically peeping through half opened fingers and cringing like a child watching a horror film.

Braving his fears, he turned the corner to be met by a crowd of bystanders encircling the pavement outside the lodging house. As he drew nearer, he made out Fred's voice ringing out from the middle of the crowd, like a market stall owner.

"Ye can see me friend 'ere lift t' gear box into place, alignin' it with, the main chamber o' t'engine wi the 'elp of 'is alignin' tool!" bellowed Fred. Tim looked over the heads of the back row of eager onlookers and saw Fred standing side-on to the car pointing like a magician's assistant towards Monty, who was holding the whole weight of the gearbox over the car's engine compartment. Murmurs of admiration attended the slow lowering of the large object under the bonnet. The crowd bent forward and craned their necks to see over the shoulder of Monty's broad back. Tim found himself leaning forward himself over the back row as the gearbox descended into the interior. As he did so, Fred caught sight of him and immediately his face lit up.

"Ah, ha!" he shouted, "An' 'ere we 'ave the receiver of this blessin'!" As one man, the whole crowd turned to behold him with intense interest. "Let's bring 'im in ter see it, face ter face!" Fred added. The crowd parted as obediently as the red sea. Fred beckoned and Tim edged uncertainly forward to stand next to Fred and Monty in front of the bonnet. Monty, who had placed the gear box on a strategically positioned wooden box support, stood up and, turning to the front, gave Tim and a disarming tobacco-stained smile. "A genius, that's wot 'e is, nowt less," asserted Fred. "The gifts wot Jesus 'as give ter this man knows no bounds. Seein' 'im work on the innards of a car is like watchin' a surgeon doin' an 'eart transplant." Without a moment's delay, Monty dropped down to the floor, turned over on his back and wiggled his way under the car with a set of spanners in his hand. "The nex' stage in the procedure," Fred pronounced in his market trader's voice, "is the af-fixin' o' the gear box ter the main body o' the engine. This is achieved by the linin' up both of 'em wi' no less than ten bolts."

Tim, with the involvement that ownership carries, bent forward in common with the whole front row of spectators, to peer down into the engine. There Monty's half obscured face looked up from the ground totally absorbed in the job in hand. He was uttering loud grunts as he concentrated on tightening the bolts in their criti-cally precise positions on the underside of the engine. He worked with patience and consummate dexterity, considering the constrained position he was in. With a last feral growl, he began to rock his way forward from under the car on his buttocks, and scrambled up to bend his towering frame under the bonnet intent on tightening the bolts the upper side of the gear box. His face shone with intense pleasure as he focused on manipulating his tools, and the crowd watched with a concerted fascination. Tim watched with some admiration tinged with anxiety as to the final outcome. He turned to Fred, who was nodding and beaming in a self-satisfied way to all around him.

"Er, how long d'you think this might take, Fred?" he asked, disguising his fears with what he hoped was a casual tone.

"Ye weren't thinkin' o' usin' it t'day, was ye?" returned Fred, in a half-accusatory voice that challenged the relevance of Tim's question.

"No, of course not," Tim replied hurriedly.

"Well, no 'urry then, eh?" said Fred with a finality that defied further enquiry. The immediate bystanders nodded their agreement, as if any haste in the matter might bring their enjoyment to an improper end. Tim sensed that Fred was more concerned to impress the audience than satisfy any concern he might have about the car, so decided he had little option other than to leave the protagonists to their street theatre.

"I'd better go and report in at the lodgings, then," he murmured.

"Aye, you clock in while we get on wi' it," said Fred. "See yer later, when all's done." Fred turned to the bystanders, produced small cards from his breast pocket, and took to distributing them to all in sundry.

"If ye've appreciated what ye've witnessed 'ere, terday, an' ye've a mind ter treat yer auto-mobile to the same cossetin' treatment, ye've only ter contact us on the

number indicated. Terms is 'ighly competitive and satisfaction is guaranteed." Cards were eagerly accepted, and
murmers of approval were carried away as the crowd
began to disperse.

Feeling summarily dismissed, Tim turned and
climbed the steps to the lodging house just in time to
catch sight of Mrs. Delaney moving abruptly away from
the window, leaving two fellow lodgers staring down at
him with bemused expressions. As soon as he entered the
hallway, his landlady confronted him, barring his path to
the stairs with arms akimbo.

"Right, young man," she began, launching right in,
"I've had just about as much as I'm going to tolerate,
today. You've a half hour, - not a minute more, - to get
those ruffians away from my frontage. The whole thing's
a disgrace, making an exhibition of themselves in such
an unseemly manner. Yes. Unseemly, that's what it is.
They're making an unseemly spectacle of themselves on
someone else's respectable doorstep."

Tim had no idea what a respectable doorstep might
look like, but was not about to argue that point. He
adopted a crestfallen expression and shrugged like a
Jewish Taylor without a measuring tape.

"I'm extremely sorry for any inconvenience, Mrs.
Delaney. Unfortunately, I cannot ask the men to leave
before they've completed the repairs on the car."

"Young man, you have not heard what I said. Either
they go or you go. Which is it to be?" Her mouth
compressed to a thin line.

"I really don't…. know…." – He sought wildly for
some magic solution – "..what to say."

"Then I'll say it for you. Tomorrow morning, you will
leave these premises. "

"Would that be before or after breakfast, Mrs Delaney?" Tim asked, inserting a plaintive sigh into the question.

"You will be served breakfast, Mr. Carter. Thereafter, you will not cloud my house with your presence; you will grace it with your departure." She turned on her heel with a "humph" and a toss of the head that expressed her satisfaction with a performance entitled to deafening applause.

When Tim got to his room, he was spent of all desire to face the world, or the idea of asking Fred to leave the front of the lodging house with a captive audience of that size. He removed his shoes, slumped down on the edge of his bed and contemplated the depths to which he had descended.

How had he got to this state? - a job that gave him little real satisfaction? - A romantic dream that had crashed round him? A car that refused to act like one? - and now homeless in a northern backwater? How?

He slumped back across the bed, staring at the ceiling in a deeply sober mood. What's the point of it all, he asked himself? He imagined aggressively putting the same question to Fred. "What would Jesus tell me to do about this, then, Fred?" He savoured the thought of Fred being completely nonplussed, and then recalled how unlikely that would be. Gradually, and for no particular reason, Tim framed the idea of telling this Jesus, what he thought of the situation. "Look, Jesus!" he started mouthing quietly to himself, "I don't know if you're there to hear this, but, if this existence is all there is, it's crap. Every move I make is blocked. You can't say

I haven't tried, because I have. What's the point of striving for anything?"

In the silence that immediately followed, either he was given the phrase, or he was simply writing Jesus' script, but he was aware of a clear message. "You've never asked me for a solitary thing, Tim." That was all that came out of the silence; nothing else. No qualification, no promises, no spiritual heart massage, no help to solve the present problem. But, it was true enough, nevertheless. Tim was not used to asking anyone for anything, actually. Perhaps you had to have more confidence than he had, in order to really ask someone else for help.

He stayed with the thought until it slowly gathered him into an escapist cocoon, like a spider drawing his prey to the web's and sent him, still fully dressed, into a deep sleep.

Breaking Out

As Tim awoke the following morning, he was vaguely aware of having wriggled out of his trousers and wrenched his socks off from a semi-conscious foetal position. He had obviously wrestled several rounds with his bedclothes that, having conceded defeat, had deposited themselves on the floor, thrown out of the ring. He prized open his eyes with his finger and thumb, and, straight-away, the 'disagreeables' of yesterday invaded his consciousness, eliciting groans of recognition. There was always something objectionable about sleeping in one's shirt and underwear, which, in itself, ill prepares one for the day ahead. He felt tainted, and as he levered himself into a sitting position, yearned for a hot tub. There was a bath, but the temperature of the water was, at the best of times indisputably tepid and, at the worst chilling to the bone.. The admitted virtue of this was that, by the end of the process, one was very awake indeed. On this occasion, he was not sure he wanted to be at all conscious, but felt soiled enough in his wrinkled underpants to feel the need to brave the rigours of the experience.

This having been endured, he felt marginally better for it, but was still conscious of his subliminal reluctance to draw back the curtains to reveal the consequences of Fred and Monty's attentions to his car. He got dressed in a fresh set of clothes and packed away his others in his suitcase ready to leave, before he finally addressed his worst fears and was able to look down from his window on to the street below. Drawing aside the curtains, he was somewhat pleasantly surprised to see the car gleaming in the oblique sunlight, its bonnet polished and windows sparkling. It had rained during the night, and small droplets gleamed on the top of the luggage section like carelessly scattered diamond necklaces. No trace of the trappings of the workforce were left, and a calm pervaded the whole scene. It seemed obvious that Fred and Monty had abandoned the whole exercise and admitted defeat, leaving him at square one again. He would confirm this straightaway by a closer look. He crept down the stairs past the dining room and three or four regulars breaking their fast, and was just about to make for the front door, when Mrs. Delaney came out of the kitchen from the other end of the corridor and caught sight of his furtive tip-toeing exit.

"Ah, so, Mr. Carter, down at last, I see. If you were not so intent on hiding your face, you might have seen a communication on the hall table left by your (spoken with heavy irony) "gentlemen" acquaintances, last night. They had the temerity to ask me to take it up to you." She sniffed her displeasure before adding, "They were informed that I do not provide a postal service."

She flounced into the dining room, carrying her tray, without another glance in his direction. Tim glanced down and picked up an envelope with his first name scrawled on it. He slit it open and extracted a single sheet of crumpled exercise paper wrapped round the key to his car. The letter read as follows:

'Trusting this finds you as it leaves us, - full of rejoicing. Monty's God-given talents has triumphed and no

mistake. Him and me'll be in the Dragon's Arms at one o'clock sharp, where, no doubt, you'll be wishing to show your appreciation for his good services You'd have had this afore if it weren't for the uncoorporational attitude of your landlady, wot I pray the Lord to forgive.'

Tim imagined the exchange that must have taken place last night on the doorstep, and sighed as he remembered that he had to find new lodgings. But even more pressing was the need to inspect the car. He descended the steps and looked it over. He observed that It had certainly been polished. He opened the driver's door and slid down into the seat. The dashboard was also immaculate and had obviously been wiped over with a chamois leather or something. He inserted the key and swallowing hard, turned the ignition. Miraculously, the engine broke instantly into life and responded with slavish obedience to the lightest pressure of his foot. Astonishment gave way to delight that turned swiftly into euphoria, and he found himself repeating the single word over and over, "incredible!" then amplified to "Absolutely incredible!" followed shortly by "Absolutely bloody marvelous!" If he had had any sort of vocal training, he would, undoubtedly, have broken into song. He took his foot off the accelerator and the engine purred like a kitten licking cream. He touched the pedal softly and the purring rose an octave like an opera singer effortlessly practising her scales. The engine slowed again and he turned the engine off. He turned it on; it sang. He turned it off, it ceased instantly and stood in golden silence. Again he turned the key; it responded with the music of the spheres. The miracle took him over, and the car and his soul sang a duet. His mind began to cast around for the words to express his enchantment, until slowly he realised that all his feelings were leading to unqualified gratitude, - a gratitude that also brought with it some guilt. He had been so dismissive, so distrustful of Fred and Monty's attentions. How he had indulged himself in wholly unmerited pessimism!

Suddenly the fact that he was about to be thrown out of his digs seemed to pale into insignificance. If it came to it, he would sleep in his car. He got out, locked the door, bounded up the steps, gaily swept through the front door and entered the dining room, smiling like a master of ceremonies about to introduce a cabaret act. Mrs. Delaney was standing arms akimbo making it very obvious that she was inconvenienced beyond measure by the delay in obtaining his breakfast order. "Good morning, all!" he exclaimed. "I think it's going to turn out nice today, don't you?" Mrs. Delaney was affronted and looked Tim up and down as if he had lost his mind to believe he had the right to deliver pleasantries, considering the dark cloud he should feel himself under. Tim ignored her silent resentment and said, "I think I'm able to take my breakfast now, Mrs. Delaney. Your full English, if you would be so kind." He sat at the table next to the window beaming with such obvious pleasure, that she was completely taken aback, and, with an immense question mark etched on her brow, retreated to her kitchen, casting murderous looks over her shoulder. Lost for any comment she was obliged to save face with a "humph!". The other residents nudged each other in surprise, and Tim, noticing their reaction, turned to them and said with amiable confidence, "This morning, I will relish breakfast, knowing it will be my last." One of the group tried to sound surprised and replied, "Are you leaving, then?" Tim stared at the fellow slightly askance and challenged him with, "Oh, come now, you mean didn't hear Mrs. Delaney giving me my marching orders last night?" The chap was decent enough to appear abashed and the second resident sitting opposite hastily added, "We did hear something, but didn't know if it would blow over. Has she really put you out?" "Oh, yes," Tim airily admitted. "Whatever for?" pressed the second fellow, looking at the others to support his curiosity. "Because her pusillanimous snobbery cannot distinguish the hoi polloi from motor mechanics with a genius for tuning cars to perfection," returned Tim with relish.

He began to hum quietly to himself which signaled to the others that he had nothing more to say. Since they were lost for a response, he had no need to say another word. Breakfast was fetched in by Mrs. Delaney in a chilling silence associated with polar ice-bergs, and Tim ate like a man breaking his fast on the morning of his release from prison. He made a point of doing everything with great deliberation, whether it was buttering his burnt toast, stirring his tepid coffee or wiping his mouth with the crumpled paper napkin. Finally, placing his knife and fork in the middle of his plate with ostentatious neatness, he rose and, with a cursory nod to those present, walked jauntily out of the dining room.

Having got his few belongings from his room, he was soon sitting in the driver's seat, aware of being the focus of a sour faced group staring out of the dining room windows. He pressed the ignition and, delightfully, she sparked into life. Revving her up in a clarion call to arms, he adjusted the mirror, dropped his window and gently putting it into gear, drew out into the road. He accelerated swiftly enough to make of his departure the boldest possible statement. It was only when he had turned the corner of the road that he realized he had left without any notion of a destination. With a kind of escapist inevitability, his mind went straight to the municipal park, and he straightway turned the nose of the car hither.

In keeping with the somber understatement of the unimaginative municipal lay-out, a short row of tarmac parking spaces was provided next to the railings. If one might be led to believe that the unpretentiousness of these facilities entitled one to park free of charge, an erect meter was standing sentinel at one end to disillusion you of any such possibility. Though never having seen a meter attendant, Tim dutifully inserted the requisite number of coins and entered the familiar asylum to collect his thoughts. He embraced the familiar worn bench next to the familiar untenanted fishpond behind the bravely defiant row of stunted pansies as the perfect location for mulling things over, and leant back on it to ponder. Where was he? In a strange place, indeed. Homeless when he desperately needed to stay in the town for the next three weeks, disillusioned about his work, and rejected, so it seemed, by womanhood. He was, however, still the proud owner of a fine status symbol and had his old friend, Fred and his burly henchman to be grateful to, for having had it restored it to perfect working order. 'Grateful'. As he mused, the word detached itself from association with the car, and he reflected on what constituted his relationship with Fred. Who was Fred Butterworth? Why did he feel challenged to reappraise himself since he met the old fellow? What was it about Fred's opinionated forthrightness that invited him to re-investigate his life? Well, for a start, he had never met anyone so secure in his faith that he appeared to want roll up his sleeves and take on the whole world around him. Tim could feel himself irritated when Fred declared himself as concerned with the next world as with the values on this one, as if it could all be taken so easily for granted. It was his absolute certainty that made Tim impatient; that and the fact that he was so private about himself. What did he know about Fred? What was his history? What his relationship with Elsie? For that matter, who *was* Elsie Wainwright, and who were the strange down-at-heel misfits they associated with? Who was Monty, smiling inscrutably and speaking in loud monosyllables when prompted, and able to fine-tune a high-powered car with consummate skill? Gratitude and dissatisfying mystery contended with each other, as he concluded that, whatever he felt, he had to get to the Dragon's Arms at opening time and offer proper remuneration before he went in search of lodging. Above the line of roofs in front of him there was a clear edge to a line of brooding clouds, forming a new front that heralded sunnier weather. He allowed himself a breathing space as he watched it slowly approach.

Taken In

As Tim made his way into the unfashionable, not to say down-at-heel section of the town, he became conscious of the effect his now gleaming drop-head coupe could have, and, by the time he reached the road in which The Dragon's Arms stood, he began to feel intrusive. If it was not exactly a feeling of guilt, it was still an uncomfortable feeling. The squat terraced houses, with one or two small shops on street corners, frowned accusatively, so that he was glad when he had turned the final corner and stopped outside the familiar white-tiled frontage. He parked just past the pub and turned the engine off, sitting for a few minutes, to take control of an unaccountable uncertainty. The few people that passed by inevitably looked down at him with a kind of half resentful interest, making him feel as if he were over-dressed for an informal party, or even that he had been given an invitation to which he was not properly entitled. However, this was not something he could or would even have wanted to avoid, and so he drew in some deep breaths and climbed out to make for the etched glass- panelled doors. He kept his eyes down and made a bee-line for them. As soon as he pushed them open, there they were, all grouped round the unlit hearth, Fred, Monty, two other men in worn mackintoshes and Elsie, dressed in a lightly checkered two piece woollen outfit, gripping a large grey handbag in her lap. The two strangers were a strange duo; one resembling a fairground prize fighter with a slightly adjusted nose and a shaved head, and the other a ferret of a man with thinning hair scraped back and a mustache, which, if it had been any more clipped would have duplicated Adolph Hitler's. It was Elsie who first recognised Tim, and giving Fred a sharp nudge with her elbow, nodded eagerly towards him. Fred followed Elsie's smile and immediately stood up to lean over and tap Monty on the shoulder. Then the whole company took Tim in, and Fred broke into a grin of triumphant satisfaction. Monty smiled as Fred punched his shoulder like a trainer would punch his boxer, having won his bout, and Monty smiled ever broader as he looked at Tim and the mackintosh brigade nodded at each other as if confirming the successful outcome of well-placed bets. "Right ye'are, then. Here's the lad, hisself," said Fred, "come ter celybrate 'is good fortune, no doubt."

"Yes, indeed, Fred. And to thank you both for the remarkable job you did on the car," returned Tim with the humble respect that the layman always feels obliged to show motor mechanics and watch repairers. Elsie patted the chair next to her and said, "Come and sit ye down, Tim, lad." Before he could respond, Fred interjected, "'E can't sit down wi'out summat in 'is 'and. An' while 'e's at it, I've no doubt e'll be of a mind ter get another round in, eh,Tim, lad?"

"Of course. What'll it be?" asked Tim.

"Bitters all round, is it?" Fred turned to the assembled company. "Half o' stout, 'ere," added Elsie. Tim nodded and went over to the bar. Standing at the counter, he was conscious of the group bobbing up and down in agitated anticipation. Monty's smile featured permanently, and all heads nodded with a clockwork persistence. His return to the group was accompanied by a constant exchange of meaningful looks. As soon as he placed the tray on the low table, everyone stared expectantly up at him, as if he was about to give a speech. "Good on yer!" said Fred, breaking in on the moment and reaching forward to pass round the glasses. The room was instantly filled with bonhomie and mutual appreciation that bubbled out in chattering small talk. Brimming glasses were raised to lips, slurping noises emitted, and grateful sighs exhaled. Once again, Elsie patted the seat next to her, and Tim sat with embarrassed reserve next to her and nodded self-consciously at Monty who responded with great enthusiasm. Addressing himself to Fred, Tim said, "I don't know how to express my gratitude. You and Monty have done a magnificent job."

"Aye, well, don't tell me, Tim lad. Tell it ter 'im," said Fred jabbing his finger at Monty. "'E's the genius."

Tim turned to Monty and shrugged. "What more can I say?" He turned back to Fred and continued, "You must tell me how much I owe you for such a priceless job. You can't begin to know how relieved I am."

"Tell 'im, not me," insisted Fred.

He was confronted once again by Monty's perpetual smile and obdurate silence. "Just say the word, Monty."

Monty looked over at Fred with raised eyebrows.

"'E's after givin' ye a reward," said Fred, mouthing the words as to a child of limited understanding. Monty immediately shrugged in self deprecation, but retained a look of triumph. Tim looked round at Fred again and noticed the two men of the belted mackintosh brigade nodding to each other in a knowing way, as they quaffed their beers. Elsie nodded encouragingly.

"You must tell me what I owe you," persisted Tim, "and make it worth your while."

Fred leant over to Monty and repeated the phrase, "Wants to make it worth yer while."

Tim lowered his voice and said quietly, "Doesn't he understand me?"

Fred gave an impatient snort. "Course 'e does. But ye' kip turnin' yer 'ead away."

"What do you mean?" asked Tim, in some confusion

"'E's ter read yer lips, ent 'e?" retorted Fred, as if it was entirely obvious.

The penny dropped. "O-oh, you mean,…?"

"Deaf as a post. Are ye tellin' me yer didn't know, then?" asked Fred. "I thowt it were plain as the nose on yer face." Elsie nodded at Tim and the two gentlemen nodded knowingly at each other and quaffed some more.

Tim was left completely confounded and embarrassed, but convinced that he could hardly be held responsible for what he had been left in ignorance of. "I'm sorry. I.. didn't know." He turned directly to Monty and, in halting deliberation, repeated his words in as diplomatic a way as possible. "I'm - sorr-y. I - did- not - know - that – you - had - a - hearing - problem." Monty shook his head and suddenly spoke for the first time. "Don't bother yerself abowt it," he said

"I - was - just - saying," Tim continued, "I- must - pay - you - handsomely - for - all - the - good - work - you've - done - on – the - car." Tim's delivery gradually induced the whole gathering to nod to the slow rhythm, and even Monty began to blink in time to it. When Tim had finished, Monty stared at him expectantly until Tim gave a last nod as if impressing on a child the importance of looking both ways when crossing the road. Monty nodded with bland acceptance and looked away. Tim tapped his elbow, and as Monty turned back said in a voice that got louder and higher, "I'm – so – grateful." Monty sighed as if exhausted by Tim's strenuous effort to communicate. At this point, Fred clucked his tongue and interjected. "Ye gods and little fishes! Ye don't ave ter speak wi' lead in yer boots. 'E's not retarded."

"Er, no, of course.. not. Sorry," Tim said, swinging round to Fred. To Tim's surprise, Monty, with slightly distorted vowels and ambiguous consonants, said, "Tha's awright. It were nuthin'."

Elsie chipped in with, "Steady up, Fred. He were nowt but tryin' ter show 'is gratitude." The two macintosh brigade members nodded and grunted their agreement.

"Aye, well, gratitude is as gratitude does. Speakin' ordinary'll do," Fred retorted, holding his ground from sheer impatience.

"Yes, Right," Tim consented. He cleared his throat and composed himself before turning again to Monty. He smiled. Monty smiled back.

"How much do I owe you?" asked Tim

Monty nodded his comprehension and replied, "Fred'll tot it up for us."

Tim turned again to Fred, who became more amiable and ready to talk finance. "Is that right?" Tim asked. Fred nodded matter-of-factly. "Aye, it is that. Monty's not overly sharp at tottin' up, so I do it fer 'im."

"Right, then, so what do I owe?"

"Well, there's the experteez for a start. Then there's 'is time, which were not just an impromptu flash in the pan, and then there's the cost of mechanical replacements and my ten per cent 'andlin' fee."

"Yes, of course," murmured Tim, swallowing hard in preparation for the sizeable bill that should follow.

"So, by my reckonin', ye've ter cough up two 'undred and fifty pound."

Tim blinked and looked round at Monty wide-eyed. He could hardly believe that he was being charged such a reasonable sum for a transformation of his car's performance, performed with such dedication and incredble promptness.

"B..b..but…." Tim stammered, completely thrown.

"O'course, if immediate payment is in-con-veni-ent, ye can cover t' cost o' the parts, an' pay the rest in instalments t'ease the situation," interrupted Fred.

"No, not at all!" Tim exclaimed. "I think that's extremely reasonable. I'm certain it would have cost me much more at the garage."

"'Appen it would, an' all," Fred agreed. "But that's nowt ter do wi' it. We 'ad a confabulation wi' Prince Jesus, an' 'E come up with that as a good round sum, - an' tha's what we've settled on."

Tim was overcome with gratitude. "Well, I must say, I am eternally grateful to you," he effused.

"An' ter Prince Jesus, I expect." Fred eyed him closely, and raised an expectant eyebrow.

"Er, yes, of course," murmured Tim.

"Seeing as 'E was our overseer in chief," added Fred.

"Yes," said Tim, lowering his voice even more.

"Fer which, yer'll be wantin' t'offer up a word on behalf of all."

"Sorry?" Tim was perplexed.

"Offerin' a word of thanks and praise fer 'is ever ready 'and in time of need," Elsie added in explanation. "It's only right, en't it?"

"Yes," muttered Tim. "Well, I'll get on to it, as soon as I find a room for the night."

Elsie's expression was instantly translated from that of admonishment to one of eager interest. "Find a room? What fer, lad? I thowt ye' was catered for."

"Truth is, I've been thrown out of the lodgings," Tim offered in a brisk way with philosophical acceptance.

"Never!" exclaimed Fred, "What did ye do ter deserve that?" Tim was grateful that he did not need to explain Fred's and Monty's part in the affair, because Fred chose just then to look across at Monty and mouthe, "'E's bin given the push at Ma Delaney's". Monty shook his head in puzzlement and pushed his mouth down in the shape of a sad clown's. He turned towards Tim with a crestfallen expression. "A sad do," he said with sympathy set deep in his eyes and a half smile on his lips. Tim was faintly curious as to how Fred knew Mrs Delaney's name, but let discretion rule him. They all deeply contemplated the consequences of his unfortunate plight, Elsie clucking her tongue, Fred shaking his head in disbelief and growling under his breath while Monty made sighing sounds. The two belted mackintoshes downed the last of their drinks. The 'prize fighter' burped in a crestfallen way, whereupon the 'Adolph look-alike' stared philosophically at the ceiling as though he might solve something by the sheer power of concentration.. Slowly, like two clockwork models, Elsie and Fred turned to face each other as an idea took slow unavoidable shape. Elsie gradually adopted an erect posture and pursed her lips, as a sublime smile of self-possession spread over her face. She had the look of saintly conviction that destiny had bestowed a prize on her. "Fred, this 'as ter be the silver lining t' black cloud.

Wot 'as that cosy little room at my place bin waiting fer, if it weren't this young fella-me-lad in 'is hour o' need? It's taylor-made fer im."

"Right enough, Elsie!" said Fred with the gusto of someone who recognises his cue.

Alarmed, Tim said, "Oh, I couldn't put you out like that!" Then, instantly aware of having responded rather too peremptorily, he added, in simulated apologetic tone, "I mean, I'll be all right, really. There are plenty of digs I can approach. I've got a list of lodgings my Manager gave me."

"As if we'd allow that!" retorted Elsie with the conviction of a town crier that made the barman swing round his head at the other end of the room. "She's give ye a rough deal, 'as that Delaney so an' so!. Any road, it's not all that easy ter find a place jes' now, on account o' the town being full ter burstin' wi' the North West Philatelists'Convention. It's always a scrum each year, is that. No, that's decided! Done an' dusted!" she pronounced, with sufficient relish to evaporate any further resistance. "An' ye'll not regret it, I can tell ye," added Fred. "She fries up t' best breakfast in t' North, does Elsie."

Sensing the futility of further argument, Tim muttered his inarticulate thanks. He tried to secure a little independence by adding, "Well, my goodness that is an offer and a half! If I can just impose on you for two or three days until the philatelists leave town, that'll be fine."

"Don't be daft!" said Fred and Elsie in concert, looking at him, as if about to be mortally offended.

"Any road, let's see 'ow we go, eh?" concluded Elsie,

"An' let's bow our 'eads and thank Jesus fer 'is timely intervention," added Fred, as if any further discussion would be offensive to Heaven. Fred made a sign to Monty, placing his hands together and jerking them heavenwards. Monty responded by instantly bowing his head, as all the others did likewise. Elsie's sideways smile at Tim was as much a challenge as encouragement, and he obediently dropped his head forward. As he did, he glanced towards the counter in time to see the barman nudge the arm of a customer and nod towards them. Four or five regulars turned and raised their glasses and eyes to heaven, as if they had seen this kind of thing many times before. Embarrassment induced him to curl forward with a frown, as the rest of the group bowed reverently. Fred launched in.

"Well, Jesus, once again we 'ave ter thank ye fer steppin' in and workin' things out. An' I know Tim, 'ere, is goin' ter say a big 'thank ye', not only fer the rescue of his auto-mo- bile, through yer inspiration in Monty's hands, but also fer the timely solution to his 'omelessness through the good offices of Elsie. Well, ye've 'eard my thanks, Jesus, so I pass the prayer over ter Tim, hisself."

If Tim had considered himself alarmed by anything that morning, no emotion could compare with the panic that overcame him at that moment. He had offered his heartfelt thanks to Monty and had responded to Elsie's hospitality with all the proper gratitude it merited, but to offer audible thanks to Jesus, that mysterious, invisible entity, called upon a heroic dive into the unknown at which he was more likely to swoon before finding the means of performing.

"Right, it's all yours," said Fred in a determined tone.

"An' we can give ye' an 'and, if it comes to it," said Elsie, in a softer voice. "That's right, en't it?" she added, turning to all the others. "Tell 'im," she whispered to

Fred indicating Monty. Fred leant forward towards him and slowly mouthed, "We're givin' young Tim a leg up wi' is prayers." Monty responded with a grave nod, which somehow expressed approval but without any responsibility to be involved. They all turned to Tim, looking as if they were about to hypnotise him into praying. Tim swallowed hard, nodded nervously several times and dropped his head. The rest followed suit.

Tim cleared his throat and gave a cough. He decided, in a second's reflection, that he could only accomplish this demanding task, if he imagined himself addressing a board meeting about a sales campaign. back in the office.

"Yes," he began, followed by a long pause, "er, ... Jesus." Another pause. "I must say how grateful I am for the help I have received from these good...friends of yours," he continued.

"An' yours," muttered Fred, "yours an' all."

"Oh, yes, indeed," added Tim. "I, er...don't know what I would have done without Fred and Monty. I was in a bit of a hole, actually."

Everyone made approving noises, and Tim decided he must be saying the right thing. "I mean, where would I be if they hadn't turned up? But, I am going to reward them properly for getting me out of a bit of a mess."

Fred clucked his tongue and whispered, "Thank 'Im direct. Don't ferget oo yer talkin' to."

"Er,..Jesus?"

"Right. Go on, then," urged Fred, still in a whisper.

"Yes,..well, as I say, "I'm very grateful."

"To *'Im,* right?!"

"Oh, yes, to Him, too."

"To *you!*" exclaimed Fred, as if teaching a child the alphabet.

"To me?" said Tim in complete puzzlement.

"To *'Im!*" hissed Fred, jabbing his finger upwards to the ceiling. Say *'You'* to *'Im!!*"

"Oh, yes, I see!" hissed back Tim, as the penny dropped. Fred groaned under his breath. Elsie retrained him with a tap on his arm.

"Go on then," prompted Fred in a slightly more equitable way.

"Right. I.. er.. want to thank You, too," continued Tim, carefully, swallowing hard "er,.. Jesus, for sending your, er…" - He struggled for the word - "agents… to help me out of my problem. And," he remembered to add, "to Elsie for offering me a roof over my head, tonight."

Elsie looked up and said, in quiet admonishment, "It were Jesus that put the idea in me 'eart. It's 'Im ye've ter thank, not me."

Tim sighed before saying in an unenthusiastic way, "Well, anyway, I'm grateful to all concerned, because I was in a bit of a hole. So thanks all round."

Fred looked up and said, with a deep frown cleaving his brow, "Is that it, then?" The rest of the company all solemnly shook their heads, except Monty, who apparently felt it necessary to nod.

"I thought,…well,.. I said, 'thank you'," Tim said, uncertainly.

Prayer was suddenly set aside. Everyone looked intently at Tim and Fred respectively, like Wimbledon spectators.

"And do yer think ye deserve all this 'elp?"

"I was jolly grateful to get it."

"But did ye *deserve* it, is what I'm askin'?"

"Deserve?"

"Getting Jesus ter go t'all this palaver?!"

"Well, *I* didn't ask him to put Himself out, did I?" said Tim defensively.

"So, all the more *gracious* of 'Im to put hisself out fer ye," pronounced Fred. "Yeou as wanted ter show off an' get yerself a classy clapped out car wi'out thinkin' it through. An' then, wi'out a single word o' suppli-cation from yerself, 'E sends me an' Monty along to sort things out. That's a fair bit more than getting' yer deserts, en't it?"

Tim felt snared and looked round at the company before saying, "Well, I wasn't showing off, as you put it, but as for the car, I suppose you're right. But..."

"Brought on by yerself, an' all," interrupted Fred, emphatically. "That's why yer've ter be double grateful."

"I'm ready to pay what I owe," stressed Tim defensively. Fred looked at him for a second before raising his arms to heaven in saintly desperation at Tim's obtuseness.

"Go easy on 'im, Fred," said Elsie, appealing to his calmer nature. Then, turning to Tim, she added, in a softer tone, "Ye've not rightly understood, see, Tim." Turning to the rest of the company, she said, in quiet confidence, "I reckon we need ter give 'im a bit of a leg up wi' this." Everybody nodded in sober agreement.

"Aye, 'appen ye'r right, there, Elsie," Fred demurred. Turning once again to Tim, he said with calculated care, "It's like this, ye see. There's many folk just' 'as a list o' requests t' 'and over ter Jesus. An' when they've done, they say, 'ta very much' in anticipation, like they wus getting' a regulation 'and-out'. Wot they don't realise is that they first 'as ter be 'sanctified'." Fred laid special emphasis on this last word.

"Sanctified," repeated Elsie with lingering relish, and they all nodded appreciatively. Even Monty joined in, having lip-read the exchange.

"So," continued Fred, in measured tones, "first ye 'ave ter confess yer unworthiness in the presence o' th' Prince. Ye 'ave ter let 'Im know you know, an' all."

Tim scowled and muttered, "I never knew praying was so complicated."

"Tha's because it's bin foreign to yer," retorted Fred. "Wot we need ter know is, are ye ready to get it right?"

Tim shook his head in some confusion, before saying, obediently, "I suppose so."

Fred scrutinised him for a second before continuing. "Well, takin' yer "supposin"' as a 'yes', please be ready ter repeat the followin' after me.

A short pause ensued, during which Fred nodded to Tim.

'Dear Prince Jesus," started Fred.

"Dear Prince Jesus," echoed Tim, in an unconvincing tone.

"I know 'ow little I deserve yer assistance," Fred intoned.

"I know how I little deserve your assistance," Tim dutifully repeated.

Elsie suddenly chimed in with, "It's closin the eyes time, all."

Everybody except Monty complied.

"but, reco'nisin' the sacrifice wot you paid fer me," Fred went on, doggedly.

"recognising the sacrifice you paid... (licking of the lips)... for me," repeated Tim in a detached voice. .

"And, in recognition of yer good services..."

"In recognition of your good services."

"I want ter thank ye."

"I want to thank you."

"An' praise yer name."

"And praise your name."

"Amen," declared Fred.

"Amen," repeated Tim.

Everyone else's 'Amen' gave the final punctuation to the session, with Monty's voice added a beat or so later.

"There!" said Elsie in the comfortable tone of a kindly primary school mistress. "That weren't so difficult, were it?"

Tim smiled wanly as the two 'mackintoshes' punched each other's shoulder affirmatively, and Fred beamed as if he had just won a prize for the biggest marrow. "That's rounded it off proper. Now we can get off ter your place, Elsie, and let the 'ound see the 'rabbit," he said.

Everyone stood in unison, like an audience when the lights go up in the auditorium. Fred and Elsie led the file to the door without any formal prompt, and they all trouped out. Tim followed after with the bemused expression of one devoid of knowledge or commitment, to wherever the crowd might lead.

Once on the pavement, Fred scratched his head and turned to Elsie.

"'Ow d'we work this?"

"Well, Alf and Bert'll 'ave ter leg it back. An' me and you and Monty'll take a lift in t' automobile." They all looked at Tim, who dutifully took his cue and unlocked the car. Elsie and Monty ducked into the rear and Fred got into the front passenger seat. Monty's bulk made him look like a trussed bull, with his knees doubled under his chin, while Elsie was forced to scrunch herself into the opposite corner. "See yer back 'ome, lads!" she shouted at the two 'mackintoshes', as she wound down the window. They grinned back, stuck their thumbs up and walked away, as Tim, without asking where they were making for, started up and pulled away from the kerb.

Open Doors, Open Windows

Tim and his bulging car drew up before Elsie's house, having completed a journey attended by vociferous contradictions about shortest routes and quietest roads. On several occasions, he had been obliged to make last minute decisions, based on sudden and conflicting directions, most of which had elicited less than complimentary comments, both auditory and visual from other road users, and, on one occasion, from an elderly lady pedestrian who, after merely three attempts to look both ways, had had the temerity to step off the kerb, to be confronted by a blaring horn and screeching tyres. On one occasion, Tim thought he saw someone take out a pen and notebook, and hoped he had turned the corner before his number could be scribbled down.

He was not, then, in a composed frame of mind to appreciate his surroundings on his arrival at number 37 Gladstone Terrace. When they had all extricated themselves from the car and he had had time to focus on his surroundings, he was presented with a narrow street of modest terraced, three up two down, bay fronted houses, most of which were in need of sprucing up with a coat of paint. A few doors down, two ladies, puffing cigarettes, leaned against their door frames, arms folded across their ample bosoms, exchanging the time of day out of the sides of their mouths. One of them nodded in the direction of the newly arrived group and the other shook her head ruefully as if nothing good could come from that direction. Several lace curtains had begun to flutter on the other side of the street and Tim began to feel the presence of a thousand hidden eyes. As he looked up past the single line of roofs, he could see two layers of clouds, the lower dark shapes rolling under the seemingly static bright silver threads. It was the sort of sky that left its options open and revealed little to decipher.

Elsie walked to her front door and gave a brief, non-commital nod to one of the gossips, before turning the key in her lock. Fred looked up and down the road to register his awareness of the interest that their arrival had engendered, and then, as Elsie led the way, indicated the door for Tim to enter. Monty, whose face contained the fixed smile of oblivious contentment, followed last, and closed the door behind him.

Elsie led them all into the kitchen at the far end of the hallway. There was an air of warm and thrifty homeliness about it; a table with six wooden cushioned chairs, a small welsh dresser with polished worn shelves with a row of mugs hanging from hooks. The small window looking out on to the back yard had floral curtains held to the sides with matching ties. There was a rack to the side of the draining board with lustrous pans leaning into each other in an orderly arrangement. There was not a trace of cooking smells, and the cloth draped decorously over the taps expressed a housewifely pride not to be messed about with; a place where strictest instructions had been delivered to make sure the status quo was maintained.

"Eeh, well, 'ere we are, then," Elsie said as she filled the kettle, and then turning to Tim, added, "An' I 'ope as 'ow ye'll be very comfortable. Soon as we've 'ad a cuppa tea, I'll show ye up ter yer room."

"'E's not brought 'is things in, yet," Fred reminded her.

"Oh, I'll get them right now," Tim hastily offered.

"No. Sit ye down and get climatiz'd," said Elsie in a tone that brooked no contradiction. "An' any road, there's some settlin' up ter do, first, right?"

"Of course," Tim responded, diving his hand into his breast pocket for his cheque book as he sat down. "I'll write it out straight away. Two hundred and fifty pounds, wasn't it?"

Fred sat next to him and lay a hand on his arm, "That's not the way we do things,'ere, lad. Cheques is fer them as 'as bank accounts. We favour cash."

"Then I'll draw the cash out tomorrow," Tim replied. "You'll have it in the morning."

"Right. Then it's easy enough ter split between us each according ter 'is deserts," continued Fred in way of explanation.

"An wot's more, there's no Mister Inlan' Revenue sniffin' round, takin' 'is greedy share o' the proceeds," Elsie added as she sat at the head of the table, and Monty set himself down at the other end of the table to get an overall view of everyone's lips. "As fer settlin' up," she went on, " I wus referrin' ter t 'ouse-keepin' kitty."

Tim reacted promptly. "Of course. Will that be cash, too?"

"Ye're very keen to pay up, I will say, " she said, as the kettle began to sing. "Ye don't even know me terms," she continued, walking to the hob with a canny smile. "Wot were Mrs. Delaney askin for lodgin? Not a cough an' a spit, I'll bet."

"It's the going rate these days," offered Tim with a rueful smile.

"'Ow much was that, then?" persisted Elsie. They all looked at him, and Monty focused on his mouth.

"Fifty pounds a night," Tim stated.

"Ye're jokin'!" she said, simulating hushed awe as she made up the tea. .

"Robbery!" exclaimed Fred. "Daylight robbery!"

"There's no justice!" Monty pronounced as moral judgement. "But she'll not thrive by it," he added, confidently.

"She's ever been that way," declared Fred, turning to Monty. Then turning to Elsie, he said soberly, "That woman's in love wi' t' ways o' this world, wi' never a mind fer t' next'un."

Tim's curiosity got the better of him and he could not resist asking Fred, "How do you know so much about Mrs. Delaney? I didn't know you'd ever met her before today."

Fred shook his head in silence and Elsie nodded wisely and tapped the side of her nose. "Least said," was her only comment. There was no optimistic inference of it being 'soonest mended', and Tim was left non the wiser.

The tea-pot was brought to table, the cups got from the dresser, and biscuits and home made ginger cake laid out in a wide fan shape on a large plate. Conviviality immediately took over and soon the principal sound was of slurping and munching and clinking of china. Tim almost felt obliged to manufacture some appreciative sounds, but balked at the loud exhalations of satisfaction that Monty and Fred appeared to think necessary. No sooner had they downed their first cups than a rap was heard on the back door. "Come in, lads!" Elsie shouted. "Ye're just in time fer a cuppa!" The door opened and the two 'mackintoshes' entered, grinning and flushed with the effort of hoofing their way home. Monty got up and pulled two more chairs to the table from the side of the room to make places for them. They sat side by side next to Tim, put their thumbs up to Monty and nodded to everyone else as enthusiastically as if it were ages since they last met. Tim could not help noting that they made no attempt to loosen their belts, let alone take their macks off.

As soon as they were handed cups, Fred addressed them. "Right, lads, it looks like there's some 'edge clippin' and weedin' ter do tomorrer mornin'. There's a Mister Spender in Broad Mead who's taken ter 'avin' a bit of a make-over fer 'is garden. 'E's a mind ter smarten it up fer t' purpose o' puttin' it on't market." The two men muttered their assent, their mouths crammed with ginger cake.

"So it's an early rise wi' the shears and trowels. I've wrote down th'address on this 'ere piece of paper." Fred pulled a scrap of paper from his inside pocket and handed it to the taller of the two men, who took it and scrutinized it for a second before giving Fred the thumbs up and stuffing it into his own side pocket.

"Fer time bein', ye can rest up an' we'll call yer in at supper time," said Elsie. "We need a bit o' time ter sort things out wi' Tim, 'ere."

The two men swallowed down the last remnants of their tea and cake, and straightway got up and went out again by the back door.

During this episode, neither men had spoken a single word, but restricted themselves to grunts and hand signs throughout. As soon as they had closed the door behind them, Tim turned to Elsie and asked her discreetly if they were also hard of hearing.

"Gracious, no!" she said. "They're not much good in company, that's all. Specially polite ones," she added, pointing her finger at Tim.

"Oh, I'm sorry they think that," Tim responded.

"Don't ye want ter be thowt polite?" asked Elsie.

"No. What I mean is, I don't want to be the means of making them uncomfortable," corrected Tim.

"Aye, well," chipped in Fred, "that's unavoidable up 'ere, wot with yeou an' yer southern ways and yer eder-cated voice, an all."

I don't see why that should inhibit anyone," retorted Tim in a slightly offended tone.

"No, well, that's 'cos yer can't 'elp yerself'," said Fred in a reasonable tone, which veered more towards sympa-thy than explanation.

"Can't help myself doing what?" insisted Tim.

"Well, since ye've asked out right, I'll come straight out wi' it. Bein' polite is fair enough, but there's times yer need ter be direct an' come ter t'point."

"Now then, Fred, steady on. There's no call ter be too personal," admonished Elsie.

"No, that's fine," returned Tim in a defensive tone that took even himself by surprise, "I'd rather hear where I'm going wrong, especially if I'm supposed to be lodging here."

"There's no call ter take it ter 'eart," said Elsie, hastily.

"It's a start, any road," said Fred, with some relish. "That's 'ow we like it up 'ere. 'Avin' it out wi' someun, is what we calls it. It's what Jesus said ter do, an' all. If ye 'ave owt against someun, go an' 'ave it out wi' 'im an' clear it up. Then ye can bet His Father'll be glad to receive what ye've a mind ter give 'Im."

Tim was perplexed. "Why does his father have to come into it, just because you've had a difference with someone?"

"Not *his* father!", retorted Fred. "It's Jesus' Father!"

Tim frowned before proclaiming, "I've never said anything against Jesus."

Fred and Elsie exchanged looks, frowned, shrugged resignedly and emitted sighs. Fred, in a quieter tone, said. "Seein' as yer not instructed in the ways o' the good book, it's better leave it there."

Tim was torn between gratitude for having had his car repaired and a roof provided over his head set against a distinct feeling of being pronounced a misfit. He was on the point of reconsidered the advisability of remaining a guest in Elsie's house, when Elsie, herself saved everyone's face in a moment by saying in a warm, motherly way, "In this 'ouse, everyone's taken as they're found, an' welcome as the spring. Whatever the diff'rences, we all play a part in t' other's lives."

Monty, who had been observing the exchange closely, broke out with a hearty, "Right 'nuff, Elsie!" and then fell to nodding reflectively to himself.

"So, Monty and Fred can wash t' dishes and put them away, while I take ye up ter yer room," she said to Tim, in a tone that brooked no gainsay.

Elsie led the way along the hallway and up the stairs. Since this was a terraced dwelling, little light fell on the landing except what escaped from doors ajar. She turned the handle of the door that immediately faced the last few turned steps, and pushed it open to reveal a comfortable room not quite big enough to be called a double.

There was, indeed, a double bed there, but it had elbowed itself into the limited space so that there was scarcely enough room to pass by its foot without bruising one's shins on the Edwardian style cast iron fender. There was a wardrobe in the corner facing the entrance and a small bedside table the other side of the bed with a lamp whose base was graced by two plaster of Paris figurines of two slumped old men looking the worse for drink, one of which appeared to be sliding under the table. As a salutary comment on such irresponsible behaviour, over the bed head was a small reproduction of Holman Hunt's 'The Light of the World'.

In the corner furthest from the door was a small table with a bible placed conspicuously in the middle, and a solid looking, round–backed chair. The tasteful floral curtains and bed-covers took away the minimalist severity and contributed to a homelier appearance. Tim was struck by the simple comfort of the room, and felt strangely relieved. It was almost as though he had not expected Elsie to be the possessor of such relatively middle class taste, and for a moment he felt almost guilty for thinking so.

"So, what d'yer think?" she asked in a quietly confident way.

"It's fine, Elsie. Very comfortable indeed," Tim readily admitted.

Elsie smiled. "Yer can 'ave it fer fifteen pound the night. Will that do yer?"

"Fifteen?!" exclaimed Tim in astonishment. "Surely it's more than that?!"

"Aye, well, it'ud be more to them I don't know. An' o'course, that don't include breakfasts, which I'd be askin' a fiver fer, if that suits."

"But that's less than half what Mrs. Delaney charged," insisted Tim.

"Aye, that's as may be. But then she don't 'ave t' same right ter choose 'er clientele." She smiled at Tim in a mixture of pride and indulgence. He half smiled back and said, "I'm really very grateful."

"Aye, well, I doubt ye'll find a better offer in this town. Now ye can get yer things in fro' the car."

She led him out again, pointing out the bathroom on his right as she went. They joined Fred and Monty downstairs, who had just finished wiping the dishes and were replacing them on the shelves.

"Now then, Fred," said Elsie, "if ye'd be so good as ter start layin' t'table ready fer supper, p'raps Monty'ud 'elp Tim bring in 'is things." She stood in front of Monty and mouthed, "Tim 'ud be glad of a bit of 'elp wi' 'is things, right?" He instantly laid down the tea-cloth and said, "I'm right with 'im," as he led the way through the hall door.

As soon as Tim had opened the boot, Monty grabbed hold of two suitcases and hoisted them under his arms, before picking the remaining two by their handles. The next moment, he was back through the front door like a bear seeking sanctuary, leaving Tim with nothing more to collect than his laptop case and a couple of files. He locked the car, glanced briefly at the row of disturbed window curtains, looked at one or two unthreatening clouds in an otherwise clear sky, auguring good weather and strolled back inside, aware that he had been scrutinized by several locals. On reaching his room, Monty was nowhere to be seen, but the cases were neatly arrayed on the bed. Downstairs, there was the sound of murmured voices and clinking crockery, a suitable background to more relaxed thoughts now that a roof over his head was secured. He sat on the side of the bed and let the accelerated events of the day file past him. He was very conscious that Fred and Elsie had rescued him from two very difficult situations, and, without them, he would have been in a bit of a tight spot. There was some irony in the fact that the solution to one problem had been instrumental in causing the second; that of having to find new lodgings. Interestingly, there were unexplained questions. How, he wondered, did Fred and Elsie know Mrs. Delaney? They obviously had strong opinions about her, but from what experience other than having darkened her doorstep yesterday, he could not imagine. How had they come to know Monty and the other unkempt fellows, who seemed to be a permanent part of their entourage? Ingrained politeness was too deep in Tim for him to pry into others' lives, yet curiosity was keenly aroused. They appeared to share the same abiding faith as Fred; either that, or they considered it worth their while to pay convincing lip service to it. Tim felt a bit of a charlatan himself when he recalled the prayer session in the Dragon's Arms, but, at the same time, he was also motivated by real gratitude. Of course, he had no desire to be engulfed by the dictates of Fred and Elsie's regime. One thing that had always been of paramount importance was his own space. He had always protected it, even from earliest friends and acquaintances. Being an only child and never having to compete with siblings had made him prone to creating his own world. Perhaps, he half admitted to himself, it had made him feel distrustful of anything that he did not organize himself. Maybe he put too much trust in his imagination, for which he paid a high price. As indignity and hurt gradually left him, he began to wonder if Lydia had not been an example of that. Was he really hurt by her rejection, or was it to do with his own fanciful belief?. Was the Lydia he had believed he was drawn to, in reality, a self constructed chimera? As he sat and mused, it occurred to him that he had not really constructed much of an idea of her, anyway, and, if he were honest, had built expectation on very little. She had appeared to lead him on, but he had been too swift in interpreting her effusiveness as significant. Oh, dear! The humiliation involved in confronting one's wishful delusions! Yet coming to terms with them contributed to easing the pain and discomfort. He was able to put them into context and, anyway, he had found escape from romantic thoughts behind the wheel on the open road. Fred and Elsie could think what they would, his car was an important boost to his self-image. It was necessary, he told himself, in aiding his advancement, and he was much more likely to impress clients turning up in style.

He was jerked out of his reverie by Elsie shouting, "Are ye up there, Tim?!" from the bottom of the stairs.

"Yes!" Tim shouted back.

"Will ye be eatin' wi' us, seein' it's yer first night? Or will ye be eatin' out?!"

Tim had not given any thought to meals, and was thrown into some confusion. Somehow, it felt as if accepting the invitation would be setting a precedent that meant capitulating to a whole regime. "I, er.. thought of.. possibly going to the fish and chip shop," he stammered "

"Aye, well, that settles it. Since that's all ye've come up wi', ye can eat in t'night!" she shouted back in a tone that brooked no argument. "We eat seven sharp!" He heard the kitchen door shut and took it as her blank refusal to discuss it further. He could, of course, rush downstairs and flatly refuse to eat in; pretend he was meeting someone, or even say he had a sudden irresistible urge to have fish and chips, but he contemplated the sustained energy this would require and admitted defeat. Well, at least, it would give him an opportunity to arrange his schedule for the rest of the week. Recent events had not given him much time to properly organise the penciled-in arrangements to meet prospective clients. He spent the next hour and a half in fruitfully working out the logistics of fitting firms in surrounding areas into a workable schedule, and by the end felt vindicated for not having turned down Elsie's invitation. It would not have been accomplished had he been driving round town searching for somewhere to eat. He lay back on the bed and closed his eyes, surrendering to the relaxed feeling that gradually spread over him.

Refuge

He only realized he had fallen off to sleep when he was awakened by Elsie's voice from the bottom of the stairs. It took a moment for him to collect himself, as he heard her coming up the stairs. He hauled himself up off the bed and got to the door just in time to prevent her from knocking.

"Oh, so ye're up an'abowt, then," she said in a slightly impatient tone. "Only I've been shoutin' up t'yer for the last five minutes. I thought ye might'a slipped out, or summat."

"No, sorry, Elsie. Fact is, I fell asleep."

"Did ye, then? Alright fer some, eh? Any road, it's just about to be ladled out, so come an' 'ave it while it's 'ot."

The aroma rising up to him from the kitchen was wonderful, and he suddenly realised that, without doing a stitch of work, he had worked up quite an appetite. He followed her down and into the kitchen to be met by a full complement at table, Fred and Monty on one side and Alf and Bert, - neither of whom had as yet been identified as having which name, - on the opposite side. They were all ogling a huge bowl of meat stew and tureens of potatoes and peas. Alf and Bert fidgeted like two young boys at a birthday party and Monty continually looked up at the ceiling as if that might help him resist any temptation to dive into the tureen forthwith. Fred, by contrast sat immutably calm and all but imperceptibly nodded, as if in benign approval of the proceedings. Elsie pointed to the chair next to Monty. "Sit yourself down there, Tim. Fred, you'll be ready to say a few words."

"Right y'are," responded Fred in his most forthright tone, as soon as Tim had settled in his seat. "So, Lord, 'ere we are again, this time with young Tim, an extra mouth ter feed int' family. I'm sure we all want ter give Ye thanks fer the good food what You 'ave provided an' Elsie 'as bin so good as t' prepare fer us, an' we ask ye ter keep the work comin' in, so's we can keep putting it on t' table. Oh, an, o' course, keep pryin' eyes out of our business. Amen."

As Tim unenthusiastically joined in the chorus of 'amens' he reflected on never having been described as 'an extra mouth in a family' before. The feeling of being accepted as a family member was accompanied by the question of what prying eyes could possibly discover if they focused on this household. What exactly had he become a member of? There was no time to dwell on the matter, for, in the next moment all the men were galvanized into energetic doling of food on plates, while Elsie stood looked on with maternal indulgence. She pointed to the tureens and said, "Get in there, Tim, before it all disappears afore yer eyes. There's no lah-di-dah upper class manners 'ere." Tim, having been identified as having lah-di-dah habits, felt even less able to take any initiative in serving himself, and Elsie, seeing his difficulty, leant over and tapped either Alf or Bert on the wrist, wresting the serving spoon from him and handing it to Tim. In a tone that expressed both firm authority and good will, "Get diggin'; it's yer only chance."

Tim dug hesitantly, casting an apologetic smile to Alf or Bert opposite him, who responded with a resigned shrug, as if being treated like a naughty six year old was 'par for the course'. They showed no resentment as Tim tentatively doled the potatoes, but twitched with nervous impatience, nevertheless.. "Give yerself plenty of everythin', afore the vultures descend," Elsie prompted, smiling over everyone like a referee at a wrestling match. Tim continued serving in what his contestants obviously viewed as impossibly slow motion and confirming to them that he had no idea of the rules of the sport. As soon as he put the spoon down, it was pounced on by his eager adversary opposite and the ladling continued in 'no-holds-barred' fashion.

The next ten minutes was taken up with the wordless business of transferring food to mouth. Guttural noises of appreciation, smacking of lips and clinking of metal on crockery were shortly followed by the scraping of spoons scooping gravy.

The next course was apple pie, which was cut into equal portions from a large flat oven dish and served by Elsie herself. In contrast to the melee that attended the first course, the bowls of pie were passed down in reasonably orderly fashion, and the jug of custard followed from hand to hand. Unexpectedly, it was poured with proper regard to the needs of fellow diners.

"This is thanks to Alf and Bert, right?" said Elsie, nodding towards them both. Their mouths by this time full, they nodded and grunted assent. "Windfalls from Mr. Murgatroyd's orchard. Twice as good as ye get in t'shops, an' all."

"I 'ope Mr. Murgatroyd wasn't there ter see ye," said Fred, looking at Elsie.

"I doubt 'ed mind, if he were," she replied, dismissively. "They weren't but fallen on't'ground."

"Aye, but 'e might take it in t"is 'ead ter ask why we'd demean ourselves ter pick them instead o'buyin' our own," insisted Fred.

"Eh, don't start worryin' yerself, Fred. If they fell from t'tree, it's got ter be the Lord's provision."

"Aye," Fred demurred, "ye're right, o'course, Elsie. I stand corrected."

He continued eating until, after some thought he added, "I'd be 'appier in me mind, though, if I knew Jesus 'ad 'ad a word wi Mr. Murgatroyd about turnin' a blind eye."

"Aye, well ye can get on t' 'Im about that later," retorted Elsie. Suddenly turning to Tim, she asked, "Now then, 'ow was that?"

"A splendid meal, Elsie. Thank you very much."

"Three poun' fifty 'll just about cover it, right? "

"Remarkable value," Tim replied with the haste that came from being taken off guard by her impersonal business-like approach to things.

"I'll put it on' t' tab and ye can pay at the end o' t' week... in cash, if it's all the same."

"Oh, right. Yes, of course."

The meal over, no time was wasted in idle banter. Elsie began to clear the tureens off the table, and as if on an invisible cue, everyone assisted in gathering the plates and bowls to the draining board, while Monty ran the taps and poured in washing liquid. Fred folded the table cloth up and put it away in the sideboard drawer. Alf and Bert pushed in the chairs and, without a moment's hesitation, went straight to the back door and wnt out. As soon as they had gone, Elsie took out a large ledger from another drawer and placed it on the table together with a biro. Tim felt marginalized by such efficient domestic machinery, managing to do no more than push his chair under the table.

"Right, Fred. We'd best get the figures done," Elsie said. Then, turning to Tim, she added, in the tone of an abrupt but well-meaning headmistress, "No doubt, ye' ll want ter be getting' about yer own business, Tim, so we'll not hold ye back."

Aware suddenly that he had been less than tactfully dismissed from what seemed to have been transformed into a place of earnest business, Tim consented with muttered ineffectual words like "Right,".."Of course,".."Yes, indeed,.." as he escaped through the hall door.

Having gone to his room, Tim mused on the rather exclusive and secretive atmosphere that had replaced the open relation there had been during the meal. There had been an undercurrent difficult to put his finger on; something they held close to their chests, unwilling to share.

He decided to clear his mind of such thoughts by driving into the town and perhaps finding a small pub or even a café, if it was not too late. He felt he needed to re-assess his position as an 'extra mouth to feed', and possibly find convincing reasons to leave and find other lodgings. It made him quite sad to consider that friendship at arms length could often be more meaningful than one at close quarters. He felt real gratitude for Fred's and Elsie's solutions to his recent problems, but maybe the limit had been reached and there was danger of intrusion on both sides. He was aware, too, that there was something in their lives that lay beyond what he had experienced; something that motivated them with a confidence that had always evaded him. It was alien to him, coming, as he did, from a very different world.

He threw on his coat and went downstairs and gave a discreet tap on the kitchen door. He would tell them he was going out to get some air for perhaps an hour or two before retiring to bed. Elsie came to the door and opened it just sufficiently to allow them to exchange looks and for her to ask him what he wanted.

"I'm just going into town for a breather. I wonder if I can have a key to let myself in?" Tim asked.

"Aye, well, I suppose that's all right. Though there's little doin' in town at this time o' night," she responded with a disdainful air. She retired into the kitchen leaving the door to swing open just enough for him to catch a glimpse of Fred, Alf, Bert and Monty seated round the table with paper money in front of them. As Fred caught his glance, he placed his hands over the money and looked away as if deeply preoccupied with other unrelated matters. Elsie returned with the key and said, "I'm in bed by ten o'clock, so be mindful when ye come in."

"Yes, of course," Tim assured her.

"That's all right, then," she said, as she abruptly closed the door.

Tim put the key in his pocket, let himself out and got into the car. As he started up he still carried the picture of the assembly round the table, but told himself firmly that however clandestine it might appear, it was none of his business. He pulled away from the kerb and was instantly overtaken by the sheer pleasure of the surge of his car in the small of his back.

He drove reasonably slowly to make a note of street names and count the number of turnings in order to be able to retrace his movements. Most of the property this side of town looked very similar, and he had relied heavily on his passengers' garbled directions when he drove to Elsie's.

As he neared the town centre, he began to look for the slightest sign of life in any of the cafes but, after a fruitless search, decided it was too late to catch anyone open. It would have to be a public house. He finally settled on one he had seen a couple of streets back on a relatively quiet corner. With no parking restriction at this time of the evening, he reversed up an adjacent side street and left the car to walk to it.

It had pretentions to being more than just a local bar, for it had a lunch-time menu on the inside of the door, and a multi-coloured carpet on the floor leading past several polished tables to a bar with tankards hanging in front of the bartender. Coloured lights reflected a warm glow on to the sheen of the dark oak counter. It seemed to be the kind of refuge to pass time with someone special, with whom one had a rapport and could spend quality time discussing how to put the world to rights without destroying anyone's reputation. He felt he had chosen well; here he could reflect in relative calm on his situation. He ordered a Guinness and a small bag of crisps and took them over to the corner furthest from the light. As he sat ruminating on the choices open to him, he became aware of two men in the opposite corner leaning towards each other and apparently taking some interest in him. Presently, he saw one of them nudge the other and they then slowly rose and came towards him. As they entered the centre of the room, their faces became clearer and he recognized them instantly as the mechanics in the garage he had initially approached. They appeared to be smiling, but he was not certain what that might signify. He smiled up at them as they stood next to the table.

"Hullo there. Remember us?" began the first mechanic.

"Well, yes, I do," Tim responded They nodded wisely and looked at each other as if pleased to be remembered.

"That's good, isn't it, Bobby?" said the same fellow.

"Yes, Ron. Very nice, indeed," replied Bobby.

"So you won't mind if we join you, right?" continued Ron. They sank down into the seats either side of him. Tim looked at them each in turn and sensed that their smiles were fixed on their lips, not their eyes.

"So, how's the car, then?" asked Ron.

"Oh, going really well now," said Tim, adopting an optimistic tone to cover the questions that were arising as to why these two fellows should seek his company. "It's a pity I couldn't get back to you about it. It was rather taken out of my hands in the end," Tim added, in as apologetic a voice as possible.

"Yes, it was a pity, wasn't it, Bobby. It caused quite a bit of grief, one way an' another."

"Yeah. I rang my Dolly to tell 'er I'd be late home. Really felt let down, she did, specially after I'd told 'er I was makin' a bit extra on the side."

"An' of course, I 'ad to cancel arrangements for the evenin', too," added Ron. "What folk don't seem to realise is that disappointments of this kind can have quite serious repercussions on all concerned."

The two mechanics delivered this information with a sweet reasonableness, that caused Tim to suspect the repercussions might also include him and began to consider ways of excusing himself from their company without unpleasantness.

"I can see it must have been a bit awkward," he offered. "I wish it had turned out otherwise, but this friend of mine arranged things for me."

"Oh, arranged 'things', did he?" said Ron, nodding. "Takin' over the work we'd agreed about ,an' which you did not call on us to personally cancel?"

"Yes, well, I can see your point of view. Perhaps it was a bit remiss, but it all happened rather suddenly. I'm sorry. Look, let me get you both a drink." He was about to get up, but Ron and Bobby pressed down on both his shoulders and held him in the chair.

"I wouldn't hear of it, would you, Bobby?" said Ron.

"Not at all," replied Bobby.

"In fact, I think I should get you a drink," said Ron. He looked round the room before fetching his elbow round to push Tim's Guinness over the edge of the table straight into his lap. Tim backed away from the table involuntarily, but took the full force of the splashed contents in his lap.

"Oh, deary me!" said Ron in mock surprise. "Oops!, as they say. How careless! How did you manage to do that? Just as I was about to go to the bar."

"You did that on purpose," said Tim, in a dark undertone, his face tightening in anger.

"I don't think you should say that unless you've got witnesses, do you Bobby?" Ron said bringing his face near to Tim's in a mock-concerned way.

"There's no point now in gettin' another in. You might go an' do the same with that, eh?" contributed Bobby.

"Still it certainly reached the parts, 'didn't it?" was Ron's witticism. They both chuckled mightily at this, and Tim nodded philosophically, as he realized he could not respond in any way that would give him any revenge without causing a ruckus. He would probably get hurt, anyway, being outnumbered. He really did not have any witnesses, and his main concern now was to leave and get out of his embarrassingly wet trousers. The more discreet his exit the better, considering the state of his crotch.

"Right, you've had your fun. I hope it gives you a lot of satisfaction. Pretty adolescent humour," was all Tim could think to say.

"Hey, Bobby, that must be Surrey fightin' talk, must that."

"Anyway, thanks a lot." Tim stood up and they both chortled as they saw the full extent of the wet patch on his front.

"Don't mention it," said Ron.

Bobby pointed directly at his flies. "I 'ope folk don't think you've wet yourself wi' fright."

"P'raps 'e 'as, an' all," said Ron, as Tim made his way with as much dignity as he could muster to the door.

"Everythin' all right down there?!" shouted the bartender, as he saw Tim go out walking rather stiffly.

"Yers!" Ron shouted back. "Bloke a bit under the weather. Didn't know 'ow to take 'is drink, so he got up and left." They dissolved into more suppressed chuckles, and lifted their own drinks to signify satisfaction.

The drive home was, to say the least, uncomfortable. He was sitting on an old piece of cleaning cloth he had draped over the seat to protect it from beer stains. But the discomfort arising from his humiliation rankled far worse, as he considered how he might have responded in a more physical and, - to put it plainly to himself, - manly way. The better part of valour may have been the sensible thing, but he tensed his muscles and the knuckles on the wheel went white as he imagined them making contact with the faces of his assailants. His school days returned to him to remind him that he had never been someone who enjoyed physical contact sports, and when obliged to play rugby had always been thankfully placed on the wing, where he could use his speed to advantage. But even if he scored a try, it was not in the style of someone throwing himself triumphantly at the ground, but as someone whose superior speed permitted him to decorously place the ball on the ground with a finesse that belonged rather to a game of bowls. How then could he be expected to defend himself physically when something in his nature seemed to rebel at the thought? On the other hand, if the odds had been more even, who knows? It was the first time that he had been accosted in such a way, so it was difficult to decide whether, taken by surprise, it was his reserved nature or simply cowardice that had held him back.

Such thoughts were unsettling, but now he had to get into Elsie's and clean himself up, hopefully without any fuss. His distractive thoughts nearly made him lose his turning once or twice. But eventually he arrived at Elsie's street and pulled up outside No. 37. with a mixture of relief and apprehension.

He eased himself out of his seat, locked the door and walked up to the door. He was about to insert the key when, as fate decreed, it opened to reveal Fred on his way out. There was a moment of silent confrontation as Fred took in the sorry picture of Tim's trousers, still crumpled and soggy with the dark stain of Guinness, and his face adopted an expression of curiosity and concern turning to suspicion arising from Tim's embarrassed attitude. Tim had hoped to escape upstairs to avoid all explanation, and now here he was face to face with the one person who would, he knew countenance no evasion.

"So?" was all Fred said as a prompt.

"Yes," responded Tim, inadequately

"I was on me way 'ome. You better come in." Fred backed in and let Tim pass.

"I must get changed," Tim muttered.

"'Appen you're right, or get a name fer yoursel'." Fred closed the door and went back towards the kitchen. "When ye've done, bring 'em down fer Elsie ter wash. I'll get 'er ter put kettle on fer a Cocoa."

"I,..I.. don't want... to put Elsie out..." Tim began to stammer.

"Don't be daft, lad. Where else can yer take them trousers wi'out being asked daft questions? Bring 'em down soon as ye've got cleaned up."

Fred walked into the kitchen and said in a loud confident voice, "Kettle on, Elsie, lass! Tim's back wi' a tale ter tell!"

The full implication of Fred's tactless declaration struck Tim with painful force. They would look for a full explanation. Should he tell them the truth or make up some story? As he climbed the stairs he could hear enlivened voices. While he got his lower half out of trousers, underpants and socks, and washed himself down with a sponge, he tried to invent a plausible reason for having come home in such a state, but, try as he might, his creative imagination fell short of anything he felt could reasonably take the place of the truth. Had it not been the whole pint spilled over him, he might have confidently claimed it was caused by his own carelessness. But he had been on his own for not more than half an hour, having said he would be out for the evening. He was not very good at fictionalizing the truth, and, in any case, the very idea of being found out by Fred and Elsie to have invented anything nearing a lie nudged him irresistibly towards the unvarnished truth. There was something about them that made him ultra conscious of the need for probity; anything but the truth would seem like a betrayal. Perhaps they would be satisfied with a short précis of events, and he could leave out details, avoiding attributing motives to the two mechanics. He carried the clothes downstairs and knocked lightly on the kitchen door. Elsie responded, with a brisk "Come on in, lad!"

The scene that met Tim as he entered was almost exactly the same as he had left. There was no sign of money, but they were all sitting round the table, ranged in the same order and looking curiously in his direction, as if ready to give their full attention to every detail. He swallowed hard and for a second felt like turning tail.

"Come on an' 'ave a cuppa cocoa. Yer'll feel ever so much better fer it," said Elsie. "An' give us them clothes ter bung in t' washer," she added, going over and gathering them from him.

"Sit ye down, lad," said Fred. "Kettle on the boil, eh, Elsie?"

"Just this minute," she replied, going out to the scullery.

"I hope I'm not the only one?" Tim asked hastily as he sat next to Monty.

"We're all up fer another ter keep 'im company!" shouted Fred.

"Aye, fair enough," she said, returning. "It'll be worth the bother while we get ter bottom of it." Tim looked round at the company. Alf and Bert were scrutinizing him with the intensity of visitors to a museum exhibition, and Monty was all smiling attention, ready to read every syllable that came from his lips. Fred looked fixedly at him with narrowed eyes, nodding gently like a friendly psychiatrist about to attend to his patient. Tim was unable to hold their looks for more than a second before casting about with his eyes in all directions. He was grateful that Elsie broke the silence with the clatter of cups on the table and the dispensing of cocoa to each in turn, busying herself pouring the boiling water and milk into each. Finally the sugar bowl was placed in the middle and Elsie settled herself into her chair with a gentle sigh of anticipation. Five spoons stirred five cups in unison as the kind of enthrallment fell on them a pianist might expect as he settles himself at the keys of his instrument in a concert hall.

"When ye're ready, lad," prompted Fred.

"Yes," murmured Tim, wracking his brains for a way to play it all down into something resembling a light-hearted episode they could all smile at. He cradled the cup in his hands and held it to his lips for some seconds. He took a sip.

"Well,.. it's like this, actually," he began. "I found this nice quiet little pub called the "Jolly Miller" near the main square in the centre of town, and thought I'd try it out." He could hardly explain that he had been seeking out a quiet pub for the purpose of pondering on how to extricate himself from Elsie's house.

"Yeah. Know it." They all exchanged significant looks. "Know it well," said Fred. "Yeah, seen it many a time," said Monty. Alf and Bert nodded to each other, and, everybody having established their familiarity with the place, they all refocused their full attention on Tim.

"So,.." continued Tim, his mind straining under the effort of finding the right words to play down the drama "I got my drink at the bar and sat in a corner enjoying the quiet and, er,.. everything."

"An' that's when it 'appened?" interrupted Fred.

"What 'appened?" asked Monty. " Did 'e say?"

"No 'e 'asn't yet," said Elsie, tetchily. "Let 'im get on wi' it fer 'eaven's sake! Go on, Tim, in yer own time."

"Yes, well, there I was, when,…" Tim began to feel the frustration felt by a parent making up a bedtime story for a group of tiny tots. "…who should come over to my table, but the two mechanics from the garage I originally invited to look at the car." (Pause) " They sat down in a sort of friendly way and enquired how things were going." (Pause) "So I said 'fine' and, so," (Pause) they seemed pleased enough, and then," (Pause) "some-how, (Pause, deep internal breath) "..my drink got spilled into my lap."

There was a second or two's hesitation as everyone waited, and then turned to each other in incredulous disappointment. Tim felt defeated, knowing that no child would have been satisfied to go to sleep after a tale as lame as that. Fred turned down his mouth in scornful denial and said with firm conviction, "That's the biggest load o' codswallop I've 'eard in a month o' Sundays."

Tim blinked rapidly and managed an ineffectual, "I beg your pardon?"

"Aye, an' so ye might, an all," Fred insisted. "I'll tell ye what 'appened, an' stop me if I get it wrong. Them two nasty pieces of work came over and poured yer drink down yer pants just fer kicks. Right?"

"Well,…I wouldn't want to put it quite like that, but, well, I suppose,…" began Tim.

"No supposin' abowt it," said Fred. "I know 'em of old. They've a mighty 'igh opinion of theirselves fer no good reason as I know. They overcharge and they're under'and, and folk are daft as brushes ter go to 'em, after I put me and Monty's card in their 'ands." He fetched a visiting card out of his breast pocket and waved it in the air.

"Aye, that's me. Fred 'ad 'em made professional," said Monty with pride.

"Just 'cos we don't have a pile o' posh equipment, they don't reckon on Monty's experteez."

"It says, 'Great work done with a clear conscience at a fair price'," Monty recited from memory.

"What could you get better'n that?" asked Fred earnestly, turning to Tim.

"No. No, you're right," Tim responded swiftly.

"I know what it is wi 'em two. We cheated 'em out 'o cheatin' you, an' they don't like it. They was cut down ter size, so they 'd ter get back any road they could."

"Aye, but it were Tim took the brunt fer you and me. Right?" said Monty, indignantly.

"So we'll 'ave ter take up the cudgels on Tim's be'alf"," said Fred. Alf and Bert were galvanized into enthusiastic nodding, and one was suddenly heard to say, "Right on, bro." to his fellow. Tim was taken completely by surprise at either of them saying a single word, but eventually managed to say, in a tone that he hoped did not sound capitulating and defeatist, "Look, I'd much rather leave the whole episode behind."

Fred expressed hurt amazement. "Ye can't just let the unrighteous walk over folk wi' their 'ob-nailed boots, willy nilly!"

Aye, it's the principle o' the thing," contributed Elsie, in a quieter, more reflective way.

"Yes, but, I mean, where is this going to take us?" Tim protested.

"Take us?! It'll take us where the unrighteous are made ter mend their ways or suffer the wrath o' the righteous!"

Monty nodded his absolute approval and Alf and Bert were almost beside themselves with anticipation of what that might infer. Fred was in full flow now and he felt it appropriate to quote, "He who lives by the sword, shall die by the sword!"

"Oh, I don't think we should think along those lines," protested Tim, startled by the image.

"Don't fret ye'self. I were thinkin' metaphorical like," Fred said in a somewhat milder tone. "Every'un should be given time ter consider the error o' their ways, an' benefit from it," he added, to give some moral tone to his intentions. "T'morrer, we shall call out the devil from 'is lair to settle accounts. Right, Monty? Alf? Bert?

"Right y'are!" was Monty's immediate response, followed by Alf and Bert thrusting their thumbs up in unqualified support. Tim suspected they were no wiser than he about what 'settling accounts' might involve. He began to imagine things getting quite out of hand, and decided he had to make a protest against any kind of violence. He swallowed hard and launched out. "Look, everyone, I really don't want anyone getting hurt over this very silly situation. After all, what is the great harm in a pair of wet trousers?"

"No lastin' 'arm in that," countered Fred, "cos Elsie'll 'and them back wi'out a stain. But the attack on yer self respect is not ter be countenanced."

"Yes, but my self respect really does not rely on clean trousers," persisted Tim. "I mean, it's not something you'd go the law about, is it?" He laughed almost sardonically, inferring it was beneath contempt to continue with the matter.

"An' that's 'cos the law don't deal with a man's spiritual condition, only what damage 'e does to property. If ye 'ad witnesses, ye could take yer trousers into court as evidence of damage, but gettin' 'em t' see 'ow yer self respec' were jeopardized is another thing all together! I rest me case. Tomorrer, it's out o' t'court's 'ands. Yer self-respec' will be restored, one way or t'other." This statement was delivered with a finality that, had it been further challenged, might have caused more than a ruckus in Elsie's kitchen, and made Tim hold his tongue.

"An' now I'm off ter me own pad, an' I'll see ye all tomorrer." He looked directly at Alf and Bert to say, "An' think on. Ye've to be at Mr. Spender's in Broad Mead in't afternoon. So we all need a good night's kip." He got up and, as he went through the door, turned to thank Elsie for the cocoa and bid everyone a good night.

They all heard the front door shut, and the group obediently broke up, Alf and Bert gave Elsie a peck on the cheek, said, "Ta, Elsie, luv," and departed swiftly through the back door. Elsie swept up the cups and put them on the side of the sink while Monty tucked the chairs under the table. Tim and Monty were unceremoniously ushered out of the kitchen, followed by Elsie, who flicked off the lights, declaring it was time to "Climb t' wooden hill up ter plank common." And this they all did, each to his and her respective room and thoughts.

Revelations

Whatever anyone else's thoughts might have been, Tim's were centred on Fred's proposed confrontation with the garage mechanics. He went to sleep struggling to come to terms with what it might involve, and awoke, conscious that he had failed to do so. He was not one to remember dreams, but on this occasion was aware that he had been swimming in a vat of beer, prodded with long sticks by brewers, who stirred the vat's contents with more gleeful enthusiasm than seemed at all necessary. He thought he remembered having seen Fred peeping over the rim at one stage and saying that it was all for his own good in the end. As he entered full consciousness, he found it difficult to decide who had been stirring and who had been onlookers. However, the overall feeling had been that no-one had fully understood his predicament. He shook his head to rid himself of the lasting effects of the nightmare, and ambled bare-footed to the small window to pull back the curtains and let in some daylight, to discover that, in fact, it was much earlier than he would have liked. Although it was still early and the light had not fully climbed above the serried roofs and chimney tops, he was able to discern two figures in pyjamas and slippers standing in the yard, stretching their arms and yawning. One of the figures having seen Tim's curtain pulled suddenly aside, looked away and quickly nudged his fellow, upon which they both darted guiltily into the shed that stood against the wall. Without question, he had just witnessed Alf and Bert, dressed in night attire, behaving like two felons on the run. It did not take a monumental mental effort on his part to work out that they both slept in the shed. It certainly made sense; they consistently entered and left the house by the back door, even late at night. But the explanation for it was beyond Tim's powers to conjecture.

There is always something disturbing about having seen something that you feel you should not. First, there is the discomfort from the thought of the next meeting with the persons involved. Next, one has to make up one's mind whether or not to let on to having been a witness at all. In this case, he knew that he was now privy to what everyone else in the house must know about. This compounded the awkwardness of his position. He made up his mind to act as if completely oblivious to the two men's clandestine behaviour. In any case, he was much more concerned about what Fred and Monty had it in mind to do about the garage mechanics. He decided he needed to get out of ther house as soon as possible, to avoid being implicated in any way. As he lay on his bed, he practiced two or three phrases as breezy prefaces to the day as he entered the kitchen. "Ah, that smells wonderful!" would be good. "That will see me off to a good start. I've got a busy day ahead," would be a suitable follow up. Encouraged by his efforts, he concocted, "What sort of a day is it going to be, Elsie?" but then swiftly decided that might open up all kinds of unsought revelations. Having, eventually got his script ready, he got up, spruced himself, practiced a nonchalant attitude before the mirror, and steeled himself to go downstairs in apparent unconcern.

As Tim entered the kitchen, Elsie turned from the stove and instantly made any script superfluous by greeting him with the information that a full English breakfast was on its way.

"I could 'ear ye movin about, so I thought, 'I'll wait till he comes down afore I start fryin' the eggs'. Is it one or two?"

"One will be fine, thank you."

Tim was about to say, "I've got a busy day ahead", when she abruptly interrupted with, "Sit ye down. The others've already 'ad theirs."

If Tim hoped that meant everyone else had gone about their business of the day and left the house, he was immediately disillusioned. No sooner had Elsie placed the plate before him than Fred, Alf and Bert all entered in single file from the backyard, and with earnest expressions on their faces, sat down at table. With some suspicion, Tim nodded in their direction, and said, "Good morning", at which they all nodded back but remained mute, fixing Tim with a baleful stare as he started on his breakfast. He looked up once or twice to see if Elsie was about to put something in front of them, but they obdurately sat in silence and watched Tim begin working his way through egg, sausage and bacon. This sombre surveillance became oppressively disconcerting, and was only broken when Elsie put a cup of coffee before Tim, which seemed to be a cue for Fred to say, "Well now, Tim lad, I think ye was up betimes this mornin' and 'appened to see somethin' that might cause questions ter rise up in yer mind, like."

Tim was at a loss to make any meaningful comment, and stared back at Fred, momentarily halted in his mastication of the sausage.

"And so," Fred continued with purposeful emphasis, "we all think as 'ow it's time ter take ye int' our confidence. An' I know I speak fer us all 'ere, when I say we're certain sure we can rely on yer discretion."

Alf and Bert looked at Elsie, who felt prompted to say, "No doubt abowt it," at which they both obligingly added, "good enough fer us,an' all" and, "I'm sure you're right, Elsie." Tim, amazed at having heard Alf and Bert utter a good deal more than their usual grunts, clung on to neutrality, trying to assess the seriousness of having been witness to them scuttling into the shed in their pyjamas.

"So," Fred went on, constructing some kind of verbal protocol in his mind, "you'll be asking yerself what Alf, 'ere", - placing a hand on the shoulder of the 'fairground pugilist, - "and Bert there," - waving towards the 'Adolph impersonator'- " might be doin' paradin' theirsel's in the backyard at six in the mornin' in night attire. It seems as 'ow they've blown their cover, as yer might say, so it seems on'y right ter speak out and lay t' cards on t' table."

"Oh, come on, Fred," Elsie interrupted, impatiently, "there's no need ter make a three course meal of it. Just tell 'im, an' 'ave done."

It was no small revelation to Tim that he was now able to indentify Alf and Bert from each other.

"Aye, right, but well these things 'as ter be done proper, Elsie."

"Aye, but we're not in court, eh?" she retorted.

"So, any'ow," Fred continued, attempting to retain some dignity, "such questions should be properly addressed." Another look from Elsie and Fred moved on to make his point, "The thing is, Alf and Bert live in the shed until such time as they find theirsel's in a place o' their own. Right?"

Tim, realizing that some kind of response was called for at this point, shook his head in agreement, and offered the safe observation, "That seems a good idea."

"Aye, That may well be," Fred swiftly continued, "but we've got the nosey parkers up to no good, peerin' from be'ind their net curtains."

"Really? Well, I don't suppose they could do anything about it, anyway, could they?" suggested Tim.

Everyone let out a sardonic laugh. Fred cast his eyes to heaven, Alf and Bert threw up their hands in mock despair, and Elsie slowly shook her heads to express how, in this life, ones shoulders were constantly weighed down with unmerited trials and tribulations. "It's no good, Fred, ye'll 'ave ter come clean," she said, as if she was bowing to some dire inevitable fate.

"Ye're in t' right, Elsie," returned Fred in the same dolorous tone. "It's t' only way."

As Tim watched the whole gathering fall deeper into apparent desperate resolve, he began to feel a mixture of alarm and sympathy, without the faintest notion of what he should be fearing or sorry about. On the other hand, since he hadn't the slightest wish to be involved in any of their troubles, the only proper thing to do seemed to be to take a forthright stance and declare his wish to dissociate himself.

"Look, everyone, I'm sorry if you've got difficulties, but I don't think it's my business to get involved, you know. I mean, it's nothing to me if Alf and Bert live in the backyard shed. It's a jolly good idea if they... I mean.." -

nodding to them - *you* can't find alternative accommodation…"

Elsie held up her hand like a traffic warden and Tim, deflated, stopped in his tracks. She turned to Alf and Bert and said simply, "Ye better introduce yersel's, an' we'll start fro' there."

At a signal from Elsie, Alf spoke first, with a fluency that amazed Tim, considering his lack of communication to date. His voice reminded one of a sack of gravel being discharged.

"Well, first off, it's not easy, see, when ye've done time, 'specially when it's fer inflictin' g.b.h. on some'un. Folk don't look too kindly on t' perpytration o' violence, even when there's extenuatin' circumstances, an' the offender sees the error of 'is ways. It takes time fer 'em ter see the change what comes over yer."

"Ter be fair, Alf, ye *was* burglarin' at the time," Elsie said.

"Oh, aye, fair enough, Elsie," Alf growled, with ready contrition. "I'm the first ter see the wrong o' that. But, comin' at me with a cricket bat afore we'd exchanged a single word, were a bit strong, eh?"

Fred broke in to speak up in his defence. "That were the extenuatin' circumstance, see, but it were too difficult ter prove."

Overburdened by the sudden revelation of Alf's criminal past, Tim sensed their expectation of some response, but bereft of words, licked his lips and nodded assent.

"Mind you," cut in Elsie, directing an ironic smile to Alf, "I'm not sure where a conversation would'a taken ye."

"There's not much time fer a verbal exchange when ye've to stave off a bloke with a bat in 'is 'and. I got me fist in first and give 'im a bashin' afore 'e did fer me."

"Anyways, that's all water under t'bridge," said Fred with sanguine confidence. "Alf saw the wrong of it when he come ter Jesus."

"Aye. An' it were Fred an' Elsie who brought me, an' all. Wi'out them, I'd still be slidin' down the path ter perdition. What d'yer say, Bert?"

"Most certainly," Bert piped up, ready to give his testimony. "They started us on the road to salvation, and that's a fact."

"That's as may be," interrupted Elsie, "but Tim 'as ter 'ave the facts. Tell 'im what *you* was in fer."

The last thing Tim required was any more facts about their criminal history, but Bert, in a voice that spoke of some education, and obviously trained to be a convincing instrument, seemed to relish telling him that his crime had been as a con man. He stressed that, though he was thoroughly ashamed of the fact, confession was now a release from the burden of guilt. Fred and Elsie and Alf all lent their support by nodding their assent throughout.

"You see, the trouble was, people's greed made it too easy for me to lead them on."

"Not that that excuses ye, Bert," Elsie said.

"Not at all, Elsie. I was making capital out of their weakness, and that is a sin, no doubt about it."

"Hallelujah. Jesus be praised!" let out Fred.

"Amen," they all said in unison.

Tim was in no way moved to share this expression of approval, and the thought even occurred to him that Bert, having considerable experience in exploiting deception, might, even now, be still employing a little of his expertise.

"So ye see, Tim, lad, we've ter keep it all under wraps," Fred explained, "an' we're relyin' on ye ter do the same."

Tim, having no understanding of the matter at all, expressed his opinion that he was very unlikely to meet anyone who would be in the least interested in the shed's two residents. Fred narrowed his eyes and leant over the table. "But ye can never tell who ye might meet. An' they could draw it out o' ye, subtle like."

"Yes," Tim asked in some exasperation, "but who are these people who are likely to question me? How would I recognise them, and what would they want to know, anyway?"

Elsie held up her finger again. "We've not explained it proper ter 'im."

Turning to Tim she said in quiet measured tones, "Alf and Bert 'ave t' ave an address so as ter sign on for social security benefit, when they're not working, like. Elsewise, they're taken to be 'omeless vagrants who're not eligible. Like as not the shed dun't qualify fer an address, so we make it possible fer the Job Centre ter believe they live in the 'ouse. Are ye clear about it, now?"

Tim had no wish to be involved in any illegal activity, but, on the other hand, he could quite see the case for providing shelter for two 'vagrants' trying to go straight. The dilemma lay in having to agree to support them in a deception that possibly enabled them to receive money not due to them. He wished fervently he had not got up too early and seen something that technically made him an accessory. However, being certain that nobody was in the least likely to approach him about the subject, he nodded his understanding, and assured them that their secret arrangement was absolutely safe with him.

"Good lad!" said Fred. Alf insisted on shaking Tim's hand, and Bert and Elsie nodded at each other smiling broadly at him. Everyone seemed to be thoroughly satisfied with the outcome of the exchange, and, soon, even Tim felt he had acquitted himself well and exchanged brief smiles with them all.

"It's a weight off our minds, I can tell you," said Bert. "Already, its a job sneaking in through the back alley."

"Aye," Alf added, with an admonitory nod. "Let's 'ope they don't cotton on. Getting' past all them flutterin' curtains is a proper do. I'd not be surprised if there's folk scratchin' their 'eads and tryin' ter put two an' two together right this minute."

"We've Jesus lookin after us, an' 'E won't let us down," Fred reassured them, with a broad wink. "An' now ter business o' the day. Lads, ye've ter be down at Mister Spender's place 'toot sweet'. 'Is tools 're all set up fer ye there. It's a good couple 'o days work at the least, an' 'e's chuffed wi' ye so far. 'E's even said as 'e'll recymmend ye ter friends. There's nowt like getting' passed on by word o' mouth."

They rose and, apart from a brief cheery goodbye and optimistic nods, left without another word. Fred stood and tapped Monty on the shoulder to get his attention. "We've ter make a little visit in t'town, right?" he said with some emphasis/

"Right enough, Fred," responded Monty.

"Ye'll be off now abowt yer own business, Tim, eh?" prompted Elsie.

"Yes, indeed. I've a number of appointments to make today. I'd better get on with it." He got up and adopted a self-conscious, business-like attitude. Thank you for an excellent breakfast, Elsie. That will see me through to this evening."

"Will ye be eating in? Ye can bring 'ome fish an' chips, if ye've a mind, but ye've ter eat 'em in t' kitchen. I don't like 'em taken up t' room."

"No, of course not. I quite see that," he acquiesced. "I'll probably eat out, anyway, thanks."

"Don't forget ter take yer key. Specially if ye're to be late."

"Thanks, yes." There was a moment of silent dithering. "Right," he said in an indeterminate way, "I'll be off then."

"Right", said Elsie. "Mind 'ow ye go, then."

"Right. Yes," he muttered unnecessarily as he got to the door. "See you later." He slid out, clambered quickly up to his room, got his brief case and swiftly left the house. He needed to sit in his car for some moments to collect his thoughts, and to consider where all he had just learned was taking him. He was possibly an accessory to a deception regarding two old lags given sanctuary by a well-intentioned old man and his... well, just what were Fred and Elsie to each other? Of academic interest was the question of how on earth Fred and Elsie had got themselves mixed up with ex-convicts at all. What appeared more pressing than ever was the need to quickly find alternative accommodation, in as diplomatic a way as possible. He started up the car, put it into gear and gently eased away from the kerb.The Immediate pressing need was to get to the bank, procure money to pay Fred and Monty and to settle with Elsie for the room till the end of the week. And then it was high time to focus on earning a living ; to get back into 'the run of things' expected by his employers.. He had made appointments which he must honour.

There were several large furniture stores in the surrounding area he had arranged to call on. He was presently involved in a campaign aimed at selling prints of well-known paintings as a decorative feature. His firm had had some success with these, although there had been a narrow choice of subject matter. Tim had wanted to introduce paintings that invited empathy; windows on the world., as it were. However, he well knew what he was up against. Most people wanted decorative art that gave colour and blended in with their personal taste in furniture, though he failed to understand why Vladimir Tretchikov's exotic female figures brazenly intruding into domestic quietude from their dominant place over the mantelpiece, could fit that bill. Nor did he know why they sometimes chose the abstract work of Jackson Pollock, whose bold statements depended on what you wanted them to mean, if, indeed, they meant anything at all. It was probably because nobody dared question why you hung him on your walls for fear of an explanation beyond their comprehension. What on earth was one to say of a painter who declared, "When I am in my painting, I'm not aware of what I'm doing". Tim was even obliged to offer Andy Warhole's Marylin Monroe and the other iconic representatives of collective dreams that formed a background as trivial as super store shopping music. Tim had a real desire to direct people to look squarely at pictures, and to enter into the world they opened up. At present, he was drawn to prints of Edward Hopper's statuesque reflective musers or Winslow Homer's powerfully understated dramatic moments of pregnant waiting. He could contemplate for hours the secret thoughts going on in the minds of the people suspended in arrested time. They would, he thought, make a perfect talking point in anyone's home, because they somehow represented everyone's story; were adaptable to anyone's life. But, of course, the script he employed had to be carefully tailored to the way furniture was sold. He would have to settle for saying that Homer's dramatic narrative, or Hopper's cinematagraphic single frames were ideal for people who wanted to be known for good taste without being distracted by the paintings, - which really came down to meaning that they were good if they looked right where they hung. It made Tim restless and dissatisfied. Such thoughts brought him distractedly round to imagine what pictures would be suitable to hang in Elsie's house. Holman Hunt's Jesus knocking at the gate was obviously wholly appropriate, but it begged some Victorian genre paintings of active daily life. He remembered Ford Madox Brown's metaphor of "Work", where four manual labourers are digging up a thoroughfare while the rest of the passing world looks on. He recognised a viable comparison with Fred's irrepressible public energy in it. He concluded that Fred and Elsie did not belong to the twenty first century, with its pick and mix philosophies. Their lives were founded on absolutes, and nobody, - at least nobody Tim knew - was as honestly outspoken and uncompromising as Fred in their defence. His performance in the episode outside Mrs. Delaney's lodging house replicated a 19th century fairground salesman making a pitch to sell bottles of the elixir of life.

He found himself standing in front of the bank teller and asking her to hand over a substantial sum to pay Fred and Monty. "After all is said and done," he told himself, "money extremely well spent", as he folded the notes and put them in his breast pocket.

Disillusion

For Tim, as for most of the male of the species, it was bad enough walking round a large furniture store with the intention of making a purchase, but entering it merely to inspect its contents was anathema to him. The female, on the other hand, regards them as an opportunity to speculate on infinite possibilities. She ambles among them, ruminating, mentally possessing and creating new empires over which to reign. Furniture is displayed for her royal pleasure, and her great delight is to move them around, like chess pieces in her mind, hovering over them, choosing and de-selecting at will. If a man wants to sit in comfort, he will buy a chair that fulfils that purpose; a woman wants not only to sit but to be seen sitting and that involves choosing shape, style, and its appropriateness in respect of the rest of her empire. A man will put the chair to a physical test. "Ah, that feels comfortable!" he will say, recognizing its utilitarian claim. "But, how will it look against the new curtains?" she will insist, inspecting it for its ability to make a comment on her good taste. In Tim's present situation, which is to say, trying to sell art as a complementary decoration, he was almost attempting the impossible. On the one hand he would prefer the man of the house to be stirred a little from his comfort by the sight of a picture, and the woman to actually stop and see a piece of art for itself, rather than as an adjunct to her own jigsaw creation. He would have liked to promote Winslow Homer's work for the way it brought into a single moment in the midst of major events. Similarly, Edward Hopper's arrested action, like a single frame of a feature film, drew you into a world of infinite possibilities stirred by memories of one' own experience. Surely, anyone with the slightest pretension to imagination could sit for hours speculating them? Well, apparently not, for that demanded involvement. People did not want to make an effort in tbeir homes, and so complementary colour and recognisable scenery were preferred; or something so abstract as to demand nothing at all except to be superficially clever during cocktails. It was on this understanding that he was about to try to sell art to the manager of a furniture shop.

Tim was conscious that he was not comfortable in his own age. He still harked back to the nineteenth century, where art restlessly searched meaning in class divisions, social struggle and human relations at all levels, all derived from a suspicion that there was something better round the corner. Fred fitted easily into this vision of life, and maybe that was why Tim was intrigued by the old man's unwavering convictions and, yet, complete lack of complacency. Tim, on the other hand was spending his life selling art to people who wanted to own it without ever being challenged by it. How many times would the twenty first century household change its furniture? Three or four times maybe? The average Victorian lived his whole life with the sticks he had inherited. Most people would have known little about art, but Tim was convinced they provided a much more vibrant legacy for it than his contemporaries. But, at the end of the day, what was Tim? Nothing more nor less than a purveyor of pictures, and, into the bargain,an unworldly bachelor who seemed unable to interpret the fundamental signals that open up human relations. Sometimes he felt like apologising for himself, at other times, aggressively defensive, and it occurred to him that that was why he was intrigued by Fred, who possessed comparatively little of the world, yet had such optimistic expectation of who he was and where he was going. And then there was Elsie had made herself indispensable by rescuing people from homelessness. Monty, Alf and Bert obviously heavily relied on her for their very subsistence. Neither Fred nor Elsie gave any indication of their intention to do good, but fell into doing it unpremeditatedly. However, underpinning it was this ridiculous belief that they were protected by Jesus, and, as Tim saw it, was a condition of others receiving their suppport. Well, that was not going to be how it was with him.. He was grateful to them both, but nothing would induce him to adopt a hypocritical pretence of faith.

Carrying a large portfolio case, he entered the huge emporium under the sign reading "TRADEWINDS FOR FURNITURE OF DISTINCTION". He had travelled a few miles to an out-of-town large shopping mall to the local branch of this nationwide company. As soon as he crossed the threshold, an assistant glided swiftly over the floor towards him, salivating with expectation.

"Can I help you, sir?" he enquired, with a polite tilt of his head.

"I've come to see Mr. Bernard Littleton."

"Is he expecting you?" asked the assistant, dispensing immediately with warm politeness in favour of efficient formality.

"He has arranged to see me in five minutes," Tim replied, drawing a card from his breast pocket,with the satisfaction that comes with eliciting an alert response.

"One moment, sir. I'll ring up to his office."

The assistant crossed to the counter and picked up the internal phone. Tim casually followed with a consciously disinterested air.

"Mr. Littleton will see you now, sir," the assistant said, carefully avoiding his eye, and pointing to the back of the shop. "Through that double door with the emergency exit sign," he added, superfluously, since it was the only door to be seen.

Tim thanked him and walked over. As he approached, it was opened by a corpulent figure whose trousers looked as if they relied heavily on the braces to which they were attached to keep them held to where the waist might have been. He was almost bald, but had let his hair grow long enough to hang over his collar. He stood ready to greet Tim, but there was no accompanying smile. Tim put out his hand, but Mr. Littleton beckoned him through the door with an impatient gesture. He was conscious of Littleton's laboured breathing and the perspiration under his sideburns.

"I can give you half an hour... to convince me with your sales pitch, Mr. ...er,..." he said breathily.

"Carter. Tim Carter," Tim said, with some emphasis.

"Right, Mr, Carter, we'd better take a gander at what you've got for us."

He led the way into his room at the foot of a flight of stairs, next to a second set of double doors with 'Emergency Exit' written on an unlit panel above. Tim resented the word 'gander' straightaway; it did not augur an intelligent appraisal.

199

"Can I lay them out on the desk?" Tim asked. "It will give you a clearer view."

"Why not, if it speeds things up?" said Littleton. He dropped heavily into his rotating chair behind the desk and waited as Tim opened the case and carefully drew out a number of large prints clipped tightly together, separated by tissue paper. He laid the small pile on the table with some delicacy, and Littleton raised an eyebrow. "You take a lot of trouble with them, I must say," he muttered.

"We like to show them as the customer would want to see them – without a blemish," Tim said, with a note of polite correction in his voice.

"Right. Well let's be seeing them, then."

Tim drew out what looked like a plastic ruler which he opened out into a collapsible frame, and placed it next to the pictures. As he revealed each piece of art he meticulously placed the frame around it to provide a finished look. The first pictures were a mixture of abstract works, including Pollock and some carefully selected expressionist canvases by Franz Marc, full of blazing swirls of opposing colours or a kaleidoscopic burst of splintered multi colours. Tim gave out the names of the artists and a few words of basic explanation, while Littleton remained silent, save for his heavy breathing, throughout, oscillating his impassive gaze back and forth between Tim and the exhibits. When Tim presented Raoul Dufy's 'The Harvest' with its dazzling chrome and red wheat fields, squiggly clouds and team of blue and red horses, and 'Horse riders under the trees', a portrait of a family seated on obediently motionless blue and orange horses, he managed, at last, to elicit a grunt from his audience, but whether of appreciation or distaste, he could not tell. Tim pressed on regardless, and finished by displaying two masterpieces by Cezanne and one by Seurat that he really liked and which he thought might, nevertheless, be generally perceived as unobtrusively decorative. They had an architectural quality which denied an immediate interpretation, while giving a sense of being true to what the mind subconsciously understands. .

It would be pointless to try to communicate to Littleton any of Tim's thoughts on the artist, but he had to convince him that they would look good hung on a wall.

"Those make up a fair selection of pictures that have already had some success," said Tim assuming an air of confidence, "and we hold the rights to make sizeable prints to suit most living rooms."

Littleton sat musing for a moment, pressing his fingers together.

"Do you have any questions?" Tim suggested tentatively.

Littleton shook his head uncertainly. He looked up at last wearing a bemused expression, and said, in the tone a crossword addict might use agonising over a clue, "What would make anyone want to hang a picture of blue and red horses on his wall? I've never been privileged to see one in real life, have you?"

Tim shrugged and smiled diplomatically. "Well, no, but that isn't the point. The colours are an expression of what the artist feels about his subject. The main consideration is whether it complements the customer's colour scheme, be it by conformity or contrast." He was conscious of speaking against his own principles; and putting forward the argument for art as a mere accessory. He knew that it was 'tommy rot'.

"That sounds very intelligent, Mr. Carter," Littleton replied, "but, at the end of the day, I'm not very interested in the artist's feelings, and I don't think the customer wants to have to explain to guests, over a gin and tonic, that the picture conforms or contrasts. They want something they can enjoy looking at, something that pleases the eye."

Tim was sensible of his role reversal and position as devil's advocate. Was it faintly possible that Littleton actually enjoyed art for itself? He lifted the Dufy aside, and placed the Seurat on top, framing it.

"Then, perhaps this is more in your line," he suggested. "The colours are less dramatic and the figures are restful and unobtrusive. It's called, 'A Sunday Afternoon at the Island of La Grande Jatte'. I'm sure it would go well with lighter coloured furniture."

Littleton shook his head. "They're not doing anything. They're just standing there like tailors' dummies," he insisted, jabbing his finger at the painting and half screwing up his eyes. "And there's something funny about them; they look as if they're standing in a mist."

"Ah, yes well, that is the impression you might get in a pointillist painting," was Tim's defence

"A Whaty painting?!" Littleton exclaimed, out of his depth.

"Pointillism is the technique of creating light and colour by applying tiny dots of different paint, thus arriving at an over-all blend of colour. It makes for a muted effect, particularly suitable for background art, when you think about it."

"Ye gods and little fishes!" Littleton exclaimed, indignantly. "The customer doesn't give a fig how the painting was made. He wants nice shapes or something he can recognise. He likes a nice bit of scenery or something interesting happening. Not that picture of a family sitting on orange coloured wooden-faced horses like cardboard cut-outs. They want something going on."

"What do you mean, 'going on'?" Tim tried to keep irony out of his voice, but raised his eyebrows to simulate interest.

"Well,...like a ship sailing out to sea, you know," - here, Littleton waved his hands about in a vague gesture, - "or people doing something together,...maybe sitting in deck chairs or having a picnic in a nice setting."

"Well, if that's what you want, Mr. Littleton, I'm sure we could provide something."

Perversely, Manet's painting, 'Le Dejeuner sur L'herbe' came to Tim's mind, with its provocative subject of two smartly dressed Parisians sitting on the grass having a picnic with a stark naked young woman staring brazenly out front. He decided on another tack.

"Surely, if customers start looking at paintings they won't be decorative any more. I mean, they would be better off going to a museum or an art shop to see pictures like that."

Littleton gave a unappreciative grunt. "Yes, well, personally, I don't mind people not looking at the pictures, but I don't want them having their stomachs turned over. That first lot you showed, I reckon my seven year old could throw paint around just as well, - or a chimpanzee, come to that."

Tim shuddered inwardly at Littleton's straight from the shoulder delivery, although he could see his point of view. Ironically, any agreement with him would be likely to discourage him from making a purchase. Tim finally displayed the two Cezannes, the first a 'Still life with Milk Jug and Fruit' and the second a landscape, 'Montagne Sainte Victoire', with a foreground of angular rocks and faint blue hills in the background. He placed the frame over each in turn and watched Littleton's reaction carefully.

Littleton sniffed and tapped the tips of his fingers together. "Aye, I'll concede that you've got something there. The fruit looks very nice, but then I can put a bowl of fruit on the table with a jug next to it any time I like. Why do I want a picture of what I've got under my nose?"

It would be a waste of time trying to explain the artist's search for unification of the work of art with the objects painted and its surroundings, nor, in the case of the present picture, his desire to give an identity to the painting, rather than creating a representation of fruit.

"Well," suggested Tim, with the given logic of the ridiculous, "it avoids the necessity of continually having to get the fruit and jug out all the time."

"True," conceded Littleton, submitting to the irrational argument, "if you felt it was important enough to keep setting them up."

Tim pressed home the suggestion. "I think the muted colours are discreet and would make a very pleasant complementary background to a room furnished in, say, your Birchwood line."

Littleton shrugged. "Do you think so?" He shrugged again. "You could be right. Well, perhaps I'll go for that, then. I'm not taken with that mountain scenery. In my experience, people want something that reminds them of what they took photos of."

"You've settled for the fruit and jug, then?" Tim asked.

"Go on, then. Put me down for a dozen to spread around and see how we go."

As Tim left the Superstore, having secured his pitiful order, chosen for all the wrong reasons he, himself, had aided and abetted, he felt a moral biliousness rise up. What on earth was he doing with his life? Although he prided himself on his knowledge of art, he was no more an artist than a music lover was necessarily an instrumentalist But the fact that he had just prostituted his love of art for the sake of a commercial deal dug into his guts. How different from when he started out with the exciting belief that he could reveal the spirituality and beauty of paintings to the world at large. He would take art to those who had never sought it out. Revelation would incite them to a new awareness of the beauty around them. He would awake something dormant in them; something their souls subconsciously yearned for. Sadly, his subsequent experience had taught him that the world's taste in art was arrived at, either by what they thought it was worth at an auction sale, or whether it lay strictly within the limits of their own worldly experience; whether it reminded them of 'what they took photos of', as Littleton had judged. Worse, he was putting art at the disposal of anyone who would use it as a utility, when it should serve nothing but itself and those who personally responded to it.

He drove back to Elsie's place, reminding himself that, for her and Fred, too, art was a mere appurtenance, which could have no significance other than to remind them of their beliefs. They would be just as disinterested in an artist's motivation as Littleton, with the exception of Holman Hunt's picture of Jesus knocking at the gate to remind them of how souls are saved. Fred, with negligible interest in art, immersed himself in the service of others. That was what, somehow, gave him the right to be so deprecatingly honest about Tim's dealings; that and, incidentally, the fact that Tim, himself, was out of love with the whole business. He could not deny Fred and Elsie had got him out of considerable difficulty, but there were attendant conditions to their helpful attention, not the least being the acceptance of Jesus's constant intervention. Fred had no right to presume Tim shared his faith. In fact, every time he shared his prayers with him, he made him feel a complete hypocrite.

He made up his mind to seek out alternative accommodation as soon as possible, and extricate himself from a situation that felt increasingly untenable.

Retribution..

Tim was once more parked outside Elsie's and preparing his polite script to refuse any offer of a meal. On letting himself in, he heard lively exchanges going on in the kitchen, and decided to tell her straightaway that he would be eating out. As he put his head round the door he heard Fred telling everyone that, "No doubt abowt it, it were a blessed outcome!".

Monty was also sitting at the table, smiling and nodding at Fred. Alf was grinning on the other side of the table, nudging Bert, who responded with a chuckle of approval

Elsie saw him first and enthusiastically beckoned him in.

"Eeh, Tim, lad, yer ears must'a been burnin'. We just been talkin' abowt ye."

"Really?" said Tim, with restrained interest.

"Come an' 'ear wot Fred an' Monty've bin up ter. Sit ye down," Elsie said, patting the back of a chair. Everybody waved him in as though he were the principal guest arriving late at a banquet. Monty even got up and pulled out a chair for him to deny him any reluctance, and he was obliged to capitulate to the inevitable with as good a grace as he could muster. As soon as he sat, they all beamed at him like a battery of footlights, and, for some seconds, he found himself bathed in an approving glare, filled with doubt.

Fred raised his hands and broke in, saying, "I ask ye all ter join me in a few words o' thanks fer the success we was blessed wi t'day." They all dutifully closed their eyes as he launched into prayer.

"We all thank ye, Prince Jesus, fer lettin' those who had a special need fer correction, ter see the error of their ways. Once again, yeours is the victory. An' we thank Ye that young Tim 'as bin give proper recompense." Tim frowned suspiciously, as Fred turning to Alf and Bert, said, "I ask me brothers to add a few words o' their own."

Alf, taking his cue, began. "Aye, thanks a bundle, Lord. We know the power of Yer 'oly name, bein' as 'ow we was once convicted oursel's, an' are now made free o' blame by Ye. Now those scoundrels've been brought out o' their evil ways, may they continue t' keep ter the straight an' narrer way. Amen."

No sooner had the chorus of 'amens' died away than everyone looked at Bert, who nodded assent and began. " Er, yes, Lord. We give thanks that although we are ex-cons, we are no longer convicted. We ask you to keep those two wayward garage mechanics from further anti-social behaviour, and to give Tim back his sense of self-respect. Amen."

Tim, by now seriously alarmed, peeped out from beneath his half-closed eyelids throughout this exchange, and was conscious of the self-satisfaction pervading the room. Fred thrust his hand in his pocket and withdrew two ten pound notes and laid them in front of Tim.

"There y'are, Tim! A token of repentance. A guilty conscience made clean."

"I don't understand. What do you mean?" said Tim, full of misgiving and made uncomfortable by the proximity of the money.

"Them two mechanics 'as seen their way ter makin' a modicum o' recompense fer their waywardness. They 'ave made due apology and wish ye t' ave this as a token o' their sincere regrets fer 'avin' inflicted 'umiliation on ye."

Tim looked down first at the money and then at Fred, allowing his imagination to take him where he had no wish to be. "You don't mean you extorted this money from them?"

"Extorted?!" exclaimed Fred with some indignation. "O'course not! Me an' Monty just paid them a visit and opened their eyes ter seein' the 'arm they'd done by their perverse be'aviour."

Tim shook his head and looked at Fred and Monty each in turn. "I'm sorry, but I find it difficult to believe that those two chaps repented of their behaviour. I hope you'll not tell me you got the money by force."

Fred frowned at Tim, and Monty, who had been reading Tim's lips, pushed his chair back from the table in indignation, shaking his head and adopting an expression of hurt pride, as he appealed with spread arms to the assembled company for their moral support. Fred, momentarily lost for words, looked up at the ceiling as if seeking divine instruction to provide him with words to express his feelings. Elsie obviously thought it was her duty to step in on his behalf, and tutted before saying, "Now then, Tim, I'd 'ave expected ye t'ave more faith than that. Fred and Monty 're sworn against violence. They rely on the stren'th o' the Lord in these matters."

Tim was suddenly made to feel like a recalcitrant schoolboy, but still found it impossible to believe in this miraculous turnabout on the part of the garage mechanics. "Well, I can't imagine why they would suddenly have a complete change of heart, that's all," he insisted.

"Then ye'd better let Fred tell ye, hisself," she concluded with a firm nod towards the old man. By now, Fred's expression spoke of accusation and betrayal and a long-suffering experience of the world's unjust judgement. Monty took to nodding reflectively, as if he was coming to terms with a world beyond comprehension. Tim grew uncomfortable and, although still very doubtful, decided he had better apologise. "I'm sorry if I've misjudged the affair. You're right. I should have waited to hear about it. I'm ready to listen if you want to tell me."

"There ye go, Fred," whispered Elsie in a pacifying tone. "'E'll see 'ow it wus, when' 'e's 'eard ye out."

"It's t' be 'oped so," muttered Fred, still holding on to hurt feeling. Elsie looked appealingly at Tim, and she made a surreptitious motion towards Fred. Tim sigheed inwardly and then, turning to him, said in as apologetic a tone as he could muster, "I'm sorry, Fred, if I spoke out of turn. Please go on."

Fred instantly brightened up at this, and Monty, who had been following every movement and word throughout, positively beamed. The moment was rescued from all incrimination, and Alf and Bert nodded at each other, the former with the enthusiasm of a five year old and the latter with a more cynical reserve. Everyone settled into their seats and looked at Fred with the expectation given to an author in a public library.

"Right," said Fred, looking round at everyone, "'ere's the truth of it. We decided, Monty and me..."- Monty smiled and nodded as if acknowledging the crowd's applause - "ter pay a call on the gentlemen in question," - Fred hesitated before adding, - " t' appeal t' their sense o' proprietee and ter touch their consciences."

"A sort o' social call, yer might say?" suggested Elsie.

Aye, ye could put it that way," said Fred, "eh, Monty?" he added, turning to him. Monty nodded. "Yeah. That sums it up," he said, in a deep affirmative growl while nodding.

"We give a polite knock afore enterin'," said Fred. "an' when they sees, me they give a sort o' smile, one t'other. 'An' wot can we do fer you?' they says, grinnin' sort 'o cocky. An I says, 'Well, I've come ter give ye the chance ter put things right what ye got wrong', I says. Then Monty comes in t'door, an' they give 'im a good lookin' over. 'E's nowt but smilin' at 'em. But they don't bother ter smile back like."

"I were nowt but smilin'," Monty assured the company.

"'Anyways', I says, 'I believe ye'll be a deal 'appier in yerselves when ye've done the right thing'. 'Wot d'yer mean?' says one of 'em. 'Makin' good the damage ye done down at the 'Jolly Miller', I says. 'Wot's that ter do wi' you?' says the other fella. 'Everythin', I says. 'The victim of the shabby deed were my friend, an' it were taken bad by 'im. It did 'arm ter t'young fella, it offended Jesus, an' wot's more, put yer own souls in jeopardy.' That don't seem ter worry 'em mightily, so I says, 'An' 'is friends, like Monty 'ere, is offended an' all.' So they give Monty the once over an' just as we agreed aforehand, 'e did nowt but smile all t' time. I'd told him ter do a lot o' smilin' while I did the serious talkin', so he smiled a lot more an' come ter stand aside o' me, the while."

Bert nodded and said, quietly, almost under his breath, "That would do it."

"Anyway, summat must've 'appened ter touch their 'earts," Fred went on, "'cos the first bloke says, 'An' wot d'ye reckon the damage is?'. So I says 'I reckon a couple o' tenners'd make all concerned feel a deal better, but more important, put ye right wi' Jesus int' bargain. 'An', I says, serious like, 'wot's more, ye'll feel a deal better abowt yersel's, when it's done.' So, after he keeps 'is eye on Monty an' me a while, he gives it some thought and goes over ter t' till and fetches out the notes an' 'ands 'em over. 'So now we're quits,' he says. I puts the money in me back pocket an' says, 'Aye, wi' us and young Tim, but not wi' Jesus, so jus' ter cleanse oursel's o'all bad thoughts, I'd ask ye ter say a few words o' prayer wi' me.' 'E seems ter think I'm 'avin' a jest fer a moment or two, an' says, 'Get on wi ye. Ye're 'avin' us on.' I shakes me 'ead and looks serious while Monty smiles an'nods. An'I says, 'Jes' repeat after me.' An' so we was able t'ask Jesus's Dad fer f'giveness fer givin' in ter temptation, an' give 'Im thanks fer lettin' us put it right. An' there y'are!" exclaimed Fred, compressing his lips and giving a final punctuating nod. Monty nodded too, as if on cue, and looked round as if seeking applause. Elsie beamed first at Fred and then at Tim, as if her heart would overflow with pride and gratitude. "Ee, the power o' prayer, eh,Fred?"

Tim tried to imagine the garage mechanics at prayer, and found it so impossible he gave up the effort. He seemed to remember having it impressed on him when young that one was supposed to forgive and forget, rather than extract recompense for the harm others did to you. But, of course, Fred and Monty would deny any intent to extort.

Alf, who was enraptured throughout, showed his delight at the outcome, and was convinced that Fred had performed miraculous evangelism. Bert, who seemed a touch more reticent, had obviously enjoyed the story and even expressed his approval in his laconic way, as he obscured his mouth by smoothing his moustache with finger and thumb. Tim, however, far from giving his approval, suspected that the matter had been resolved in a somewhat unconventional way. The two ten pound notes lay in front of him,bearing palpable witness to what they had all just heard. If he accepted them he would feel he was accessory to coercion, and if he did not, he would offend Fred, whose self-styled victory would, inevitably be depreciated. The dilemma needed careful handling.

"What do I say?" he began. "I really must thank you for going to all this trouble on my behalf." Monty shrugged and seemed suitably embarrassed. Fred wore a look of pride and satisfaction. "But," added Tim very slowly. as if reflecting, "I think....", -the windmills of his mind turned ever faster, - ".that to accept this money..." - Oh, heavens, where was this taking him..? - "would be..." Suddenly a burst of inspiration broke through., and he found himself saying, "not favoured by Jesus."

Everyone looked at him as fixedly as if he had just declared the end of the world that afternoon. Tim sighed with relief that his ability to speak off the cuff had served him.

"Yes," he said with emphasis, "I'm sure He would want the money to go where it is more needed."

The looks of rapt astonishment turned to admiration and proprietary pride. Elsie took up a knapkin and wiped her eye, Monty was so affected he scrunched up his face like a reformed gargoyle and Fred nodded repeatedly like a jew at the wailing wall. Alf whispered that 'a willing giver is blessed', and only Bert looked as if he might be weighing up the pros and cons. There were a few seconds of silence before Fred spoke, in sombre undertones, "If ye've been spoke ter, then there's nowt ter do but obey."

"Was ye given any word about where it should go, Tim?" asked Elsie.

"Not exactly," Tim said carefully, "but I got the feeling that Fred would know best."

Everyone looked at Fred, who betrayed first surprise, then pleasure, both of which feelings he swiftly replaced with a contemplative look, as if he had momentarily been immodest. He nodded slowly, in a way that suggested ethereal communication, before saying, in a measured voice that appeared to be relaying thoughts that mystically came to him, "Aye, well, it seems as 'ow new ways are opened,..new roads fer journeyin'. I've 'ad it placed in me mind t'money'd be best spent on a pilgry-mage." He turned purposefully to Tim and, scrutinizing him with great deliberation, put down the challenge' "It's time ter go the las' mile. Are ye up t' it?"

Tim had not the faintest idea what Fred meant, and with a defensive shrug, said, "Up to it? What does that mean?"

"We'll invest the money in a little trip in t' hills ter complete yer eder-cation."

"I've no idea what you're talking about," insisted Tim.

"Nay. Trust me, Tim, lad. Trust me. Tomorrer ye best take t' day off an' I'll show ye summat special."

"Can't you give me any idea what?" asked Tim.

"Trust me," said Fred, repeatedly tapping the side of his nose, until Tim finally capitulated, shrugged and muttered, "Right." He was aware, after all, that he had handed Fred the initiative by the very attempt to disassociate himself from the money.

"Right," repeated Fred. He spat on his hand and offered it for Tim to shake, like a horse trader clinching a deal at a gypsy fair. Tim took it, without spitting, and resigned himself to a day off in pursuit of heaven knew what.

Fred's triumph was abruptly interrupted by a knock on the front door. Everyone looked at each other, mystified, and Elsie asked if anyone was expected. After a further exchange of puzzled looks they all turned to Tim, who shook his head. "It couldn't be for me. No-one knows I'm here."

"Ye best go and find out, Elsie," Fred prompted.

"Elsewise we'll never know," was Elsie's tart reply, as she went, closing the kitchen door behind her.

Everybody strained to listen as they heard Elsie's muffled exchange at the door, but were unable to make any sense of it. It sounded as if she had stepped out into the street and closed the door behind her. Elsie's voice was raised as she bid the visitor goodbye. Then her steps clic-clacked back to the kitchen. As soon as she entered, everyone knew something was wrong. She slumped down, without a word, in one of the chairs, and with the tight lipped glare of an outraged headmistress, uttered an aggressive "humph!"

Fred was the one with the courage to put the question. "Whatever's up, Elsie? Ye look like ye've bin told ter demolish yer 'ouse.

"They've bin at it, that's fer sure," she growled.

"Oo 'as?" urged Fred.

"The neighbours. That were the man fro' t' Employment Centre wantin' ter speak ter t'lads 'ere." She indicated Alf and Bert, who instantly sat bolt upright.

"I told 'im they was out. But 'e said 'e'd be back later .. 'ter get things cleared up' is 'ow he put it."

Alf and Bert froze, and while Alf swore under his breath, Bert pronounced it to be an example of "sod's law. Intolerable interference by some snooping fatherless grasser, who had nothing to do but peer through lace curtains all day." Elsie silenced them with a wave of her hands. "Hush! We've ter get us thinkin' caps on. I told 'im ye both lived 'ere, so we got ter make 'em believe it. There's but one way ter do that."

"What's that?" Fred asked.

"We move 'em upstairs the whilst."

"Whilst what?" Bert interjected.

"While they're snoopin' roun'," Elsie said, with raised voice to quell any resistance. "Soon as they're convinced that Alf and Bert are residents, we can move 'em down ter t' sheds again."

"D'yer mean take all us beds up, an' all?" asked Alf.

"O' course, I do. We'll 'ave a general move, afore 'e comes back. Come on,Fred!" she barked, "Let's get it done smart like!"

"Right!" Fred bellowed, like a sergeant major passing orders down the line. "Let's get t' beds out o' t'sheds!"

"But where do we install them, when we've got them out?" asked Bert, frowning quizically.

"Er,.." Fred muttered, turning to look at Elsie.

Elsie shook her head impatiently. "Don't be daft. It's obvious. They go in Tim's an' Monty's rooms. Right Monty? Tim?"

Tim aghast at the idea of this sudden invasion of privacy, hesitated, but seeing no way out, gave a brave acquiescent smile and nodded. Elsie mouthed it all again for Monty, who instantly smiled and put his thumbs up.

Galvanised into action, Fred led the way out to the shed, followed, first by Monty, then Alf and Bert, with Tim bringing up the rear, while Elsie went upstairs to organise reception of the beds. Fred fell into the role of overseer with more gusto than efficiency, and reminded Tim of scene's from "Dad's Army", in which stoicism wrestled with eager incompetence. They gathered up the bedclothes before finding they had nowhere to deposit them while they were man-handling the beds. They returned the sheets and blankets to the mattresses, but discovered that they fell off as soon as they upturned them to get through the shed door. Bert was inspired to suggest that,first, they take all the bedclothes upstairs and deposit them, before coming back for the mattresses and truckle beds. This done, they trundled the beds along the hall and round the bannisters at the foot of the stairs, Elsie stood, arms akimbo at the top, issuing dire warnings against scraping the bannisters on the way up. At last, having got the truckle beds unfolded, the mattresses laid and the bedclothes thrown over them, everyone, with the exception of Tim, stood panting and smiling their mutual congratulations. Tim's bedroom had been transformed into a depository with the narrowest passage between the beds, and Monty's, a mere box room, resembled the interior of a delivery van, in which access to either bed was via the other. Alf's and Bert's clothing was hung from various hooks and hangers, suspended from dado rails all round the rooms. Propriety and comfort were sacrificed to create the semblance of an overcrowded doss house.

Elsie wore an exultant expression and said, "Right then, that oughta do it! Jus' let 'em try it on, an' they'll go away wi' a flea in their ear."

To this point, Tim had been caught up by the community spirit and the enforced effort. Now, with the result visible to the naked eye, he felt swamped by the implications. He mentally reviewed it, and summed it up as 'intimate proximity with Bert, a convicted con man, to substantiate a fabrication which deceives the authorities'. Far from meriting congratulation, it was something he had to extricate himself from at the earliest opportunity. To preserve his sanity, he would have to find alternative accommodation. Unfortunately he would not be able to do this before he returned from,..well,.. wherever Fred was taking him the following day.

Trials and Tribulations

The night following the upheaval of the sleeping arrangements was not one Tim would leap to remember. He was far from happy about the invasion of his privacy, having never before shared a bedroom with anyone. He would certainly not have chosen his inauguration to be with someone who had spent time 'inside'. It was not his choice that he was 'banged up', as the phrase had it, with one who had 'made his living', if you could call it that, inveigling others into revealing things that possibly worked towards illegal gain. Tim was suddenly conscious how sheltered his life had been, and how different it would be, if he had not encountered feisty old Fred, seeing his friend, Tom, off to the Elysian Fields on a fateful murky day in the local municipal park.

Tim went ahead to get undressed before Bert joined him. The space allowed for this was decidedly cramped, and he had just time enough to fold his clothes at the foot of the bed, and to sink under the bedclothes before he heard Bert and Alf climb the stairs together, chuckling loudly on the landing, and expressing their appreciation of the way things were looking up for them. Monty joined them and there were further exchanges. Alf thanked Monty "a bundle", shouting at him with over-emphatic enunciation, as if this would aid his deafness.

They finally separated, and wished each other "good night" as enthusiastically as drinking partners at closing time. As Bert opened the door, Tim turned his back, hoping he could encourage his fellow lodger to get into bed as soon as possible. It was obvious Tim was not asleep, but, as if to make assurance doubly sure, Bert launched into a stream of chit-chat. He expressed his gratitude for the way Tim had 'willingly' allowed him to share his room, and, then, went on to explain the injustice of the social system that made such moves necessary. Tim's over-the-shoulder response was a series of grunts, 'ah'ha's' and 'mmm's' that he hoped might dissuade further exchange.

The sound of boots being dropped on the floor and pushed under the truckle bed punctuated a constant flow of chatter. Bert made sure Tim missed none of the narrative, raising his voice while he pulled his sweater over his head or bent down to take off his socks. He opened the squeaky hinged wardrobe to hang up his trousers, and finally pulled on his pyjamas, huffing an puffing with the effort. When he was fully ready for bed and had switched off the light, Tim gave an inward sigh of relief. Within seconds, however, hopes of a respite were dashed. Having been used to companionable exchanges with Alf in the shed, Bert obviously thought they would be similarly received by Tim.

"The thing is, you know, old son, you have to survive, somehow; bending the rules a bit, I mean. It goes against the grain, but there's little alternative, the rules being what they are."

Tim, pulled the bedclothes down over his ears, and thought, cynically, that Bert might just be the one to bend the rules with ease. "I mean, 'going straight' means taking a few bendy curves at times. The authorities tend to judge you by your past. 'Give a dog a bad name', as they say. A great blessing to meet up with Fred and Elsie, you know, they being ready to give us a 'leg up'."

"Hmm," agreed Tim, emitting a gentle drawn-out groan to suggest someone sinking into exhausted stupor.

"It's harder for me, your know, because I'm not used to manual labour. Unfortunately that's all there is at present," continued Bert, ignoring Tim's unsubtle 'put-off'. "Tomorrow, there's a full day's gardening to get through. Still, at least I can put something away each week. I'm going to set myself up as a consultant in the security business before long. Funny thing is, when I was being a naughty boy, I could tell if someone worked manually or with their brains just by the way he shook your hand. Now I've got the same problem. My hands are a give-away to people I've got to impress."

"Look, Bert," said Tim at this point, "I'd be very interested to hear your story, but, just now I need sleep. Can we leave it till tomorrow?"

"Absolutely, dear fellow. Quite understand. Feeling a bit sleepy myself, as a matter of fact. Just socialising, you know, that's all."

"Good night," Tim replied with a note of finality.

"Sleep well, old chap," Bert replied.

Tim drifted into slumber filled with ethereal dreams, and had just floated into a Constable painting of a valley inhabited by grazing cows with friendly clouds gliding over gently sloping hills, when, from the distance, thunder broke into the scene. The idyllic world of gentle flowing rivers and rolling country was threatened by am approaching storm, and suddenly he was searching the skies for glowering clouds and forked lightening. Forced to seek shelter, he dreamed he was climbing out of the rural scene into a huge echoing drum, and as he did so, he became aware of a loud real world awaiting him, a world in which he was tossing and turning to the accompaniment of vibrating tonsils. Bert was a snorer of a particularly creative kind; one who, having emitted the long deep booming resonant sound of waves entering a cave, followed it by using his lips to simulate water receding over pebbles, and, occasionally, by smacking them together to suggest the sloshing of waves against rocks. It was, altogether, worthy of an old time music hall impersonater, wholly unacceptable to an audience of one in a bedroom. After half hour of this, the pregnant silences between the snores became as stressful as the noise itself. Tim began clearing his throat very loudly, and, when this got no response, emitted repeated stoccato coughs and punched his pillow with a murderous intensity that very closely expressed his feelings. After an hour of gradual unabated crescendo, Tim had reached breaking point. He sat on the edge of his bed, leaned over Bert, and poked him sharply in the ribs. He had to repeat this three or four times before he got a response, and Bert emerged into the semi-conscious world of personal responsibility.

"Wassamatter, then?" Bert enquired, with the vulnerable look that bleary eyes give.

"You're snoring." There was a pause for Bert to take this in. "Very loudly,"Tim added. Another pause until, having considered this, Bert remarked, "Well, I didn' know that."

"No, you wouldn't," said Tim, stemming his exasperation. "So the only way to get you to stop was to wake you up. Otherwise I wouldn't get any sleep at all."

Bert considered this for a moment, as he smoothed his moustache with his finger and thumb. "That's never been a problem before. Alf never said anything."

"Maybe he snored, too," suggested Tim.

"If so, we'd have woken each other up," Bert insisted.

"In this case, *you* woke *me* with your snoring," retorted Tim

"Yes, but we're both awake now, 'cos *you* woke *me*," was Bert's response.

Tim lay back on the bed and tucked his legs under the covers again. "Look, there's no point in having a meta-physical debate about it. I just want to go to sleep, and so I'm asking you to try not to snore."

"Well," muttered Bert, "It's not something you try to do." - then, after a moment's refelection, - "It's not some-thing you try *not* to do, as a matter of fact."

"Please, let's leave it now, and get back to sleep."

Tim put his head under the sheets and made an effort to blank off the world. Bert scratched his head and yawned and let his eyelids droop,[and before long, heavy drawn out breathing abbounced the prelude to sleep again. Tim was ready to drift off, himself, but had become so accustomed to counting the seconds between each of Bert's outbursts, that he found himself listening apprehensively even in the silence. He was not disap-pointed in his expectations, for after ten minutes or so, the snores began again. This time, however, rather than go through the rigmarole of prodding, waking and exhorting Bert to stop what he did not know how to, - or was it what not to do? – Tim took the grim decision to get up, take his bedclothes and pillow, and seeke asylum downstairs. He found a settee in the front parlour and laid himself down, body curved in the shape of an ancient celtic burial, and drifted eventually into a surreal dream, in which his limbs detached themselves from his biody and floated off in all directions, obliging him to snatch them back from the air before they went out of reach.

He awoke the next morning, feeling as if his arms and legs really did not belong to him. He was numb all over and there was a crick in his neck from being pushed up against the arm of the settee. With a groan, he unfolded himself into a sitting position, and, with the bedclothes draped over his shoulders, moved his head from side to side, while he vigorously rubbed the circulation back into his legs.

When he finally climbed the stairs back to his room, thankful not to be accosted on the way, Bert met him with a cheery enquiry as to his health, as soon as he entered the bedroom, expressing that he was shrouded with bedclothes. His alert face, shining, his hair brushed, and his person fully dressed intimidated Tim into merely grunting and leaving unspoken the unsatisfactory night he had suffered.

"Ah, not so chipper in the mornings, I see!" Bert offered as friendly banter. It was obvious that he had not the slightest remembrance of the night's disturbance. Either that, or he was avoiding the subject and would pretend, as his defence, the denial of all knowledge. Tim nodded, threw off the bedclothes and slouched his way to the bathroom. He brushed his teeth, ran the face cloth over his neck and shoulders, combed his hair out of his eyes, all the while studiously avoiding his reflection in the mirror. When he returned to the bedroom, he was relieved to find that Bert had already gone downstairs, and so he could, at least, get dressed in peace. How he was to dress was still a question, considering he had no idea where Fred was taking him It could hardly be formal, surely? On the other hand, clothes said a lot about one; one could not be too careless. He fished out his grey slacks, the pale mauve shirt, the sleeveless maroon pullover, the lightweight sandy coloured jacket and slipped on his elasticated light tan shoes. He felt more relaxed and at home in these clothes. If not fashionable, at least they felt safe. They said nothing about anything, which gave him a feeling of anonymity, behind which he was his own interior self.

They were all seated at the table when he entered the kitchen.

"Did ye sleep well?" asked Elsie, taking it for granted.

"Er, yes, not too bad," Tim replied, sliding into his chair. He caught Bert's eye across the table, and detected a suspicion of a sceptical smile behind the smudge of hair above his lip, but managed to pass it off as paranoia.

"Will it be the full breakfast?" Elsie enquired.

"Just cereal, thanks," he returned.

"We 'ave ' Frosties', 'Chocoweats', 'Raspberry Crispies' 'Honey Clusters' or 'Cranberry Bran Flakes'. Ye can mix 'em if yer like."

The last thing Tim wanted was to be confrontated with a complicated choice of cornflakes.

"On second thoughts, a boiled egg would be nice," he said quickly.

"Three minutes and two slices of toasts?" suggested Elsie helpfully.

"Lovely," murmured Tim.

"Not much to see ye through a full day," said Fred, pressing a forkful of bread into the fried egg of his full

English breakfast to emphasise his point. "I'd 'ave a breakfast wi' a bit pro-tein, if it were me," he added

"Not awfully hungry in the mornings," Tim said

"Aye, well, tha's 'cos yer not over used t' activity," Fred admonished. "When I were a young'un I needed me vittals ter brace me up."

"'Ere's yer tea," said Elsie, placing a cup in front of Tim. "Ye look as 'ow ye need it." She could not know how much.

"I reckon we ought ter be off in quarter hour, so we can make t' best o' it," urged Fred.

"Oh, fer 'eaven's sake, let the lad 'ave 'is breakfast in peace, Fred. Yer not but an hour an' a 'alf away. There's not such a rush as all that to get there," remonstrated Elsie.

"Get where?" asked Tim, hoping he might get Fred to come clean.

Fred and Elsie concertedly raised a finger and said, "Ah, ha!"

"Wouldn't ye like ter know?" added Elsie, tapping the side of her nose.

"Darker t' cave, brighter t' sun when ye come out o' it," recited Fred with tantalising complacency, as he finished off his plate.

As Elsie put the egg and toast in front of Tim, Fred turned to Alf and Bert with a brisk tone. "Now, lads, ye better get down ter Spenders' place an' do a good job. I'm 'opin' ye'll 'ave finished by t'evenin'. 'E's fair chuffed wi' ye, but 'e don't want ye 'roun' 'is place indefinite, like." He tapped Monty on the shoulder and mouthed to him, "It looks like ye've ter sign on t'day wi' nowt turnin' up. Ye can put another card in t'corner shop, an' see if it pulls some'un in. Right?"

Monty nodded. "Righto, Fred. I'll do another card in me best 'andwritin'."

Alf and Bert took their cue from Monty and rose and went out into the hall, leaving Tim to finish his token breakfast, and fill his head with vague speculation. As he finished his tea and Fred was about to rise and chivvy him on, there was a knock at the front door. Fred and Elsie froze. Then she slowly edged herself towards the kitchen door, and just as she was about to turn the handle, it opened to reveal a wide-eyed Alf, who whispered, hoarsely, "They're 'ere!"

"What? You mean..?" Elsie whispered back.

"Yes!" he broke in. "We peeked through t' lace curtains. It's them right enough. They said they would, an' they 'ave."

"Right!" she burst out, with a frown like a bloodhound's brow. "They've asked fer it! They'll get a piece o'me mind!"

"Steady, Elsie!" warned Fred. "If ye get all 'eated up, ye'll make 'em think they're on ter somethin'."

"They're just as like ter get suspicious, if ye take it sittin' down, an' all. Well, leastwise, we know what ter say, don't we?" she added, looking over directly at Tim and giving three staccato nods, as if to prompt mutual agreement. He was competely taken off guard, and nodded uncertainly back.

"Jus' finish yer tea an' look natural," she said over her shoulder to him, as she went through the door, and, pointing to the parlour, she told Alf to 'get t'other two an' bring 'em ter kitchen'. She marched boldly down the passage to the door, as another knock came, and she shouted, "I'm comin'! No need ter break t'-door down!"

She opened the door to a man in a dark grey suit, with a thin smile that spelled out efficiency, attended by a prim young woman carrying a thin briefcase, looking as if a smile would do irreperable damage to her face.

"Good morning, Mrs. Wainwright," the man said. "We're from.."

"I know where you're from." Elsie interrupted. "Come in an' lets get on wi' it'."

As Elsie took the visitors down the hallway to the kitchen, Alf, led Bert and Monty out of the parlour to fall in behind them As everyone made their entrance, Fred nudged Tim and pointed to his toast, intending to mean that 'acting naturally' involved eating. Tim made a particular point of spooning out the marmalade with studied carelessness and spreading it nonchalantly on the toast. As Elsie got everyone to sit at the table, he continued to munch and sip, as if he found it beneath his dignity to even acknowledge the visitors.

"Now, what's it all abowt?" Elsie asked, folding her arms and sitting back as soon as they had settled in the chairs.

"I'm sure you understand that we have to follow up any information given us regarding possible unfair and illegal practices," began the gentleman. Fred glowered, and Elsie raised her eyebrows almost to her hairline. He paused. "I use the word 'possible' advisedly, because we always assume innocence before we establish any evidence of wrong-doing." There was obdurate silence from all, and Tim went on assiduously munching and sipping.

"My name is Parkinson. I hope you won't mind my assistant, Miss Penworthy taking notes during the exchange. It provides us with a basis for our decisions,..something we can refer to in any later dispute concerning what passed between us."

More silence. All eyes were focussed on Miss Penworthy now, who took out a notebook from her briefcase, and poised a pencil over one of its pages.

"I'll come straight to the point. I take it that Mr. Alfred Mooney and Mr. Albert Ferns are present?" he said officiously. There was silence, and he continued, "Perhaps, they would like to answer to their names, if so."

"That's me," responded Alf.

"And me," said Bert,

"You are?.." Mr. Parkinson prompted Bert.

"Albert Ferns. Pleased to meet you." Bert extended his hand over the table, and Mr. Parkinson held his finger tips for a brief second.

"And you will be Mr. Mooney?" he said to Alf.

"Aye. Well deduced," let out Alf, smiling round at the company at his own wit.

"Thank you." Mr Parkinson looked down at a piece of paper in front of him before continuing. "From our records we see that you put this address down as your domicile." He gave both men a concentrated look. They did not respond. "That is so, is it not?"

"Well if that's what ye've got in yer records, it must be, right," said Bert.

"Unfortunately, the information people provide us with often cannot be taken too literally, Mr. Ferns." Penworthy's smile was as thin as a pencil shaving. "I am told that you already have a lodger with you, Mrs Wainwright." - He looked down at his paper again. - ".. a Mr Barfield, who also claims unemployment benefit from time to time."

"Tha's me, is that," growled Monty from the end of the table. "Only, I've bin in gainful employment, so I 'aven't signed on fer two weeks."

"Fine, fine." Parkinson gave a curt nod, and looked to see that Miss Penworthy was getting it all down.

"We have it on some authority that there is now a fourth lodger in the household."

"I'd like to know on who's authority, if I may be so bold," Elsie said, in a tone that stressed her rights. If she believed she had any, she was soon disillusioned.

"We are not entitled to disclose the names of informants, Mrs Wainright. We are merely here to establish their authenticity." Mr. Parkinson raised his eyebrows in a pseudo polite way, but his veneer of social aplomb fooled nobody; it masked an efficient inquisitorial mind intent on scraping the very bottom of everything. "Have you four lodgers in the house?"

"Yes, we 'ave," retorted Elsie, with aggressive alacrity. Everyone was aware, from the corner of their eye, of Miss Penworthy assiduously scribbling away. Tim spread more marmalade on his toast, painfully conscious that he was the fourth lodger referred to.

"Doesn't that appear excessive, in view of your having but three bedrooms?"

"No. Why the 'eck should it?" Elsie challenged.

"If I were to say that we were informed that two of your lodgers sleep in your shed, how would you answer?" asked Parkinson, abruptly, hoping to take her off guard. Miss Penworthy's biro was poised, everyone sat as still as waxwork models, until Fred broke in with an uncharacteristic humourless laugh, "Fer Pete's sake, we keep tools in t' shed."

"More to the point, where do you keep the lodgers?" asked Parkinson with steely insistence.

Elsie looked astonished and outraged that anyone should ask such a question. "Where else would ye normally sleep but upstairs?"

There was a pregnant pause. Parkinson nodded, unconvinced. "I take it, Mrs. Wainwright, that you have no objection to an inspection of the shed?"

"I take it, then, as me word is not taken," Elsie countered.

"It would help to resolve the matter if I could see for myself." Then turning suddenly to Tim, he enquired, "Would I be right in surmising you are the fourth lodger, sir?"

"Me?" Tim pulled his eyes away from the toast, and blinked his way to a full regard of Parkinson.

"Yes, sir. The fourth lodger?"

"Just now, you mean?" Tim responded, followed by a humourless laugh at his own ineptness.

"Well, we could start with now and go back in time, if you wish, sir," Parkinson said in an affected tone. Tim sensed a mind honed by a cynical interest in irony.

"I've only been here two nights."

"Really? May I have your name, sir?"

Tim felt as if he were being asked to give his soul away. "Timothy Carter."

"You don't sound as if you're from these parts, sir."

"I'm from Surrey."

"Do you sign on for benefit here or down there, sir?"

"Oh, I don't sign on anywhere. I visit the area from time to time."

"Full time 'gainful employment' is it?" asked Parkinson with emphasis.

"Well, er,...yes."

Parkinson paused to reflect. "And you lodge here with Mrs Wainwright?" He screwed up his eyes, as if willing Tim to think twice before replying.

Tim paused to think twice and then nodded. For some moments Parkinson wore the look of having seen many things that challenged belief, then, turning peremptorily to Elsie, suggested that this might, indeed, be the right moment to inspect the shed.

"If ye insist," she said, huffily, getting up and leading the way out to the back yard. Parkinson and Miss Penworthy rose and followed. "Will ye be comin', Fred? Like as not, I'll need ye ter witness what's bein' recorded!" shouted Elsie over her shoulder, implying total lack of trust in the probity of her visitors. Fred, uncharacteristically reticent and grim faced, followed in the wake of the inspection party. Elsie, opened the shed door with a flourish, and stood next to it, arms akimbo, while Parkinson and Penworthy peered inside. They were faced with a spade, hoe and rake, an upturned wheelbarrow, a small bench,on which stood a jamjar full of half-used candles and two old jackets hanging from a line of hooks.

"Satisfied?" asked Elsie with a prim, triumphant smile.

"It does appear to be used for purposes suitable for a shed," admitted Parkinson. "You can record that, Miss Penworthy."

"Suitable for a shed," she repeated under her breath.

Fred muttered under his, and threw his eyes to heaven. Elsie's head shook involuntarily and was just about to unleash a tirade, when Parkinson, reflecting on the singularity of the situation, said, "I observe that, for a small terraced residence, you appear to have a large clientele, Mrs. Wainwright." Elsie looked at Fred, and Fred looked at Elsie and then, as if on cue, both took up a pose that suggested any problem lay in Parkinson's impaired imagination.

"I doubt that concerns anyone else but me," Elsie rejoined, jutting her chin. Parkinson spread a thin humorless smile across his face. "It might concern the Employment Centre, if no evidence of lodging was provided."

"What d'yer mean?" Elsie spluttered with indignation.

"Perhaps we could go back indoors, Mrs Wainwright," suggested Parkinson, "to avoid the neighbours overhearing."

"I don't give a tupenny cus who hears me!" Elsie shouted. "An' I'd give 'em somethin' ter make their 'air curl, if I was ter find out 'oo took it on theirselves t' inform on us."

"Nevertheless," Parkinson said, dismissively, as he led the way back indoors.

As they entered, the four lodgers looked up and searched their faces. Monty smiled amicably at them, Alf appeared very guarded and his eyes flicked back and forth to discern any clue, while Bert sat bolt upright, looking officious. Tim, after a cursory look at Parkinson, stared down at his cup and stirred his tea with great dedication, yearning for invisibility.

"Aye, well, now ye've seen what ye was sent ter see, I'll wish ye goo'day, Mr. Parkinson," Elsie barked as she walked to the hall door to open it. Parkinson, however, stood immobile and Miss Penworthy stood next to him, as if attached to a lead.

"In the interests of clarity, Mrs Wainwright, I think it would be politic to show us the sleeping arrangements of the parties involved," Parkinson pronounced, in a well rehearsed formal manner.

Elsie began to turn a purple shade, and Fred, who until this point had deferred to her status as mistress of the house, intervened. "Are we ter take it as 'ow ye don't take 'er word?! It's a disgrace t' invade a body's residence an' make aspersions wi'out proper evidence!"

"That is precisely what I am proposing to establish. As soon as I am presented with the evidence of the sleeping arrangements, I will have fulfilled my obligations," countered Parkinson.

"Right!" bellowed Elsie, "Come on then! Let's all troupe upstairs an' get it over wi'!" She marched forcefully into the hall and yelled back, "Come on, then! Let's go an' satisfy doubtin' thomas!"

Fred pointed upstairs and motioned to everyone to follow. Upstairs they all obediently climbed, Parkinson and Miss Penworthy first and the rest following on, to gather on the landing. Elsie turned to the assembled party and shouted out her orders, loud enough to quell a revolution.

"Right!" She pointed at Monty. "Enter yer room and stand by yer bed!"

Monty ducked his huge bulk under the doorway and scrambled over Alf's truckle bed to take up his position. "Alfred! Your turn!" Alfred moved to the doorway and having contemplated the impossibility of negotiating the gap, stood pointing pathetically at his bed. "Albert and Tim, ye can both sit on yer beds," barked Elsie. They duly obeyed, like schoolboys in a dormitory. Tim stared round the room as if it were a prison, and Bert sat with a nonchalant but defiant expression directed at Parkinson.

"Now are ye satisfied?!" Elsie almost bellowed. "I 'ope as 'ow ye've got all that down in yer little book!" she hurled at Miss Penworthy. Parkinson, who was obviously immune to this kind of reaction, returned her look with a bland expression, and said, "You appear to have established bona fide evidence of the sleeping arrangements, Mrs Wainwright, although I have to comment that they do not seem to be ideal." As Miss Penworthy scribbled more notes,he turned to Tim and, with a cynical sidelong glance, asked, "Are you entirely happy with them, Mr. Carter?"

"Er..yes,"Tim murmured, incapable of the least vestige of enthusiasm.

"Really?" Parkinson raised an incredulous eyebrow. "I would hardly have thought it was conducive to a good night's sleep." Tim studiously avoided his eye. "But if you say so." He turned back to Elsie, who was eyeing him with venom. "Well, Mrs. Wainwright, thank you for your patience." He started clomping down the stairs, followed by Miss Penworthy as he continued. " That seems to be it, as they say. Our report will effectively close the inquiry on Mr. Mooney and Mr. Ferns."

They arrived at the front door, and Parkinson opened it himself before turning and leaving his parting shot. "But I'm sure you realise that it can be re-opened at any time on receiving further information. Good day, Mrs. Wainwright." With that they closed the door behind them, leaving everyone speechless.

Fred broke the silence. "Well, we got 'em off our backs, any road. Good on us!"

"The infernal cheek. An' them neighbours wi' nowt better ter do," muttered Elsie, gnashing her molars.

"I told ye we'd ter keep a look out, did'n I?" said Alf.

"We can't revert to the shed again, with the nosey parkers at it," warned Bert, smoothing his moustache.

"Any road, I'll put kettle on afore we do anythin'else," Elsie said, as she led them downstairs.

"An' young Tim 'ere done well, an' all," Fred asserted. "'E's earned 'is colours, 'e 'as".

"That 'e 'as!" agreed Alf. "Thanks a bundle," added Bert.

As they all assembled once more in the kitchen, Tim nodded resignedly and left all his thoughts unsaid.

They all seemed suddenly to have revived their cheerful spirits, and Fred turned to Tim again and, as if all worries were behind them, said, "There ye go, then! We can be off soon as we've supped us tea."

The Miraculous Journey

Recent events had carried Tim along without the least willing input on his part, and he was disgruntled to put it mildly. It seemed to him that he had relinquished his freedom in the service of a regime that had the mark of madness on it. What on earth was taking him over? Even now as he drove along the now familiar High Street, he felt his autonomy leaking away. He had surrendered to some mysterious whim of Fred's and now he was being directed by him from the passenger seat of his status symbol. It was also somewhat disturbing from another practical point of view. Fred's nose just reached above the level of the dashboard, and Tim suspected he did not have as clear a view of the road ahead as safety demanded in the matter of giving clear and timely directions.

There was no denying, however, that Fred made every sign of knowing where they were making for, even if he was holding his knowledge close to his chest. Apart from his occasional curt directions, "Take a left 'ere", "Take a sharp right", "Take care an' keep an eye on't road", communication was minimal. As they reached the outskirts of the town, Tim began to look at the roadsigns for any clue as to their destination, but none of the names meant anything to him, and, after Fred's direction to "Keep goin' on this' un, till I tell yer different", he began to recede into his own thoughts. Fred seemed satisfied to look at the scenery, which soon substituted the rural for the urban, with farms standing at the ends of long single tracks, and cows grazing in slow motion. The terrain in the distance ahead was more undulating and, as they approached, became hilly enough to attract clouds round the summits. The sky was a transparent blue that made you believe that, if you had a pair of wings, it would part and draw you up into another invisible universe with air as sweet as wine. That might have been more appealing to Tim, if he did not feel such smouldering displeasure with himself for allowing himself to get into such a situation. Yet, he would have felt more annoyed if he wasn't also intrigued. Fred's irritating secretiveness was, another example of the continual suspense he brought into Tim's life. However annoying it might be, it stimulated and challenged. As he drove, he caught Fred out of the corner of his eye, and, from the mercurial changes in his expression, sensed nostalgia, as if the journey were taking Fred away from the present. This somehow made Tim feel more relaxed, and he began to put recent events in some perspective. Practically everything that had happened to him was instigated by Fred and Elsie, always with best intentions and seemingly inevitable unfortunate consequences. Rejecting the garage mechanics, inciting them to express their resentment, repairing the car and getting him thrown out of lodgings, giving him a roof over his head that resulted in acute embarrassment and sleepless nights, and involving him in illegal activities in order to protect ex-cons from the due process of the law, and now, well, - how was he to phrase this? – blackmailed into undertaking a car ride to, 'go the last mile' to God knows where. All this was painfully true, and yet just to look at Fred, you knew that there was not an ounce of guile in his whole fibre. He was as straight as a die with those he knew intimately, and as benevolent as a saint in his intentions to them. On the other hand, he did not use Queensbury rules when dealing with oppressors and bullies of the world.

Tim was jerked out of his reflection by Fred blurting out,"Take turnin' on yer right up ahead", a hundred metres from a narrow road that obviously led into the rolling hills. Tim had to put his brake on quite hard so as not to drive past, but the car responded well and he swung it round off what had been largely a dual carriageway to that time. .

"It would be helpful if you gave me a little more notice of any change of direction," Tim muttered.

"Aye, 'appen," Fred replied in a low, almost submissive tone, which took Tim by surprise. It lacked his characteristic forthrightness. "I were nigh on day-dreamin' fer a bit, there." He looked up through the windscreen at the sky, as if to put his thoughts into some kind of balance. He sighed after a bit, and looking sideways at Tim for a second or two, nodded as if he had come to some new conclusion. "It's bin a while sin' I were in these parts. Whatever change comes over folk, the fells stay ever the same. It's enough ter make ye weep".

"Fells?" repeated Tim.

"Aye. Them 'ills up front," Fred said, as if his thoughts were so transparent they needed no introduction.

For some reason, Tim needed to understand."Why do they make you weep, then?"

"Why?" Fred halted for a second or two and looked sideways at Tim, as if it was strange to be asked such a question, and then moved his mouth from side to side as if he was practising the words he would emit. "Well, 'cos them 'ills tell the story of bein' wot they was made fer." There was another pause before he added with emphasis, "which is a deal more than ye can say fer most o' mankind."

By now the car was climbing and negotiating increasingly tighter curves. Tim enjoyed the gentle sway as the camber of the road guided the car round in arcs, this way and that. Fred showed a morose pleasure in everything he looked at, and Tim sensed that he belonged in this terrain, or perhaps the terrain belonged to his memory. The most eloquent evidence of this was his uncharacteristic silence. Suddenly, however, Fred stared over the bonnet, and with a stabbing motion of his finger, indicated a sign which said, **'Panaramic View Ahead'**.

"Pull over in t' sidin' when ye get t'brow o' this 'ill," he urged Tim. They came up to the brow and slid the car over into a pull-in, overlooking the valley they had just climbed.

"We've ter get out 'ere, an' drink in this place," Fred said, as he opened the door. "Turn t'engine off, an' feast yer eyes". He got out and walked over to the edge of the parking area to look down at the valley, resembling a huge counterpane, with the winding road making a tear in its fabric. Tim climbed out and followed over to the thin wire barrier that defined the edge. The fields made a patchwork quilt of greens, yellows and browns stitched together with low hedges. The leaves on the few trees that stood in the hedge line showed the beginning of autumn with slight touches of yellow. Fred gazed down on it all, and breathed in deeply. "Ye got ter breathe this in t'yer," he said, placing his hands on his breast, like a general gazing over a victorious battlefield,to feel it inflate. Tim stood at his side and attempted the same, and became aware of a chill in the air "D'yer know wot 'inspeeration' means, Tim lad?" There was something proprietary in his tone, not only of the scene before him but also of Tim.

"I think so," Tim answered, "unless you've got a new definition. For me it means suddenly getting a great idea and making the best of it."

"Not bad, far as it goes," Fred said, without seeming too condescending. "But there you go, see. *How* d'ye get 'old of this idea, eh?. An',.." - Here he paused for emphasis, - "what makes ye *want* ter make best of it?"

"Er..pass." Tim shrugged.

"Ye're breathed inter, That's what."

"Sorry?"

"The livin' presence o' t'Almighty breathes int' yer. Look at that bea-oo- tiful valley, will yer? Tha's not jus' air I'm breathin' in; I'm breathin' in 't'Almighty's bea-oo-ty."

"Right," Tim concurred tonelessly.

Fred turned to him and shook his head impatiently, "Ye don't see anythin', if ye don't feel t' Father in it."

Tim decided he would not submit to another sermon from Fred. "Sorry, Fred, but, as far as I'm concerned, a thing's beautiful, whether or not I think about someone's Father."

Fred punched the air sideways, and jerked his head forward, almost making his five foot five frame totter. "Then ye're missin' out, lad. Bea-oo-ty's not just shape'n colour, an' that. It's sharin' it wi' 'Im wot made it."

"Well, to tell the truth, I'm quite able, in fact, to find something beautiful without sharing it with anyone at all," Tim said, with an insistence that clearly showed his intention, this time, to contest Fred's self-assured authority.

Fred looked fixedly at him for some moments. Tim returned the stare, forcing Fred to blink and turn away before saying in a low voice, "Then ye're marooned on yer own island, lad. Ye're lookin' out from the inside, stead of standin' outside yersel' lookin' in." He frowned, as if contemplating a huge failure, or an imminent struggle, Tim could not decide which. Fred looked over the valley and up to the scudding clouds and mouthed something Tim could not hear. He felt they had reached an impasse and the silence that ensued between them was invaded only by a sighing wind. They stood like two Epstein figures; as if something as inflexible as marble had been carved out of them. For a moment, Tim felt guilt at having confronted Fred, not because he had refused to capitulate to his argument, but that he felt his sadness at their not being able share the same vision.

"We can't all feel the same thing, Fred. We're made differently, all of us."

Fred nodded almost imperceptibly and muttered, "Aye, 'appen ye're right, there." Then, shooting a quizzical look at Tim said in a more positive way, "But I still 'ave 'opes. Let's get on, then." He turned back to the car and Tim followed, scuffing his feet like a scolded child.

"This isn't where we were making for, then?" asked Tim, as he got into the car.

"Nay. It's at t' bottom o'next valley," Fred replied, in a disinterested way.

Tim turned the key, and to his surprise, nothing happened. He pressed it again, and the engine did not respond. A look of dismay came over him and he turned to Fred with a look of helplessness.

"Wot's up, then?" Fred enquired, innocently.

"The car won't start."

"Try again."

Tim turned the key again and there was a dull whirring sound that clearly suggested automotive fatigue.

"Dead as a doornail," said Tim, with an aggressive acceptance of sod's law.

"That's a call ter prayer, is that." Fred opened the door, and added, "Open t' bonnet. I'm goin' t'ask Jesus ter put it right fer us."

"Oh, for Pete's sake!" muttered Tim under his breath, as he pulled the bonnet release catch and climbed out of the car. "More to the point is looking to see what the trouble is."

"Hold it!" Fred ordered as if he were standing sentry. He pulled up the bonnet and secured it with the stay. "I'shall lay 'ands on t' engine an' ask Jesus ter put it right."

Tim raised his voice against the malignant fates that had reduced him to being at the mercy of this old fellow, who looked as if he were going to perform an experiment straight out of Frankenstein. "I never knew Jesus was a mechanic!" he shouted.

Fred ignored the facetiousness and, laying his hands on the engine, said quite calmly, "Jesus is everythin'. I'd be glad if ye'd stand quiet, while I say a few words ter 'im."

Tim thrust his hands defiantly in his pockets and glowered.

"Well, Jesus, 'ere we are in a bit of a pickle," began Fred, "an' I'm throwin' us on Yer mercy, in despite o' t'skepticism of one among us. As Ye know there's a bit o' bother in t'engine, and I'm, askin' that Ye reveal Yer power by givin' it a kick-start. I thank Ye that Ye 'ear our requests, an' Ye know all abowt us,... which reminds me ter ask Ye ter fergive them as turns away fro' Ye in unbelief." Tim looked disgusted and scuffed his feet on the grass. "I'm trustin' Ye ter show a thing or two," he added, as a final plea. Then he took his hands off the engine and turning to Tim, said, "Try startin' 'er agin."

"You think putting your hands on the engine and saying a few words...?"

"Try startin' it up," Fred insisted.

"Oh, for heaven's sake!" Tim flounced as he got into the car, and took his keys out with an exaggerated gesture that expressed his total disbelief in what he was being asked to participate in. He thrust the key into the ignition as if he were stabbing someone, and turned it with a violence that a psychopath reserves for his victim. The car burst into life, and Tim sat bolt upright in alarm and disbelief.

"Praise ter ye, Jesus!" Fred shouted, as he slammed down the bonnet and raised his arms to heaven in gratitude. They regarded each other through the windscreen, Fred with a look of triumph and challenge, and Tim full of confusion and suspicion. He got out of the car and, leaving the engine running, walked slowly up to Fred, carrying a question in his furrowed brow. Tim stopped in front of Fred, who looked up at him triumphantly. Tim stood in silence eyeing him for some betraying sign.

"An' there ye' are, young Tim. Prince Jesus has revealed 'is 'and on yer life."

"What did you do to make the car go, Fred?"

"Do? Me? I did nowt but have a word wi' Jesus."

"Come on, Fred. I wasn't born yesterday. You did something under the bonnet, right?"

"I did nowt o't'sort!" Fred protested.

"So you want me to believe it was a miracle? Is that it?"

"Ye'll believe what ye like. I'm jus' tellin' ye 'ow it is." Fred began to flush with indignation, and he stared defiantly at Tim, who turned away and walked to the side of the car looking into the distance. There was a pregnant silence, except for the soughing breeze that flicked Tim's hair. Fred narrowed his eyes and approached the other side of the car. There was a mixture of hurt and resentment in his face.

"I take it bad that ye'd think I were lyin' ter ye. After what me an' Elsie 'as done t'help ye."

Tim wheeled round and they glared at each other over the bonnet.

"Well, as as a matter of fact, Fred, I have to say, what you've done for me is a very mixed blessing."

"What's that supposed ter mean? Ye'd better come out wi' it."

They had reached a point of confrontation from which neither could retreat. This was stand-off at the not so OK Corral. An age worn north country sherrif versus the Surrey young gun fighter putting himself to the test.

"Well, for a start, I resent what you did with the garage mechanics. What took place between them and me was *my* affair. You had no business to interfere."

"'Ow d'yer know it were on yower be'alf? It were me what turned 'em down in t' first place. An' as a matter o' fact, I were thinkin' o' their welfare."

"That's ridiculous! How does going round intimidating them, help them?".

"Intimidatin'?!"

"What else is it, when Monty, the size of a grizzly bear, stands grinning down at them?!"

"Gerout wi' yer!" Fred threw his eyes to heaven and back. "Monty woudn' 'urt a fly!"

"Right! But you relied on those fellows not to know that!"

"I rely on 'em ter know what it's like to be ganged up on. I 'ope they're glad to 'ave learned summat by it." He nodded to emphasise his point.

"I thought we were supposed to turn the other cheek." Tim was complacent enough to think he had scored an incontestable point, but Fred let out a humourleess laugh. "That don't mean ye've ter lie on t' floor and invite them ter walk over ye like a doormat!"

"You didn't make any friends by doing that."

"Is that all that's worryin' ye?"

"No it isn't. I don't like sharing a room with someone I look over my shoulder at."

"'Ow d'yer mean? Bert's straight as a die."

Tim adopted an aggrieved tone. " I've nothing against him apart from his snoring, but I was forced into the odious position of lying for him."

When did ye lie? I never 'eard ye."

"If telling the man from the employment centre he didn't sleep in the shed isn't a lie, what is?!"

"They was sleepin' indoors at time o' t' investigation."

"But Elsie said they slept upstairs permanently."

"Not in my 'earin'.. She jus' asked where else they expected 'em ter sleep. A fair question, en't it?"

"It was still deceit."

"As I sees it, Mr. Nosey Parkinson saw what 'e saw, an' made 'is own judgement. Nobody lied. We jus' didn' tell 'im any more than we 'ad ter."

"Well, I didn't get a proper sleep, that night."

"That's a bad do. But ye don't 'ave ter take it out o' me."

Tim, suddenly aware that the engine was still ticking over, opened the door and threw himself into the driver's seat. "And you needn't think I was taken in by that trick of yours," he said, defiantly.

Fred, about to get into the passenger seat, was halted in his tracks by Tim's remark. He bent down and peered in at Tim. "Trick? What trick are ye on abowt?"

"All this mumbo-jumbo with the engine. It doesn't fool me."

Fred scowled and straightened up. He seemed to be considering Tim's accusation for a moment, and then strolled away for a few steps, stopped and then turned back to confront Tim like a counsel for the defence about to grill the plaintiff. "What d'ye mean by 'mumbo-jumbo?"

"All that laying on of hands and praying for divine intervention."

"So, if it weren't divine intervention, what would ye call it?" Fred challenged narrowing his eyes.

"I don't know what you did! I don't know enough about cars!" Tim retorted, increasingly angry.

"An ye don't know what Jesus can do if ye're faithful ter believe!" Fred said, beginning to pace up and down, agitated. "It's there afore yer very eyes, an' ye're dead set on not seein' it!"

Tim felt helpless and angry at his inability to explain the occurrence in the face of Fred's insistence. "For heaven's sake, get in and let's get on to wherever we're going," he blustered. "We'll be here all day if we go on like this."

"Nay, lad," said Fred lowering his voice with quiet, cold conviction. "I'll not get in t' car while ye think so bad o' me an' so little o' Jesus."

Tim shook his head, slumped and stared at his knees for a moment before raising his head again and, in a half resigned, half conciliatory way, saying, "I don't think bad of you, Fred. But I won't believe what you believe."

Fred threw down the gauntlet. "In that case, I'm not fer getting' in t' car."

"For Pete'sake, what do you want me to *do*?!" Tim burst out. "Be a hypocrite and say Jesus started the engine?!"

"Course not!" Fred shouted back. "I jus' want ye t'admit ye can't explain it!"

"Right!" He raised his arms to shoulder height and blew his cheeks out. "If that will make you happy!" Tim said, in surrender.

"Aye, Jesus'll settle fer that," Fred conceded, but added, "fer time bein'," as a final punctuation. He walked to the car and got in without another word, and they got under way.

The next five minutes were filled with silence, as the unspoken thoughts widened the barrier between them. They glued their eyes to the road ahead and resolutely refrained from glancing each other's way. Tim's mind could not disentangle itself from the mystery of the car's performance. He had never before felt able to doubt Fred's sincerity or to suspect him of duplicity. But something was a bit weird. There must be some simple explanation. Either Fred had fixed something while his hand was on the engine, or it was a simple coincidence that the engine righted itself. Was this another example of Fred saying no more than he had to, because Tim had not asked the right question? It could not be any kind of,... well..., supernatural happening. That was ridiculous, and not even worth entertaining a second thought. The only thing was, Fred's integrity was being questioned, and something in Tim's judgement refused to believe that Fred would try to deceive even in the interests of claiming his soul for Jesus. Tim was not in a debate between 'either or' or even three choices. He was on the side of reason against fantasy, and yet he could not give any substance to either, and had to resort to accepting coincidence. And then you had to admit coincidence had worked wonderfully well in Fred's favour.

Fred broke the silence abruptly with, "Turn 'ere."

Tim didn't see the turning until almost right up to it, for the entrance was framed by two high hedges.

"This one?" asked Tim.

"There's nowt but one."

Tim was about to ask Fred to give more notice in future, but thought better of it.

He turned into a narrow lane that promised a winding and undulating journey through the hills. He had just time to see a thin signpost with "Lower Netherfold" written on it. The road could not have been more than a cart track in the past, and Tim had to drive with extra care, knowing that if they met anyone coming the other way, it would be a tight squeeze. Hopefully, in that event, he would find a cut-in or a gate entrance to a field to solve what might otherwise be an impasse. Within a short time, however, the road dipped into a valley and he could see the huddled roofs of a village with two or three thin spirals of smoke coming from their chimneys. He continued winding down into the centre of the village, which as he approached turned into a hollow bowl, like a delicate treasure cupped in a giant's hands, out of which several roads climbed in all directions into the nudging hills, which gave to the village a feeling of a secret protected charm. There was a raised column in the centre of the main square with a memorial tablet at the base. He heard a tinkling bell, and, to his left, he noticed a woman coming out of a small grocer's with a basket over her arm. An old man hobbled up another road some way ahead. Otherwise, the village seemed deserted.

Tim glanced sideways at Fred expecting some direction, but Fred seemed buried in his own thoughts.

"So, which way now?" asked Tim.

"Eh? What? Oh, aye." Fred brought himself back into the present. "Ye climb a few paces up the second off and look fer a narrer entrance wi' a notice hung nex' ter a buldin' sayin', 'Fer customers of Green Lantern Tea Rooms'." Fred gesticulated broadly with his right hand.

"How far up?" enquired Tim, straining his eyes.

"No but a cough an' spit. There!" he almost shouted, "It's afore yer eyes!"

Tim slowed down and, seeing the turning, eased the car round to the right and into a narrow entrance next to a double-fronted café with mullioned windows that spoke of an age before he was born. It had a discreet charm about it, but Tim's thoughts were centred on the possible reason for having been brought to what he had supposed was, in some way, a significant venue. What had Fred in mind? Merely to take afternoon refreshment at the Green Lantern Tea Rooms? What could Lower Netherfold mean to Fred? Was it part of his youth, and what could it possibly say to anyone else? He drew up next to a fence overlooking open fields that clambered up round rocky outcrops on which the occasional stocky tree poised to give the scene a populated look. Fred was still uncharacteristically quiet as they got out of the car.

He seemed to be inhaling everything around him, as if re-appropriating things half recalled. He slowly led the way to the back of the property, past what looked like a large store shed or garage with double doors and on to a small door at the rear. Tim followed, aware that Fred's silence related to something that would remain unspoken for the moment.

Fred opened the door, and passed through. Tim had to stoop under the lintel, and straightened up to find himself in a beautifully fitted spacious kitchen that smelled of hygiene and efficiency. Racks of cups and saucers were tidily ranged along the full length of one wall and a double sink and two draining boards stood under the window that looked towards the fields. Adjacent to the sink area was a range of kitchen cupboards and drawers and a worktop supporting food processors, cake stands, whisks and teapots, all implying a practical caterer's conveyor belt.

As Fred moved to the door at the other end of the room, it opened and a young woman stood framed in the entrance. As soon as she saw Fred, she rushed towards him and threw herself at him with an excited cry and hugged him as if he had just returned from the battle front. It was some time before she condescended to release him and allow Fred, who had, - all five foot six of him,- been physically shaken as he mumbled in her ear during the embrace, to back away and enable her to see Tim behind him.

There was an arrested moment exchanged between them. Tim found himself surprised and delighted with what he saw; a young woman with blond curls shaped round ears that protruded just enough to give her a girlish look. Her wide open eyes promised frankness, and her pert nose was an attractive smudge that spelt humour. Perhaps most noticable was her mouth, full and generous with a slight wrinkle at each corner, that somehow, bore witness to a face that had been used to register her feelings.

How had Fred made no mention of such a person? There was something about her so alarmingly appealing that Tim found himself smiling and exhaling breath of pure pleasure. As she looked at him, it felt like standing before a hugely appealing portrait that he would hang in his own home. Still without emitting a sound, she looked at Fred and pursed her lips in a wry, half-accusing way, to which he responded by shrugging slightly and adopting what, for Fred, was astonishingly like a sheepish look, tempered by what might also be detected as a proud and proprietary gleam in his eye.

"And so this is..?" she asked, turning to Tim with a barely detectable smile.

"Tim. Tim Carter," Tim offered, not sure whether he should return a smile so subtlely given.

"I'm Alicia." She came towards him offering her hand. Tim took hold of it, as if it were porcelain, though when it gently pressed his, it pulsated with warmth and energy. She was dressed in a thin maroon coloured pullover that clung to her trim bust, and a knee length light weight cream skirt that fitted snuggly over her hips and enhanced the curves of her waist.

"Welcome to my little country seat. We aim to give pleasure to all who come," she said with a hint of inexplicable irony, as she looked sideways at Fred. For some reason she stressed the word 'all', as if there might have been some disagreement about it. Her open manner made nonsense of any such thought, but, nevertheless, left Tim with the impression that there was something more behind it than he could fathom. He also noted the hint of a Northern accent, without the missing consonants or squashed vowels. And there was practically nothing of the Northern brash about her.

"Dear Uncle Fred, you and Tim, will take tea in the café. Very few come out of season." If she had been older, she would have been described as gracious.

She moved to the cupboards and brought out a tray and some tins from which she extracted crockery, knives and spoons, together with scones from a bread bin and a bowl of obviously home made jam.

"You can give me a hand taking these out, while I boil a kettle. Put them on one of the window tables, where I can show you off to the locals." She placed cups, saucers, plates and cutlery on the tray. Fred pointed at Tim and, with uncharacteristic reticence, indicated with a wave of his hand for him to do the honours. Tim moved swiftly to take hold of the tray as Alicia lifted it towards him. They exchanged a look, and again he detected that gentle irony. Her pert retrousse nose gave her a self-possessed, independent look. Her pretty face had an openness, with large, wide-spaced hazel eyes and elfin ears that appeared to peep out from the nape length blond curls encircling them. She seemed free of all fashion. He had to break away from his absorption in order to carry the tray into the café. Fred following in a sombre mood that Tim found strange, silently indicated a window table with a wave of his hand. He placed the tray on the table, and they sat. He tried to catch Fred's eye, who seemed to consciously avoid meeting his. Curious, Tim began with, "She called you 'uncle'. So she's your niece, Fred?"

"Closer than that," Fred answered, settling into the opposite chair and pressing his lips together. Tim tried to interpret this, and imagining she might be his grand-daughter, began, "Do you mean…?"

"'Appen she'll tell ye," was all Fred was prepared to say.

"Right," Tim muttered. "Look, Fred," he started, changing the tone,

"I'm sorry if you're disappointed in me. Maybe I shouldn't have said what I did. Maybe I got it all wrong,.. you know… about what happened back at Elsie's with…"

"Ye don't 'ave ter worry yer soul-case abowt that," interrupted Fred. "An' I've reflected on yer unbelief. It's not yer fault when it comes down ter it."

"Well I just thought you'd gone a bit quiet on me, that's all," Tim said in a contrite way.

"There's other things is on me mind is all," Fred said with a sigh. Tim was importunate. As Fred had given the journey some considerable importance, he felt entitled to press him. "Is it this place?"

"It's nowt ter do wi' anyone but me," Fred replied. Possibly feeling that this was too abrupt, he added, "We've all got ter go t' last mile fro' time ter time." Tim knew that was all he would get out of Fred for the time being, and kept his silence. He gazed out of the window and observed two middle-aged women gossiping on the corner of the road opposite and a man with a pipe leisurely exiting from a newsagent, a paper under his arm. The whole scene suggested a gentler and less intrusive schedule than he was used to. Even the gossipers stood patiently listening to each other, taking their turns in a civilized, orderly fashion. The man puffed on his pipe and looked up at the sky with no more than a passing curiosity that spoke of an acceptance of things as they were. Although Fred faced the window, he seemed to be gazing unblinkingly into himself, and his facial muscles betrayed, from time to time, something of an internal debate. Their thoughts were interrupted by Alicia bringing the tray with teapot, jug and bowl, which she ranged on the table before seating herself between them directly facing the window.

"So, how do you like it? A dash of milk , sweetened?"

Tim looked at Fred. "I know how Uncle Fred likes it. What about you?" she asked, looking straight at Tim.

"Oh, that's fine."

"One or two spoons?"

"One, thanks."

"Usual three spoons and poured when fully brewed for Uncle."

"Aye. Right on," Fred responded.

"Everything good at home?" She asked him.

"Right as rain. Elsie sends 'er love, as ever."

"Squeeze her hand for me." She gave a chuckle at the image she had of Fred's limited range of emotional display.

"D'ye prosper, Alicia, lass?" He looked straight into her eyes, as if to test the truth of her response.

"I'm as contented as a cat with a bowl of cream, Uncle." She returned his look with an assuring and slightly challenging tilt of her head.

"Then tha's fine an'dandy," he returned.

Tea poured and scones buttered and spread with jam, they settled into eating with little need for social convention.

"Yer work goes well?" Fred asked.

"I'm pleased with what I'm doing. Whether it pleases others is another thing. " She smiled, and shrugged to dispel any notion that she really cared one way or the other.

So, there was something more to be learned of Alicia, thought Tim, something that, maybe, mattered to her more than running a café.

"Are you working on something?" he asked.

"Well, I can show you in a while, if you like," she said.

Fred shifted in his seat and tipped his head back to drink the last of his tea.

"That were champion," he declared, and instantly stood up. "I'll leave ye for a while, Alicia, love. I've a mind ter do me tour, whilst ye give Tim 'ere an eyeful."

"What?! So soon. You've only just got here," she said. She raised an eyebrow and smiled knowingly.

"Don't I alus take me stroll roun'? he responded defensively. Then in a tone that tended towards affectionate, but was not obvious enough to most to be termed such, Fred said, "So, I'll go an' do it fer t' umpteenth time, an' be darned." He stood unceremoniously and nodded, then ambled over to the front entrance, drew back two bolts and, with a brief salute over his shoulder, went into the street and was suddenly gone.

Alicia watched him through the window with a tender look of concern as he walked up the hill, and then turned to Tim smiling brightly. Tim found himself smiling back more transparently than he would ordinarily have allowed himself to do.

Put in the Picture

The smile lasted some seconds in silence. Tim was quite disturbed by the intense way she searched his face, and, accordingly, sought for an opening gambit. She pre-empted his effort.

"Do you know why Uncle Fred brought you here?" she asked abruptly.

Tim was taken off guard. "I'm afraid not. Fred didn't say."

"He said nothing at all?"

"He mentioned going the 'last mile'. It didn't mean anything to me."

"Dear Uncle Fred. He does like keeping things close to his chest." She observed him closely as if making a psychological assessment. "Why did you come, then?"

Tim felt obliged to attempt an unconvincing explanation, like a defendant in court with an inadequate defence. "It's rather complicated, but,.. well,.. I agreed to drive Fred as a recompense for, .. I mean ... well, he did me a favour."

"What was that?" she asked.

Tim struggled to find words that would give least away. "He,.. er, obtained some money owing to me."

"Mmm, he's pretty good at that." She smiled and, to his relief, appeared satisfied to let it drop.

She leant back in her seat and clasped her hands together in the manner of a professional deciding to deliver the diagnosis. "Fred brought you here for me to look you over as a potential husband."

Tim, completely floored, sat transfixed and helpless for some seconds before coughing, emitting a nervous laugh and blustering, "But.. but..oh, that isn't possible!"

"Why? Are you worried?" She raised her eyebrows and smiled theatrically.

"No, not at all!" he fell over himself to assure her, and then, still flushed, added, "I mean,.. that is.. well, I can't believe he intended ...such a thing. He probably just wanted me to drive him here to see you."

She gave him what Northern people call 'an old fashioned look'.

"How long have you known my uncle?"

"It's more than a year now."

"Doesn't he strike you, as at all unusual?"

"I've never met anyone like him. But, I'm from the south."

She laughed in a musically appealing way, and leant forward to place her hands on the table like an inquisitor.

"Wherever you're from, Tim, what makes you think he couldn't have brought you here to match-make?"

Tim felt like a swimmer trying to touch bottom with his toes. "He didn't even mention you," he offered as evidence.

"He's too wise to do that," she returned, smiling affectionately. "Would you have come, if he had?"

Tim frowned. "I don't know." She raised an eyebrow. "Possibly not," he admitted, and then added hastily "But I'm glad I did, of course."

She nodded and shrugged non-commitedly. "I believe I am, too."

After a brief pause, she said, in a matter of fact way, "Would you like to see my workshop?"

"Yes," he said, entirely curious and relieved to have the subject changed.

"Come on, then." She abruptly stood up and led the way through the kitchen into the rear yard. Tim followed compliantly, noting her confident stride and observing her bouncing curls, petite frame and the flounce of her skirt over her impertinent little bottom with particular pleasure, now he was not under her direct scrutiny. Her unconventionality must run in the family, he thought.

She strode over to the double doors of the large shed, and thrusting one of them wide, ushered him in with a wave of her hand. He was instantly confronted by an amazing array of art work illuminated by a large roof window and comprising a mixture of unframed paintings and clay figures. The paintings were ranged round three walls and the figures stood in the centre of the room next to a large kiln, a slip bin and slab table.. He estimated there to be nigh on a hundred pictures, and, at least, a dozen clay figures.

Tim stared, speechless. He approached slowly, unable to do more than absorb a general impression of the paintings' flamboyant colours, contrasted with the opaqueness of the clay figures, before turning to ask her, "Is this all *your* work?"

"Yes," she returned, in an unaffected way.

Tim approached the first wall. The pictures were of various rural scenes, painted in vibrant irridescent colours, all containing female figures of all ages travelling on roads, tree-lined avenues, mountain tracks, garden paths. The figures were all making their way towards entrances of some kind or another, doors and gates, or to a bend ahead that would hide them from view. Some were about to turn a corner or make their way through an arch, and one or two had half disappeared. All the paintings guided the eye to a similar focal point, just short of the edge of the frame round which the observer could not see, and beyond which one could only speculate what was to be discovered. Some of the figures were looking back over their shoulders towards the viewer. One or two were waving, and one, having half turned the corner, leant backward to take a last look out towards the spectator. One that particularly held his attention was of a nymph-like girl dancing towards an arch, both feet clear of the ground, her flowing diaphanous robe and hair flaring out in incandescent yellow and orange hues reflected in the surroundings, as if they took their colour from her presence. Tim looked back at Alicia for a moment, and she folded her arms patiently awaiting his comments. He came upon one picture of a girl turning back to look at the silhouette of a man, standing at the side of the road, partly hidden by the shadows of some trees. She was walking up a hill, beyond which a setting sun sent out brilliant shafts of light in a fan shape. The silhouette had no discernable face or bodily features.

Again, Tim looked round at Alicia, and she cocked her head to one side with a mock rueful expression.

"This one isn't finished?" he asked.

"Inevitably not," she said.

"Inevitably?"

"I have no idea what he looks like."

"So, it remains unfinished?"

"For the time being. What's your general impression?"

"I think they're wonderful. The recurrent theme.is fascinating."

"Which is?" She raised her eyebrows.

"I'm not sure," he offered cautiously. "It's a journey of some kind."

"Right," she conceded.

"My impression is, the figures are on a kind of pilgrimage."

"Go on."

"And," he pondered, "the figures reflect the colours of the surroundings, suggesting they are happy to be on the journey. But,.." He hesitated, holding something in check.

"But, what?"

He felt obligated to interpret meaningfully. "Their destination is either a secret kept from us,... or,.. is unknown even to them."

"Very good!" she said, enthusiastically. "What makes you think they're 'happy?"

"I'm not sure. I think the feeling goes beyond 'happy'; more like joy. But why, I don't really know. The scenery itself seems to reflect it."

"Do you mean, a transference of feeling from the figures to the surrounding scene?"

Tim looked at several of them, one at a time, before carefully venturing a circumspect opinion.

"Not necessarily. Now I look more closely, the figures seem to derive their colour from the surroundings."

He looked at her again for her reaction. Alicia's demeanour relaxed, and she smiled at Tim in a way that recalled the radiance in her paintings. She, too was

radiant, he told himself. Everything about her contributed to an impression of an outgoing energy that
invited him to admire, but also to wish to embrace.
Oh, dear, was he falling into that trap again? Had he
learned nothing from the Lydia incident? How long
had he been with her? Less than an hour, and already
susceptible and letting his imagination go beyond reasonable expectation? Yet, it was she who had freely
stated Fred's reason for bringing him.

"I'm delighted with your first impression."

"I got something right, then?" Tim asked, not sure in
what he had been perceptive. "Are you saying the same
thing with your sculpture?" he asked.

"What do *you* think?" she countered.

He focused his attention on the clay figures. They
seemed to represent a similar journey into the unknown,
going through arches, doors in walls, and some half
hidden behind pillars, but forced by the solidity of the
medium, to keep their feet on the ground. As far as Tim
could see, the effect was limited by the concreteness of
the clay. Instead of directing the eye to a mystery beyond
entrances or round corners, the arches, doors or gates
seemed merely an obstacle in the way of the figures.

"Sculpture and modeling is not my forte," he
ventured, "but I think it falls short of the sense of
mystery in the paintings."

"Absolutely correct!" She beamed at him. He felt
bathed in her approval. "The solidity of clay doesn't give
the same freedom that the theme demands and the two
dimensional representation permits."

She sauntered over to him and gently took his arm.

"I'm impressed. I believe we'll be good friends," she
said, complacently.

The word 'friends' inexplicably stung him. Apparently, she was not drawn to him in the way he found himself being attracted to her. It provoked him to engage with her in a way he had never done before. He raised the stakes.

"You mean, ignoring your Uncle's intentions for you?" He raised his chin in a pseudo-challenge. She released his arm and smiled up at him before she replied. "How splendid! You're flirting, aren't you? Good heavens, no! Uncle Fred doesn't have 'intentions' for me. He knows me too well. He opens up possibilities; that's all." She leant away and with a challenging smile, added. "But, in any case, why would friendship rule out greater intimacy? Separating love-making from friendship means nothing's left when passion dies."

Good Lord! Here she was talking about intimacy and the death of passion in the same breath. Tim felt as if in a game with rules completely foreign to him. Her self–assurance was both intimidating and exciting. Surely, when you were attracted to someone, you sent subtle messages and signs out, didn't you? Well, as a romantic young fellow, he had always imagined that you had to succumb to being vulnerable and having irrational thoughts when you became emotionally involved. How could she talk about the decline of passion before you had entered on a relationship; and, anyway, surely passion only faded after a considerable period of delightful madness? Ah, well, it must mean she wasn't really attracted to him. He must not allow things to lead him to embarrassment and hurt again.

"What *are* you saying in your painting?" he asked, escaping to the subject where he felt safest. She released his arm and went over to the wall to stand before the picture of the girl looking back at the unfinished male silhouette. She looked as if she were a spectator rather than the creator of the painting.

"It's about searching."

"Searching for what?"

"For who I am, maybe for who we all are in this world."

"Don't you know who you are?"

"One half of me does…" - She smiled at her own enigmatic inference, - "..the half not consciously engaged with the world."

"That's too profound for me," Tim said, pushing his hair back from his forehead. "It sounds just as if you don't know where you're going?"

"That's partly true."

"Then, how do you know where to look?"

"It's about the search for the part of me that *does* know."

"How do you know there is one?"

Here she turned to hold him in a steady look. "Because I want there to be."

Tim nodded, recognising something rather than agreeing with her.

"You sound like your uncle Fred."

"That would hardly surprise you, if you knew how much he had to do with my education and upbringing."

"Really?" Tim was intrigued. "

"He funded my studies at art school. I wouldn't expect him to have mentioned that."

"He never mentioned you at all," he said, with a shrug.

"Hmm." She mused for a second. "He mentioned you to me. Maybe he thought you'd be frightened off."

Tim thought how impossible that would have been had he known whom he was to meet. He had to admit he would probably have baulked at the idea, having experienced several of Fred's 'helpful' schemes.

"From your expression, I see that you would," she added.

"Don't be mistaken, but I'm not always entirely comfortable with your uncle's good intentions," Tim said, with an apologetic frown. "I know he's an amazing chap, but he lives in a different world from mine."

"What world is that? Yours I mean?"

Tim smiled ruefully, as if admitting to a failing rather than claiming superiority. "I suppose I'm conditioned to living a safe, ordered existence."

"I know what you mean," she agreed. "I used to order my life until I realized I was getting hemmed in." She paused to reflect and then moved towards the door. "Let's go into the house. We'll be more comfortable."

She took him to a small living room, which in former times would have been called a 'parlour, arrived at through the kitchen to one side of the café. It was a cocoon, with a sofa and easy chair that took possession of most of the space. The sofa faced a small black grate, and was near enough to able to reach forward to stoke the shiny Victorian hinged hob that shone with years of un-use. All warmth emanated from a radiator set below the window giving on to the fields at the rear. She stood to one side of the door to let him enter and then closed the door behind her. "Where would you like to sit?" Tim looked at the sofa, the chair and Alicia. He chose the chair. She smiled to herself, and sat at the opposite end of the sofa. .

"I do all my thinking here, after I've finished work."

"It's very cosy," he observed, for want of anything else to say.

"Perhaps too cosy," she reflected. "It's a bit small for guests who want their own space."

"This seems fine to me," he said, brightly.

"I noticed," she said. "Tell me. How do you feel about Uncle Fred's motive for bringing you here?"

"Well, if Fred did bring me here to meet you,..." Tim began, hesitantly.

"With the aim of igniting a relationship," she reminded him.

"Well, if you say so," he murmured in a circumspect way. "I suppose I feel rather ill-prepared."

She smiled at the thought. "I would have thought there was no way in the world to prepare for meeting someone you know nothing about."

He shrugged defensively. "Well, at least, I wouldn't have been taken off guard."

"But then I might have been denied the real you. You'd have hidden behind a façade you wanted me to believe."

Tim was, strangely and unexpectedly, enjoying the exchange. It was slightly risky, and potentially significant. He found it easier than he thought to voice unedited thoughts. "But there's something unfair here, isn't there?" he pointed out. "You knew I was coming and so had time to prepare yourself. Am I seeing the real you?"

She laughed with a musical peal that hit his solar plexus as its rallentando descended to a lower register. "What possible advantage would it give me?" she replied. "How do you prepare? Is it something you do in front of a mirror? Physical exercises?"

Tim found himself laughing in return. She joined him and it felt like clinking champagne glasses. When they stopped, they looked at each other with renewed interest.

"That is a relief, Tim. I thought you were going to be a very serious chap with a rooted objection to finding life amusing," she said with a cautionary sideways look.

Tim looked down at his feet and compressed his lips. "I suppose things matter too much sometimes," he returned.

"Do they? I often find the things that matter can be hysterically funny." She paused for a moment. "It's usually when I compare what I intended with what I manage to accomplish."

"You've accomplished something amazing," he responded immediately with warm sincerity. She seemed genuinely delighted. "Really?" she asked, searching his face. He nodded enthusiastically. "Thank you," she said. "I think you have remarkable interpretive insight. So, obviously we are a mutual admiration society." He smiled at the idea of a mutual anything at all between them. She appeared to find this encouraging, and leant back in her cushions, surveying him for a moment before saying abruptly, "At the risk of embarrassment, I can tell you, you are an attractive man."

"Really?!" He responded, aware that he was blushing slightly. "That's rather embarrassing for me!"

"Why? I'm not in the least embarrassed," she retorted. "Perhaps *you* will be, if you find me unattractive."

"No! I mean, yes, … I mean I don't," - he swallowed - "actually."

"But I have the impression that I'm making all the running." She smiled with something of a challenge.

"I'm sorry. I recently had an unfortunate experience with someone."

"Yes, I know."

"You do?"

"Uncle Fred said you were disappointed in love."

"I didn't say that."

"Perhaps not. Were you?"

Tim looked down at his feet. "I made a fool of myself."

"And you're afraid you'll do it again?"

"Maybe," he said, reluctantly

There was a moment's impasse, broken again by Alicia.

"Wouldn't you like to come and sit here?" She patted the sofa seat. "That chair seems miles away."

Tim recalled his conscious choice to sit in the separate chair. He was also aware of the move he had just been invited to make by this self-assured, attractive girl. It felt like crossing the Red Sea to bridge the gulf between the chair and the sofa, and he felt angry with himself for having handed Alicia an initiative, which somehow demoted him. Crossing to the sofa meant complying again, instead of initiating. As she said, she was 'making the running'. He could hardly resist her smiling invitation; it was both the polite thing to do, and highly desirable. He settled himself at the other end of the sofa and smiled thinly, which had as much to do with a feeling of ineffectuality as with pleasure.

"I think it might help if we ticked a few boxes," Alicia said, in a matter of fact tone, looking down, "to get hang-ups out of the way." Tim stared at her, like a schoolboy listening to a well-intentioned careers advisor. She looked up at him and suddenly raised her hand to her mouth. If she thought she could hide her mirth, she was hopelessly given away by the creased corners of her eyes. Tim looked perplexed, which only intensified her reaction. She began to shake and finally exploded into laughter that left Tim hopelessly bewildered. His look of apparent hurt elicited an instant change of mood and she shifted her body next to him and reached out to hold his hands.

"Tim," she said with feeling, " I'm not laughing at you. I just heard myself, and it all suddenly got to me." She leant in to him, and lowering her voice, said, "Forgive me, but I can't think of anything else better to do." She kissed him full on his lips.

There was a moment's silent visual exchange. Tim was unable to express the pleasure he felt at her intimacy. He opened his mouth in sheer incomprehension that this lovely young woman should kiss him like that without the least encouragement.She studied his face and asked simply, "Did I go a step too far? Perhaps I didn't have the right?"

"The right?" he whispered tonelessly.

"It would be a gross miscalculation on my part, if you didn't find me attractive."

"Oh, you're very attractive!" he burst out, before adding in a quieter tone, "But I think you know that."

She ignored the blandishment. "So you don't mind the liberty?"

"No," Tim responded with alacrity, and then added softly, "As if I would."

"Good," she said, settling back again. "That's established. There's always the question of compatibility." She reflected for a moment before continuing. "We're both involved in art, but that's an academic matter."

"You've got a remarkable talent," Tim offered as a contribution to 'compatibility', hopefully reminding her of his 'amazing interpretive insight'."

"That's very nice. Thank you. But it's not particularly relevant."

"Oh? Really?"

Alicia smiled. "I want to know what you believe, not what you think."

Tim searched for her meaning. "I **believe** you're very talented," he offered, feeling, even as he said it, that it was a shallow observation. Alicia looked at him sideways and puckered her mouth.

"Obviously we've got a little way to go." She nodded slowly for emphasis.

"What you believe about art is based on what you believe about life," she said, trying not to sound didactic. "And I believe that depends on where you put your faith."

Tim felt on very shaky ground in foreign territory without any coordinates. Any faith he might have was based on decisions he derived from experience. He had always put his toes in the water before going any deeper; and put his trust in what worked for him.

"Where do you find your faith?" she asked, eerily reflecting his own thoughts. He looked up and found her eyes searching his face.

"It depends what you mean. I tend to trust what's tried and tested."

She nodded slowly, as if hoping he would qualify it. He shrugged and compressed his lips, at a loss.

"If we were to be more than good friends, I'd need to know you have faith in yourself."

"I know what I'm doing," he hastily assured her. "I think I'm pretty good at it."

"It's nothing to do with confidence in 'doing'. Faith comes with going beyond incontestible evidence. That's what searching for meaning is all about. It's for what you know you lack, without knowing what it is precisely."

"How can you search for what you don't know?" he insisted.

"With faith," she said, ingenuously. "We might get to like each other very much, but it takes more than what we learn about each other to make a real commitment."

"That sounds complicated," Tim said. "I mean, surely, people get to be sure about each other, when they know each her."

"To be really close you rely on a much greater mystery than that."

"You mean, falling in love?"

"Oh, that's easy." She waved the concept aside with her hand. "Maybe too easy."

Tim's past experience suddenly came flooding in. Alicia seemed to be aware of his reflective struggle. "We've all been there," she said, without any implication. "It seems to me, it's more important to know what to do with your feelings."

"Do with them?" he echoed.

"Yes. Deciding where to go with them, if you're to make an irrevocable choice."

Tim mentally shifted this theoretical consideration to the particular possibility of becoming involved with Alicia, and liked the idea more than he could possibly have imagined. On the other hand, he remembered vividly the farcical episode with Lydia, and a cloud of mistrust descended. He decided that the only way to continue was by skirting round 'the particular' for the time being.

"How do… people… know when it's irrevocable?"

She smiled at his disingenuousness. "I don't know about anyone else, but *I* get a clearer picture when I've shared the possibility with Jesus."

Tim was immediately shocked into a state of help-lessness, a feeling of being out of his depth, and, in a way, outnumbered. Two against one. At all events, it hardly seemed romantic to have it confirmed by Jesus that you were entitled to be in love. Obviously, Fred had indoc-trinated her.

Alicia continued in that self-possessed way of hers, "I think you could do worse than consult Him, too."

Tim nodded slowly, partly to assure her that he was taking what she had said on board, and in part, to assist the orchestration of his thoughts. He struggled for an answer. Finally he shrugged and said, apologetically, "Last time I tried praying, it was just like talking to myself?"

"Then don't pray. Just talk to Him," she said with a fleeting smile.

"Will he answer?"

She shrugged and then searched his face. "If seeing me again is important enough, I think you'll hear him."

They looked at each other for some time, each asking the other an unarticulated question. She broke the moment.

"Maybe we should leave it there, and let you decide whether you want to come again."

"I do," Tim said instantly.

She smiled. "Lovely. I'm glad. Try to come with some faith."

The intensity of her gaze at that moment bore into a part of his soul that he had not known existed before. It ached like muscles that have been unflexed for ages..

"I wish I knew how to find it," he almost growled.

"Excellent beginning. Faith in yourself. Not in what you do, not even in what you believe, but in what you are." She became conscious of pontificating and added, "Sorry, I think I'm quoting." She stood abruptly and, as if to shake off a mood, reverted to her business-like persona. "Any minute, Uncle Fred will be back from his regular rounds. We'd better go back to the kitchen." She moved to the door and Tim got up from the settee. She turned to him and, like a doctor giving advice to a departing patient, added, with a touch of gentle irony, "Ask Elsie about my uncle. It might make you more comfortable with his good intentions'."

Tim followed her into the kitchen, pondering the inference, and found Fred already sitting at the table in contemplation. His mood persisted even when they had entered.

"Did you see anyone, Fred?" she asked., placing her hands on his shoulders.

"I doubt there's a body left ter r'member," he replied in a stoically resigned tone. "I went the rounds, any road, an' it were good ter do,he said, bringing himself back into the present. "But I never met a soul who'd re-member."

"Well,..." Alicia looked at him with tenderness, and came round to face him. "..maybe that's for the best. It was a long time ago, and some things are best let to fade." She took her hands off his shoulders and said, "You should've come back before the dew settled. You're quite damp."

Fred looked up at her an' nodded. "'Appen."

Her tone brightened. "So, another cup of tea before you go." Without waiting for an answer. She got a tray ready and put the kettle on. Tim suddenly felt marginalised, left to engage with his tumbling thoughts revolving round the afternoon's events. He was conscious of being outside something they shared with each other; something that had evidently left Fred in a sober, reflective mood, for he sat without a word, seemingly wandering in the past.

This time they sat and drank tea at the kitchen table, and Fred picked ginger biscuits out of a large tin, while Alicia asked him questions about home. His replies were invariously short, and varied little between "Fair ter middlin'", "No more'n ye'd expect" and "Right enough", responses that would not satisfy anyone who wanted details, but, apparently, sufficient to satisfy Alicia, who knew she would not receive more, anyway.

He condescended to initiate a brief exchange by enquiring when she would be opening properly for the season. She told him it would not be until the following Easter. "That's the earliest that folk visit round here". Meanwhile, Tim, looked on, conscious that these were family matters. He could not, for the life of him, make small talk with Alicia, after what had taken place between them. It would have been a retrograde step, almost as if it denied the intimacy. He caught Fred glancing at him from time to time, and then shifting his look to Alicia, as if making some kind of assessment. Of what, Tim was pretty sure he knew. The less he said, then the more able he was to keep cards close to his chest.

The tea supped, and the biscuits munched, a pause prompted the cue to leave. Fred pushed his chair back and stood. "Time ter get back, I reckon. T' light fails early this time o'year" He looked at Alicia, then Tim. "Tha's if ye've nowt else ter cover."

"No. Tim's seen everything we've got to show," she said in an equable tone, looking at Tim, in a way that gave no hint of anything extraordinary having taken place that afternoon. In the face of this air of closure, Tim felt helpless to express any real feelings.

Minutes later, he found himself ushered to the car, exchanging a brief shake of the hand with this splendidly disturbing girl, before being waved off, notably without the least display of customary family affection from Fred. Tim could sense a tangible emotional bond between Fred and Alicia, but saw Fred betray none of it at their departure. The affection was visible in Alicia, who held Fred to her and hugged his undemonstrative form almost fiercely as he prepared to leave. Tim, at that moment. was aware in himself, of a deeper involvement than he could ever have imagined.

New Perspective

As soon as Tim turned out of the rear yard, with a last sight of Alicia waving them off in his wing mirror, Fred settled into his seat and the journey descended into sombre silence. Tim sneaked a glance at him now and then, as he gazed abstractedly out of his window at the dusk gathering over the autumnal fields. The light had begun to fail so that his reflection could be faintly seen lit up from the dashboard lights. Tim was content with the silence, feeling that, on this occasion, it was not so much a barrier, as a temporary refuge for Fred's private thoughts. In any case, Tim was exploring his own feelings. He had just come away from this excitingly attractive girl whose work had impressed him, whose humour had stirred him, and, primarily, had unsolicitedly kissed him. Not only had he never met anyone like her, he could not imagine ever having dreamt up her kind. Delicious though the memory of her lips on his might be, her face had disturbed him. There had been something exquisitely alive in her look, as if searching for something in him she was already familiar with. He sensed it came from a daunting self-knowledge. His mind dwelt on her kiss. She had asked him if she had had the right to that intimacy. Had he been the one to initiate the kiss, it would never have occurred to him to ask retrospective permission. But then it was unlikely that he would have had the temerity to kiss her. As it was he had not had time to return her kiss, it having been delivered so spontaneously. He turned his mind to Fred. How likely was it that he was trying to match-make? Was he capable of such romantic intentions? In any case, was it romantic? Wasn't it just an experiment to test Tim's suitability as a spouse? How suitable had Alicia found him? These thoughts almost caused him to overshoot the junction at the main road, and he was forced to brake very hard. Fred was jerked out of his reverie as the seat belt dug into his shoulder.

"Sorry," Tim muttered, as he turned sharp left into the dual carriageway.

Fred, shaken into full consciousness, sat up and began to take an interest in his surroundings.

"We bin past the pull-in where we 'ad the contry-temps, then?" he asked brightly.

Tim feeling the least said the better, simply nodded. Fred shifted round sideways, before squinting up and saying. "She's a sharp'un, en't she?"

Tim resisted a response.

"Didn' ye not find 'er so, then?" Fred pursued.

"Alicia's a very talented artist," Tim responded.

"Aye, an' sharp wi' it, eh?" Fred insisted.

"She's got a keen mind, certainly," Tim added.

"Oh, aye, all that. But sharp an' all," Fred emphasized a touch impatiently.

Tim was keenly aware that Fred was not so much making a judgement as searching for clues. He was also aware of his own ambivalent feelings towards this old man who had inveigled him into visiting his niece without any notice of her existence. He felt a mixture of resentment and gratitude, the former from the deception of the whole thing and the latter from the sheer delight at having met with Alicia.

"Did ye not find 'er sharp, then?"

"I'm not sure what you mean by 'sharp'."

"Ee, by 'eck, but summat's lost down south, if ye don't know that."

"So, tell me," Tim said, perhaps more curtly that he had intended. Fred looked at him with more interest than resentment of his tone.

"Righto, then. 'Sharp' 'as a load o' meanin's. It says some'un's full o' theirsel's an' knows 'oo they are. They can read other folk like a book, an' all. It comes fro' bein' theirsel's wi'out fear or favour. An' they're not afeared ter let their feelin's get an airin'."

"That's a lot for a small word to mean," Tim said, looking fixedly ahead. Fred looked at him for some time before nodding. " 'Appen it does. 'An I'll venture ter say I think 'appen ye might 'a picked up a bit yersel', on yer visit ter Lower Netherfold."

"What d'you mean?" asked Tim, alert to the inference.

"It can be catchin', can this 'sharp'. That's if ye've a mind ter be open t'it." Fred adopted a knowing look.

"Open to it? What does that mean?" Tim, suspicious of Fred's motives, had to know where this was taking them.

"Ye've ter want it, tha's all," Fred replied.

"Want what?" asked Tim in an exasperated tone. "Are you being mysterious on purpose. Come out with it, for heaven's sake!"

"There y'are, see!" retorted Fred. "that a fair bit of it, clear ter see!"

"What?!"

"That outburst o' yourn. The first clear sign o' things ter come." Fred adopted an expression of smug confidence that intensely irritated Tim, who nodded determinedly to himself before breaking out to say, "I think it's time we did some straight talking, Fred."

"I'm al'us up fer that," Fred responded, in the tone of a boxer accepting the challenge of a bout. "Let's be 'avin' yer, then."

Tim licked his lips and briefly rehearsed the words in his mind. "Perhaps, you'd tell me why we went to your niece's place. I mean what was it all about? You don't give me a clue beforehand, and then, as soon as you introduce me, you slope off by yourself."

"It weren't like that, at all. I were on one 'o me reg'lar trips back in time. An' anyways, 'ow was ye ter get acquainted like, if I were sitting there twiddlin' me thumbs?"

"All very well, but why didn't you say a single word about Alicia before we went?"

"Didn't ye get on, then?" Fred asked, jutting his chin up at him.

"What's that got to do with it? You made a mystery out of it. And, what's this "going the last mile' all about?" insisted Tim with some force.

"That's nowt but a sayin', is that?"

"Maybe so, but what did *you* mean by it?"

"The last mile," said Fred, with a mysterious smile playing on his lips, "is what you make o' t' visit."

"Let's not beat about the bush, Fred. What was I supposed to make of it?" Tim discovered that his foot had pressed harder on the accelerator than he had intended, and instantly had to ease back. He glanced sideways briefly to see Fred wearing an inscrutable expression of self-satisfaction. "Yes, Fred! Come on. Just what?!" Tim's question was grimly earnest, and Fred reflected for some seconds before finding an answer that would serve the need of the moment.

"All I'll say is this. Sometimes its better ter let the whippet see the 'are, afore ye put yer money on it."

"Please don't give me that baloney, Fred, because it doesn't work any more!" Tim burst out. "I'd be most grateful if you'd stop speaking in riddles."

"By 'eck, but ye've picked up summat back there," Fred pronounced, almost to himself.

"I've picked up nothing at all, except a conviction that I've a right to a straight answer to a straight question." Tim was almost exhilarated by his own commanding tone and determination to get to the bottom of Fred's motives. Fred sighed and gave a wry frown at Tim's insistence. When he next spoke, it was with a markedly less confident and aggressive manner.

"Some 'un us get driven by wot we can't escape, an' don't rightly know 'ow t'explain t'others."

Tim kept his silence, sensing that he should leave Fred to reveal as much as he would.

"There's some things as'll not go away till ye face up ter 'em. Ye might think ye've got summat licked, but in' t'end it comes down ter knowin' wot ye've done an'givin' it over ter 'Im wot cares, - my mate, Jesus."

Tim let Fred's words pass by him, catching the smallest glimpse of a confession from his past. He also recognised the touch of sadness that accompanied Fred's self-assurance as he referred to Jesus.

"We've all ter find t' space wot needs fillin' afore we find faith. An' wi' me it were as I were bottom o' t' pit."

Fred turned a look of mild admonishment on Tim, tempered by fellow-feeling.

"It seems as 'ow ye're 'avin' a struggle ter come ter faith. An' I know as 'ow Jesus is yearnin' t'embrace ye an' take ye ter 'Im. But ye'll 'ave none o' it, till, maybe, ye've summat bad enough ter speak t'Im abowt."

He appeared to ruminate for a moment, working out how to proceed. "It came ter me as 'appen, ye might find t'answer back there wi' that lass." He shrugged and gave a brief nod. "That's all I've ter say."

Tim was rendered mute by the sudden realisation that Fred really cared about his welfare. He was also touched by Fred's trust in him in regard to his niece. Whatever faith Tim was unable to espouse at that moment, it was clear to him that Fred cared deeply for both him and his niece.. He was instantly infused by something he had never felt before, a humble recognition of the old man's good intentions.to him. Alicia's advice to approach Elsie about her uncle occurred to him, and he began to see something common among them all; - Fred, Elsie, Alicia and even Monty, Alf and Bert. They were bound together by a single cord; which they could reach out to and hold any time to connect with each other. Fred gazed out front with a bland face, as if determined not to divulge any more. Tim stole another look at him, to assess his mood. Fred looked tired and more passive than he had ever seen him. A sudden desire to be gentle and forebearing came over Tim, almost a wish to protect the old man. He searched for the phrasing of his next question with care..

"Fred?"

"Aye?"

"Do you think I might really get to know Alicia?"

Fred smiled a thin smile to himself. "How serious are ye?"

"I'm very serious,….actually." Tim looked at Fred as he said this, as if asking permission to pose the next question. "I'm not sure I'm right for her, I don't have her faith."

"'Appen she's enough fer two o' yer." He paused a moment then added, "Ter begin wi', any road."

Tim felt again the need to tread carefully. "Did you really take me to meet her. I mean, was that the reason for going?"

"I go, whatever. It's summat I've alus done, ever since…" He petered out and stopped, before ending with, "It don't matter jus' now."

"But did you have it in mind?"

Fred looked up at him and tapped his nose as he interrupted. "It matters nowt what I 'ad in mind. Wot ye've ter decide now, is wot's in yer 'eart."

Fred delivered this so emphatically that Tim lost courage to press him further. He recognised what Fred said was true. It really did not matter, in the least, what Fred's motives were in the face of the emotional awakening he had just undergone. Without any question, he did want to see Alicia again, - badly. He remembered, fleetingly, how he had wanted 'badly' to see Lydia. But, there was no comparison. Alicia radiated peace with herself and openness; she showed not a single cultivated attitude in her whole being, but was all truth and transparency. Yet, she was also a mystery; she was self-assured but not self-contained; confident of her own journey but ignorant of what the future held. And the greatest mystery was why she should offer him any intimacy on their first meeting and make what might seem unattainable, entirely possible. Such an exceptional girl had to be deserved, and he began to doubt whether he was worthy of her.

He was suddenly aware of the beams of oncoming cars and turned on his headlights. He turned to look at Fred, whose silence filled the car with unspoken significance. This old man could probably explain everything about the eponymous character of Alicia's story, if he wanted to. And, contrary to his earlier view of Fred's machiavellian conduct, he felt, tangibly, the cord that bound them all to each other.

By the time they reached Elsie's house, Fred had fallen asleep, slumped against the passenger door. Tim had to prod him before he slowly emerged into the world in a half dazed way. Tim got out and went round to open Fred's side. It was a laborious effort for Fred to climb out, and Tim had to give him his hand to pull him on to the pavement. Tim expected him to amble over to Elsie's front door, but he stood for a second or two and then, as if coming to a resolution, gave Tim a cursory glance before shuffling down the street, waving a hand over his shoulder, saying, ""I've need ter get back and get me 'ead down a while. Tell Elsie I'll see 'er tomorrer."

"Right," said Tim, taken by surprise. He was not even sure if Fred had heard his reply. He watched him go down the road, temporarily lit up each time he passed under a street lamp, and Tim was drawn to wonder what was preoccupying him as he clumped his determined way along the pavement, until he turned the corner and was lost to view. Tim felt odd at Fred's sudden departure and was disturbed by the possibility that maybe something between them had caused him to want to escape. He strolled towards Elsie's front door and inserted the key, glad to get to a place where he could commune with himself and gain some perspective of the day.

More Revelations

Once inside the hallway, all thought of retiring to his room was instantly thwarted by Elsie opening the kitchen door, obviously alerted by the sound of his return. She had an air of smiling expectancy, but was obviously surprised not to see Fred. "So where is 'e, then?"

"He left as soon as we got here," Tim answered, trying to hide his own curiosity and confusion.

"'E went down t' road?" She puckered her brow slightly. " S'not like 'im ter slope off, such a time as this. 'Appen e's 'ad enough t'day, an' needs ter get 'is 'ead down. I'd a thought 'e'd a stayed ter report in, though." She shrugged philosphically and added, "We-e-ll, 'e can catch up wi' t'news termorrer."

"Yes, that's what he said. Has he got far to go?" Tim enquired as nonchalantly as he could manage.

"It's a good 'alf mile ter 'is residential 'ome. But tha's nowt ter Fred." She shrugged away her own curiosity, and with a proprietary smile, beckoned Tim into the kitchen, whose instant inclination was to excuse himself and plead fatigue. Elsie, however, continued to jerk her head imperatively towards the door, which disempowered resistance. Hiding his reluctance, he followed her into the kitchen and, at a wordless summons of her finger, found himself sitting at the table, while she put the kettle on. He let her start the conversation.

"So," she said, as she lit the hob, "'ow did it go, then?"

Lifting his voice in feigned enthusiasm, he replied, "Er,.. a very enjoyable outing."

"Enjoyable,eh?" She looked at him inquisitively, bending forward, as if to read every delineation of his face.

"Yes." Tim nodded, and, catching her focused attention on him, sought to amplify his response. "Very interesting, indeed."

There was a pause. She eyed him closely, before echoing his phrase.

"Very Interestin', ye say?" She mused on this for a few seconds before prodding, "'Ow come?"

Tim opened his mouth several times before he found himself saying, "Well, it's a very picturesque part of the world."

Elsie shook her head, and sighed as she wore an expression of patient disbelief. "Pictureque is as maybe, young Tim. I were thinkin' more of acquaintance ye made."

"Oh, I see!" Tim exclaimed, attempting innocent ignorance. "Oh, yes, well, Fred introduced me to his niece,... of course."

"And...?" She stared at him as if he were undergoing a lie-detection session.

"It was a pleasure to meet her." He delivered this with an air of finality and bravely stared back with a strained half smile.

Elsie turned away to fill the teapot and set the jug and cups out. There was silence until she had set all out on the table. She sat opposite him, as if she were about to enter a chess competition.

"Ee, but ye give nowt away, d'yer?" There was a puckish quiver in the corner of her mouth. "T 'ear *yeou* speak, it were nowt but a bit of an outin'." She pursed her lips.. "An interestin' pleasure." She let out the phrase with some distaste, followed by a staccato laugh. "Is that t'best ye can do, then?" she challenged.

Tim felt like a small boy caught with his hands in the biscuit tin. He coloured and looked down, wondering if Elsie had, by some mystical means, been watching him during his entire visit to Lower Netherfold.

"Nay, lad, don't mind me. I say what I mean, but alus wi' best intentions. I can see fro' yer face ye've bin touched."

"How's that?" he asked, as nonchalantly as he could.

"Fred didn' take ye all the way out there jus' fer the good o' yer 'ealth. I bet ye knew it soon as ye got there. So, best stop messin' abowt an' come clean."

How much did Elsie know of what had happened with Alicia? He felt naked under her fixed and challenging stare.

"Come clean about what?"

"Oh, give over," Elsie muttered as she poured the tea out in slow precise movements, occasionally looking at Tim and smiling to herself. She pushed a cup towards Tim, and bent forwards, resting her elbows on the table.

"What did ye think on 'er?"

Tim hesitated before murmuring, "Alicia?"

Elsie merely nodded and raised her eyebrows, as if waiting for a confession from a recalcitrant schoolboy.

"I thought she was…"

Elsie raised a finger, and drank from her cup. "Don't gimme "interestin', whatever ye do."

Tim looked at Elsie as she drank and looked at him over the cup's rim and decided he was incapable of any further circumvention. "To tell the truth, I thought she was".. he sighed .. "one heck of a girl."

Elsie beamed at him, and within a fraction of a second he found himself smiling back and nodding as if he had just been relieved of a huge burden.

"That were jus' wot Fred an' me was after 'earin' ye say. I'm jus' a bit take aback that 'e sloped off like that. We was both 'opin' t' 'ear t' same thing." She frowned reflectively. "'Appen there's summat on at 'is place; residents 'avin' a bit of a do, But 'e never said nowt ter me."

"A party at his house?" asked Tim

"Not 'is 'ouse, lad. He 's got a room in 't, tho'.

"You mean an old people's home?"

Elsie nodded. He struggled with the idea of Fred being taken care of, and certainly with notion of his obeying institutional rules.

"Do they allow him out all the time?"

Elsie laughed very loudly before controlling her mirth and leaning over the table to pat Tim's arm. "Ee, lor bless ye. 'Ow in t'world d' ye think they could stop 'im?!" She sat back and shook her head, philosophically. "But, 'ow could ye know otherwise. There's a lot ye don't know about our Fred." She sized Tim up again for a second. "I think it's time ter know a bit abowt 'im…. if ye've a mind ter."

Tim remembered Alicia suggestion that he should approach Elsie for the truth, and here she was about to reveal it unsolicitedly. He wanted to know everything, now that he had met Alicia; wanted to be immersed in everything that pertained to her. He tried to hide his fascination, however.

"Of course, so long as he wouldn't mind, that is."

She smiled at him in a maternal way. "Ye're a fair bit of a gentleman, I will say. Nay, bless ye, 'e wouldn't mind yer knowin' abowt 'im, now 'e's got t' measure o' ye."

For a second or two, she adopted a serious manner, before continuing.

"I'll tell ye summat else, an' all. Ev'ryone in this 'ouse thinks as ye've passed muster. An' tha's the livin' truth."

It was strange to be given such praise, without quite knowing what it was for. It was a bit like getting a certificate for good behaviour and general progress at school. He had received one or two in his time, and never quite knew what they meant. He never knew how to respond to anyone who complimented him on receiving them, and he was no less confused now.

"I'm glad everyone thinks we get on," he said, diffidently. "I hope they don't think I'm a bit,.. you know,.. toffee-nosed, or anything."

She shook her head adamantly. "Nay, lad. They just think ye're different, tha's all. They don't take any mind o' yer bein' southern. Fred an' me's got used ter it, an' don't mind it too much at all, now."

"Oh, good," was all Tim found to say.

"So, - wot I were sayin', - it's time enough fer ye ter know the real Fred. First off, ye've ter know he were in clink five year fer manslaughter back in forty six, jus' after t'war."

Tim was astonished, his breath taken away. "In prison?"

"Tha's wot I said," asserted Elsie. "'E come back int' civvies an' foun' Brenda, 'is affianced, wi'..." She swallowed hard... "someone else. 'E found 'em t'gether in t' Black Bull Pub 'in Lower Netherfold 'igh Street."

A rueful expression passed over her face for a second, as if she was accommodating the pain of the memory.

"'E were a passionate young fella in them days, 'avin' carried 'er photo through t' war, an' it were a shock ter see 'em t'gether there, 'im turnin' up as a su'prise, not lettin' on as 'e were demobbed, till 'e got 'ome."

Tim, absorbed, began to assimilate her moods, as she re-lived the past.

"Ter cut a long story, 'e reacted like a madman, an' there were a fight, - an' it were summat ter be'old. Furniture thrown abowt, folk scatterin' out o' it,... an' then,... 'e 'ad ter get 'is 'and on a bottle, an bring it down on 'is 'ead." She went silent for a moment, gathering strength to continue. "It were all up, then. Police came roun', 'e were arrested. An ambulance took me brother away, but 'e were pronounced dead on arrival at' 'ospital."

Tim was brought to a sudden violent halt in the story. He shook his head to make sure he had heard what she said.

"Your brother?" he whispered, awestruck.

"Aye.lad. Eric were no more nor twenty three comin' up ter twenty four."

Tim cast his eyes around in some bewilderment, before attempting to express it. "But, if Fred was responsible for...."

She nodded. "...fer endin' me brother's days?"

Tim nodded back. "How could you forgive him for...?"

Elsie pursed her mouth and shrugged. "I were just fourteen when it 'appened. Eric were ten year older nor me an' we'd not 'ad much ter do wi' each other, save causin' a ruckus at dinner table. I mean, I liked 'im a fair bit, an' 'e 'ad is funny side, I s'pose, but we weren't that close, like."

"But didn't you hate him at all? Fred, I mean."

"I were caught up wi' t'family grief, an' all that. But I never took it like t' rest. Me dad were angry and me mam were stricken wi' grief. Nancy, me sister were angry an' wanted justice. She were seventeen." She shrugged. "I s'pose I shared summat they felt"

Elsie sighed as she recalled the domestic upheaval and the sense of loss in her family, before looking at Tim' crestfallen expression.

"I s'pose it'll seem funny, me an' 'im bein so close, nowadays. But it were fate as 'ad an' 'and in it all." She smiled as she recalled. "No-one saw 'ide nor 'air o' 'im fer the 'ole time 'e were put away. Me mam an' Nancy said sentence were too short, 'cos t'judge put it down ter manslaughter on account 'o t'extenuatin' circumstances. I think me dad were 'grieved wi both o 'em; Fred fer lashin' out, an' Eric fer takin'up wi' 'is girl be'ind 'is back."

There was silence, while she let her mind return to those days, and Tim struggled to take in the full import of her story. When she began again, it was as if she had to remind herself of the whole affair. Tim, now enthralled, left his tea to go cold, and sat silently agog.

"Then one day, - May, nineteen fifty-one, it were, - 'e marched int' village and sat 'isself' down, large as life, in t' bar of t' Black Bull, like 'e'd never been gone. It got roun' t'village like a dose o' salts, as 'e'd turned up again. It were no time afore the men got t'gether and marched up ter t' pub 'in a brigade, ter get t' measure o' things. Me mam wouldn' let me dad go, fer fear o' trouble, so 'e stayed 'ome, chunnerin' on abowt 'ow Fred ud been let out early, an'what was the law thinkin' abowt."

She paused to reflect.

"I went up ter see if I could catch a glimpse, wi'out knowin', rightly, what it were I were after seein'. I stood on t' seat outside and peeped in on t' 'ole thing, - I were fourteen, then, mind, - an' there were Fred at one end o' t' saloon, an round fifteen o' t' locals at t'other, all starin' at 'im, wi'out a word. 'E sat starin' back fer a while an' then 'e raised 'is glass and wished them all God's blessin'. They all looked at each other, flabbergast, an' it were left to Old Blenkinsop, who 'ad t' men's outfitter's shop a few doors away, ter speak up, an' ask Fred if 'e thought 'e were welcome in t' village."

Elsie reached out and gripped Tim's arm for a second, as she recalled the moment and prepared herself to do justice to the drama. "Fred stood up an' addressed 'em all, like 'e were at a meetin' o' t' local council. First off, 'e said 'e were not expectin' ter be welcome, considerin' what 'ad 'appened, but then, he said, he were not even askin' fergiveness wi'out they all knew 'e were penitent. Third, he said 'e weren't ever goin' ter tell 'is side o' t' story, but it were best they all knew 'e'd fergive 'isself.

Old Blenkinsop were riled by that, an' said it were too easy ter fergive 'isself, an' it showed 'e weren't in t' least penitent. There were lots o' shoutin' agreement on that. Then, when t'babble 'ad died, Fred said, all quiet like, 'I've come 'ere ter say sorry t' ye all, and to show penitence by givin' o' me best. But ye'd best know, I've fergive meself, 'cos Jesus 'as fergive me."

She sat back in her chair and emitted a long sigh.

"Well, Fred sat down again, an' ye could'a cut the air wi' a knife. There were lots a chunnerin' and growlin' till Blenkinsop gets pushed t' front again, and says as 'ow 'it were more t' point that the Wainwrights fergive 'im', - that's me mam and dad an me an' me other brother, Dave – ' 'cos it were them as 'ad lost a son, not Jesus'."

Elsie stopped to muse for a moment, as if something had occurred to her for the first time.

"I think it were next that I knew 'e were special, 'cos 'e got up again and it were like 'e were deliverin' a message. 'E were all calm an' collected, an' said 'e were ready ter do whatever were needed to be fergiven by t' Wainwrights, - meanin' us family, - 'cos it were much more in their int'rests than 'is."

Elsie chuckled at the outrageousness of Fred's remark.

"Eeh, well, that riled Fletcher, the butcher, who said 'e'd feel a darn sight better if 'e gave Fred a duffin' up. Fred stepped aside o' t' table, an said Fletcher were free ter duff 'im up, if it 'ud make fergiveness easier. Fletcher started t'ward 'im, - six foot two, 'e 'were - an' towerin' over Fred, but when e' was stood right next ter 'im, face ter face, an' saw 'im standing wi' 'is 'ands hangin' by 'is sides, - all five foot six of 'im - 'is anger got drained away, an' after glarin' at im fer 'alf a minute, e' shook 'is 'ead, flapped 'is arms about a bit, and stepped back. There were more chunnerin' and when it died down, Fred said, quiet like, that 'e'd come ter serve t' community, ter repay the debt 'e owed. Blenkinsop said they didn't want nowt fro' 'im, so 'e could beat it. Fred said it were not up ter Blenkinsop, it were up ter Jesus, 'cos it were Jesus what 'ad asked 'im ter do it."

Elsie gave a laugh as she revelled in the moment.

"Ye should a seen' em all, then. There were no-one seemed ter know what ter say back at 'im, till Mr. Bertram, the draper at bottom o' t' hill, jutted 'is chin for'ard and asked Fred what 'e proposed ter do about the young girl as 'ad been left unfathered. That floored Fred fer a bit, 'cos 'e 'ad no idea that Brenda 'ad give birth. It knocked the wind out o' 'im at first, an' he stood castin' 'is eyes abowt till 'e got 'isself t'gether again. Then 'e said, simple like, 'e'd be very willin' ter support the child, till Brenda found 'erself an 'usband. Well, there were lots o' disputation among 'em all, an' Fred were sittin' drinkin his glass the while. Any road, in't end, they all marched out, an' Blenkinsop shouted back as 'e'd tell Brenda wot 'e'd said, an' 'e'd best be serious abowt it.

When they'd all gone out, I watched Fred sittin' there, alone, drinkin' 'is beer quiet an' calm, an' 'e seemed like a young 'ero seein' off an army, single 'anded. When 'e come out o' t' pub, I followed 'im at a distance, till 'e got t' top o' t high street, an' 'e went out o' sight." She chuckled quietly to herself. " It were years later 'e tells me 'e'd found a cattle barn to rest 'is 'ead fer t' night."

Elsie sat gazing into the distance, down time's pageant, and Tim was given a moment to assimilate what he'd heard. Her story presented Fred in an entirely different situation, in an age that had vanished, but, at the same time, gave some insight into what he had become now. Tim cleared his throat to signal his question, which seemed an intrusion on her memories.

"And did Fred support Brenda's child?"

Elsie stirred and looked at Tim as if he had betrayed the image of Fred, just by asking the question.

"'Course 'e did. Fred's alus been a man o' 'is word," she said, in an affronted tone.

"Oh, I know," he sprang to assure her. "I was just thinking that perhaps he would find it difficult to get work in the village."

"It weren't in t'village 'e worked. It were Grindle-ford ten mile away. 'E got a mechanic's job in t' local garage, an' 'e were wi' 'em fer more'n ten year. An' all the while 'e were sendin' money fer Brenda's young girl."

"That's amazing," Tim whispered. "What did Brenda's family think about it?"

"First off, they was sceptical, like, but after three year, an' the money kept comin' in, 'er dad invited Fred 'ome, one day. When 'e goes, they want 'im ter consider marryin' 'er. But 'e wouldn't,'cos 'e said it were like step-pin' in t' shoes o' t'victim. That's 'ow 'e put it ter me, later on, any road."

She related all this with a kind of proprietary pride, and Tim was aware of her relationship with Fred exceeded what many married couples felt. He even contrasted it with his own parents.

"When did you get to know Fred, properly?....if you don't mind my asking."

Far from minding, she embraced the opportunity.

"Well, after 'e'd been ter Brenda's, t' village got a diff'rent picture o' Fred. There was plenty who thought 'e'd 'ad some reason to lose 'is rag, even if it 'ad led ter me brother's death. O' course, me mam an' dad never saw it like that, and never went near 'im. Any'ow, 'e started ter come over t' pub and drink a glass wi' t'locals, an' bit by bit 'e were accepted int' t' community. Local garage even offered 'im a job, 'cos o' is repertation in Grindleford. But 'e wouldn't take it on account o' it bein' too near us. I were eighteen by now, wi' a job at Old Blenkinsop's ladies' department."

Elsie lowered her voice, as if there were hidden earlopers behind the skirting boards.

"One day Fred comes int' shop, like a bolt out o' t' blue, an. asks fer a pair o' mittens at the men's counter. An' 'e looks over at me, casual like, an' asks after me family. Well, ye could'a knocked me down wi' a breath o' air, 'cos I didn't think 'e'd know me from Eve. I turns away an' says, 'I been asked not ter speak t' ye by me dad'. 'E nods an' says, 'Aye, I reckoned on that'. An' then 'e asks me 'ow I felt abowt that. I were tongue-tied, but says I didn't know. An' then 'e says 'e'd be greatly relieved if I'd fergive 'im fer what 'e'd done. An' I thought back ter that first evenin' in t'pub, an' wi'out thinkin', I say I did, right out. 'E gives me a smile. It were first time I'd seen 'im give one. So I smile back. An' then 'e says 'e wished I'd take it back home ter t' rest o' me family. I says "take what?" 'E says, "Yer smile". I says, "Why". 'E says, "'Cos a smile o' fergiveness is catchin'." An' 'e goes out o' t' shop wi' is mittens, an' gives me a last smile as 'e shuts t' door be'ind 'im.

Elsie sighed and looked over to Tim in a motherly way.

"Ye've let yer tea go cold. I'll jus' make ye another one"

Tim tried to protest, but she got up and crossed to light the gas under the kettle. Tim reflected on the legendary nature of what he was hearing. She returned to her seat.

"Aye," she sighed, "I took that away wi' me, an' thowt on it fer a fair time. I never told me dad and mam I'd spoke wi' 'im, o'course. An' it were three year later an' 'e come in t' shop again, only this time 'e come straight up t' ladies counter an' said 'e wanted ter speak ter me. We'd not passed a word since last time, so I were taken aback. Any road, I says, 'what can I show ye?', an' 'e says, 'T' kindness ter listen'. I says 'Listen ter what?' an' e' says, 'Brenda's family's movin' out t'Australia, an' she's goin' wi' 'er new fiancee, an' me obligations is at an end there. I'm wonderin' if there's owt I can do fer yower family.' I knew that me dad 'ud 'ave nuthin ter do wi' 'im, so I say, straight out, that there were nowt. He looked at me fer a few seconds afore sayin', "Are yer courtin' yet?". An' I look at 'im back an' say, 'yes', - cos I were goin' out wi' Dave Brocklebank at t' time. So 'e asks me is it serious, an' I tell 'im we was plannin' ter get wed, 'appen in a year or two. So 'e nods once or twice and then, earnest like, 'e says 'e's glad t' 'ear it."

She reflected and gathered her thoughts together as she got up to fill the tea-pot again. She stirred it and poured into another cup, before continuing, and Tim caught her mood of nostalgic regret in the way she expressed herself.

"It were then" – she poured milk into Tim's cup – "'e said 'e'd alus be of a mind ter 'elp me in time o' tribulation, an' I were alus ter remember that."

She poured the tea and pushed the cup over to Tim.

'E left, straight after, givin' me a friendly wink, an' I never seen 'im again till just afore t' weddin' day."

She pushed the sugar bowl over to Tim, gazing abstractly at the corner of the room, as if it were an important coordinate in her memory's chart, and spoke as if taken again by surprise by her own recollection.

"The next time, 'e were leanin' on t' rail-post, waitin' outside o' t' shop, ter waylay me soon as I were goin' 'ome. 'E steps for'ard as I come through t' door, an' plants a bank book in me 'and, an' says as 'ow it's a gift on me weddin' day."

She poured his tea, and pointed to the cup.

"Don't let it get cold this time, lad. Where was I? - oh, yes, as I were sayin', - Well, I were flabbergasted. I didn't know what ter say, at first, - like ye wouldn't, would ye? I say, "What's this fer? 'It's a reward fer fergivin' me', 'e says. I says, 'Ye don't get paid fer fergivin' someone.' 'E says, 'It's not payment. It's a gift fro' Jesus. I looked at 'im sideways, an' says, 'Wot?! Jesus sent ye this ter give ter me? 'E gives me a look back an' a grin, an' says, 'It were 'Im what give me the nudge'. An' 'e turned roun' and went off wi'out another word." Elsie jabbed her finger at the cup again. "Drink yer tea, lad, afore it goes cold again."

Tim jerked himself back into the kitchen and complied. Elsie shook her head and took her next cue from the ceiling, as she recalled the event.

"When I opened the book, there was nigh on five 'undred pounds written in t' last column. An' ye could see as 'ow 'e'd paid in deposits every week. When I looked up again, 'e were gone."

Tim peering over the rim of his cup, saw her visibly reliving the narrative, and dissolving into a deep, almost painful gratitude. She sat there like someone in a cinema, who had just seen a tear-jerker and was unable to face the real world until she had come to terms with her emotion. Tim tried to see Fred as the young man described in Elsie's story, the same age as Tim was now, but with a generous heart prompted to act as his conscience dictated. It was a 'young Fred' whose motives clearly pointed to those that drove him now, as an old man; motives that had not, till now, been properly appreciated by Tim.

"But now you're together again," he said in a voice that gave away his intense curiosity and emotion. "So, when did you next meet?"

Suddenly, Elsie started. "Oh, 'ecky, what time d'ye make it? The lads 'll be in fer their supper, an' I've not done a thing abowt it. Eeh, what with ye getting' me at it, it completely slipped me mind."

She got up and started to arrange food on the work-top, bringing them both into actuality with a brutal dismissal of her tale. Tim felt like a cheated theatre-goer when a curtain has been brought down before the end of the act. He yearned to be able to pick up the story where they had left off.

"Will ye be eatin' in t'night?" she asked, without looking at him.

"Er no,… actually. I thought I'd try the Indian Restaurant in Tyler Street." Tim had no idea he would mention that place before he opened his mouth. He only knew that he was in no state of mind to be plagued with any questions from Bert, Alf and Monty. He needed time on his own to put the whole day, including Elsie's graphic journey into the past, in some kind of perspective. He desperately wanted time to assimilate this and the clinging presence of Alicia into the melting pot of his mind and heart. The inevitable curiosity of his fellow lodgers would be sacrilege.

"Right. Well, don't get yersel' inter trouble this time," Elsie said brusquely, and focused on the meal preparation. Tim got up and left her to chop, scrape and slice on the wooden board, feeling that he had been dismissed without need of further formality.

The room was just as he had left it that morning, except for the neatness with which the bedcovers had been tucked under the mattresses by Elsie. No attempt had been made to move Bert's bed back to the shed, but although Tim felt it was far from ideal, it now paled into insignificance, in the face of everything else that had happened. Only last night he was vowing to move to another residence, and now he was bent on staying, on finding out who they were, for, as he saw it, everything led back to Alicia. Alicia had asked him to find out the truth, and that was enough to convince him of the need to become part of it all. Elsie had already radically changed his understanding of who Fred was. He was also touched by the trust Elsie had shown in him by revealing so much of Fred's and her story. But there was so much more to know about them all. As he sat on the side of his bed, he was also aware that what he was learning about them was forcing him to learn more about himself. They were opening new doors, and he was drawn to pass through them to escape from the vicarious world he was living in, where he put himself in a marketplace for which he had no respect.

When he went out that evening, he felt very satisfied that he had a home to return to, a home where he could wrestle with his feeling for a girl, who had seriously disturbed his equanimity..

No 'Because' About It

The following morning he awoke with an amazingly light heart, not fully understood until the memory of the previous day invaded his consciousness. A rush of blood from his head to his heart, made it pound, as he resurrected the sensation of Alicia's lips on his. The tactile memory had lingered with him all last evening. He returned early from town and had managed to retire stealthily without having to face intrusive questions. He had let himself in and climbed the stairs without detection while everyone was in the kitchen. Thankfully, Bert had not disturbed him, when he came up, and now Tim was making every attempt to return the favour by creeping round as he washed and dressed. He had drifted into sleep with Alicia's expression of gentle irony, as if she were searching his soul, and emerged from sleep, recalling dreams of embraces and intimacies that now he almost blushed at. At this early hour of seven, he was intent on leaving Bert, snoring gently, undisturbed beneath his pile of bedclothes, and thus avoiding inevitable matey conversation. He was determined to exit the house before Elsie started cooking breakfast, to protect his memories from intrusive curiosity.

He had, in fact, got a man to see, and, although, he did not, ordinarily, derive much pleasure from his self-serving misrepresentation of art, he felt, today, that the pictures he was taking with him, were ones he personally admired, and that he was carrying round with him a new found encouragement. He felt brighter than he had done for some time, for the man he was going to visit, seemed to be genuinely interested in art reproductions. Having been pressed by his firm to find new outlets, Tim had arranged with a bookseller in the nearby town of Blackbridge to meet at his shop and discuss the possibility of supplying him with pictures and prints. From the initial exchange by letter, he got the clear impression that the bookseller was someone more informed than the usual client. The response had been friendly and enthusiastic and a meeting was duly arranged. Tim was pleased to be driving some twenty miles to the venue, for it gave him the feeling of escaping to his own space.

He found Blackbridge a bustling little town, with metropolitan pretentions. There was a large sheltered bus centre with single decker vehicles lined up, and a taxi rank. The streets were made up of a nice mix of privately owned specialist shops and well known nationwide superstores. He observed that no-one turned heads to look at his car, suggesting an urbane and sophisticated centre that was not easily impressed.

Tim left his car in in a three-storey car park, and walked to the shop with the aid of the local map. He found it in a bustling street, full of people taking a lively interest in windows or striding purposely out. There was an air of urban enlightenment and communal purpose. From the diverse styles of the buildings, the town declared itself to have grown organically. He sensed a challenge to his usual feeling of southern superiority from a town with civic pride.

The book shop was a sizable two-storeyed building with a wide double glazed front and two steps leading to iits entrance, giving it a slightly 'nose in the air' look. There was nothing 'toffee-nosed' about the shop itself, however, for, he was impressed by its friendly open shelves set in the middle of the floor, with large notices in broad italics indicating the subject matter. There were three shop assistants, two young women with professional politeness and discretion etched on their faces, leaving customers to browse at leisure, and a man, whose face was half hidden behind a wiry beard, and topped by a mop of thick hair, left to part itself in any direction it had a mind to. His eyes, framed by rimless glasses, spoke of middle age, but his movements were quick and expansive, like an eager waiter in an Italian resort. The two women offered the thinnest of smiles, as Tim gazed round the shop searching for the section on art. As he made towards it, carrying his portfolio, the man sidled up to him. Tim said he was not looking to buy a book, at which the man declared it to be a great loss to them both, and assured him that books were all the shop was equipped to sell. "Please, do browse, nevertheless," he offered. "We often find reluctance to buy overcome by temptation."

Tim smiled and explained that he had come to see a Mr. Nathan Steadman. The man extended his hand, and introduced himself as, "the very same, sir". Tim, surprised, shook his hand. "And you will be Mr. Tim Carter." Tim nodded.

Mr. Nathan Steadman turned briefly to the girls. "Will you hold the fort, my dears? I'll be in the office with Mr. Carter, but I'll not forget your coffee break."

He beckoned Tim to follow him to the back of the shop and into a large, comfortable room with a leather button-backed settee and a desk with a revolving executive chair behind it. The floor and desk and surrounding shelves were littered with books, in untidy piles, some of which had toppled over, left to their own devices like ruins of an ancient city. The atmosphere was of cheerful chaos.

"Sit, sit, sit you down, Mr. Carter, and call me Nathan, because, you see, I'm very pleased to meet you."

Tim sat on the settee. "It's my pleasure, Mr,.. er,.. Nathan."

It was an informal introduction to a business meeting, but he felt obliged to respond in kind. "Please call me Tim."

"Good, good, good. Glad to, must say. Can't stand formality. Gets in the way, don't you think?"

"Er, yes. But it's more usual than not."

"Really? Well, no point in starting from past experience. Always make a fresh start I say. That's always been my way with these things."

Tim smiled politely, unable to think of a reply, and wondering what 'these things' might be.

"Yes, well, what you wrote me sounded very interesting. Must say, we could well find ourselves of the same persuasion. A good start in any venture."

He sank peremptorily into his seat, leant forward and raised his eyebrows to the height equatable with a startling revelation.

"Don't you agree?"

Tim had never met such positive reception within such a short time, and was practically lost for words, except to admit that he did, indeed agree.

"Good," Nathan said emphatically. "Very good. Well, straight off, I'm sure there's a definite future in art repros. Worth exploring every possibility. So," - He made an expansive gesture with his hands - "what have you got for me to see?"

Tim launched into his over-rehearsed sales spiel.

"The examples I brought with me today are only a small selection of what we can offer. I can send you a brochure, or you can go on our website and browse a comprehensive gallery from all periods up to modern day."

"Good, good, good. So, wide selection, many styles, Good. But, how d'you see this going forward? You provide me with the pictures and I sell them,...... how?"

Tim felt his way carefully. "Well, this is a book shop..."

"Yes, that's true. Hadn't gone unnoticed, but thanks for that."

A slight hesitation and a smile to accommodate the levity.

"So, if you were going to sell pictures, you'd have to give over some space to them up-front, to create inter-est".

"Yes, you would." Nathan nodded in enthusiastic agreement. "You would, indeed. To create interest, yes."

"Then we would have to consider how a book shop would sell pictures," Tim suggested.

"Ah, well, there you are. As I see it, I'd be diversify-ing. And that's a good thing. Society is definitely becom-ing more visually orientated, these days."

"Yes, but the visual goes hand in hand with words, don't you think?"

"Absolutely! Quite right! Point taken!"

"So, perhaps we could synthesise them in some way."

"Excellent! Let's do that!" Nathan exclaimed. There was a silence during which he looked on the floor with an intense expression like a detective pondering a clue, before abruptly posing the question, "How?"

Tim nodded wisely, as he struggled to give birth to the idea.

"You could give one of your window displays over to the reproductions, with maybe some relevant art books arranged next to them. That way you would not look as if you were a book shop selling pictures, but a shop selling books and pictures with a clear relation between them."

Nathan slowly opened his mouth throughout Tim's suggestion. By the end, his eyes complemented his mouth, and he laughed from the depth of his diaphragm.

"That's .... Absolutely...brill! You've got it, haven't you?! That's it, isn't it?. Absolutely! Not a book shop but a shop selling books and pictures. Unified diversity, that's what it is!"

Tim regarded this as the main chance for cutting to the chase.

"Yes, well, perhaps we should look at some of the pictures, and see if they appeal to you," Tim offered.

"Yes, yes, yes, let's do that. See if they appeal."

Tim opened his portfolio of pictures, and laid them on the table, one by one. He had included Manet's wistful 'A bar of the Folie Bergere', 'The Cheat with the Ace of Diamonds' by Georges de la Tour, 'A Maidservant Pouring Milk' by Vermeer, 'The Hireling Shepherd' by Holman Hunt and 'Nighthawks' by Edward Hopper.

"How splendid!" Nathan clapped his hands together ecstatically, as each one was laid out. "How diverse!

How historically appealing! Each one a captivating arrested moment! What made you choose these?"

"They seemed accessible to the general public," Tim said. "The figures are all behaving in a recognisable way. They speak of everyone's world. One can see oneself reflected."

"Yes, you're right! Yes, I can see that! The artist has arrested these universal moments for close inspection. Nothing special or significant in themselves, just highly focused fleeting moments."

Tim beamed, relishing the prospect of clinching a contract.

"So you like them?" he asked confidently.

Nathan, for the first time, following his voluble bursts of enthusiasm, sat back in his chair to reflect. He took his glasses off and wiped them with a tissue from his pocket, replaced them, joined his fingers together and pressed them against his lips, before exhaling a deep sigh.

"But you know,... and I say this with due deference to your taste, ... I think there are more compelling examples of your chosen artists. Take your George de la Tour, for instance. He was especially renowned for the way he lit his subjects from below to give dramatic effect. It was his trade mark. How still and moving is his 'Penitent Magdalen' where Mary's eyes peer through the candle-lit moment of enlightenment at the memento mori skull, or 'Christ with St. Joseph in the Carpenter's Shop', with the young child Christ holding the candle that pushes back the shadows so that his Father can see clearly to work. As for Vermeer, don't you think that perhaps his 'Lace-maker' shows better the absorption of the girl in a more intricate and demanding task than the 'maidservant pouring milk'? One is drawn into the picture by wanting to peer under her inclined head to see the face. She is focused on her work but also on her own resources"

It was Tim's turn to slacken the jaw and bulge the eyes. It was obvious that Nathan was a connoisseur and was intimately acquainted with the subject – and – he was passionate about it all. Tim swallowed hard as Nathan suddenly jumped out of the chair.

"Let's have a look, eh?"

He burst out of the office and returned seconds later with two volumes, which he opened on the desk and then handed to Tim to inspect. He continued to make compelling arguments for examples that competed with Tim's offerings, and persistently made forays to the bookshelves, and returning with armfuls of books like a frantic delivery man. In no time, the floor round Tim's feet was littered with volumes and pamphlets, ranging from coffee table tomes to thin publications on individual artists. They pored over them together, comparing them, with such mutual infection that, within half an hour, Tim was persuaded that Nathan's knowledge and enthusiasm was unchallengeable. Nathan's selection of pictures was a salutary experience for Tim, for he had to recognise that they involved deeply personal moments, chosen for their introspective, but less self-contained, focus.

At last Nathan sighed, and nodded his satisfaction.

"It's time for refreshment, right? The girls would like a cuppa, no doubt."

He bounded out of the office for the umpteenth time, exclaiming, "Coffee on girls!"

In the interval, Tim's mind whirled with ideas and opinions that interconnected with the events of the last two days. In the midst of all these thoughts, was established the certain knowledge that he had just been introduced to an amateur in the best sense of the word, someone who, far from being amateurish, loved art. Nathan had given him a new prespective that demanded new insights of himself. He recalled the delight he had felt at Alicia's paintings, and was convinced they, too, had the same kind of focus. What had Alicia said? 'What you believe about art is based on what you believe about life'. Maybe a deeper inspection of art would lead to a clearer knowledge of who he was, which, in turn, would bring him nearer to Alicia. Fred's accusation of his being 'on the inside looking out' had sounded facile at the time, but perhaps it did have some substance. Nathan returned with a tray of coffee and biscuits and a lively inclination to chat, this time with less intensity.

"So, Tim, how long have you been trading in art?"

Suddenly Tim was defensive about admitting to 'trading', even if it was true. His first impulse was to pretend to forget, or throw a remark away and change the subject. "Oh, for quite some time." Then hastily added, " But how long have you had the shop?"

Nathan laughed. "Since two years ago, when an uncle left it to me in his will. He has my eternal blessing for releasing me from teaching. I bounce around all day, hardly able to believe my good fortune."

"Do you mean this is all new to you?" Tim could hardly credit it.

"Depends what you mean by 'this'. The shop, yes; books and literature and art, no, no,no." He wagged a finger.

"But, you obviously know a great deal about them," Tim said, unable to fathom his expertise.

"Well, you don't think knowledge comes with suddenly owning a book shop, do you?" He wore a pseudo-suspicious expression, chuckling, as he handed Tim a coffee. "I've loved art and literature since I was able to read 'Chicken Licken', my school primer." He caught Tim's smile at the idea. "I see you don't think 'Chicken Licken' is literature. I do. The first book to open the door to language and pictures in the mind, is a good entry to literature and art. I read it from cover to cover at four years old, and still vividly remember how all the animals feared the sky would fall on them.. My first great lesson in life was from a warm, ample-bosomed young teacher who told me that we don't need to fear the sky, and anyway chickens and their farmyard friends don't have much of a brain." He looked intently at Tim. "And what about you?"

"I don't think I've got much, either."

Nathan laughed uproariously, and Tim, caught up in the hilarity of the comparison, found himself laughing, too. He couldn't remember making a joke quite like that, and felt liberated.

"Ha,ha! Heavens!" Then suddenly serious. "You know what I mean. Where did you get *your* love of art?"

His love of art. Where did he get it from? What did 'love of art' mean? Did he love art? In what sense did Nathan mean it?

"I suppose I was good at recognising style and technique, characteristics of painters. My art teacher told me I had an eye for it, and so it seemed natural to pursue it." He halted and Nathan sat watching silently. "I suppose," Tim added, lamely.

"It sounds as if art was chosen for you," Nathan suggested, raising a quizzical eyebrow.

"I suppose so, in a way," Tim admitted.

"You seem to suppose quite a lot, if I might say so," Nathan said, with a smile.

"Yes…"

"I suppose so." Nathan added his voice in unison with that of Tim.

He smiled, then threw his eyes to heaven and pulled a confused grotesque face, which made Tim smile, too.

"So, my dear fellow, I can see you have a wonderful grasp of all the technicalities, but now perhaps you need to let go of them." He looked startled at his own audacity for a second, before adding, "I say, I hope I haven't offended you?!"

"Not at all." Far from being offended, Tim felt invigorated, if somewhat chastened. He liked Nathan's easy, confident manner, and recognised a mind that brought a combination of mental appraisal and introspection to his love of art. He looked at Nathan, framing a question. Nathan looked away, sensing the internal debate. Tim resolved on asking the simple question, "What do you mean, 'let go'? Of what? What for?"

"My dear chap, to allow your instincts freedom. Open up the Pandora's box of feelings and let them invade the pictures. Let them speak back to you, directly. It's too easy to know what the world's already said about art. It's more important to find out what *you* think and feel about it."

"That makes it all completely subjective."

"Yes, yes, yes!" Nathan lifted his eyebrows to his hairline, smiled broadly and nodded sufficient to lift his head off. "Exactly! If we don't start from there, we'll never reach an honest agreement with anybody about art. We'll just be echoing what we've filtered through our brains from sources handed down to us."

"Is that what you think I'm doing?"

"I don't know. Are you?"

Tim thought perhaps he ought to resent the implied rebuke, but could not manage to in the face of his suspicion that there was truth in it.

"Well, I'm only concerned with works that'll be popular with the buying public. I mean that's what you want, too, isn't it?"

Nathan threw his hands out, as though about to break into song. "Well, of course, dear fellow, but what has that got to do with it?! I have always convinced readers to buy books I recommend. I think I can promise to do the same with pictures. I wouldn't get any satisfaction from offering them art that doesn't speak to *me*."

"Supposing they don't share your taste?" Tim said this more in the way of keeping his end up, than to make a meaningful contribution.

"Then we must convince them to change their mind."

"How?"

To start with, I'd write a critique in big letters on card, with quotation marks, and put it next to the painting in the window."

Tim frowned. "But people will think you're referring to some art critic. Suppose they ask you who you're quoting?"

"I'll bet you the cost of a four course supper at the local posh restaurant that most people won't give a rude raspberry who says what. They'll believe someone said it and that, in itself, will be seen as a seal of approval."

"Is that honest?"

"Oh, for Pete's sake, dear fellow, it would only be dishonest if you didn't like the painting. And anyway, I'd come clean, if they asked. If my customers are prepared to take my word for a book, I bet you anything, they'll take it for a picture."

There was a pause as they fixed each other, Tim with his doubts and Nathan with his challenge.

"So," Nathan asked, breaking the silence, "are we in business? We can discuss the paintings, then you choose some, I choose others – you bring as many of them as you can secure rights to - and I'll give 'em window space. Strictly a joint venture. Right? And please don't say 'I suppose so." He smiled.

Tim capitulated. "Right. We can do that" Then, as an afterthought, he asked, "Are you interested in seeing new artists?"

"Why not?" Nathan said, with an expansive shrug. "Anyone in mind?"

"Might have," Tim threw out, carelessly.

"Bring it on, dear fellow."

In the next half hour they conjured up a mix of their respective suggestions, and at the end, Nathan insisted they shook hands over a verbal contract reached by compromise. Tim felt he had a client with whom he had much in common, even if, in some measure, they differed in taste. After all, they at least had in common the belief that art was not for decoration, but contained beauty for all to discover. In addition, Tim had something to take away with him and reflect on; namely Nathan's insistence that, in good art, interior life went beyond subject matter or style. He left conscious that his new acquaintance's eccentric informality fronted a fertile mind that challenged him mightily.

On The Outside Looking In

As Tim left Blackbridge behind him, his mind sped immediately back to Alicia, whom he now knew he could not dismiss from his thoughts, even when conducting business. If he were honest, she had been present throughout the whole affair in the book shop. In fact, as Nathan and he had exchanged looks, he also saw her eyes peering back at him in a similar challenging slightly ironic fashion.

She was at the same time a mystery and a beacon to him. The mystery had much to do with her uncontrived overture to him, at odds with her ostensibly controlled and philosophical view of the possibility of greater intimacy between them. But, he was drawn to her, not because she was an attractive and sensually exciting girl, undeniable in view of his erotically convincing dreams; but by the aura of enlightened purpose that emanated from her. It wasn't just to do with her paintings, with which he was immensely impressed; you didn't fall in love with someone because they were good at art. No, it was more than that. He was irresistibly attracted by his conviction that she knew exactly the direction she wanted her life to take, while, at the same time, leaving exciting possibilities open. Since he had never met anyone with that same kind of single-purposed direction, he found it incredibly sexy and challenging. And yet..? Was he truly in love? Had he been bamboozled by Fred and Elsie into becoming obsessed with a girl, whom they had persuaded him to believe was a romantic candidate? It seemed like vicariousness gone mad. Here he was, contemplating returning to visit a girl whom he had met once and who had prompted him to ask Jesus how he should go about approaching the prospect of intimacy.

The dilemma stared him in the face. If Jesus was important in her life, how was he going to cross the bridge over the gap created by his own scepticism?

He was half way back to Elsie's when he pulled into a lay-by, switched off the engine and sank back into his bucket seat to ponder. He gazed out of his side window on to a field of grazing sheep, contentedly nibbling at the turf, hardly needing to move except to lift their heads and stare with unsearching, self-satisfied eyes at the surrounding world, unmotivated by any thought beyond their immediate needs. How fortunate, in some respects, the mindless beast was. Yet, on the other hand, what a great loss never to be able to be hurt by love. What Elsie had told him about Fred was largely about triumphing over pain. What a mystery Fred was. Yet Fred was a simple man with a single-minded approach to life. He had something that took him above the struggles he had been embroiled in. And, there was no way of escaping the possibility that it came down to faith. The reality of Fred, that Tim had experienced, was at war with the suspicion that Fred was deceiving himself. Why did he suspect Fred was deluded? If he was, then his faith flew in the face of what the world and he had done to each other - violent things, it was now revealed. And yet, the suspicion was growing that Fred knew himself better than Tim knew himself. Fred acted from an assurance that was foreign to Tim, who had to own to groping his way. And what had Nathan been so insistent about? That he should approach the paintings by searching within himself. He sensed a connection between his meeting with Nathan and Alicia. He positively thirsted to look again at her work to see how they would communicate themselves to him. Or, no, - he would communicate with them. He would look at them, searching within himself for his feelings for her, both as an artist and a woman. He felt the need for inner strength to take the initiative, to declare his feelings without incitement from her or anyone. He debated with himself. The fear of rejection required self-assurance to overcome it, but maybe, in an affair of the heart, you couldn't be assured until you could resist seeing it as a matter of life and death. Nothing seemed a matter of life and death to Fred, Elsie or Alicia. Why? Was it because they were not alone; they had their mate, their friend, their prince, Jesus? He stared at a sheep standing near the wire fence, as it looked back at him chewing contendedly. It had no idea it was on its own; no concept for loneliness. Yet, perhaps it felt comforted in some irrational way by the presence of other sheep, taught, from birth, by the need for mother's milk. Is that what drove him to love someone? Taught by his mother from birth to avoid being alone? That would make love a mere dictate of Nature over which he had no choice. He did have a choice, but had to come to terms with an impulse to be with somebody, to share life with a woman. It wasn't his loins telling him this; it was something that filled a vaccuum in his whole being. Was Fred right in believing he was accompanied? What did Alicia mean by prayer? Why did she ask him to pray? The last time he tried, Fred was convinced, - how did he put it? – that Jesus had got him on His books. Tim looked up at the overcast sky, obstructing any view of the heavens. They pressed down on his psyche, as he sat there. He remembered the last time he tried conversing with his idea of God, beginning with 'If you're there…let's talk'.

"So, are you there,Jesus?" Tim's lips barely took the shape of the sounds in his head.

"Good heavens, Tim, what do you expect me to say?"

"How do I know? I suspect I'm only going through the motions, here"

"And, *how*, in those circumstances, do you think I'm going to talk to you? Do you expect me to boom out from the clouds?"

"No." Tim smiled at the idea.

"Right. That would frighten you to death, and, furthermore, would convince you that I am somehow obliged to resort to the five senses to speak to you."

"Yes, I suppose I can see what you mean."

"That's a start. Let me ask you another question. Leaving me out of the equation for the moment, - just the moment you understand, - what do you want from life?"

"Life? You mean, what do I want to achieve in my life?"

"Partly, but it goes further than that. What does life mean to you?"

Tim pondered on the implied difference between succeeding in life on one hand and giving it meaning on the other. He struggled with his thoughts.

"It means being conscious of myself, and doing what I believe it is right for me to do. Does that cover it?"

"That view has its merit, but how do you achieve this? You say 'believe what is right' How do you judge that?"

"Well, I largely follow the rules generally accepted by most people."

"Have you any idea where most people get their rules from?"

"Well, .." - Tim struggled again to help the thought climb out of the wrestling ring - "we all accept what has proved to have worked through experience."

"So you take on trust what others before you have experienced and handed on to you?"

"Yes,..well, yes,.. I suppose so."

"Now, bringing me back into the equation, what do you think would make you believe I really exist? Could you believe in me, if someone told you that it was a good thing, because they have experienced me?"

Tim smiled ruefully to himself. "No, I don't think so. Well, it might make me think it possible, depending on the sort of a person who told me, I suppose."

"Hmm. 'Suppose'. Useful word for staving off conviction. However, it's often a door left ajar, too. Very well, what sort of a person do you think that might be?"

"It would have to be someone I liked, who did things I approved of, someone I looked up to, … I suppose."

"I see. So, it's your approval of what sort of person he is and what he does that gives it all credibility?"

"Sort of."

"Very well. Now, I want you to think carefully. Where do you think you get your right to approve from? Put another way, against what are you measuring the person you approve of?"

Tim screwed his eyes up at the effort. "Against...my understanding of what is good and right to do?"

"That sounded like a question. Are you wise enough to know precisely what that is?"

"I didn't mean...well I know I'm not perfect in these matters, but...." He petered out.

"When I once said, 'there is no-one who is good, save my Father in Heaven', I wasn't being disingenuous. Tim..."

Tim was startled for a second by his name.

"...it's the human condition to see goodness from a subjective and personal point of view. That's what I came to be part of when I entered the world of flesh. That's why I needed to listen to my Father all the time. Do you get it?"

For a moment Tim thought he was losing his grip. How was he allowing himself to be involved in an internal debate like this? Where did these ideas come from? Was he recalling days studying 'divinity' in school? His own thoughts were intruded upon again.

"Isn't it interesting that you talk about 'goodness' without once mentioning love?"

"Didn't I?" Tim put the question to both Jesus and himself.

"No. Despite thinking you are in love with Alicia."

"Yes. Alicia. I think I must be in love with her."

"Really? On what basis? That she's good, and you approve of her? How do you know she's good, or worthy of your approval?"

"Well, it goes beyond approval doesn't it I mean you don't love someone because they measure up to your standards. You might do that with a friend, but not..."

"...Someone you want to make love to?" Jesus completed the thought.

Tim wore an almost rueful expression as he returned with, "You're beginning to make it seem selfish to want someone for myself."

"Depends what you want them for. To own them is ridiculous; to serve them with love is sublime. And when two people make love to serve each other, it is sublime pleasure"

"So pleasure is O.K.?"

"Why not? But have you asked yourself *why* you fell in love with Alicia?"

"Must there be a reason?"

"Not one you'll necessarily understand perfectly. But don't you suspect something beyond understanding?"

"What?"

"She made you feel on top of a mountain, when she kissed you. She showed you she thought you were worth crossing a boundary for."

"She might just have been sorry for me."

"Is that why you didn't return the kiss?"

Tim wanted to escape that thought.

"Or is it because you didn't have the courage? You left her to have the courage for both of you?"

"Oh, did I really lack the courage?" Tim frowned at the thought. "It would have been so good to return the kiss, wouldn't it?"

"Yes, but you need to feel your way into someone else's space. Great care is needed to ignite a great and lasting love."

"Easy does it, you mean?"

"That's my way, most of the time."

Tim had to think about that for a second, before taking it on board.

"We seem to be doing pretty well, here. Just one last question. Why do you think Alicia had such courage?"

"Brought up to be self confident?"

"Yes. She's been taught to know she isn't alone. She has me with her. We're both coming at you. But before you start that nonsense about being outnumbered, why not share me? You'll have to listen to me, of course, because if you don't, she'll know." There was a pause for thought. "Do you want to give it a try? Surrender yourself to the possibility, at least?"

"I suppose I could," Tim decided. What choice was there, if there was any chance of losing Alicia?

"What have you got to lose?" whispered Jesus, as His voice drifted away.

Tim looked at the sheep nuzzling up to the fence line. It stopped nibbling the grass and looked straight at him for a moment, asking the same question. Tim heard himself chuckle.

He started up the car and pulled away. Tomorrow, he had to go down South again to make arrangements to obtain commercial rights to the pictures. But tonight, he was going to his home in the North, to Elsie's, to the haven for the homeless, to the blessed gateway to Alicia. There was, oh, so much more to be learned about them all, and, it seemed, about himself.

The Language of Flowers

As soon as Tim got through the door, Elsie was out of the kitchen to put a stop to any chance of his creeping up the stairs, which, in fact, this time he was not contemplating.

"Eeh, ye're a sly 'un, slippin' away like that wi'out a bite ter eat. Come in t' kitchen. I've ter tell ye Fred caught a bad chill yesterday at Netherford, an' 'e's in bed wi' the resident nurse."

Tim was startled by the picture that invaded his mind. "Good heavens!"

Elsie pursed her lips and tutted to herself. "I'm that flustered. Wot I mean is the resident nurse is attendin' ter is needs while 'e's poorly." Then she broke into a laugh at the implication of what she had said. "Poor ol' bloke. 'E'd be little use ter t' nurse in 'is present condition."

Tim smiled back, then asked, "Is he bad? I thought he went a bit quiet as we arrived back here."

Elsie returned to her preparation of the evening meal, nodding to the table. "Sit ye down while I get on wi' things, an' we can catch up."

Tim sat, much readier to exchange information than before. He knew that there would have to be a trade off; the price for his own curiosity would be the news about his visit to Netherfold. His attitude to this struck him as curiously uncharacteristic of himself.

"Aye, well, it's never been like Fred ter rest up wi'out a reason. So, its got ter be summat makin' 'im feel low. I rang 'is place, an they said as 'ow 'e'd caught a chill wot 'ad settled on 'is bronchials. I said, 'ow long will 'e be abed, an' they said they didn't know, but they were keepin' an eye on 'im, continual like, an' they'd let me know if there was any developments."

She stopped chopping and turned to Tim.

"'Ow was 'e, when 'e sloped off, did ye say?"

Tim played it down so as not to worry her. "Oh, he seemed all right, except that he went quiet towards the end of the journey, and then, when we got here, he suddenly went off saying he had to rest, and he'd see you next day."

Elsie ruminated a moment. "It says summat when 'e 'as ter rest. Anyway, the next day,'e didn' come down ter breakfast, an' when they went up ter 'is room, 'e 'ad a temperature an' were glad ter be under t' covers." She spooned some minced meat into a saucepan with an air of finality. "So, any road, that's 'ow we left it."

Tim sensed a greater concern in her delivery than she wished to reveal.

"I expect it's just the long day that's done it. He went for a walk while Alicia showed me her paintings. The air got damp before he returned, so maybe that's it"

"Aye, 'appen." She brightened her tone to shuffle off her worry. "Anyway, enough o' that. About you, now,... wot am I ter tell 'is lordship when I pop in ter see 'im?" She gave him an old-fashioned, maternal proprietary look, challenging him to be evasive if he dare. Tim found he liked the feeling of belonging, and smiled back at her. Elsie was almost taken off guard, but looked away to hide her own smile.

"Today, I met a client that I am going to enjoy supplying. Splendid chap…"

"Aye oop! That might be great ter listen ter, if ye was a mind ter give it yer time. I want t 'ear 'ow ye got on wi' Alicia. Ye got me on about Fred las' time; now it's yower turn to spill the beans."

Spilling the beans would make for a complicated rigmarole, and was the last thing Tim wanted just yet. But, keen to hear the saga of Fred and Elsie, he knew he would have to offer trade to satisfy her thirst for his experience. He could sense her involvement with Alicia, but had yet to understand what that was exactly.

"An' while we're chattin' I'll put the kettle on." She sat opposite him and smoothed her apron on her knees. She looked directly at him and jutted her chin out, claiming undefined rights.

"So what d'you want to know, Elsie?"

She gave a low chuckle. "Eeh! I've got this phrase runnin' roun' me brain, wot ye let slip las' time. 'She's an 'eck of a girl'. Tha's it en't it?"

"She is." Tim nodded. "I think she's very talented."

"Tha's nuthin' we didn't know. The art school raved abowt 'er. She came back wi' prizes and diplomas the len'th of yer arm. I'll bet she never showed ye any o' them, eh?"

"No, she didn't. But I'm not surprised. What is strange is that she stays in an out-of-the-way village, running a café."

"We'll come ter that." She got up as the kettle came to the boil. "Wot I'm out to get ter the bottom of, is 'ow you two got on."

Tim resorted to his public school banter. "Absolutely famously. We had such a lot in common, she being an artist, and me being a dealer in art."

Elsie remained silent as she poured the boiling water and arranged the tea things on the tray. Tim tried to think of some continuation of the conversational line he had adopted, but found her silence impenetrable. When she finally placed the cup before him, he detected a change in her demeanour and expression. When he looked at her, she smiled in a coy, almost evasive way. As she stirred her cup, she gazed into its depths as if a crystal bowl. Finally she spoke in a low tone, with which Tim could never have associated her before.

"I can see ye've a mind ter keep yer feelin's back, lad." She shook her head philosophically. "Maybe it's time ye knew a thing or two abowt me an' Fred. Us destiny were twined like thread in a spinnin'jenny." She looked up and gently reached out to hold Tim's arm. "Did Alicia say owt abowt us?" She peered closely into his eyes to detect the slightest evasion on his part.

"No. Nothing at all," he leapt to assure her, "except…" He halted.

"Wot?" Elsie was on the alert.

"She told me to ask you about Fred. I think she wanted to leave it to you."

She withdrew her hand, and lowered her voice again. "She's a canny lass, is that one." She shot a swift glance at Tim and then cast her eyes down again before adding, "A catch in a million."

Tim attempted to avoid further implications by simply nodding. Elsie sighed.

"That five 'undred pounds wot Fred give Dave an' me were a godsend at' t' time. We put 'alf down on a terrace 'ouse on outskirts o' Grindleford, an' t'other in t' bank fer a rainy day. Dave 'ad a job at a small workshop mendin' farm machinery an' fittin' tractor tyres, an' such. We was 'appy as Larry ter begin wi'."

She paused, searching for a clue.

"I don't know 'ow it were wi' 'im, but 'avin' money in t' bank seemed t' unsettle 'im. 'E didn' seem too 'appy in hisself abowt getting' money from another fella. I put it down ter that, any road. 'Cos, ter cut a long story short, 'e got 'is 'ands on the bank book, an' started treatin' 'is mates at t' pub. I found out jus' afore I was due wi' t baby. 'E'd got through most of it by t' time I found out. I went ter t' bank ter buy baby stuff, an were rocked on me 'eels. When I got back 'ome there were an up-an'-downer." Elsie let out a prolonged vocal sigh, and pursed her lips, philosophically. "In a nutshell, it were down 'ill from there on. Eighteen months later, Dave were gone fro' t' house."

Elsie gathered the crockery and put it on the tray distractedly, as if she were revisiting her memory. Tim felt a wave of sympathy for this life-worn woman, whose story gave rounded flesh to her domestic outline. He was watching an extrovert personality turned to self-absorption.

"That must have been frightful for you."

"It were that. Payments on t' 'ouse, an little Nancy ter feed an' clothe."

She laughed at a private joke. "It were a daft situation, that's fer sure."

"It can't have been funny."

"No. I were laughin' at t' way things 'appen." She laughed again. "It got roun' t' village like wild fire, o' course, an' cross t' whole county. 'Dave Brocklebank 'as left 'ome! Elsie's up t' creek wi'out a paddle!'.

"Did you have to leave your house?"

"That were on t' cards, right enough. Then, out o' t' blue, knock on t' door. Opens it to see breezy smilin' Fred on 't doorstep. 'Heard yer news. Let's talk.' Tea up. Quick chat, an' 'e 'ad t' whole thing worked out." She smiled and shook her head. "It weren't as if I 'ad a choice, when it come down ter it. But, as it goes, it were pretty good."

She sighed, slipping into her own world again. Tim prompted.

"So, what did he propose?"

"Sounds out o' order, when ye come out wi' it. 'E were ter sell 'is 'ouse, wot 'e'd renovated and move in wi' me an' pay t' mortgage. We'd both 'ave a roof over us 'eads, an' young Nancy 'ud be took care of."

Tim's face betrayed his surprise at the thought of Fred and Elsie living togoether.

"Aye, I know wot ye're thinkin'. That's wot the world thought, an' all."

"No. I was just thinking that he saved the day."

"'E did that, awright. " She shook her head in disbelief, as she looked into the past. "An' 'e never asked a thing' fer 'is self." Tim sensed that she said this with some regret.

"Well," she said more brightly, launching into the story, "'e moved in, an' 'e'ad 'is own room an' he stayed more'n fifeen year all told. As it turned out, 'e didn' 'ave ter sell 'is 'ouse. 'E let it out ter a mate o' 'is, while 'e were scrapin' up enough ter lay down on 'is own 'ouse. That paid fer Fred's mortgage, which weren't a fortune, 'im 'avin' got it cheap an' done it up. An' 'e were doin' all right at t' garage in Grindleford, so's ter put money aside fer t'mortgage on *my* 'ouse. 'E said 'e were only payin' me fer rent and board, but 'e'd a' got more 'n that, if 'e'd wanted."

Tim looked a little puzzled, and she smiled roguishly at his naivety.

"I made it clear 'e'd be welcome ter share me bed, but 'e said it were not fer 'im. I were a bit put out ter begin wi', 'cos I were young an' 'e were a nice lookin' fella, an' I 'ad a taste fer it. I ask 'im straight out, 'wot's wrong wi' me?' 'E says, 'nowt'. I say,' Then wot's wrong wi' you?'"

She smiled with reminiscent regret.

"Then he comes out wi' it. 'E says, 'Elsie', 'e says, ' 'ev'ry time I got betwixt the sheets, I'd be seein' the sister o' the man I did fer.' I could see 'is point o' view, o' course. But I says, 'So ye're jes givin' me charity, is it?' An' 'e says, 'Elsie, love, if I were ter choose, ye'd be top o' t' list. But I feel it a favour jes' ter be wi ye'."

Elsie got up and went to the draining board and took a piece of kitchen paper to blow her nose. She kept her back to Tim, while she discreetly recovered herself. Tim was touched and somewhat awed by the confidence that had been placed on him. When she turned round again, she directed a solemn, earnest expression at him, and in a soft and broken voice, said, "Tim, lad, if Alicia's a mind ter take up wi' ye, don't give 'er too much o' yer politeness. Get 'er a ruddy big bunch o' roses an' gather 'er up wi' passion."

As if the emotion had got the better of her, she suddenly threw all her energies into peeling and chopping vegetables at the sink.

"An' now I've ter get on wi' preparin' t' supper. Will we see ye at table, then?"

Tim responded without thinking. "Yes, please." He was obviously dismissed, with still so much of her story with Fred untold. He edged towards the door, keeping his eye on her back, watching her staccato movements as she attacked the vegetables.

"Till later, then," he offered ineffectually.

"Aye," she replied, without turning to him.

He left, feeling he had been appointed a mission, attended by a mood of dissatisfaction with himself. He would be going South tomorrow for a couple of days, in order to secure the rights over pictures that he had chosen with Nathan. There were things that felt unresolved. The very idea of a journey taking him further away from Alicia was anathema, and he felt an overwhelming need to rid himself of feelings of inadequacy. Elsie had mentioned flowers. He knew they had the power to express many emotions, such as grief, sympathy, devotion and gratitude, often speaking more eloquently than words. He would send a large bouquet to Alicia with a card that spoke of....what exactly? Well, he could not leave flowers to imply everything; he would have to send a message with them.

He changed into something comfortable, and left the house for the nearest florist. This turned out to be practically in the centre of the town, requiring him to park the car in a side street and retrace his steps to the one he had noticed as he passed.

An old fashioned bell overhanging the glazed door chimed out as Tim pushed it open, and a young woman of about twenty-four, with a pleasantly attentive face came out of the back, the sleeves of her blouse rolled up, wiping her hands on a towel. Stalk ends clung to her apron, and Tim could see vases full of arranged flowers beyond.

"Can I help?" she asked brightly with an attentive smile.

"I want to send some flowers to a lady," Tim said, without reserve.

"I see. Is it for a special occasion, perhaps?"

"Not particularly."

"Then perhaps she's a special person," she said with calm presumption.

"Definitely," Tim returned without a blink.

"Ah." She paused to voice decorously. "Very special?"

"Absolutely."

"Had you anything in mind?"

"What would you advise?"

"Roses never fail."

"Do they have a perfume?"

"The Pink ones have more smell than then red ones." There was a reservation detectable in her voice,

He interpreted her information. "But the red ones are preferable?"

"Oh, that's not for me to say." She smiled apologetically.

"But you would prefer them?" he insisted.

She compressed her lips, opened her eyes wide and nodded. Then hastily, she protested, "But only you know the person you're buying them for."

"I wish I knew her better." He reflected before taking the leap. "I'll take a dozen red, so long as you can send them."

"Of course. They'll be twenty-three pounds. Is that all right?" He nodded. "I'll put a card with them. Who are they to be sent to and where?"

"To Alicia. The Green Lantern Café, Lower Netherfold."

"Alicia who?"

Tim suddenly realised he had no idea what her surname was. "No,.. urm.. it doesn't matter. Just Alicia will do."

"You're sure?"

"Absolutely. There's only one."

The assistant smiled in an understanding way. Tim braved the smile and held on to an uncharacteristic assertiveness.

She consulted a long list on the wall and ran her finger down it, before turning to him to say, "I see Netherfold is right in the middle of the dales. I'm afraid the delivery'll cost a bit more. We don't have an Interflora shop nearer than twenty miles. Five pounds extra, I'm afraid."

"Fine." He took a deep breath of satisfaction.

"Would you like to choose a card from the rack?"

She pointed to a far corner of the shop, and he went over and chose a card engraved with an emblem of bird perched on two entwined branches. He took it back to her, and she offered the pen and pointed to the counter.

"You can write it out and send it as it is, or we provide a free printed out version in 'Aristocrat', 'Buckingham' or 'Calligrapher' font." She pushed a sheet of examples in front of him. He liked the calligrapher font, as being stylish in the service of a bold statement.

"Right. 'Calligrapher' it is. If you write it down on this piece of paper, we'll print it out on the card you've chosen."

The pen was poised and the mind prepared for boldness. He began slowly.

'A *small token of...*' No! What's a token?! Something you put in a machine, or pay for your mobile with. Keep it simple, for heaven's sake!.. 'This is to say thank you for a... What?! A lovely afternoon?! How pathetic! Do you say 'thank you' to someone you want to make love to? Start again. 'These roses are to say.... What?! Who's saying what?! Roses don't say anything!. They accompany what the lover says from his heart. Well, yes, but flowers touch the heart of the loved one, too, don't they? Otherwise why send them at all? 'I want these roses to tell you that... 'that, if I'm honest, I desperately want to see you again. You've sent me into a spin. I can't stop thinking about you.' He remembered Elsie's warning not to be polite. He looked at the crossed out attempts and, as if mesmerized by his own honest thought, wrote, 'I think I'm in love with you. Next time, I'll know.' It was honest, but not quite right. In the end he wrote simply. 'Here's to our next time. I think I'm in love with you.'

He pushed the paper towards the assistant, got out his cheque book, and began to write out the name of the shop. She picked the paper up, and glancing at it, briefly, let out a short breath of surprise. She looked at Tim, visibly radiating pleasure. "Oh... how lovely!" she whispered.

"Really?" Her reaction was gratifying.

"Aren't you sure, then?"

"I'm sure. But I'm not sure whether she can feel the same way."

"She must. I wish my boyfriend would send me a message like this...just once,.... even if it wasn't true."

"Really?"

"I would fall all over him."

Tim began to blush. She gave a wry smile, as she began to gather the roses together.

"I don't think men send flowers to florists. They think it's coals to Newcastle, or something," she said regretfully. "At least, I hope that's what it is."

On an impulse, he took a red rose from the vase and extended it to her. "Please, have this rose from me. Add it to the bill."

It was perhaps a foolish gesture to a stranger, and the effect of such gallantry can be misinterpreted or evoke emotion that few fellows can cope with, let alone, have the slightest inkling of the consequences. She held the rose for a moment in silence, before looking up at Tim in quiet wonderment, letting a tear well slowly up. To say that Tim was rendered ineffectual is an understatement; he began to shuffle his feet, looking down at the floor.

"So, the full amount is…?" he garbled.

"Twenty-eight pounds,.. including delivery," she murmured softly.

"And the extra rose?"

"I'm sorry. I can't." She sniffed, "It would spoil it all."

"But surely…?"

"I'll keep it in a separate vase."

"You must let me pay, or it won't be a gift."

"You'd just be a customer being nice. I'm going to pretend it's from my lover."

Tim was now seriously disturbed by her emotional display. He cleared his throat and completed the cheque. In the silence that ensued, he gave a nod, turned awkwardly on his heel and edged to the door, keeping her in his peripheral sight. "Thank you for getting that off, then," he said, as nonchalantly as possible.

She nodded without looking at him, as he left the shop.

As he marched back to his car, he experienced a mixture of pathos and elation. He was affected by the idea of a young woman thirsting for her lover's gift of a bouquet, but felt complacent pleasure at the obvious effect his gesture had had on her. He had to admit to himself that it augured well for his next visit to Alicia. But now, he was on his way back to Elsie's and there was bound to be some intrusive questioning at table. He reflected that he did not care half so much as previously, and decided he could engineer himself through the minefield of inquisitors ahead.

He supposed that Fred would, by now, have recovered enough to be there too. But, he was, at least, satisfied that he had prepared the way to Alicia's heart, and that Elsie was unreservedly his ally in the affair.

Running The Gauntlet

As he opened the kitchen door they were already assembled at table, waiting to be served. Alf and Bert, alert, smiling and newly scrubbed down for the evening after a hard day's work, and ready to eat horses. Monty sat at the far end, half turned towards Elsie with hands the size of the plates she extended to him to pass down the line. Fred was conspicuous by his absence.

"Come in fer bein'out!" Elsie exclaimed at the sight of Tim in the doorway. "Not a moment afore time, an' all."

She ladled out large portions of stew, and, no sooner had Tim sat, than Bert was reaching across the table to place his plate in front of him. The bowls of potatoes and greens were the immediate focus of everyone's attention, as they liberally and efficiently helped themselves. Having piled their plates high and cut bread for themselves, they set to with ferocious preoccupation until, gradually, the smacking lips and discreet grunts of pleasure subsided and attention orientated, little by little to Tim, still masticating. They had wiped their plates spotless with bread slices, while he was only two thirds of the way through his meal. He was acutely aware of everyone's silent focused attention. What had, moments ago, been a cacophonous symphony of scraping cutlery and appreciative murmurs, became now a tinkling solo. Tim bravely attempted to block out the staring eyes followed every movement of fork to mouth. In the palpable silence, every time he looked up, he was greeted with a familiar nod. To break the silence, he turned to Elsie and murmured his appreciation of the meal. Elsie nodded her agreement and leant her elbows on the table in stoic patience. Bert and Alf constantly exchanged wise looks and Monty grinned like a child at a Saturday morning children;s cartoon film. Finally, Tim forked the last vestige of the mopped up gravy into his mouth and placed his knife and fork in the middle of his plate.

"Very good indeed." Tim nodded. They all nodded in silent accord, fixing him with the expectation of a wedding party awaiting the groom's speech. It was Bert who took the initiative. He pushed himself back in his chair, and in spoke in a comfortable tone of one who knows he will meet with general approval.

"Well, I'm sure we'd all like to know how things went, Tim. We were all rooting for you."

Yes. Thank you, Bert. Well it was a good day, actually. One of the best and most memorable days I've ever had, actually."

Everyone leant forward and elbowed the table, as if proximity would ease collective deafness.

"Yes," Tim continued, "I think I've met someone who really understands who I am."

"So, ye really got on, then?" Alf prompted.

"Without a doubt," Tim said with unabashed certainty.

"An immediate rapport, then?" Bert said, with a wink directed to the others.

"That about sums it up, Bert, yes," Tim said, in a matter of fact way. Elsie seemed surprised at first, looked askance at Tim and then went quiet.

"So, 'ow did ye leave it? Are ye goin' back again?" Alf asked with undisguised excitement.

"Oh, I think we'll be making a permanent arrangement, without much doubt. We share a lot in common."

"Well, I'll go t'our 'ouse!" exclaimed Alf. "Is it done an' dusted then?!"

"We haven't put our names on a written contract, yet, but that's on the cards."

Bert eyed Tim carefully. "That sounds a bit calculating for someone who's making a lifetime commitment, old son, if you don't mind me saying."

"Oh, I hardly expect it to last a lifetime, Bert. Though,".. - Tim smiled in a concessionary way, - "I'm not saying that's impossible."

Monty, who had been looking closely at each in turn, suddenly spoke up.

"Aye-oop! It's got ter last, or it's awready up t' creek!"

"Good gracious. It's only a business agreement!" Tim looked at each in turn in affected resentment.

Alf's face was clouded with bewilderment and accusation, Bert gazed at Tim as if he were a strange exhibit in the Natural History Museum, and Monty's habitual smile changed to one of glowering disapproval. Elsie, swivelled round on her chair to confront Tim. "Eeh, ye're a slithery customer. We're after findin' out 'ow ye got on wi' Alicia."

"Good heavens! I thought you wanted to know how I got on with the chap in the bookshop."

The three men gestured their disblief and sighed heavily.

"Codswallop!" Elsie barked. "We don't give a brass farthin' fer yer bookshop! What 'appened at

Netherton, is what we're after knowin! An' well, ye know it!"

Tim tried to look amazed, but faced with Elsie's constant scrutiny, he capitulated. There was no chance of fooling her with his evasive chat. And now, all four at the table were on to him.

"Well,…" Tim looked at each of them in turn, reading their thirst for romantic involvement. It recalled days of old when literacy was available to few, and travelling story tellers were invited to entertain round the hearth. He felt a sudden powerful responsibility to satisfy their longing for drama. It was not a tale to be told without embellishment. How much his own deep feelings could be revealed was another matter; they were too personal to share. He would tell them a story.

"Well, I think I can say, it was one of the most life-changing days of my life." The fishes prepared themselves to swallow the bait. "The journey gave an opportunity to appreciate some beautiful scenery. There was one occasion when…."

"Let's leave out t' journey, if ye don't mind, Tim. Ye got there an' ye got out t'car and she came out ter greet ye, right? What did ye think, soon as ye set eyes on 'er?"

"Aye," Alf interrupted, "wus she a looker?"

Bert winced a little and added, "What we mean is, were you struck by her looks."

Tim gave a resigned nod. "She's very pretty. I remarked on that, as soon as she welcomed us."

Monty bounced in his chair and grinned from ear to ear.

"I thought…well, she impressed me, as a strong-minded and yet sensitive woman. She invited us into the kitchen and, straightaway, offered us tea."

"An' Fred left ye together while 'e went on 'is rounds," Elsie urged aggressively, determined to push the story forward.

"Well, yes that's true. How did you know?"

"'Cos 'e said 'e would. Anyway 'e alus goes on 'is own. So..?"

"We sat first to have a nice cup of tea in the café."

Elsie groaned, and the others looked as if taking tea was a heinous crime.

"Then afterwards, Alicia invited me to inspect her art. She took me over to her studio." All their eyes lit up again as they leant forward. "and her paintings were wonderful, figures journeying through splendid scenery, as good as I've ever seen in modern art. I remarked to her on the message they seemed to be sending."

"After t' paintings? What then?" Elsie asked in an exasperated tone. "Were t' whole time spent chattin' 'bowt paintin's?"

"Er, no,..we talked of.. other things."

"Such as?" Elsie started tapping the table with her forefinger. "What did she say abowt you an' 'er?"

"Well, I think that's a bit private, don't you, Elsie." Tim was about to adopt an expression of hurt sensibility, but Elsie launched in.

"Don't be ridiculous! This is t' family we're talkin' 'bowt! An', anyway, d'ye think we don't know wot was set up ter 'appen?! 'Course we do! Wot we want ter know is 'ow it went!" She thumped the table during the last words.

Tim looked round and was left in do doubt that not only was everyone aware that Fred had taken him to meet Alicia, but was wholly aware of the scheme to get Alicia and him married off to each other. Nothing was under wraps, it seemed.

Bert took the initiative in a remarkable fashion, and with an unexpected diplomacy, possibly learned over years of professional duplicity.

"You see, old son, we actually care about the outcome, because we take a brotherly and sisterly interest in you." His expression was of earnest concern for his welfare. It had the tones of a doctor, earnestly involved in his patient's welfare, and asking him to persevere with unpalatable medicine. Tim thought how good he must have been as a con man. But on the other hand, in a funny way, they all did really seem to care. His story was big in their eyes, and they had placed him in the centre of their lives. Also, in the last couple of days, he had, subconsciously, grown strangely fond of them to the point at which he now felt a reluctance to disappoint them. It wasn't as if he had found anything distasteful in Fred's intention; he would have probably fallen in love with Alicia, even without the unsubtle scheming. He looked at Bert, who raised his eyebrows to suggest the reasonableness of his case, at Alf, who pursed his lips and shrugged, at Monty who returned a tobacco-stained half-smile, and finally at Elsie, who had that calm determined look in her eyes.

"All right! I'd better come out with it."

Everyone eased forward like a tide coming over the sands.

"Right away, I can say, Alicia is the most wonderful girl I have ever met."

A second later they erupted into exultant appreciation of the confirmation they had hoped for. The whoops of happiness and the shared delight was overwhelming. Elsie clutched his arm and squeezed it with a fervour he had never thought possible of her. Bert kept nodding at him, smiling like a toy dog in the back window of a car. Alf slapped Bert on the back as if it was all his responsibility, and Monty kept jerking himself up and down in his chair. It was a moment of unconfined joy, which took Tim completely by surprise. He did not feel it an exaggeration to believe he was experiencing, for the first time, the love of a family that desired the very best for him. It was a moment in which he felt cherished and adopted beyond any reasonable explanation, and, as he looked round, he felt emotionally humbled. He felt that somehow, they were expressing something that released feelings in him unknown before. He smiled first, and then, as they laughed at their happiness, he began to laugh also, until, for no reason that immediately came to mind, tears of joy began to flow. Later, Tim was to explain it as hysterical relief that his inhibition had been wiped away and the folly of pretended indifference made manifest.

"Eeh, at last we've got t' blood out' o' t' stone!"

"I think that says it all. 'The most wonderful girl, I've ever met'," Bert repeated.

"Well, it's not as if I've met that many, in my time," Tim felt it necessary to add.

" 'Ey, don't spoil it!" Alf objected.

"No," Tim immediately responded. "I only meant, well,.. that, I'm all the more fortunate to meet her."

" 'Blessed'," corrected Elsie. "I'll tell yer wot, young Tim, this'll buck Fred up no end. I can't wait till I tell 'im, when I go down there t'morrer afternoon." Her face lit up. "Aye-oop, ye can come wi' me an' tell 'im yersel'!"

Tim shook his head. "Sorry, Elsie, I can't. I'm off to Surrey again on business, tomorrow."

Everyone stopped smiling. "Fer 'ow long, then?" Elsie asked.

"Just two days. I'll be back by the end of the week."

"That's considered a fair time away for someone who, we take it, is enamoured of a young lady." Bert sounded like a pretentious marriage counsellor, and Alf and Monty looked unconvinced. "I mean," he continued, "it's not good to leave things too long."

Tim smiled at Bert's attempt to offer avuncular advice, and was grateful he could say, "I've sent Alicia flowers."

Elsie beamed, and everyone made noises of approval. Bert nodded again as if Tim had just got the answer right in a quiz programme.

"Right, now then!" Elsie proclaimed, "It's on'y right ter cover this wi' Jesus. If ye'll jus' bow yer 'eads, I'll say a few words on our be'alf."

The men all obediently bowed their heads and closed their eyes. Tim hesitated, but under the supervisory eye of Elsie, quickly followed their example.

"Now, Jesus, as ye will 'ave 'eard, Tim's made a proper confession of 'is amorous inclinations to our Alicia. Now's the time fer 'im ter take on board t'importance o' keepin' in constant touch wi' Ye ter get 'is progress reports. 'Cos, when all's said, there's nowt ter be took fer granted in such matters. So, I ask ye ter keep remindin' Tim to check in, so's not ter lose yer 'eaven sent blessin' in respect o' their amorous intentions. An' I ask ye to 'elp 'im ter know that wi'out yer blessin' nowt lastin' can come out o' it. Amen."

Everyone repeated 'amen', and then, with the business of the day completed, Elsie announced that there was an apple pie in the oven waiting to be served. She got up from her seat and went to get it out, while each, in his own way, declared himself to be the luckiest person in the world to have landed in her culinary oasis. The pie was scrumptious and they now veered away from Tim's affairs and talked of their own day with satisfaction.

That night, as they lay in bed, Bert was generous enough to give Tim some valuable advice on how to handle women; lessons, if he was to be believed, he had learned from his own wide experience. It included among other things a clear warning not to be over scrupulous in telling the truth in all matters, and especially when it came to making reference to the loved one's appearance. "Just remember, dear fellow, whatever she looks like, she is always 'lovely'. Well meant intention to advise her about her appearance will never go down well. You remember that, and you'll be fine, especially if she's a good looking girl, because she'll easily believe you."

It was to Bert's droning admonition that Tim fell asleep, secure in the belief that he was embarking on the adventure of a lifetime.

Out of Need Comes......

As Tim left the house the following morning, after a full breakfast, that Elsie insisted on, to combat the fatigue of the journey to that foreign country, 'the South', he felt as if the only foreign country he was entering that day was his own turbulent mind. His thoughts were bouncing back and forth between the world of art, love and dramatic revelation. He was elated by the new ideas implanted by Nathan, the call of an amorous relationship with a delightful woman and the challenge thrown down at his feet by what Elsie had revealed about her life with Fred. In each area, he had learned so much, and the more he discovered, the more he knew how much more there was to learn. In the world of art, where he had based his appraisals on the dictates of traditional values, he was suddenly compelled to explore on a much more personal level. Nathan had presented art as a religion to him. Paintings were so personal to Nathan that he almost left the world behind and climbed into the canvas. Tim had always had strong feelings about paintings, but they had somehow always emerged from his instructed knowledge of art. One wild enthusiastic afternoon with Nathan had taught him that looking at paintings was an act of re-creation. He couldn't wait to return and enter that world again with his free-wheeling, child-like book-seller

And then, there was Alicia. Her phrase kept echoing,. 'What you believe about art is based on what you believe about life.' Fine. But then on what do you base your life? Surely, you base it on where you decide to start the internal debate, - where you decide everything starts from, doesn't it?. Either the whole truth is what your senses inform you of, or you seek a faith in something beyond. The Renaissance painter saw nature as the second Bible, providing proof of divine ordinance. But, even so, to believe you were seeing something better than a mere shape of beauty, you had to make a leap of faith beyond the senses. That seemed to echo Fred's insistence that you have to be on the outside looking in? - because 'looking out', or relying on the senses, ultimately stands in the way of faith? But what started Fred on his….?

As he careered along, deep in such thoughts, Tim had to remind himself, from time to time, that he was in charge of a high-powered vehicle, that was very unforgiving to an absent mind. Half way down the motorway, he felt it advisable to pull in at a service station for a coffee and a Swedish pastry. He sat at a window seat, watching the files of motorists and passengers moving through the doors, to form obedient queues slowly inching forward on the retail belts, as on moving belts of time, itself. He recalled a picture of the mythological sister Fates; Lachesis deciding the role and status of each earthly soul, Clotho spinning the coloured threads of its life, and Atropos, measuring out the longevity and snipping the threads off with her dreaded scissors. That was the finality with which the Greeks viewed life. While Tim had tolerated Lachesis and Atropos, he shied away from the idea of Clotho deciding the shape and colour of one's life. It implied the futility of personal desire. But, how does that kind of beginning and end, give any value to wanting anything at all? Was it a purposeless exercise, fuelling in one moment the ability to open up the possibility of the next? Was it a conveyor belt of cause and effect only brought to a stop when the power to make any decision was taken away? Or was there a higher purpose? Was there something else round the corner, as in Alicia's paintings of figures making for indefinable possibilities? Perhaps that was what faith provided: release from merely serving the moment. It occurred to Tim that living *for* the moment prevented you from properly living *in* the moment. Maybe, seen from the viewpoint of the believer in something beyond, a moment is timeless. Maybe what faith gives you is not a driven desire to serve the moment, but access to a state that already exists within you. That seemed, on reflection, to be what motivated Alicia; - and Fred, if he thought about it. Personal desire did not seem to control either of them, and they cared little for what the world thought of them. They were motivated by the needs of something outside themselves, seen from inside. Put baldly, they were living a life that did not wholly belong to them. Then to whom? How had Fred come to believe in Jesus? Was he living out guilt for the crime he had committed? That seemed unlikely in view of the energy that Fred expended with such zest, and the confidence with which he exercised it. And Alicia, who now seemed the most desirable but hardly attainable person in his life, offered the challenge of a new vision. How could he reach her without taking up that challenge? How was he to do that? He would have to do it, whether feasible or not. Alicia had invited him to take the challenge, and that was all that mattered to him.

Refreshment consumed, Tim was on the road again. The way ahead was straight as a die and the engine as smooth and purring as a kitten on a lap, the sky static and washed with acrylic grey, reflecting nothing.

"Well, Jesus," he thought, "here we are again, but this time on strong recommendation. I'm not sure what I'm doing here, or whether you're even listening. But you are obviously real to the people I am learning to care about, and especially Alicia, the woman I'm losing my heart to, so I'm starting the ball rolling again. Over to you."

"All right. But, keep your eye on the road, or there might be a closer and earlier proof than you look for. So, then, why have you come back for this chat?"

"You once said I'd never asked you for anything. I can't deny that, I suppose. But then, it's not easy asking something of someone you're not sure is there?"

"True. So, how do you feel about that, now, Tim?"

"We-e-ell, I think something has happened that changes my perspective a bit. There is a strong inclination to believe in you, motivated by wanting a life with someone who has no doubt about you at all."

"Well, that's a start."

"It might mean I'm creating you in my mind just in order to reach the woman I love."

"Yes, that's possible. It could work that way. It sometimes does. My followers witness to me, so I am not in the least surprised if people approach me through becoming close to others. Any which way you like is my way of things. I allow the mustard seed of faith to germinate where it will."

"You mean, because I see faith in others, I think it'll work for me?"

"Not quite. But seeing me in others can create a void, which makes you want what they have. And, - if you must know, - falling in love can often do it. It's one of the things I thoroughly endorse. "

"Your seal of approval, so to speak?"

"Absolutely. One thing that brings people closer to me is the knowledge, - often surprising to them, - that I am constantly in love."

"You mean, falling in love is reflecting what you do?"

"If you like."

"We are talking about the same thing, are we? I mean, I want to possess Alicia in every way, you know, physically as well as emotionally."

"Of course. You want to possess her, as I want to possess her because of who she is. You love her for who she is, and so do I."

"She's perfect, isn't she?" Tim thought indulgently.

"No. She isn't. But that isn't the reason for loving anyone, anyway. You love her because she showed love to you, not because she's perfect. Anyone who thinks his beloved is perfect is suffering from romantic delusions."

"Why do you love her, then?"

"That's an irrelevant question. I don't love 'because of', or even despite anything. I just do. But I am specially pleased when someone *wants* to be perfect for me, just as, if all goes well, she will want to please you. That is why you will love her. Not because she's perfect, but because, for you, she will want to be."

"So we'll be sharing her?"

"Oh, yes."

"We'll each have a part of her, then"

"No we'll each have all of her. But the more you surrender her to me, the more she will be yours."

"I don't understand that."

"Look at it this way, and be kind to yourself. Since she has already given herself to me, you don't have an option but to share. But by freely letting her be mine with you, you will be letting her be herself. And, if you give yourself to me, you will be closer to her by being yourself. "

"That begins to sound rather like a contract."

"It's much more binding than that. It's a covenant, and we both solemnly agree not to break it."

"No going back, once entered into?"

"Not on my part. Hopefully not on yours. But the price for doing so will not be visited on you by me; it will be on your own head and in your own heart. But, just think what strong ground you will be on."

Tim thought hard on that, and his desire for Alicia convinced him that it was a path he had to walk down. That he wanted to possess her was indisputable, but how did his love of her equate with Jesus's sort of love? Tim wanted to make love to her? Jesus' possession could not involve anything carnal. They could both see her as a part of beautiful creation? He compared her to a wonderful painting he would stand in front of for ever. But, she was more than beautiful in the conventional sense; she was an awesome mysterious 'other', that challenged him to complement her. It would be futile to worship her. Alicia would insist on approaching each other from both ends of a level playing field. That was the challenge. She had asked him to come back with faith in himself, and that was what he most craved.

"Jesus, are you still around?"

"Right with you, Tim."

"I think I've found what I want to ask you for."

"Go on."

"Can you give me some confidence in myself?"

"*Some* confidence? Why stint yourself. You couldn't have asked me for anything better. It's what I yearn to give everyone, - the freedom to be entirely themselves."

"Warts and all?"

"So long as they recognise they've got them."

"But I thought you wanted everyone to be perfect."

"Yes, I know what you're referring to. 'Be perfect even as I am'. Let me ask you a question. Do you think you ever could be perfect?"

"Not in a million years!"

"Good. That's out of the way. Do you think you should try to be?"

Tim mused on the idea before reluctantly replying, "Yes."

"Rather took your time about it, didn't you?"

"Sorry."

"Accepted."

"So, you just want us to try to be perfect?"

"If you're looking for confidence, there's no better position to be in. But there's one thing even better."

"Yes?"

"Wanting the best for others."

"Everyone?"

"Why not?"

"That's a tall order, isn't it?"

"I never said it was easy."

"But easy to want for Alicia."

"Of course. That should give you confidence, as nothing else could. If you stop thinking about the happiness you want from her and concentrate on the happiness you can give to her, you'll be entirely yourself. And when you know yourself, you need never fear anything."

"Thank you,... Jesus,...if you're there."

"You're welcome... And trust me. I am."

As he arrived in more familiar southern surroundings, he decided that, next time he stood before Alicia, he would see her as he saw a lovely painting that he wanted to own and enter into, like Nathan climbing into a picture. He would overcome fear of rejection by thinking only of her. He remembered the flowers he had sent and the message with them. Would they melt her heart or would they seem sentimental to her? The urge to see her again invaded him. He needed to show her that the flowers and the less than passionate message were no more than a shadowy metaphor of his real feelings. But, in a strange, inexplicable way, he imagined for the first time that he might not be going to see her alone.

The Full Gamut

In the evening, two days later, Tim drew up outside Elsie's house and let himself in. He walked to the kitchen door and rapped on the panel. There was no answer, and the conspicuous silence told him the house was empty. He went upstairs and put his suitcase on the bed. This was ordinarily the time that Elsie would be in the kitchen preparing a meal for everyone. Since she was such a creature of habit, he had to conclude that something unusual had detracted her from her regime, for she had offered to have supper ready for him when he returned. Having mused on this, he decided that the only thing to do was to eat out, and leave a message in the kitchen for Elsie to find when she got in. He hastily scribbled a note, and, having got his coat on, went downstairs again and entered the kitchen. About to place the message on the table, he noticed that there was already one there. It was addressed to him and read as follows;

"Tim, this is just to let you know as how me and the lads has been called down to see Fred Because He has been took extra poorly. He had the home call us because he wanted cheering up, so we took him some flowers and a slab of parkin. We wiill be back later. Make youself a cup of tea. Regards,

Elsie'.

The reason for everyone's absence having been cleared up, Tim decided he would go to a little pizza place this side of town, and come back about nine o'clock, to hear how Fred was getting on. More importantly, he had to post a letter to Alicia, asking her if he could visit her in the next week. He had put a huge amount of thought into the letter. He had never written to a woman he was in love with before, but, more importantly, he found it difficult to capture the tone which expressed enthusiasm without importunity, a declaration of his feelings without effusion. He had agonised for some time over the persona that he wanted to present, and was far from sure that he had got it right. But send it he would, before his nerves gave way and he chickened out. He had already begun rehearsing what he intended to say when they stood face to face. He had audibly repeated his script several times over while he was driving up North, and, in the service station on the motorway, he had attracted strange looks from nearby customers, when he muttered over his coffee and doughnut. At one point he considered writing himself a script that he could memorise, to give himself the appearance of fluent sincerity. But, in the end, fearing that he might suddenly dry up during the rendition, he decided to opt for memorising cue words, aiding him to make what would seem his impromptu declaration. But he could not disguise from himself how contrived, and pre-emptive it was, not to mention illustrative of his insecurity. He found himself asking, - or was it pretending to ask, - invisible Jesus for some moral support. As he sat munching his pizza in the 'parlour', he began to mentally review his cue words and run them before his theoretical Jesus for approval.

'Love's growth through absence'…. 'Gestation'….. 'Beyond comprehension'…. 'Combination of beauty and talent'… 'Meeting of minds'…. 'Compatibility' ..

The ham, mushroom and pepper 'special' stared up at him from the plate, and he sighed.

"Don't you think they're just a bit prosaic?" Jesus asked. "Are true feelings that straightforward?"

"Well, the trouble is, I'm not a poet."

"You might be, if you didn't try so hard. Why don't you let your heart feel what it wants, instead of wrenching explanation from your conscious mind?"

"How do you do that?"

"Relax and let the words come to you."

"They might not."

"Then think of your favourite painting, or remember a favourite piece of music."

"I can't do that when I'm face to face with Alicia! I'm just afraid of being tongue-tied."

"Reflect for a moment. What does being tongue-tied come down to?"

"Not being able to say anything at all."

"Another word for it is 'silence'. Given a chance, it can often say much more, when the mouth gives the message over to the eyes."

"I'm just afraid that deafening silence will be seen as stupidity."

"Look, you had a good thought the other day in the car. You realised that you can't live *in* the moment if you're living *for* it. That was a moment of true enlightenment. Maybe it came from me. Have you thought of that? It came unbidden, didn't it? So, why don't you stop rehearsing? In the end it doesn't bring you true feeling; the heart doesn't want love explained. It's much wiser in the matter of love than the mind. It trusts without knowing. That's what you must do. Take courage from just being in love."

"You're right, Jesus. I'm being a coward, aren't I? Dying many deaths before I die."

"Oh, come.now! Really! You're so dramatic!"

Tim laughed into his pizza.

"That's better," Jesus said with a chuckle. "Now enjoy the rest of your meal, and leave till tomorrow what belongs to it."

As Tim drove back to Elsie's he did have to admit that he was feeling more confident, though still retaining the equivalent of stage fright. He let himself in with his key again, and this time, he heard subdued voices from the kitchen. He knocked on the door and opened it to find Elsie and her 'tenants' seated in sombre mood staring disinterestedly up at him. He was surprised by their mood, and quite alarmed when they all looked away in unison. He must have looked confused, thinking that, possibly, he was the unwitting cause of their disapproval, for Elsie waved him forward and said, "Come in, Tim, lad, and sit ye down. Ye'll not 'ave 'eard, but it's not good."

The three men nodded and shook their heads.

"Aye," Bert exhaled in an interminable sigh.

"What's happened?" Tim enquired, trying to gauge the seriousness from their expressions, as he sat himself down next to Elsie..

"Fred's gone an' done 'fer 'isself?" Alf said, with a voice of doom.

"What?!" Tim, with chilling images suddenly engulfing his mind, reacted with such uncharacteristic violence, that they all looked at him for a second or two in silence.

"It's that trapsin' roun' t' village wot done it," Elsie said lugubriously. "'E will go rootin' out t' past, every time 'e goes back there. An' it never does 'im owt good."

"What's happened?" Tim hardly dared to conjecture."

"'E's got 'isself chilled ter t' bone," Elsie pronounced with a mixture of doom and rebuke.

"But, is it just a chill?" Tim asked, frowning. "I mean, a few days in bed with hot soup and medicine, and he'll be fine,… won't he?"

There was silence. Monty stared unseeingly, nodding almost imperceptibly, first at one corner of the room and then another, as if he was communicating his anxiety to unseen ghosts. Every time his eyes met Alf's or Bert's they would hoist their eyebrows up to the ceiling in recognition of the inevitable course of inscrutable fate.

"It's worse n'than that," Elsie said. "It's on 'is chest an' lungs. E's breathin' bad and don't take 'is food."

"I'm terribly sorry." Tim spoke in subdued tones. "But they let you see him, anyway?"

Elsie nodded.

"So perhaps I could visit him, too?"

"Great 'eavens, no! 'E's ter 'ave complete rest and solitude the while. 'E weren't good to look at, I can tell ye."

"But, I'm sure the doctors'll put him right," Tim offered as encouragement. "They do wonderful things these days with anti-biotics."

"Aye, well, that's as may be. It's all in t' mind o' t' patient as lies t' cure, an' if Fred 'asn't got t' heart fer it, it'll be all up wi' 'im."

"Oh, but surely he can't be as bad as all that."

Elsie kept silent, but stared at the table in deep contemplation of the worst possibilities.

"Bert?" Tim addressed himself to perhaps the one who would give the least fatalistic opinion.

"It's bad, Tim. He didn't look at all chipper, and that's a fact. There was no fight left in him. He wasn't the same man, when we left."

"Tim." Elsie turned her face to him, suddenly aged by premonition. "I think ye've ter go an' fetch Alicia. It's maybe t' one thing as 'll give 'im t'strength ter carry on. Can ye do that fer 'im?"

Tim looked back at her and while eager to make contact with Alicia, thought it unfortunate that it was prompted by such circumstances. In any case, he was not sure they were not being over-dramatic. He could not imagine Fred being defeatist about his own illness. He would fight to recover his health with all the conviction that his faith brought with it.

"Can ye do that?" she repeated in a tone that implied that only the hardened heart of a Victorian landlord evicting a single mother with a babe in her arms from a rented hovel could refuse. Tim had intended to go to see Nathan with news of the pictures he had procured, but, in the face of such pleading, he could hardly refuse.

"Of course. I'll go first thing in the morning"

Elsie applied an even more mournful expression. "It 'ud be better t'night, lad."

He stared at her in disbelief. "But it's after nine! I wouldn't get there till after eleven, and it would be too late to bring her back tonight."

"No, but ye could stay over an' bring 'er back tomorrer," she said in a voice that implied the sweet reasonableness of her suggestion. She widened her eyes in supplication. "Couldn't ye?"

Tim swallowed hard and thought of a thousand objections. He settled on, "She'll not be expecting me" as an argument that would satisfy most people.

"She'll bless ye fer it, Tim. She'll bless ye, I know she will."

Monty boomed out with, "She'll bless ye, an' so will Fred an' all."

Tim was suddenly aware that he rarely saw Monty without a smile, and this did seem to give the situation some authentic gravity.

"Well, at least can you contact her to let her know I'm coming?"

Elsie jumped up out of her chair and made for the phone in the hallway. "I've got 't'address of 'er neighbour, three doors away. She'll let 'er know."

"Doesn't she have a phone of her own?" Tim asked.

"No. Not in t' winter season. There no call fer it when she shuts t'café up. You get off soon as ye like an' I'll tell 'em ye're on yer way."

Tim got up, went upstairs to get his suitcase, fortunately still unpacked and found himself making once again for his car, throwing his things into it and starting it up, earnestly hoping that he would remember the way Fred had directed him last time. It was night, and nothing looked the same in the dark.

He was concerned about Fred. The collective anxiety had ignited feelings in him that he realised went deeper than he had imagined possible. What effect would all this have on Alicia, when she heard? Well, at least he could dispense with all that script. This message took precedence over any personal romantic notions. Concentrate on the road! Yes, otherwise he could end up in the middle of nowhere.

He used his full headlights as often as he could, which, as he got further out of town, was made possible by the thinning of the traffic. Finding the main road out of town proved easier than he remembered, but he had to give full concentration as he drove further into the countryside. He slowed down to a crawl passing several lanes off to the right, for fear of missing the all-important turning. Being on a double carriageway, made it difficult to see turnings from the slow lane, so it was with greatest relief, that, at last, he recognised the one he sought; the one he had so nearly overshot when he was with Fred.

Once on the narrow winding road that led up to the fells, he felt more confident, and his thoughts focused more on Alicia, Fred, Elsie and all their adopted 'family'. It struck him that he had been adopted, too. But, whereas Monty, Bert and Alf had been adopted for altruistic reasons, it was not so obvious why they had adopted him,... unless....(and here he hesitated to believe it possible) they had ear-marked him as a candidate in the Alicia marriage stakes at an early date. His response to the whole idea was ambivalent. He partly resented such manipulation, which gave their kindness an ulterior motive, and partly he felt honoured to have been chosen for such a wonderful prize, if only he could deserve her. When his thoughts dwelt on their relationship, Tim was very conscious that Elsie had only told half the story. There was something binding them together closer than just the early history in Lower Netherfold, which intrigued him. Just what was Fred's connection with Alicia? Why did she call him 'Uncle Fred'? He had seen how attached she was to him, and now, it appeared she was crucially important to him in his supposed critical state, if he was to believe Elsie.

He came abreast of the pull-in where he had stood with Fred overlooking the valley and where Fred had restored the engine to life. (Or are we really saying it was you, Jesus?), and he had had his first real contretemps with him. He slowed down briefly to register the place and consider how unimportant their altercation really was. The fact that Alicia shared the same faith as Fred seemed to give greater credibility to the idea of a minor miracle. The even greater miracle was that he had met a woman who possessed his thoughts in a way no-one had ever done before. She was a miracle in herself, hidden away in the middle of nowhere, with a talent that ought to be seen, but with no greater ambition than to be true to herself and to create art without any view to marketing it. He remembered Fred asking her if she 'prospered'. Well, if she did, it was not from what she took from the world.

He continued on down the last narrow snaking lane to the valley, where Lower Nertherfold's tiny streets snuggled together to protect themselves from modernity. His heart beat faster as he approached the turning into the Green Lantern car park at the side of the café. There were no lights on, and he assumed that Alicia must be somewhere in the rear of the building. He drew up and extinguished the headlights. The silence was tangible, as he got out of the car. He pressed the door shut for fear of intruding on the dark peacefulness, which closed in like a womb. He had to proceed with care towards the barely perceptible outline of the building and the rear door. There were no lights to offer any kind of welcome, and the silence was intimidating He groped his way to the handle of the door and tapped lightly on the glass pane. A few seconds passed before he rapped a little harder. Silence. This time he banged hard against the glass, wincing as the noise echoed round. Something akin to panic began to overtake him, as the deafening silence yelled at him. Then suddenly a light appeared in the recesses of the house, and he felt the same relief as the beseiged of Mafeking must have felt. Another light in the hallway was illuminated, and he discerned the figure of Alicia, gathering a robe around her, a she approached the back door. She stepped down into the kitchen and put the light on, peering towards him through the glass. Her lovely face, framed by her tousled hair, made him breathless for a second. Her eyelids were heavy, and she needed some moments to take in the image of Tim that impinged itself on her. When she fully comprehended, she unlocked the door with a huge question mark spread across her brow. Tim knew instantly she had not been contacted by the neighbour as Elsie had promised.

"Tim? What on earth are you doing her at this time of night?!"

Tim was thrown by the fact that she could know nothing. "I…came, because.."

"Oh, come in, come in, you dear boy. I'll put the kettle on." She ushered him in and closed the door. For a moment she looked fixedly at him and wiped sleep from her eye. "Take a chair."

"Thank you." He sat, trying to accommodate his understanding of her ignorance with the violent feelings he was undergoing. More than anything, he wanted to take her in his arms, and tell her everything the flowers had not, but with such a message as he carried, it felt grossly inappropriate. His news stood in the way of intimacy.

"I woke you up?" he asked apologetically.

"Well it is half past eleven, and I usually go to bed about ten o'clock, unless I'm burning the midnight oil in the workshop."

"I'm sorry," he grunted.

"Oh, I'm delighted to see you. I'd be even more delighted if you hadn't arrived in the dark, and I wasn't in a deep sleep."

She sat opposite, agonisingly untouchable, and now he had to tell her what had really brought him here.

"Are you being wonderfully impetuous?" she asked with that gently ironic smile playing on her lips.

"I...er,.. I intended to come and see you tomorrow,.. if things had been different."

"Oh, I see. Well no, I don't, really. I thought the flowers were lovely, by the way. "

He looked sheepish for a moment, before murmuring, "And the message?"

"It left room for some speculation – but it touched me. Has anything changed?"

She had that slightly ironic smile again, and it took him some time to realise that there was a real question there. The irony slipped away. He swallowing hard.

"Oh, God! I'm no good at this!" he muttered. "I wanted to say it differently...to tell you that I fell in love with you. The flowers were a clumsy way of covering up for lack of courage."

She smiled at his honesty. "Tim, are you sure you aren't succumbing to suggestibility. If I hadn't told you about Fred's purpose in bringing you here, would you still think you were in love with me?"

"Ah, ..so you don't feel the same." He gazed down at the table, looking as if he were leading troops out of defeat.

"Silly boy, I cherished those flowers; they said all that needed to be said."

She stood, preparing to come round to him. He held up his hand, leapt to his feet and uttered, "Don't move!"

She was alarmed, at first by his outburst, but gradually relaxed as he came slowly round the table, his mouth twitching at one corner. They held each other's gaze as he approached her until he finally stood before her, and she searched his intention and her imaginings. She remained immobile but alive, as he extended his hand and brushed her cheek, as if he were testing the texture of a work of art. He cupped her face, and watched her head incline towards it, which made him draw in breath. A slow motion dance followed; arms entwined and contours embedded themselves in each other, and most sublime, the encounter of breath and lips, seeking possessive intimacy. Her mouth was open and as he kissed her, her tongue moved gently on his. An instinctual compulsion to possess her took him over, and he aggressively crushed her lips with his, as they tasted each other's need. He felt as if he might swoon at the tangibility of what, minutes before, had seemed so distant. They remained submerged in surrender, until, like revellers filled with potent wine, they leant back in drunkenness, to gaze at the vessels from which they had drunk their fill. He was powerfully aroused by her look of gratification and surprise, but, as they took each other's face in, he also read her desire for something all embracing. It wasn't reserve, - far from it, - but it contained a need for total commitment. He intuitively understood their ecstatic kiss was precursor to something sacred; a sensual metaphor for a union yet to be understood.

The kettle started to whistle on the hob, and she slowly withdrew her body from his, and returned silently to the mundane task of spooning tea and pouring water into the pot, transferring milk from carton to jug. Every simple motion was translated into a poetic expression of a potentially sacred bond. Silence turned to an admission that words were inadequate and inappropriate.

She poured the tea, gave one to him and he returned to the other side of the table. They sat, letting the silence flow over them. She placed her elbows on the table and cupped her face with one hand, as she studied him. He smiled back at her with the suppressed exultation of a card player with a full house. She basked in his pleased look, and leant back with that slight ironic twist to her mouth, as if she were about to put finishing touches to a painting. .

"That was a lovely surprise," she murmured thoughtfully, expressing contentment more than excitement, as if, already, she were searching a perspective on her own emotion.

"I rather took myself by surprise." He was still smiling, but there was also a passionate need to amplify his feelings, to make clearer their intensity.

"I wish my flowers could have let you know what I feel."

"You dear sweet boy, you're too afraid of being hurt. Considering we'd only met once, your message was above and beyond the call of what could be expected. I thought it was lovely. I suspected, from the first, that you're a romantic. It makes for timidity."

"Is that how you see me?"

"That's not the right word. You were a little self-protective, perhaps. But now you've driven over the hills like a knight on his charger in the dark to make love to me. That's a brave move."

Suddenly Tim remembered why he had come and was painfully uncomfortable. How would she see his advances when she learned what he had come to tell her? In his sudden passionate need to reveal his love for her he had neglected to tell her of Fred's condition. Would she think him insensitive? He had to take the bit between his teeth.

"Alicia?" He was startled by the thought he had never called her by her name before.

"Tim?" Again that half ironic smile, basking in their new intimacy.

"You didn't get a message from your neighbour?"

"I'm sorry?" She shook her head in some bewilderment at the sudden diversion.

"A message…from a neighbour."

"Here in Netherton?"

He nodded.

"No. When?"

"Elsie said she'd ring a neighbour here to tell you I was coming. Look, I'm sorry, but…" He winced, recoiling from what he had to tell her, "…. I came to bring you news of your uncle."

"What news?" Her face instantly clouded with concern.

"No, don't get upset, please…. it's all right, I think,.. but he caught a chill when he came here the other day, and it's laid him low. He's resting up in the home."

Alicia frowned, withdrawing into herself and scrutinising Tim with an impersonality, that alarmed him.

"Ah, … not so spontaneous, then," she said, quietly

"No! Wait. I would have come soon, anyway. It's just that Elsie wanted you to know earlier. So my reason for coming has nothing to do with how I feel… well, no, I mean, yes, I suppose it does. But my feelings for you are separate from.... Look, you can hardly imagine I'd drive over at this time of night if I didn't care about... " He took a breath. "Alicia, I'm in love with you."

"You only came out of love for me?" she challenged.

He shook his head, straining again to get it right. "Not put like that, of course. I did it for everyone, Elsie, Fred and the others, as well as you."

To Tim's relief, she relaxed, and he seemed to have said the right thing.

"Did *you* see him?"

"I only just got back from Surrey tonight. But, in any case, they didn't want me to."

"Elsie asked you to come straight over?"

"Yes." Tim shrugged.

Her voice softened and she gazed at him, recognising his commitment and generous spirit. "Thank you, Tim." He watched her mood shift. She frowned in a vulnerable and dependent way that Tim had not seen before. It filled him with a desire to protect her.

"Is he very ill?" she asked reluctantly.

He wanted desperately to enfold her in his arms, not only with passion, but with protection. "Elsie thinks you should be there."

"Do *you* think so?"

"I think it would be good. I think they all need you."

"It's too late, tonight."

"I'll take you first thing."

"So, you stay here tonight."

He smiled wryly. "I was rather depending on it. It's all right, isn't it?"

She reached over the table for his hand. "Tim, you make me smile. You're my gentleman beau."

He felt tears of relief stinging the back of his eyes, now that she was reconciled to his news. "I'll be anything you want me to be."

"A little extreme, isn't it? It sounds as if you're making a vow."

"I am."

"You're ready to do that, already?" She cocked her head to one side and took him in.

"If you'd let me."

"Dear Tim, I'm very tempted, but Fred used to say, 'never make promises under the influence of drink or strain'. We're both tired, and we must go to bed, me in my bed upstairs and you on the parlour settee."

"Of course. Thank you." Tim nodded in his 'gentleman' role.

She shook her head in pretended reproof. "You don't have to be enthusiastic about the arrangement, or pretend you're not open to temptation. I'm presuming you would like to share my bed."

Tim emitted a laugh of embarrassed pleasure. She smiled back at him.

"Yes, I'm tempted, too." She flicked her eyes over him provocatively. "So, there we are. We both have to resist temptation."

He recognised her outrageous flirtation from the safety of moral protection, and smiled ruefully.

"I can resist temptation so long as you know I don't want to." He was struck by his own boldness, before adding, "Needs must when the angels drive."

"Yes." She shrugged. "Please believe me, my lovely beau, I'd love to sleep with you. Unfortunately, surrendering to the pleasure without sacred promises won't work for three in a bed."

He was confused for a second, but it became clear when she added, "I know Jesus would forgive me, but I wouldn't give myself any peace for ages after."

He nodded philosophically. "I think I knew that."

"Did you really, Tim?"

"I guess so."

She sat back in her seat to appraise him. "You are still guessing, aren't you?"

"What about?"

"Life's purpose. How it fits with mine. I must tell you, if you lived with me, you'd be living with Jesus, too. Would you be happy with that?"

"I would be happy under any circumstances." He looked at her with such tenderness that she frowned, as if about to cry. She prepared her words carefully before she leant forward again and spoke in a measured but earnest tone.

"Yes, I think you would." She gave herself some time to find her words. "I don't want to make house rules, my sweet, lovely Tim. I'd rather you understood before merely accepting it. I want a life that permits me, and the man I share my life with to be totally honest with each other. I would want you to tell me if you thought I was wrong. just as I reserve the right to tell you. Loving someone doesn't mean surrendering to their faith. All I could ask you to do is to try to learn to love both of us, - me and Jesus. If that seems like a tall order, I can only say that loving Him would make me love you all the more." She paused and Tim remained silent, trying to make sense of it. She looked hard at him and then leant forward to lay her hands on his. "Would you try, at least?"

"Maybe I have, already."

"Maybe?"

"I've started speaking to Him. At least, I think I have. I'm waiting for Him to answer, I suppose."

"If you've spoken to Him, then he's already answered."

"I'm sorry, but I didn't hear Him, I'm afraid."

"Listen to your thoughts. Ask Him to enter them, and He will." She shivered excitedly. "Oh, Tim, I won't promise, but I feel some expectation in what you've said. Let's leave it now. Get some sleep."

She stood up and began to resolutely focus on the sleeping arrangements like an efficient hospital matron.

"First, let's get you some bedding. I'll find you a coverlet and a couple of pillows, while you bring your things in from the car."

Within minutes, she had laid everything out on the settee, ready to be slept on, and Tim's suitcase stood next to it. The task complete, she slowed down, and stood motionless, as if she might have forgotten something. She passed him and stood in the doorway.

"Will you kiss me goodnight?" It was an invitation to tenderness, and he realised perfectly where such a kiss lay in the gamut of love's expression. He came over, bent down, cupped her face in his hands, and lay his lips on hers with a gentleness that angels bestow on those to whom they owe eternal devotion. She breathed a low moan of pleasure, before relinquishing him, and with a whispered, "good night", left him.

Lights out, he lay under the coverlet and tried to make some rational sense of this heady relationship, in which, after two whirlwind meetings, they were implying the possibility of marriage. Bizarrely, he felt as if he had known her for ages, and yet his reservation was that he.. and possibly Alicia... had become enmeshed in a relationship, which in Fred and Elsie's minds was destined. He had, without the slightest doubt in his mind, fallen in love with Alicia, but had he, as she inferred, been seduced by suggestibility into so doing? He was overwhelmed by the possibility of a marriage with Alicia, but he could neither believe his good fortune, nor understand how he could deserve it. What did they know of each other, when it came down to it? He was conscious of having seen two Alicias; one the confident self reliant, artist, who seemed to want so little from the world and cared not to be judged by it, and now, this other softer more vulnerable woman, who had betrayed her need for passion and shared commitment. The more he felt able to take initiative with any confidence, the more she showed her vulnerability. She was still forthright and honest, but gentler in her irony. It was as if she wanted to hand him authority. But, overhanging all this was the complication of having to come to terms with Alicia's commitment to a spiritual marriage with Jesus. He wondered for a moment what effect that might have on his physical desire for her.

As he faded into unconsciousness, he wished – or was it some kind of conversational prayer? - that he might encounter Jesus in his dreams and receive a word or two of explanation.

The Confession

At seven o'clock in the morning, Tim was awakened by a rap on the door. Alicia came in with a cup of tea and two innocuous dry biscuits. She placed the tray on the small low table without even looking at him.

"That will get you to the bathroom and then the kitchen in fifteen minutes. Under starters orders."

She left as swiftly as she entered, leaving him to ease himself up and wipe the sleep from his eyes. He was aware of having dreamed of being at an auction, where he was bidding for all kinds of artifacts and objects. His mother had shown up, telling him that he was choosing inappropriately, because they wouldn't look right together. But the auctioneer kept nodding and laughing as he brought the hammer down on the block. He had been angry with his mother for interfering, but was also confused when the auctioneer kept selling him things. Dismissing his dreams with a grunt, he slid his legs off the couch and drank the tea, gratefully. He hoped he had had enough sleep and didn't look too awful when Alicia came in. He scrabbled around in his suitcase, extracted his toiletry bag and padded to the door. As soon as he opened it, Alicia shouted from the kitchen, "Shower room second door along the corridor to the left!" Thankful to have been spared a search for the amenities, he sloped along to his ablutions.

By the time he had showered and shaved, he felt invigorated and delighted with the idea of being served breakfast by this beautiful, talented, bright, sexy and unpredictable girl. He entered the kitchen, and there it was laid out on the table; toast in a stainless steel rack, butter rolled into individual portions on a saucer, marmalade in a jar with a spoon sticking out of the lid, and a white jug embellished with a blue pansy motif, from which emanated the rich aroma of freshly brewed coffee. Stylish and domestic, she had magically conjured it up within ten minutes.

"Did you sleep well?" she asked, glancing at him with an expression that held a subtext.

"Yes. I got off pretty quick. And you?"

"I crashed out and slept like a log," she said in a somewhat defiant tone, as if she had made a decision to ignore what had happened between them. Immediately, he sensed that she was actively attempting to quell any emotion and creating an atmosphere of detachment. She appeared to protecting herself behind a screen of efficiency such as she might employ in her teashop. It was like being treated as a customer. Tim's confusion turned to hurt as his self-esteem drained away. Was she deeply concerned about Fred's illness? If so, was it not reasonable to suppose she would want to share it with him.

"Please help yourself to coffee. There's milk in the jug and sweeteners or sugar there." She pointed to the centre of the table. "The marmalade is home-made."

"Oh, good. Splendid. Thank you." The prospect of domestic intimacy with passionate undertones had faded into the distance, and he couldn't account for the separation that denied they had ever touched. He found himself looking for a reasonable explanation; maybe she was just temporarily stepping back to get some perspective, but he was not convinced. Nothing seemed to explain the invisible gulf he detected.

They poured their coffees, buttered the toast, ladled the marmalade, and munched on it in silent very separate preoccupation. Alicia suddenly broke in on the silence with, "Shall we start in a quarter of an hour?"

"Yes. That's fine." It felt like walking along a hedge, unsuccessfully searching for a gap to break through.

Breakfast finished, they went to their respective rooms and packed their suitcases, and while Alicia washed the few breakfast dishes up and locked the rooms, Tim prepared the car and placed their cases in the boot, all with a wordless efficiency that belied the turbulent running commentary running through his brain.

Once seated in the car, Tim asked her to fasten the seat belt, and helped her secure it to the clasp to the side of the seat. She thanked him in a decidedly formal way. He asked her if she was comfortable, hoping to elicit some complimentary comment about the car. She merely assured him she was, and straightaway, fell back into silence, leaving him to feel slighted and his proud possession snubbed.

The soft purr of the engine, which, ordinarily, he would have taken pleasure in, now made the lack of conversation more obvious. He wound through the country lanes with none of the delight that natural surrounding usually elicited, while he sought desperately for a suitable subject with which he could approach her. She was seemingly engrossed in her own thoughts, and conversation for its own sake would be an intrusion. He recognized some of the curves and bends ahead, and remembered the crest of the hill overlooking the valley, where Fred had stopped and claimed his miracle. On an impulse he decided to stop, to see if he could initiate some response relating to the view. He pulled in onto the lay-by and slowed to a stop. Alicia looked at him for the first time. He turned to her.

"I thought I would take in the view, and a breath of fresh air." He made his voice expressionless for fear that she would detect some purpose. "Do you want to see it?"

She nodded, and he got out and opened the door for her. They strolled over to the edge and looked over the valley.

"How did you know?" she asked, looking straight ahead.

"Know what?"

"About this view?"

"Fred stopped here the other day."

"Ah, yes, he would. So he told you about it, then."

"Sorry. What d'you mean."

There was a pause, as if she were trying to clarify something in her mind.

"Tim?"

"Alicia?" The relief at hearing her speak his name and being able to voice hers came over him like a flood.

"Did you speak to Elsie?"

"Yes, as a matter of fact I did,..or rather she spoke to me."

"What did she tell you?"

"I suppose it was mostly about how Fred came to her rescue."

"And about me?"

He hesitated, wondering if he should say it. "Nothing."

Alicia frowned. "I wish she had. Though I suppose I knew she wouldn't."

Something akin to a cloak of mystery descended like a cloud, making Tim feel a mixture of apprehension and curiosity. There was nothing to say, and he could only wait while the silence compounded the suspense.

She began with a tone of self-absorbed reflection, looking out over the valley beneath.

"I'm the end of the story, really. That's how I see it, anyway. And it's crucial you know it, before we go any further."

She looked at him, as if searching for an answer before the question was put. "You see, Elsie's my grand-mother."

Tim was taken completely by surprise, but he managed to nod his understanding and say, simply, "I see. She didn't say anything about that."

"Her daughter, Nancy, was my mother."

Referred to in the past, Tim thought she must be dead.

"But I don't remember her."

"I see."

"What do you see?"

"She died?"

"She's probably still living somewhere in the southern hemisphere. At least, that's where she went, when she left me" The unimpassioned way she stated this was nevertheless loaded with significance. A slight breeze ruffled her hair, and she lifted her hand to control it.

"But you don't know for sure?"

"No. And I'm never likely to. She left when I was born."

"I'm sorry."

"You needn't be. I'm not, any more."

"You don't care, then?"

"I might have cared if Fred hadn't taught me to look beyond the past. I'm indifferent.now I've made this life of my own."

She turned and looked long and hard at him as if he were a page she was about to write some indelible fact on. He held her gaze, asking his own unformed questions. At length, she nodded and, in a softened tone, said, "I'm sorry about this morning. I know you think me odd."

Tim was about to say something dismissive, but she shook her head to prevent him. "Please don't say anything bland. It's confusing when you reject someone you're drawn to. I knew I was doing it, and why."

Tim's relief at her sudden confession was qualified by the helplessness he felt, fearing to break the thread of communication.

She smiled at him faintly, recognising his patience.

"You don't ask me anything about me, do you Tim?"

"You'll tell me if you want to."

"Yes, I will." She began to gently pace her thoughts, and decided to begin with a question. "I know practically nothing about you, except what Fred and Elsie have said. Did you have a happy childhood?"

Tim frowned. "I suppose I did. I mean, nothing traumatic ever happened. I was bullied a bit at school for a while, not because I was timid, but probably because I didn't understand other children's aggression."

"I'm guessing you were the only son."

"An only child, actually."

"That makes two of us. But that's where any similarity ends. I'm the illegitimate daughter of a father, sentenced to life for murder, and a mother who chose him to get pregnant by."

Tim was rocked on his heels, no less by the dramatic nature of her revelation, than by the unimpassioned way she imparted it. She continued with relentless detachment.

"When my mother discovered at his trial, two and a half months into her pregnancy, that my father'd been seeing three other women, one being his murder victim, she tried to have me aborted. My grandmother found out in time and called on Fred to help. He took control and insisted I was allowed to come into the world."

She looked at Tim, as if to emphasize the importance of what she was about to say. "He convinced my mother that she should give birth to me, by offering to take on the responsibility, with my grandmother, of bringing me up. She agreed so long as she could leave England to escape all the publicity that would inevitably accompany the scandal. And that was what happened. Fred and my grandmother brought me up in a stable home where I never knew the word 'bastard'."

Tim was shocked more by her use of the word, than any meaning it carried. He was also vaguely aware of the formalities involved when a mother surrenders her rights to bring up her child, even to someone in the family.

"So Elsie adopted you?"

"On condition that Fred married her..." Tim raised an eyebrow, which she registered, adding, "..which he did."

He logged in her bald statement and blinked back his astonishment. It took a moment to reclaim his balance. Alicia continued with relentless determination. "They moved away from Netherton to where Elsie lives now, and Fred sold his house and bought one in the same street."

They stood side by side looking over the valley; the silence became eloquent. Very softly, she continued, " Fred used to come here to 'turn things over in his mind', he used to say. This place is significant in all our lives. I think he made most of his decisions standing right here."

Tim swallowed hard before intruding on her resurrected world.

"Do you mean Fred and Elsie are married, still?"

"Legally, yes. They keep their own names, but it's all above board, if somewhat unconventional. I never knew if they ever consummated the marriage; they didn't cohabit in the accepted meaning of the word." She gave him that gently ironic smile. "It's bizarre to anyone who doesn't know Fred. But he's been everything to me, father figure, adviser and protector, and so now, here I am, the illegitimate daughter of a violent criminal, and rejecting mother."

She turned to him and, jutting her chin defiantly, thrust the question at him in a bantering tone, but with underlying serious implication. "How do you feel about taking on a girl like that?"

He sensed a vulnerability in her, and his heart responded. At the risk of turning him away, she had decided to tell him the unsavoury truth. Overtaken with male protectiveness, he looked down at her, and desperate to let her know nothing she had said made any difference, said, "You're not a girl like that! You're not a girl like anything! You are you! I'm in love with you as you are."

"And what would you say to your parents? 'Hullo, this is Alicia, my girlfriend, deserted by her mother and fathered by a murderer'."

"Stop it! I forbid you to say that!" The violence of his voice echoed back at him, and took him by surprise. He had discovered an unexpected strength in himself, an overwhelming need to convince her of the strength of his feelings.

"Forbid?" She said it partly in surprise, but also in challenge. He was willing to take the challenge up.

"Yes, 'forbid'! It's you I love, not your history. You are *you,* not the result of your past! That won't make me fall out of love!"

The earnestness of his protest and the intensity of his gaze arrested her, and she registered it by relaxing her features into a *Mona Lisa* smile. With slow deliberation, she drew close to him and, lifting her lips to his, kissed him as if she were coaxing a fire from embers. He responded, gathering her form to his, moulding them together. She had to bend away from him in order to look at him and whisper, "I prayed that you would say that." She placed her finger on his lips and gently detached herself. "Forgive me. I had to know if you were in love,or infatuated with an idea."

Tim was melted by her earnest gaze, releasing an urge in him to make honest confession. "I have never met anyone as real as you. For the first time in my life, I know I can trust what I feel. I love you Alicia, with a certainty I've never felt before."

She smiled coquettishly. "Even though dear Uncle Fred engineered it?"

Tim laughed involuntarily. "I'm nothing but grateful." His mood adjusted to his thought. "I suddenly realize how much more I owe him than I could ever have imagined."

"Yes, he's an amazing old man, and I love him dearly. Maybe we should get on and see him."

She held his arms and kissed him lightly, before walking briskly to the car and getting in. He followed, his heart immeasurably lightened. He was elated as he sat next to her, excited by the undisguised proprietary looks they exchanged. He couldn't prevent himself from smiling like a clown. She began to hum a tune.

"Music?" he asked, pointing to the radio. She nodded, and he pressed the programme selector till he found a station with bouncy nostalgic tunes from the sixties and seventies that would offer accompaniment to the humming tyres on the road. From time to time, they stole glances at each other, but felt no need to make conversation. As they neared Elsie's, he said, nonchalantly, but with earnest intention, "I've met someone I'd like to show your pictures to. Do you mind?"

"Sounds interesting. An art critic?"

"He's an art *lover*. I think he might be in a position to help you get your work seen."

"How wonderful! Yes please! I'd be delighted!"

He, in his turn, was delighted by her enthusiasm, and basked in her smile as in pure golden sunlight. As he gave his full attention to the road ahead, it occurred to him that when they arrived at Elsie's it would be the first time she would have seen them together. He took a deep breath and steeled himself to face the onslaught of her warm maternal optimism.

Flowers and Grapes

As soon as they entered the house, Elsie heard them, and was out of the kitchen like a terrier. She and Alicia fell into each other's arms and Tim watched them like two wrestlers strangling each other with neck hugs. When, after sniffles from Elsie and whispered repetitions of her name from Alicia, they were able to release each other from their mutual grasps, Tim was marginalized. They entered the kitchen, leaving him to follow discreetly, feeling he had to take care not to intrude. There was no way he could, for they were, just then, oblivious of his presence. Elsie gazed rapturously on her granddaughter, repeating, "Well, my lovely, well, well, well", and Alicia kept smiling back through half-sad eyes, nodding and softly intoning, "Yes, indeed. Here we are then. " He was made profoundly conscious of the unbridled affection, unrestrained by southern conventions he normally experienced.

"Well, now then," Alicia asked in a chivvying tone to break the mood, "what's up with our Fred?"

Elsie imparted the news with more enthusiastic excitement than foreboding. "It's bin bad wi' 'im, an'no mistake, but 'e's givin' the 'ome the run aroun', so 'e must be getting' better. E'll buck up no end, soon as 'e sets eyes on ye." She turned to Tim and added, "Both o' ye."

"Is he out of bed?" Alicia asked.

"Not yet. 'E's takin' 'is time. It says summat abowt 'is condition that 'e lets 'em keep 'im there. I don't remember 'im givin' inter sickness afore, an that's a fact."

"Tim says he caught a chill at Netherton."

"That's as may be. 'E's probaly bin doin' more'n 'e should."

She immediately took the role of solicitous hostess, and grabbed Alicia's sleeve.

"Let's get yer coat off ye. Ye an' all, Tim, while I put t' kettle on."

Tim, once more gathered into the family, stepped forward and helped Alicia off with her coat. Having removed his own, he threw them over a chair, and they settled down, facing each other across the table. As Elsie busied herself at the worktop, Tim felt he was on call ready to be useful when they had made decisions. He was unsure whether Elsie was playing down her disquiet about Fred, but felt that she was trusting on Alicia's ability to contribute to Fred's welfare. In any event, he detected an undercurrent of concern put to one side, and a reliance on Alicia's presence as a psychological support.

The tea brewed and biscuits laid out, Elsie joined them, sitting at the head of the table, where she had a perspective on them. She looked at each in turn, as if establishing an artists's vanishing point between them on the horizon. The inference was obvious, and Tim simulated preoccupation as Alicia smiled back at Elsie as if to confirm her thoughts. This obviously encouraged Elsie, for, with the least concern for tact, she came out with, "Can we say ye've become mighty pleased wi' one another?"

"Yes, we can, grandma, and we can leave it there for the present," Alicia warned.

"Well, Fred'll need ter know, I can tell ye," Elsie emphasised. "Ye'll be seein' 'im, this afternoon."

"He needs to know no more than he needs to know."

"What abowt *yeou*? 'Ave ye nowt ter say fer yersel', young Tim?" persisted Elsie.

"Grandma!" Alicia admonished her in a low voice, glancing over to
Tim.

He felt strangely comfortable, and shrugged calmly. "Oh, I don't mind. It's pretty obvious what I feel, I expect. I haven't got used to flaunting it yet, that's all."

"Tellin' 'er gran'mother en't exactly flauntin'!" protested Elsie. "Any road, that's what ye do, when ye share feelin's."

"Feelings are shared between those who have them," Alicia pronounced firmly.

"Aye, an' what abowt them as 'ad an 'and in bringin' it ter fruition?" Elsie broke into a proprietary smile, before adding, "Fred'll be glad ter see ye side by side. It'll buck 'im up no end."

"Perhaps he'd like to see Tim and me in a passionate embrace. No doubt that would really have him skipping about."

"'Old on, That's goin' a bit far!" Elsie said reproachfully.

"I should hope so!" What do you say, Tim? Should we go into a clinch at the foot of his bed?"

Tim grinned uncontrollably at the image, embarrassed but pleased beyond measure at the very idea of such intimacy.

He pretended to reflect, smiling. "I think the gentleman should take his cue from the lady."

Alicia laughed. "That's the most blatant cop-out I've ever heard."

Elsie watched them, smiling and interpreting their laughter as confirmation of her best dreams for them. Getting up from her chair she went impulsively, first to Alicia and then to Tim and, hugging them round their shoulders planted a resounding kiss on both their cheeks. "Well, if ye 'aven't a mind ter 'ug each other, I'll do it fer ye!" She continued on round to her worktop and began to sort things out for lunch. Tim stood and with a determined look, suggested, "What say I treat us to a meal out?"

Alicia's eyes lit up, but Elsie reacted as if her domestic authority was being challenged. "Wot? After I've got all t'food ready?"

"Oh, come on, Grandma. Let's call it a celebration."

"Celebration?! With Fred in 'is sick bed?!"

Alicia got up and put her arm round her shoulder, adopting a wheedling tone. "Fred's going to be no worse for our having a meal out, and I know he'd be happy about it, anyway." She gave her shoulder a gentle shake and kissed her cheek. Elsie hesitated with a wry look before responding with a concessionary shrug. "Aye, well, put like that, I suppose…"

"Good. Then we'll all get our coats on and…" She turned to Tim.

"Where have you got in mind?"

Inspiration came. "What about Harvey and Bagnold's? We could have a lunch and then get some flowers and fruit to take to Fred.

That shop sells everything."

"By 'eck, yower fella's got 'is wits abowt 'im, eh?" Elsie said to Alicia in a lowered voice, as if attempting to impart a confidentiality, but making sure it was audible to Tim.

"It's a good sign, isn't it?" Alicia responded with mock seriousness.

Tim felt the full warmth of their shared dry northern humour, which confirmed his acceptance into a familial intimacy he had never known before.

As they drove into town, he caught sight of Elsie in his mirror, sitting in the back bedecked with her anachronistic hat and glanced at Alicia's trim form next to him in the passenger seat, and felt as proud as the chauffeur of an eastern potentate. His satisfaction continued to flow over him as he ushered them to the table across the carpeted floor, handed them the menus and sat listening to them chat as if already accustomed to taking him for granted. It was women's essential small talk, handed down the generations; the insubstantial female subject matter reflecting recognition of each other's daily survival strategems. That he was not expected to contribute gave him time to reflect on the amazing speed with which his life had been re-orchestrated. An unbelievably short time ago he had been sitting in the Dragon's Arms drinking with Elsie and Fred and their homeless hangers-on, being offered homespun philosophy on his love life. Even less credible was the fact that, hardly more than a week ago, Fred had taken him to meet his heart's nemesis, as he now thought of Alicia. It was as if he had discovered a map hidden under his nose.

When the meals were served, the conversation eventually veered from the purely domestic, and Elsie impetuously turned her attention on Tim. "Will ye be keepin' on wi' them pictures o' yours, then?"

He was unprepared for such a question, and couldn't think why she had asked him. "My job, you mean? Well, yes, I hadn't considered giving it up."

Elsie turned to Alicia. "Would 'e be any good 'elpin' out at yower Place?"

Alicia laughed. "I hardly think Tim'd thank me for that."

"Why not? It'd give ye more time fer yer paintin'."

"She's going to be famous," Tim said suddenly.

"Really?!" exclaimed Alicia.

"Oh, aye? 'Ow's that ter be?" challenged Elsie.

"I'm not sure yet. But I've made a promising contact." Tim took himself by surprise, but nodded emphatically at Alicia. "He's agreed to look at your work."

"Seriously?" Alicia looked earnestly at him.

"I wouldn't say it if it wasn't true. I think he should see it as soon as possible."

"I thought you were just saying it."

Tim shook his head. "Your work is amazingly good. I'm sure he'll think so, too."

Alicia fixed her gaze on him as if she were studying one of her own Portraits. "Isn't this you being entirely subjective, Tim?"

Tim smiled confidently, as he remembered what Nathan had said.

"All art appreciation is subjective. But it's got nothing to do with *knowing* the artist. You have something special. I just know that."

"You lovely man. You don't know how dishy you are." She laid down her knife and fork and came round to him, beaming. "You say just what a girl wants to hear." She bent over him, whispering, "I've just got to do this", and kissed his upturned mouth with deep preoccupation. As she returned to her chair, Tim was acutely aware of a wide-eyed, middle-aged gentleman on the adjoining table nudging his wife, whether in disapproval or enthusiasm he was unable to decide. While Alicia sat with cool aplomb, Tim smiled embarrassedly at his elderly neighbours, who were instantly absorbed by their plates, as if gazing into crystal balls.

Elsie, with a tear in her eye, sniffed into her handkerchief, taking Alicia's gesture as part of the ritual confirmation of their relationship.

"She were alus the one fer doin' that, was Alicia." She turned to the adjacent elderly couple, adding, " It in't even 'is birthday." The lady smiled bravely back, and said, demurely, "That'll be something to look forward to, won't it?"

A warm undercurrent of excitement shone in Tim's and Alicia's faces. He was enchanted by her unrestrained demonstration, and while recognizing it as just this side of eccentricity, knew it was entirely real. She smiled on him as if he were the victor of a joust, wearing her favour, and as Elsie gazed on them sentimentally, they stole frequent glances at each other, letting the world recede.

After lunch, they went to the lower floor to choose flowers and fruit for Fred. Everyone agreed that grapes were the obvious choice. The flowers were more problematic, and appeared to depend on what each thought they signified.

"Fer 'eaven's sake, don't get 'im lilies," Elsie stressed, "or e'll think 'is time is come."

"What about roses?" Tim suggested.

"They're too romantic. He'd be embarrassed by them," Alicia advised. "I think he'd like those carnations over there." She pointed at several buckets of them. "He was fond of wearing them to celebrate certain times of the year."

"Aye. Ev'ry Saint George's Day, wi'out fail. They're not too showy, neither," Elsie concurred.

"Carnations it is, then," Tim said, and ordered a dozen red and white mixed.

Appetites satisfied and gifts obtained, they drove off to visit Fred in high spirits, in full expectation of bringing him new life and vigour with lively banter and moral support. When they rang the visitors; bell, a carer came out of the parlour, and having received their names, rang for the matron, whose footsteps were soon heard clattering on the landing, accompanied by the swishing of starched apron rubbing against grey linen skirt. Without formality, she launched into Fred's latest condition.

"Mr. Butterworth should not be over-excited. He needs rest. We tell him this, but he doesn't seem to understand the seriousness of his condition. He's caught a very bad chill, which lodged on his chest and affects his breathing."

"I thowt 'e were getting better," Elsie said, with some resentment.

"It will take more than thinking to get him back to health. In fact, it'll probably not do him much good to have you all visit at the same time."

Alicia was instantly alarmed by her cautionary advice, and looked at Elsie for her response. Elsie's face tautened into a stoic scepticism. "Is 'e eatin' up 'is vittals?" she asked, adamantly refusing to accept any gloomy diagnosis of the situation.

"Well, he's never taken to eating with us most of the time, except in the evenings, sometimes. But, since he's been in bed, he's become very choosy, complaining about the food, as if it was a hotel, or something."

"Aye, well, that sounds like 'e's getting' ter be 'is old self," Elsie retorted. "I think we can chance seein' 'im. Come on," she prompted Tim and Alicia, "let's put a bit of life inter 'im."

Well acquainted with the place, she led the way upstairs under the disapproving scowl of matron, who turned on her heel with a flounce and disappeared into the kitchen area, muttering under her breath. Elsie knocked on the door of Fred's room and without waiting for permission, crossed the threshold, to announce the presence of them all. Fred was slumped down on a pile of pillows behind his head, but he instantly struggled into a half-sitting position as soon as he saw them filing in. Alicia slid past Elsie and swiftly bent over Fred to kiss him on the cheek.

"So, you did the grand tour of Netherton once too often, Fred," she said, hiding her concern. "I'm glad to see you're being sensible about it. You're obviously in the best place."

He held on to her, staring into her face intensely. "I don't know 'ow ye can say that, me lovely. It's a fair treat ter see ye, any road."

She leant back from him and turned to reveal Tim holding a bunch of flowers and a basket of grapes. "Hullo, Fred. Sorry you're not well," Tim said.

"We've brought you a bit of cheer, and something you can enjoy after we've left, said Alicia."

"Wastin' yer money, like that, " Fred growled.

Alicia took the flowers from Tim and placed them in the basin, while she searched for something that would serve as a vase. Tim placed the basket on the side table, and stepped back as Elsie edged forward to stand over the bed with her arms folded against her breast to prevent any danger of a demonstration of affection. Her face told the story of her feelings, however, for her smile was twisted by inner turmoil at seeing him looking so helpless. "'Ow do, then?" she murmured. "'Ow do, yerself, Elsie, love." Fred looked away and screwed his eyes for a second or two. "Fair ter middlin'," she replied "Pretty much where I am, an' all." He averted his eyes from contact, like a small boy unready to confess a misdemeanour.

"Sit ye down," he said, waving a finger at an easy chair. Elsie slid into it as Alicia planted the vase of flowers on a small table at the side, and then stood next to Tim, at the foot of the bed. He nodded at Fred and pursed his lips, as if words would have intruded on mute eloquence. Alicia stood next to Tim and slid her arm round his. Fred registered the move with the raising of an inquisitive eyebrow, which Alicia answered with a nod.

"Yes, Fred," she said in a firm and measured way, "I think we can say," - looking up at Tim, - "we've taken a liking to each other."

Fred closed his eyes for a moment, as if in silent prayer, before asking, "'Ow big a likin'?"

She laughed. "Big enough."

Fred looked at Tim, then directed his comment to her. "'As 'e owt ter say abowt it, then?"

She shrugged and nudged Tim as a prompt. Tim smiled confidently. "I can't think why you chose me to take to Netherton, Fred."

"That's daft. 'Course ye do."

"I'm still surprised it was me." Fred gave a non-commital grunt. Tim paused before adding, "I'm glad you did."

Fred searched Tim's face. "There's no chance o' goin' back on it?"

"Not if Alicia'll have me," Tim announced.

Fred beckoned Alicia to him and patted the bed for her to sit there.

She slid her arm from Tim's, settled on the counterpane, and took Fred's hand, lying limply at his side.

"I hope you're behaving yourself, and doing what they tell you. We want you to get well soon," she offered.

"Aye, well, I 'ave ter do what I'm told when there's no other way out." He looked at her closely and drank in her energy. "Are things well fer ye, then?"

"They're as good as they can get."

"'Ave I done well by ye?"

"Very well." She squeezed his hand.

" 'E's a fair bit ter learn, but I reckon 'e'll do."

She turned round and looked back at Tim. Fred followed her gaze.

"He'll do very well, indeed," she murmured.

She smiled and Fred shaped his mouth into a wry attempt at qualified approval, which Tim received with a modest nod. Fred sighed and closed his eyes for a second or two. "If ye can bear wi' me, I've a word or two ter pass on."

Elsie leant forward. "'Ere Fred, don't be tirin' yersel' wi' all this gabbin'."

"Don't be daft, Elsie, love." He raised his voice as if to assert his male prerogative. "Never put off t'day what ye might not do t'morrer."

"Fat chance o' that!" Elsie countered with pursed lips.

Fred lowered his voice. "Well, any road, *ye've* no need ter listen." He breathed hard and patted his chest as if to prevent himself from coughing. "Ye've 'eard it all afore."

He turned his attention to Tim. "This young lass 'as, maybe, spilled t'beans abowt me."

Tim felt helpless, not wishing to say more than was proper to reveal, bearing in mind the sensitive nature of the subject. By any standard, it was impossible for him to know how to respond.

Elsie took it upon herself to chime in. "I put 'im in t' picture as much as 'e needs."

"Just so 'e knows," said Fred laconically. "An' wot's more t' point, 'e knows who t' lass is." He jerked his thumb towards Alicia.

"I told him, Fred," she interjected

"An' ye're content wi' it?" He directed the question at Tim with a jut of the chin.

Tim took in the old man's challenging stare, and for a moment considered all the replies he could make, all of which would come to the same unflinching affirmative. Yes, he would be supremely 'content' to take Alicia. He would feel so much more. Elated, entranced, raised to heights that life had hitherto never even hinted at. He would dedicate himself to her happiness and strive to prove that romantic love in the world could be perfected. How could he say all that to a man of so few words as Fred? The old man raised an eyebrow.

"I'm content," Tim said.

"I tell ye, Tim, the world can know all t' facts of a man's life, but 'is reasons belong ter' im alone. An' 'is reasons come fro' where 'e puts 'is faith. D'ye get me meanin'?"

"I think so," Tim said, less with certainty than with a desire to please him.

"Ye may know summat o'me sin, but ye know nowt o' t' savin' o' me. I took a man's life an' I were made ter pay me dues. But payin' up, don't even t' score. I 'ad ter be browt ter a dark, low place o' guilt fer Jesus ter find me an' sort me out."

The two women looked down at the floor, Elsie with her eyes closed and Alicia with the grim smile of recognition. They must have heard it all before.

"An' I daren't pretend t' understand 'ow it 'appened, but 'E come and stood next o' me in that cell, an' said I were precious ter 'im. An' I says, 'get away wi' ye! Me? Precious? After wot I done?' An' 'e says, 'Ye've lived thro't' shame on it, an' reached the sorrow of knowin' what yer sin were. Jus' say sorry ter me, - an' it's sorted.' An' I got on me knees an' I said sorry ter 'Im, and, by 'eck, I got up, knowin' fer sure I were fergiven."

He stopped to cough and had to spit into a handkerchief he pulled out from beneath his pillow. Elsie started to move towards him, but he brusquely waved her away, took some deep breaths and continued, "That were t' start o' t' new life, 'cos t' moment I got straight wi' Jesus, were t' moment I knew I were loved. Soon as that 'appened I began ter accept others."

"Aye, tha's right enough," interrupted Elsie. "An' 'e's never stopped givin' 'em a leg up."

"Give over, Elsie love," he growled, but with a hint of deep affection. "Ye make it soun' like I were tryin' ter even things up, or summat. It weren't like that. Ye can't bring a man back ter life; ye can do nowt but give summat back by fillin'in fer 'is absence. An' it's not out o' guilt ye do it. It's out o' wantin' ter thank Jesus fer lettin' ye live wi' yersel'."

For some seconds, he squinted obliquely at Tim, who stood patiently under the scrutiny. Finally, Fred coughed again and adjusted his position. "I tell ye, Tim, I never dealt wi' folk wi'out getting' 'Im ter stand next o' me. There were many a time, I 'ad ter ask 'Im ter keep me lovin' 'em. There was times, 'E 'ad ter do it on me be'alf. D'ye get me drift?

"I think so," Tim murmured.

"Is that one better 'n supposin'?" Fred asked, with a glint in his eye.

Tim shrugged sheepishly.

"I will say ye're a gentleman, Tim. Alus known that, I 'ave. An' ye've come through a testin' time wi' us." He gave a little cough and winced slightly. "I alus thowt ye'd come through wi' top grade."

He coughed again, and Elsie was about to move to him, but he lifted his hand against her and took a deep breath, like a swimmer coming up for air.

"An'now ye've ter love our Alicia," he continued, "an' there'll be times when ye'll need some 'elp ter do it."

"I doubt she's that difficult ter love," Elsie broke in.

"Ee, Elsie love, ye're so quick ter jump. 'Ave I said she were? She's God's own daughter, - I know that." He shook his head impatiently. "What I'm sayin' is, - what I', tryin' ter say, is - well, - she's got a start on Tim. She 'as Jesus standing wi''er, an' Tim's on'y got 'isself at present time."

Alicia smiled. "That doesn't make it a doddle, exactly, Fred," she said, looking round at Tim with a warning nod.

"Maybe not," Fred retorted, "But 'E taps yer shoulder when ye're not that easy." He adjusted his position in an impatient movement, as if adjusting his body prompted his thoughts. "Are ye getting' any o' this, Tim? Am I makin' mesel' clear?" Tim nodded. Whatever else he found difficult, it was clear that Fred cared deeply for them all. To be included in that care was deeply moving to him. "I'll get there eventually, I suppose."

"Ye will an' all.! I've 'ad a word, an E's on ter ye. An' I'll tell ye why. – 'cos my lass 'ere".. patting Alicia's hand,... "won't be loved proper wi'out 'Im." He stabbed the air in front of him. "Ye'll not be contented wi'out lovin' *all* of 'er, - an' that means Jesus included'."

Tim did not know whether he spoke the next words out of gratitude for Fred's concern, or whether it was, perhaps, to protect him from worry in his debilitated state, or even, - dare he conjecture, - he was beginning to capitulate to Fred's Jesus, but he said, "I've started a conversation with Him."

In the silence that followed, they all turned towards him. They all looked as if they were making a collective judgement of his sincerity, peering into his very soul, and ready to dig as deep as it needed to bring out the nuggets they sought. Tim looked at each in turn, braving their scrutiny.

At length, Fred cleared his throat and, without any of his customary flamboyance, "Tha's a good straight answer, an' ye've give it wi'out flinchin'. Good on yer, Tim, and praise t' Lord."

Elsie looked as if she was about to shout out, but, instead, closed her mouth, as a tear fell down her cheek, which she instantly wiped with a handkerchief from her handbag. Alicia stood and walked to Tim's side, took his hand, and smiled back at Fred from the foot of the bed.

"You're happy to give me away now, then?"

Suddenly Fred looked tired. He sank back deeper into his pillows. "'E awready told me ter do that, me lovely." He looked Tim straight in the eyes, and, hoarsely but with quiet conviction, said, "I give 'er t' ye, Tim. Ye'll love, cherish an' support 'er wi' Prince Jesus' 'elp." He sank even deeper into his pillow, which began to curl round his cheeks. "Ye've ter start knowin' what ye want. Ye've ter find summat better'n all this traipsin' roun' t' country, lad. Search fer Jesus, 'stead o' folks who don't know why they want what ye're sellin' 'em. 'E'll introduce ye ter yersel', as yeou, an' this lass of ours gets ter know each other, warts, an' all."

Tim and Alicia exchanged looks, as if the bed end was an altar rail. Fred shifted his head to Elsie. "It 'ud be best ye left me. Ye're all more 'n I'm up ter, jus' now."

Elsie gathered herself together and stood, looking down at him. "We better do as matron says, eh?"

"Aye. 'Appen when there's no choice in t' matter. I've ter shut me eyes fer a while."

She took his hand and held it for a moment and then let it drop again on the counterpane. Tim was conscious of the deep bond of affection that filled the space between them, but also of the boundaries that they had never crossed.

Alicia bent over him and kissed his cheek, Elsie held his hand and patted it gently before backing away to the door. Tim, still at the bed-end said, "Get well, soon, Fred."

"I'll be right as rain, whatever 'appens," was the reply from the pillow. There was a fraction of a pause and then he added, "Don't never become a politician, young Tim."

" 'Politician', did you say?"

"Aye. Life's too big ter be certain abowt things. Don't get chivvied inter makin' yer mind up too early. Jus' keep searchin'. Right?"

Tim hesitated a moment, bemused. "Right."

He closed his eyes and they were dismissed.

A sombre mood descended on them as they filed out of the room; Elsie and Alicia were sad to see him in his condition, affected, too, by the lethargy of a man ordinarily filled with such passionate energy. Matron was standing at the end of the corridor, her substantial frame blocking the light from the window that faced them. She raised an eyebrow as they neared, and asked, "Well, and how did you find him? Not so sprightly, I'd say."

Elsie nodded to signify her submission to the nurses assessment. "'E's not 'isself, that's fer sure."

"He'll only be himself if he's left to himself. You'd be much better leaving him rest for two or three days, before coming back."

Having seen him, they had to concede the truth of her judgement. They had visited with the idea of 'putting new life into him', as Elsie had phrased it. Now they recognised the necessity of leaving him to the tender mercies of the matron, and felt helpless. Matron recognised their depressed mood, and said, in a tone more 'bedside' than before, "He'll be fine. If you give me a ring each day, I'll give you an update. It's rest that'll bring him round. He's just got to do as he's told for a while, and that's not easy for him."

They were all somewhat reassured by her efficient matter-of-fact manner, and Elsie responded with a nod. She expressed their fellowship in common experience by saying, "'E's never bin easy. 'E'll be no better fer being poorly, that's a fact."

They left the home, sorry to have seen Fred in a lower state than they could remember, but generally feeling easier that there was an open line of communication, and that he was in good hands.

Journey Into Passion

Both women had spent lifetimes with Fred and their concern for him went deep. Tim's feelings, though involved, were wider and more circumspect, and so he felt able to take on himself the responsibility for providing practical support from his comparative detachment.

As they sat in the kitchen cradling their cups of tea and chatting each other into an optimistic frame of mind about Fred's condition, Tim felt it incumbent upon him to remind them of the dictates of normal daily life.

"Well," Elsie said in a conspicuously philosophical way, "maybe 'e'll learn summat fro this 'ow-d'yer-do. 'E can't jes go gallivantin' roun' at 'is age."

"I think it would take more than this to make him change, bless him," Alicia said, attempting to keep the atmosphere light.

Tim broke in with a complete non-sequitor by suddenly saying, "I tell you what, Elsie. I think we'd better settle tonight's sleeping arrangements."

The ladies both looked at him as if he had broken wind.

"I mean," he stammered, "the arrangements,..you know,.. up to now have been, well,.. you know…"

"Ye gods an'little fishes!" exclaimed Elsie, "What are ye worried abowt? It's all took care of. Alf an'Bert agreed ter get back t' shed, knowin' we 'ad another body stayin'. There'll on'y be Monty in t' next room."

"The next room. Yes, I see." He searched his mind for the full explanation, before adding, "Yes, well that's fine. I can sleep in the living room. No problem."

"Beg yer pardon?!" Elsie said, obviously deeply offended, "When ye've a perfectly good comfy bed upstairs?"

"Yes, but where is Alicia going to sleep?" he asked, remembering his trial of the settee, with its less than satisfactory springing. "I'm quite happy to give it up to her."

"What's wrong wi' sharin' t' same bed?" Elsie demanded to know with a confused expression at his obtuseness.

"You mean...?" Tim's mind refused to provide the words. If he resisted the suggestion, he would appear narrowly prejudiced, and, if he showed eager acceptance, Alicia would think him presumptuous. In his ineffectual state, he turned to her, but she returned a wholly unresponsive look, turning a bland smile to Elsie and then back again to Tim, like a spectator with no particular affiliation at a tennis match.

Elsie tutted, as if to dismiss all opposition. "We can all 'ave a good night's sleep, that's what."

Alicia turned to Tim, who tried to retain some aplomb as he caught her look.

"But,.. well,.. it's not exactly... I'm sure Alicia will have something to say about it." Tim nodded at her, like a team member on 'University Challenge'.

Alicia compressed her lips and shook her head simulating deep regret at not being able to help him out. Tim's eyebrows met in the middle, as Elsie looked like an irate mother waiting for someone to own up to a misdemeanour. Tim recognised Alicia's gently ironic smile again, just before she relented and addressed herself to Elsie.

"Elsie, dear, have you considered the temptation of the flesh you place before us? Tim and I are physically attracted to each other, and might have trouble keeping control. Unless, of course, you are giving your blessing to surrendering to our lustful inclinations before the nuptials?" Her eyes twinkled and the corners of her mouth twitched. There was a pause, and Elsie appeared to give the question considerable thought.

"D'yer mean, ye 'aven't yet....?"

"No, we haven't." Alicia simulated indignation at the very idea. Elsie retained her composure and without compunction, came back with, "Well, in that case, all we've ter do is do a bit o' bundlin'." She smiled cheerfully as if the problem was completely solved.

"Oh, it's that easy, is it?" returned Alicia

"What's bundling?" Tim asked in all innocence, hoping that a solution was found that avoided further embarrassment.

"Elsie?" Alicia handed the explanation over with a wave of the hand, as if introducing the next variety act on the programme.

"Bundlin"s a way o' lettin' t' 'ound smell t' rabbit, while keepin' 'em at bay, so ter speak."

Tim shook his head in total confusion.

"Ye gods an' Little fishes, do I 'ave ter spell it out?!" Elsie said, indignantly.

"I think you do, Elsie dear," Alicia said with heavy emphasis.

Elsie sighed. "Bundlin' is when ye split t' bed down t'middle. In old days, it used ter be wi' a plank, but anythin'll do, like rolled up blankets or summat. An' there's ter be no crossin' over, see?"

The image of lying next to Alicia with 'nowt' but a rolled up blanket to restrict his advances, did not offer the prospect of 'a good night's sleep'. Something had to be done to rescue them from the situation.

"I think,…" he began. They looked at him, Elsie with aggressive challenge and Alicia with academic interest. "..in view of my movements tomorrow, it would be better if we went back to your place," He looked at Alicia desperately seeking the support that, till now, she had, it seemed to him, reluctant to provide.

"What? And leave Elsie alone?"

Tim gritted his teeth and swallowed hard. "She could come with us, couldn't she? Couldn't you, Elsie?"

"Ee, nay, lad. Not if I'm ter stand by t' phone, ter take t' calls from t' nurse."

"In any case," Alicia added, nonchalently "what have your movements got to do with it? My place is hardly the most convenient place to work from, in the middle of nowhere."

"The fact is,…" Tim gave himself a pause to let the whole idea firm itself up, "…I'm going to see this fellow I spoke about, the one who's interested in art. I thought it'd be an opportunity to show him some of your work. We could pick up some pictures and take them along." He held his breath. "What do you think?" he asked, addressing them both. They all exchanged looks, until, after a brief reflection, Elsie came to the rescue with, "Aye, p'raps 'e 'as a point. I think ye should go, love, 'cos ye never know where it'll lead ye.

"Would you be all right here on your own?" Alicia asked.

"Alone?!" Elsie laughed. "Wi' all t' lads expectin' their meal on time?! No," she said, becoming serious, "it's best ye go, an' call in tomorrer after ye've seen this fella."

"Well, it seems we've avoided a gritty problem, then," Alicia pronounced, with a twinkle in her eye. "For the time being," she added with an even bigger twinkle.

"An' after all, ye never know where it could lead," repeated Elsie.

Tim had to sort out the ambiguity of her remark before saying, "Yes! Right! Good," Tim said, sighing inwardly, partly from relief and partly from satisfaction at his own presence of mind. "Then that's settled."

"Ye'll 'ave a cuppa afore ye go," Elsie insisted.

The journey to Netherton turned out to be a cocktail of emotions. Tim was convinced Alicia had been playing a game by pretending to accede to the idea of sleeping together. He felt he had been put to some kind of test, but wasn't sure what it was or how well he had responded to it. Yet, mysteriously and to his considerable satisfaction, he had the strong impression that she needed his support, and the way she kept smiling at him suggested he had deserved some kind of approval from her, whatever that was. As soon as they got in the car, she linked her arm with his, making him feel intensely proud. When they were leaving Elsie's, the hugs and kisses of grandmother and grandchild had had a touch of consolation about them, as if compensating for uncertainty. Alicia assured Elsie that they would be back before you could turn round, and there was no need to worry about Fred, which suggested to Tim that the opposite had been tacitly contemplated. And, as they started off in the car, Alicia's repeated opinion that Elsie would be able to cope sounded as if she were convincing herself rather than stating an opinion.

They fell into silence for the first five miles or so, and Alicia nestled against him, humming a tune, which evoked in him the warmth and tenderness associated with domestic familiarity, something he had read about but not experienced in his parents' house. When they got to the dual carriageway, however, she withdrew her arm sat forward, folding her hands round her knees. Relaxed but alive, she peered sideways at him as she spoke.

"Would you have absolutely refused to sleep with me?" she asked, looking at him with a directness that prevented him from deciding whether she was earnest or engaged in a flirtatious game.

Suddenly, here was another facet of Alicia, he thought. He adopted a self-assured smile to show her he was ready to engage in repartee. Maybe this was another test?

"Since you mention it, I think you sailed dangerously near the wind with Elsie." – 'Ah', he thought as soon as he said it, 'couldn't I have come up with something more interesting than that?!'

"You mean, you might have been forced to sleep with me?"

"'Forced' doesn't come into it." - 'How difficult it was to deliver the right intonation'. – "But I suppose I knew you'd find a way out."

"Hmm, 'a way out'?" she echoed, pulling her mouth into a wry doubtful grimace. "Oh, so you're quite sure I was looking for one?"

Was she being purposefully enigmatic? He would have to parry more vigorously.

"Well, weren't you? I was pretty sure you'd be letting Jesus down, if you didn't." He was taken by surprise by his own abrasive frankness, but in her present persona, she appeared to ignore any irony.

"Ah." She nodded. "I see. You think I'm on the hot line every second to decide what I have to do."

"I don't know. Aren't you? Isn't that the way it works? I couldn't believe what Elsie suggested. I don't know what impression she took."

She laughed. "Elsie certainly wouldn't get any 'impression' from whether we slept together or not."

"Then why were you outraged when she thought we might already have?" He was enjoying the cut and thrust, and felt he had scored a palpable hit. She also gave every impression of being drawn into a pleasurable bout, playing on the edge of things, a verbal foreplay that excited them both.

"Hardly outraged," she insisted breathily. "I just didn't want her to assume she knew everything about us, that's all."

Tim was suddenly aware he did not know enough about her to assume anything, either, - which was precisely what excited him.

"Since you asked the question, what about you?" he asked.

"Me?" she asked, disingenuously.

"Yes. How would you have avoided sleeping with me?"

"That's to assume I would, isn't it?"

She had an answer for everything. She was, as Fred had said, 'sharp'.

"Anyway,.. what are we talking about here? Sleeping with a rolled up blanket down the middle. It's all a bit academic, isn't it?" He shrugged to suggest that he had put the final punctuation to the subject, hoping he had not.

There was a silence, in which resolution still hung in the air. He was excited by things unsaid, and felt the unconsummated relationship increasingly pressing in on him. He could not be sure if she was being provocatively flirtatious, or challenging him to be more importunate. Alicia settled back into the seat, relaxed, as if she had taken light refreshment, and slid her arm round his again. "I'd like to stop when we get to the hill," she said, carelessly. "I always think that view belongs to Fred. I'm going to say a prayer for him."

The engine purred its meandering way through the hills. As he sneaked glances at her, he reflected that, from the perspective of an inhibitive middle class southern counties upbringing, he was travelling in uncharted territory. One minute she was provocative and titillating, the next devotional and self-contained.

He pulled the car over into the parking bay and turned the engine off. She released herself from him, opened the door and walked slowly ahead to the fenced off vantage point. He held back, sensing she was treading her past. She turned back to him and tilted her head to invite him to join her. They stood next to each other, inches apart, drinking in the view, which was just beginning to fade into early evening obscurity. The cattle in the field below shifted imperceptibly, as if some unseen hand was moving them like models on a child's toy landscape. The distilled air flowed into their lungs like sparkling wine, giving substance to the cliché, 'feeling alive'. To a person with artistic sensibilities, it was enough to admit the possibility of God, Tim thought. He was, after all, appreciative of beauty, even if his involvement in art was as a business. But here he was standing next to a woman he wanted to take in his arms, whose lips he wanted to crush and part with his. He wanted to explore every inch of her with intimate licence. The mystery of how to reconcile beauty and his male impulse was elusive to him? He had never met a woman who had evoked in him such admiration for her talent, incited such longing by her ostensibly immodest approach to life and who now intrigued and touched him with her innocent reliance on faith.

"Will you join me in a prayer, Tim? I don't expect you to have any conviction that God is listening, but just to wish Fred well."

"Yes, of course." He was happy to join her simply because she had asked him. They would share something, even if qualified by his scepticism. Anyway, he explained to himself, it was unthinkable to dismiss such an intrinsic part of her life.

As she spoke, her voice floated over the scene, mellow, low toned and in a sincere vernacular he had never heard before, even from Fred and Elsie.

"Jesus, we're standing in a place where Fred has spoken to you many times. He shielded me and many others from the hurts of the world, and I know you're in his heart and he's in yours, just as I try to be. I ask you to keep him safe right now." She turned to Tim and in the same tone, said, " If you agree with anything I say, you can just say 'amen', if you want."

"Oh… right," he murmured.

She addressed the valley again. "I'm fine with whatever You decide," she said, "but if it's your will, I ask that he gets well soon." There was a pause, until it dawned on Tim that this was an unspoken nudge for his response. "Amen," he said, in a respectful grunt.

"Fred has always been with You, and has taught me how to approach You, too. I thank You and him for that. And now, he's brought Tim and me together. I'm trusting this is all right with You, because it's what I want. If we need to know ourselves better, please help us to do that. Make our love good in every way, keep us interested in each other, help us to always find ourselves in each other's faces and to share what we have with others, - and give us the gift of a passionate love that satisfies our desire for each other."

Fred started at what, for him, was a complete non-sequitor. Here she was, ostensibly in a prayer for Fred, involving God in the intimate details of their relationship.

"Amen," she said. The pause that followed gave Tim just enough time to consider the comprehensive nature of what he was endorsing, before he echoed her.

She turned from the valley with a satisfied sigh. "Well, I feel better, having left it in His hands. We can go now, if you like." It was like acknowledging a good meal.as you left the restaurant. She walked round him without looking at him, and he followed, relishing the way her hair curled round her ears and the nape of her neck grew ornamentally erect from her shoulders. He dropped his eyes to the rounded apple buttocks and trim waist, that complemented her Grecian bend. This disturbing female had a fertile mind as well as a seductive body, and she had confessed herself his. How did this happen? He hurried to catch her up and taking her shoulder, turned her towards him. Her look was without surprise or response, as they held each other in their gaze for an instant, before he pulled her towards him and kissed her with the hunger of a famished spirit. His ardour came from a desire to possess and to protect, drawn from both his male sexuality and his feminine tenderness. She responded by clinging to him as if surrendering her soul, and it was an age before they could bring themselves to make the physical break. She gave a short convulsive sigh as their lips parted, and he impulsively drew her to him, cradling her head and inhaling the smell of her hair. She dug her hands into his back as if gathering him in, and her breath on his shoulder came in urgent but gentle gusts. When they were able to relax the tension in their bodies, he held her away from him, searching for something decipherable from her eyes. He was dissolved by her look of gratitude, a recognition that he had claimed his place in her soul, and affirming his right to take the initiative. That kiss had earned him entitlement to an equal footing.

"Oh, I can feed off that," she said, at last. "I so want to make love with you, Tim."

He was aware of being very aroused, and conscious that she must have felt him against her. "You can't want it any more than me, Alicia." He said these words without the least consciousness of having been theatrical or contriving. Her passionate response had entitled him to say whatever he felt at that moment. Was he also entitled to think she might be inviting him to satisfy their desire now? She placed her hands on his chest and pushed herself away from him, like a ballet dancer in a duet. He was answered; this was all part of an interpretive dance, and all the steps had to be undergone before the finale was reached. He took hold of one of her hands, lifted it and pressed his lips to it, like a medieval knight about to take her favour into the joust. He now fell easily into the role of romantic courtier, avowing to carry her emblem patiently, until she was ready to surrender the greatest gift she possessed.

The rest of the journey to Netherton was attended by the clinging memory of their embrace, but there was no sense of urgency, just a silence filled with comfortable exchanged smiles, confirming their mutual engagement.

Tim handled the car with skill round the tight bends, and took pride in knowing that, although she had never confessed it, she must be impressed. As they arrived at the little house-cum-café, he felt that he was, this time, oh!, so much more than a guest. The way she smiled as she opened the door; the slow and easy way she walked around, filled the kettle, dropped the bread in the toaster, and invited Tim to sit at the table, all spoke of domestic familiarity, which filled him with a yearning to be always in her company. He could almost imagine the delight he would have in discussing domestic trivia. They would be so comfortable with each other that they would reserve deeply meaningful verbal exchanges for the evenings, and take their intellectual discoveries into the bedroom to be resolved in passionate love-making. Even smiling at each other over small things would be part of the fore-play of their sensual life together.

As they made their preparations for the night, there were no disturbing questions. Sleeping together, though eagerly anticipated - and in Tim's case, graphically imag-ined, was not an option. He smiled as, out of the blue, he suddenly remembered what a school mate, professing to know more than his years would suggest, had told him behind the cycle sheds, - that delayed love-making increased gratification. As Alicia and he supped, drank, smiled at each other across the table, laid their bedcovers out, they chatted animatedly over the day and then about her work and how they would choose the pictures that best represented her artistic vision. Tim described Nathan and tried to make real to her the experience he had with him. Then as they came to the moment to retire, they embraced with such unaffectedness, and kissed with such gentle surrender, and relinquished each other with such gracious exchange of amorous looks, that they knew love-making, when it came, would be phenomenally satisfying on many levels.

Links

Tim awoke to what promised to be a invigorating day. As a preface to the exploration of her paintings, Alicia led him on a brisk walk through the sloping meadows that formed the backcloth at the rear of her property, scenery that played a large part of what she portrayed in her paintings. Then, arm in arm, blood coursing through the veins and cheeks flushed with fresh air and intermittent kisses, they returned, their lungs and minds refreshed, to discuss the merits of her paintings, and choose ten. Carefully skirting round any religious inplications, Tim focused on the aesthetics and technical excellence of her talent. They discussed her brush technique, the spatial ordering and the emotional content of her subject matter. He listened avidly as she led him into her paintings, revealing personal insights of her life-experience, symbolised by the diverse paths that led through the scenery that subtly changed in each subsequent picture. The exits to which the figures travelled, or round which they disappeared marked the unknown future. She spoke fluently and confidently about what she aimed to portray, and he related the painterly skill to the artistic purpose, priding himself on finding the 'mot juste' to show how art works. He flushed with pleasure each time she recognised his tutored skills, and he heaped praise on the vibrancy of her work. Choosing ten frames out of all those displayed took a whole morning of heated debate, full of wide-eyed appreciation and surprising agreements.

Having sublimated all amorous feelings during their passionate critical involvement, and with ten frames now gathered on the table, she flung her arms round his neck and shouted, "I love you, Tim Carter, connoisseur extraordiaire! You were sent to me! We're the best team in the world!" He basked in the reverberating echo of this rapturous hyperbole with all the naivety that comes with being insanely in love. "You've made me come alive," he said, with the transparency of an innocent.

They laughed like children, not only at the daring arousal of sensuality by touching each other's body but confirming each other's sensibilities. They embraced and kissed with an unabashed passion, that allowed him to make some intimate exploration of her body.

"I never imagined such happiness!" he proclaimed, throwing out his arms in a flamboyant gesture intended to include her, her work and the whole world opened up to him.

"That's because none of us ever can," she said, "and we must live it to the full, because when it fades, we can never bring it back. Oh, what a wonderful mystery!"

The world of abandoned joy was halted in its tracks. How could this be wonderful to her?

"Why fade? Why must it ever fade?" he said from a feeling of deep resentment.

"Everything in this world does! That's the beauty of our experience!"

Seeing her so exultant was unbearable, and his face crumpled. "How can it be beautiful if it fades?"

His question was more real and serious than mere contradiction, and seeing the hurt in his face, she knew it was not to be made light of. Patting his arm, she withdrew from his embrace and sauntered some steps away to gather her thoughts. "Just because we won't feel like this for ever, doesn't mean I love you any the less."

"Why do we have to think about what might change in the future?"

"Our love grows into something greater. If it didn't it would become too familiar." She turned to him smiling and frowning at the same time, willing him to understand. "If what we feel now didn't change we'd take it for granted, and you and I,…"

He attempted to deny her claim, but she held up her hand.

"No, listen, Tim, darling, we would start to look past each other, desperately trying to hold on to what we feel now." She waved a hand to indicate her paintings. "Even all this will change. I'll see it from a new perspective. Every time I come back to a painting, it will have something else to say to me. The gift of hindsight, if you like. "

He felt weighed down, but was more intent on expressing his mood than coming to terms with his understanding. "That is the saddest thing," he whispered.

"No, it isn't! Not in the least!" she declared. "The joy is in the journey, itself not at any stage."

"Right," he murmured dismissively, almost resentful of her apparent levity. "But where will this 'joy', as you call it, go?"

She came back to stand in front of him, challenging him. "It doesn't go. It just changes all the time."

"Into what?"

She shrugged. "Memories…wisdom, satisfaction, regret, pain, and everything else that makes us love each other more."

Tim shook his head, confused. She nodded impatiently.

"Believe it! It's the best part!" He was consumed by a mixture of pleasure and pain. He rejoiced in her spirited face, a volatile work of art in itself, but could find nothing but bitterness in the idea of its sacrifice for something better. There couldn't be anything better than this.

"It would be better not to have happiness, if we have to let it go in the end," he muttered.

For a moment his frown reminded her of a small boy refused an ice- cream.

"Never say that, Tim. Happiness isn't something to grab on to." She contemplated him for a moment, exhaling her frustration in a single breath. She took control of her voice, conscious of the danger of sounding didactic. "You haven't really understood my paintings without understanding the nature of change," she said patiently. "They're all about the journey." She came close enough to lay her hand on his arm. "I was making it alone, until you came, and now my painting will change, and you'll be an inevitable part of it. You will change me and my art." - here she nodded reassuringly as if to a child, before adding with slow emphasis - "And that's precisely how it has to be. How I want it."

He felt some consolation in the eager sincerity written in her face, and he reached out to touch it. She stood impassive, allowing him to cup her chin as if he were inspecting a precious vase.

"God knows, I love your face," he mumbled,

"God does indeed know, but that's now."

"I always want to see you like this."

"No. Don't ask for that." She cocked her head to one side and squinted at him. "That's too romantic. It's trying to make earthly love eternal. Fred once said to me..how did he put it?" She made an amateur attempt at mimicking his voice. " 'They say ye can't tek it wi' ye when ye've gone. By 'eck, ye can't even tek it wi' ye on yer way'. He never held on to things."

"That old man's very important in your life, isn't he?" He spoke with respect, but also some resentment, for his radical influence.

"He and Elsie have been everything; mother, father, friends, confidants, and tutor. I owe everything to them. They taught me how to be me and then let me go. I love them for that more than they can ever know." She shook her head and changed mood. "I'm beginning to sound like some narrator of my own life!" She moved to the paintings they had chosen. "You must stop me, when it gets too much."

He stood drinking in her form and sensuality, but also disturbed and challenged by her confident vision, "I'll never stop listening to you," he said tonelessly. She turned.

"Nor I to you. We'll listen and we'll also hear."

"What's the difference?

"You always listen when you're in love. But you only hear if you sometimes stand apart." She paused. "I pray that for us."

He smiled ruefully. "I've a way to go, yet, haven't I?"

"A good start!" she replied, dramatically changing her tone and suddenly bursting into energetic action. "Let's pack these paintings in the car!"

They left all those intense feelings behind as soon as they were on their way. Alicia was excited at having her paintings shown to someone, whom Tim so obviously admired, and, Tim was boyantly proud of his part in the matter, believing it gave him some status to make up for his ignorance of the world. He was elated but apprehensive. He knew Nathan would be honest in his appraisal, and it could not be taken for granted that he would like her pictures enough to display them in his window. What if he rejected her work? It was a disconcerting possibility.

For Alicia, Blackbridge was not entirely a new experience; she had visited it on one or two occasions, looking for labour-saving kitchen appliances. On those occasions, she had taken the opportunity to window shop, peering at the fashion boutiques, swiftly deciding she could easily do without all the nonsense that goes with it. She vaguely remembered the book shop, and presumed it must have been more than two years since she had last walked past it. As it was, she relied on the fortnightly travelling library to enable her to keep abreast of the *'zeitgeist'*, or as much of it as she wished.

Tim planned to pull up outside the shop to unload the pictures and leave Alicia with them, while he found a parking place. The speed, with which he had to make the delivery, turned it into something resembling a commando ammunition drop. He was ready to appease any lurking traffic warden, by leaving the boot open and the car jack on the pavement and wore a contrite frown to show he knew the offensive seriousness of parking on a single yellow line.

As he carried the first two wrapped frames up the steps and into the entrance, Nathan came out from behind the counter at the far end of the room, and marched forward to welcome him.

"My dear fellow! Good to see you! And what have we here?! Framed pictures, no less!"

Alicia walked up behind, and Nathan was about to step aside, thinking she was a customer, when Tim straightened up and introduced them. "This is Alicia, Nathan. Nathan, Alicia. Look, sorry, but I've got to get the car away before I get nabbed for illegal parking. There's eight more to bring in and then I'll drive it to the multi car park. Are they all right just here?" He nodded to the side of the door.

"Yes, of course. I'll give you a hand into the shop and then we can talk at leisure," he said, smiling broadly at Alicia to include her in the welcome.

They had the rest of the frames inside the shop in a very short time, and, with a quick wave, Tim drove off, leaving Nathan and Alicia to properly introduce themselves.

If Alicia was in any way embarrassed, she gave no sign of it. It was Nathan, who, having been abruptly invaded, was put in the position of having to entertain this attractive young woman, who, by her fixed regard and confident smile, looked as if she expected him to cope with the same equanimity as she possessed. He was bemused first by the framed pictures and now by her, having been give no prior notice of either.

"I'm delighted to meet you," he offered, "I'm Nathan, the owner of the shop."

"Yes, I know. Tim's told me a lot about you. He thinks you're very good with pictures."

"Really? How kind of him." He touched her elbow and indicated the room at the back. "Would you like to go through to my den. It's private there, and I can get the girls to make a mug of tea."

There were two or three people browsing among the shelves, and he asked one of the girl assistants in a discreetly lowered voice to put the kettle on. As they continued to the back of the shop, he tried to imagine why Tim had included this attractive lady friend on a business trip.

"Are you in the same business as Tim, then?" he asked, as he opened the door to usher her in.

"No." She entered the office, and he brushed past her to tidy some papers and books off the three chairs.

"No, I run a small village café," she said.

"Really?" He paused to imagine how he might construct some meaningful response. "Do take a seat. This one's not dusty. A café? How very interesting."

"Not really, but it serves the purpose. Thank you." She lowered herself into the armchair and looked round at the floor and surfaces littered with books and magazines.

"Quite," Nathan said, repeating himself inaudibly to see if it he could detect some significance in what she had said. He sat behind his desk. "So you're a friend of Tim's." He settled himself behind his desk, peering at her over the piles of books, as if under seige.

"I think we owe you an apology, Mr,....?"

"Oh, please call me Nathan. I never like formality. It gets in the way.

Why?"

"Why?" She looked perplexed.

"Why an apology?"

"Oh, yes, well, Tim said he was sure you'd want to see the pictures."

"Splendid. Always glad to see them. I always say if a man's soul starves without books, it will certainly shrivel without art. I stock lots of children's picture books."

"But he didn't inform you he intended to introduce the works of an unknown painter."

"Ah, not quite true. He did mention the possibility, and I gave him the nod on that. Do you know who it is?"

She laughed. "It's me."

His eyes widened. "Oh, I see! You've.. he's brought... heavens to betsy! Why didn't he say?"

"I don't think he had time, - to be fair."

"Well, of course not," he admitted, as he slapped his thigh. Then, with a twinkle in his eye, and a knowing smirk, he added, "But *you* could have let on. Perhaps the game was to let me make a judgement, before you confessed to being the artist," he said, playfully."

"Not at all. I would expect you to give an honest opinion, whatever."

"I say, dear young lady, I hope I didn't offend you. Of course, I always respect people with my honest opinion, for what it's worth. But I'm not an art specialist, you know. I hope Tim told you that."

"You're in an important position, Mr....."

"Nathan. Call me Nathan. Can't be doing with formality."

"Well, Nathan, you're in the position to show my work, not just give an opinion on it. That's a sight more important."

"Yes, so it is, so it is. What if I don't like it?"

"Then I'll go on doing what I believe in, and take it somewhere else."

"Splendid! The mark of a true artist! At the end of the day, creating for yourself." He got up out of his chair in a bound and said, in a voice that could have opened a gala. "Right, then, let's bring 'em in here, and have a look!"

He swept out of his office and was soon back with two of the frames. As he returned he asked the assistant how the tea was getting on. Thereafter, he marched back and forth with gusto until all the pictures were gathered in one corner. Then, breathing heavily and setting himself down behind the desk again, he gestured to Alicia, like a conductor prompting the entry of the soloist, and exclaimed, "Over to you, my dear lady!"

Alicia, who had been left to marvel at the frenetic activity with which the frames had been collected, took a moment to adjust herself to the role of exhibitor extended her.

She went over, uncertainly, to the pictures leaning against each other. "I'm not sure how you want me to do this."

"One at a time seems to be a good idea. Let's put the first on the desk here." He brushed a pile of papers and magazines on to the floor with a sweep of his hand. "Then you can range them round the skirting over there."

She unwrapped the first painting, and laid it carefully on the desk top. Leaving Nathan with this, she started to arrange the rest against the wall opposite the desk. For someone used to governing her own exclusive world, it was a new experience to comply with someone else's requirements, and, for the first time, she felt vulnerable; as if by having her work valued, she was being asked to put *herself* up for sale. There was only room for five along the wall, and she turned to Nathan, who was still peering closely at the painting on his desk. She halted and froze, watching for the slightest reaction in his expression. His face was immobile and totally uncommunicative.

"I've managed to get five in the space," she offered.

"Ye-e-es. Right then." His voice was languid, absorbed, as he was, in the scene before him. "You go right ahead."

What that was supposed to indicate, she had no idea. She stood watching him closely as his eyes slowly wandered over the whole breadth of the canvas, the silence invaded only by the sound of a pinging cash till in the shop. Then he stood and stepped back to get a wider perspective on it. He squinted, pursed his lips and cocked his head slightly to one side, murmuring to himself. Suddenly he said, "Right, let's be having another one."

"They're over there." She pointed to the floor, and he looked momentarily disoriented. "Ah, yes. Right. Ah,ha.. um. I see." He stood over them, scanning all five pictures with one continuous slow turn of his body.

He homed in on one in the middle and bent down to scrutinize it minutely. Shortly he picked it up and took it back to the desk, placed it next to the first one, and proceeded to cast his eyes back and forth between the two. Just then the assistant came to the door carrying two cups of tea, unsure where to place them. Nathan waved airily at the side wall and said, "Put them somewhere on one of the shelves, Deidre, there's a good girl. And thank you."

"That's all right, Nathan." She spoke as if, despite the familiarity of her address, she might be about to curtsey, and then went, leaving the cups on a shelf together with a small sugar bowl and spoon. Nathan continued to focus impassively on the paintings, leaving Alicia to guess his reaction. From the deep concentration he applied to the task, he might have been working out annual expenses for the Inland Revenue. His face revealed nothing as he appeared to survey every detail. He moved his head from side to side, as if he were weighing up two sides of a crucial argument, before crossing once more to the other paintings against the wall.

"Do have your tea before it goes cold. There's sugar in the bowl," he mumbled, without glancing her way. He proceeded to kneel and work his way along the whole row on his knees, as she took one of the mugs off the shelf. She stood and sipped her tea, watching for the slightest indication of his thoughts.

At length he stood up, went slowly over to his seat and sat with a sigh. "The light's not good," he said with a reflective nod.

"What's wrong with it?" She was defensive, but also receptive; Nathan had, after all, gone to some trouble to scrutinise her work.

"More light would accentuate the vibrancy of the colours. I can see that. I made allowances for it."

"You don't like them, then?" She could feel stoicism descending on her. He looked at her directly, seeming to come out of abstracted thought, and frowned.

"Like them?!" he said, as if he had been insulted by their very presence, and then added, with a flamboyant gesture, "I think they're wonderful! They moved me!"

"But you said the light…something's wrong?"

"The light in this room!" he exclaimed, pointing to the window behind them. "It doesn't do them justice. I had to get close to them, too close, to feel their passion!"

"Oh,… I see!" She laughed with relief.

"Sit down, Alicia, dear young lady." He waved his hand at the chair facing the desk. "You must know that I am not trained in art, and, at the end of the day, haven't the least right to make any judgement at all. But if my sensibility serves me, I believe your paintings have such strong potential to affect the viewer they'll certainly be sought. There is passion, a vibrant involvement in life and a challenge that one rarely sees today."

She was overwhelmed by his response, and they looked at each other in silence for some moments, as if each measuring the other's visual presence against their judgement and talent. A tear ran slowly down her face, and he was instantly moved to say, "My dear young lady, you should be smiling with pleasure at the gift you've been given."

"I am smiling inside." Impulsively she stood and went and kissed him on his bearded cheek.

"I say, steady on, dear heart!" he exclaimed leaning back in his chair.

"Tim was right," she said with conviction, retiring back to her seat, "You are a true amateur. Someone who encourages with your own enjoyment."

Nathan was preening himself at her compliment when through the door he could glimpse Tim coming into the shop and striding towards them.

"Ah, I see our friend coming." He stood and, turning to Alicia, put his finger to his lips to indicate secrecy. She was surprised, but nodded her assent.

"My dear fellow, did you have some difficulty?" he asked, as Tim arrived breathless at the threshold. Tim nodded as he caught his breath back.

"Another mug, Deidre, please, if you would be so kind!" he called out to the shop. "Sit down and get your breath back. Heavens! The price we pay for civic order on the roads! However, we've managed to kill time aimiably enough here. When you've recovered, I'll have your assessment of your friend's pictures."

Tim sat in the remaining chair at the side of the table and blew out his cheeks. "I had to go right to the top of the multi-storey car park, and I couldn't wait for the lift." He smiled a little nervously at Alicia. "I see you've had a chance to look at her work," he said to Nathan. "So what do you think?"

Nathan hastily broke in to prevent Alicia from replying. "Well, since you're the expert, I thought it best to hear why you think it's worth giving space in the shop."

Tim looked again at Alicia and then back to Nathan, before asking, "Don't you like her work?"

"Leaving aside what might be likeable, what makes you think people'll want to buy 'em? You're the one in the selling business, after all."

Tim suddenly felt himself in an inquisition, and bridled at being put on the spot in front of Alicia. "Well, I'd have thought it was obvious. They show maturity in the handling of paint. Her subtle blending of colour, the control of the fine brush work and the textural richness created by the layering in varying density speaks of her talent for visual detail within the broad statement."

"Ah here's your tea. Thank you, Deidre." Deidre handed the cup to Tim and left as swiftly as she had come.

"You were saying?" Nathan said casually.

"Well,....I think I've more or less answered your question." Tim replied, in a tone that implied his lack of attention to something that was self-evident.

424

"Oh, right, my dear chap. Could you write that down for me, do you think? Maybe the general public passing the window might want to read it."

Alicia laughed and immediately placed a hand over her mouth. Tim turned to her suddenly perplexed, and then back to Nathan, for some response. Nathan looked at him and posed in his chair as Rodin's 'Thinker'. "That would be just a little beyond the power of most clientele to relate to," he said soberly, straightening up again. "Look, if someone comes into the shop, having asked questions about one of these pictures, how would you try to convince them to buy it?"

"Well, for a start, I would expect them to have thought them beautiful or possibly dramatic, so I wouldn't need to say that."

"Absolutely right. So, what *do* we say?"

"I'd probably say that these pictures,".. looking round at Alicia in a proprietory way, seeking moral support ... "were a very good investment, and will increase in value over the years."

"I doubt that would make them want them, unless they were merely art punters, as I call them."

"Look Nathan, what are we saying here? Don't you like them? Because if you don't, we shouldn't waste any more of your time."

Nathan smiled, confident that Alicia had recognised the point he was making, and said gently, "Tim, my very good partner, I adore them all."

Tim stared back at him and then at Alicia. "You do?"

Nathan nodded and smiled at them both.

"So you really agree with me."

"Well, not quite. If you'll allow me, I think people will see what they want in the pictures, for themselves."

Tim was dismissive. "Most people haven't a clue about good art, when they see it."

"Yes, of course. Lots of people aren't even faintly interested in art, any more than they are in religion. So,..," He spread his hands out to beg indulgence. "...we prompt them to enjoy what they see in a picture, not its excellence, which some," he added, "will see for themselves and some won't." He turned to Alicia, who had been listening avidly to both sides but still addressed himself to Tim.

"Why don't we ask your artist friend what she's selling?"

They turned to her and she half-smiled back at them for some moments, which disconcerted them to the point at which they began to shift in their seats. Tim still held an untouched mug of tea, and Nathan leant forward like a family doctor, waiting to listen to a description of the symptoms.

She broke the silence. "I think you're both right within your own terms of reference."

"You're a diplomat, my dear," said Nathan with a wink and a knowing smirk.

"And you're also completely wrong. Tim speaks of artistry and you speak of pleasure. That's fine, as far as they go, and you can throw your respective doctrines at each other as long as you like. But, to answer the question you put, Nathan, I'm not *selling* anything at all."

Nathan sat back and spread his arms out expansively. "But you want to be recognised, don't you? And that means being bought by people who like what you paint."

"Liking is only a part of it, - a means to an end. I paint what I know and feel about myself. What I want is for people to like my pictures enough to draw them into seeing something they recognise in themselves."

Tim silently admitted to himself that he was denied this aspect of her painting, but Nathan was drawn deeper into the need to define. He was like a ferret, foraging down a burrow, looking at alternative tunnels to explore.

"Which comes first, then, the liking or the recognising?" he asked "Yes, all right," she conceded. "But what the pictures say is more important, - to me, anyway."

"What *do* they say?" Nathan challenged.

"Well, *you* say you like them. What do they say to *you*?"

Nathan smiled. "This artist friend of your is very canny, Tim, my dear fellow. We must watch and learn."

Tim, very conscious of what this might mean in their relationship, settled for a nod and a raised eyebrow. He was aware also that there were things to be learned from this exchange between two people important to him in different ways.

"Well?" Alicia challenged.

"All right. First, I see you, the artist, in the paintings. I see you, - or maybe it's someone you identify with, - travelling through changing scenes, in various seasons, and this suggests that both the figure and the country are metaphors. Of what, I don't know."

"And you like that?" She pressed him to respond.

"Yes, because it involves me, empathetically," he said.

"Right. Do you mean, you identify with it, or you find it interesting?"

"Well, I can't say I identify, otherwise I'd be more certain of the what they represent, you see, wouldn't I?"

"So, you have a detached view of the pictures," Alicia suggested, as if this was the only alternative.

"I wouldn't say 'detached'." He mused for a second. "More curious to be a part of something that I don't understand, without knowing what it means. That is," he hastily added, "I want to be a part of it."

There was silence. Tim looked at each in turn. Nathan searched her face for the response. She sat immobile, and, to the amazement of both lover and new-found friend, a tear trickled down her cheek. Tim instinctively leant over to her and took her hand, as Nathan dropped his lower lip and opened his eyes wide with concern. When he recovered himself, he murmured, in a gracious and apologetic tone, "My dear young lady, I hope I haven't offended you."

She sniffed and half smiled as her chin quivered. She looked first at Tim and withdrew her hand to pass it across her cheek, and then at Nathan, to whom she looked as if she was going to accuse of some terrible fault. Her voice, when it came, was broken, as if grief-stricken. "I'm sorry." She swallowed hard before continuing. "I don't think you will understand how what you said, affected me."

"I wouldn't have said anything to hurt you, dear lady," Nathan hastened remorsefully to assure her.

"Oh, you haven't! You haven't at all!." She shook her head vehemently.

Nathan pulled out a drawer and handed a tissue to her, which she gratefully accepted, and instantly used to wipe her nose. "You said what I wanted most in the world to hear."

"Did I?" Nathan looked amazed and Tim, completely confused.

"Yes. It's as if it spoke to someone, and it's been called into the world."

Tim felt in that moment the greatest desire to communicate with Alicia, her painting and her whole vision of life. It was as if the worst fate to befall him would be to be outside her world, Jesus and all.

Nathan, somewhat bewildered, and with a timidity that he had not shown before, said, "I'm sorry, but what exactly did I say?"

"That you didn't understand but you still wanted to be part of it."

"And that's enough to get you all emotional?" Nathan asked, intrigued.

"It means you share my acceptance of the mystery."

"Mystery of what, dear lady/"

"Everything that's wrapped in the hands of my well-wishing God."

Both men retired into their respective caves. For Tim, this was the revelatory painful moment, when he understood this lovely woman's need for companionship even in her voyage of faith. He saw, for the first time, a vulnerability behind her confidence. In a flash of hindsight, he saw what she had been telling him about their life together, and only the fear of making an inappropriate gesture before Nathan prevented him from embracing her. His intense focus on her, however, had been observed by Nathan, who smiled and nodded his recognition.

His voice, when he gathered his courage, was gruff and warm. "I say, good people, I'm going to stick my neck out again, and congratulate you on having found each other."

Alicia emitted a half-laugh, half-sob of emotional release. Tim nodded back at Nathan, saying quietly, "Yes, you've guessed. It's obvious, I suppose."

"It is, rather." He stood abruptly. "I'd like to congratulate myself for having been found by you, dear hearts. There seems to be only one way to do that. I insist on taking you both to a little trattoria I know round the corner and celebrate,..well,.. just about everything. What d'you say?"

They all looked at each other and, in dumb joy, nodded agreement.

Vicissitude

Tim would look back at that afternoon and see it, not only as a turning point, but also a stile he had climbed over. Not only was he drawn to express his love for Alicia in a more commited and protective way, but he had established a friendship involving all three of them. They were an 'amitie a trois', involved in an affair of the heart and mind and artistic soul.

During their 'celebration' lunch, which lasted three hours, by courtesy of Nathan's efficient assistants. they offered each other their antecedents. It transpired that Nathan was Jewish, with an unorthodox inability to resist all possible philosophies and religions. He quoted William Blakes's dictum, 'Anything possible to be believed is an image of the truth', and Alicia instantly leaped to recommend her voyage with Jesus, countering with C.S.Lewis's insistence that since Jesus was neither bad nor mad, he was, and is, in fact, who he said he was. The Chianti accompanied the courses and loosened tongues to confess to all kinds of determining influences in their lives. Tim found himself discovering all kinds of significanct effects from past experience, especially childhood ones. Alicia said she believed that what a child is taught becomes what he faces the world with, and took the opportunity to laud Fred's role in her life. Tim informed them he had read Freud and proceeded to explain things to them about himself that he had not fathomed until the moment he opened his mouth. When he expressed surprise at having promounced this, Nathan confessed that very often he didn't know what he knew until he said it. And, as new friends will often do, they explored and commented on each other's lives, opening up to each other with a licence freely given by the wine. 'In vino veritas' had never been more clearly exemplified, and words said slightly slurred were shown to be entirely credible or was it creditable, or even 'cred-ibited...able'?

The excitement of their association in the artistic venture led Nathan, after his fourth glass, to offer Tim to become a partner in the running of the art side of the shop, and Tim after his third, reflected for at least two seconds before accepting. Alicia, who kept to one glass, looked on them both with a heightened sense of communion, and loved them both in different ways, Tim, because he was now her man, and Nathan because he was not only their friend but an excellent prospective candidate for finding faith. She went quiet for some minutes, and Nathan asked if anything were the matter, to which she replied that she was taking a moment for silent prayer of thanks and supplication. They all went quiet and, in their individual ways internalised their thoughts, maybe in prayer, but more probably in dialogue with themselves.

When they left the Trattoria, Nathan invited them to have strong black coffee at the shop, and everyone agreed that it was not only an agreeable but also essential suggestion to end the afternoon.

Were they all happy that the paintings should begin the display in the window to be allocated to art? Yes,

Absolutely. Were they all happy to let Nathan write something to place next to the paintings in the window? Yes. Indubitably. Were they happy to join Alicia in a short prayer to inaugurate the association? Er,..yes, they were indeed, so long as *she* delivered the words. She did; they joined in spirit, and there was an emphatic 'amen' to round it off. Nathan left them with his opinion on the importance of what they were about to embark on. and referring them to T.S.Eliot's assertion that 'without religion or history there was no culture', adding that, "Without art, neither history nor religion have a visible umbilical cord... to hand on the DNA of the... dialectic progression of man's spirituality.". Whether he would have phrased it that way on another occasion was speculative.

Good strong coffee made the journey to Elsie's place feasible, but it was only Providence that covered Tim until he arrived, without the least danger to his car or reputation, at her door.

He let them in, and they burst into the kitchen to impart their latest good news to Elsie, only to find that she had left a note on the table, which read,

I have gone down to the home on account of a message what I got from the matron. Don't know when you will be coming home, but it's best to join me when you've made yourselves a cup of tea. Not to worry. love. Elsie

Ignoring Elsie's reference to tea, the panacea for all ills, they instantly agreed to go straight on to the home to find out the state of affairs. Alicia judged it to be something to do with Fred resistance to the matron's good advice, and Tim hoped she was right.

"He just isn't the kind to buckle down to taking orders, especially when it entails lying in bed doing nothing," Alicia asserted. Tim agreed that it went against his nature, and they turned on their heels and drove straight to the home without another word. Alicia was quiet and ruminative on the short journey and Tim tried to catch her attention by smiling at her. Her lack of response clearly indicated she was more worried than she was ready to admit.

When they reached the office and gave their name, the young receptionist rang an internal number to call matron down. Within half a minute the clicking heels resounded down the corridor and she came into view round the corner of the corridor at the far end of the lobby. She wore a sorely tried and philosophical expression that hinted at the story to be told.

"Miss Wainwright, I'm glad you've come. I've told your grandmother that someone needs to knock some sense into your grandfather."

Tim thought how ill-conceived that idea was. But then how could anyone know the nature of the relationships in this family, or the idiosycracies of Fred. Surely Elsie had already corrected her on that point. Neither Tim nor Alicia were about to make an issue out of it, however.

"We're just having a confabulation in my office as to what it would be best to do with Mr. Butterworth. We really must sort something out, so if you'll follow me."

She led them back along the corridor to her office, and there they found Elsie, sitting with a face as serious as a spiritualist conducting a séance. An air of discomfort hung over the room. Elsie rose and came to hug Alicia, and Tim held back, marginalised. Matron closed the door, and went round behind her desk.

"Mrs Wainwright has heard what I've had to say about the situation, but I'd best repeat it, so we all know." She paused a moment to give weight to her statement. "Mr. Butterworth refuses to keep to his bed, and takes no notice of my warnings. He is likely to do himself real harm carrying on like this."

"Trouble is 'e's alus bin active, and 'e's not partial ter 'is bed," Elsie said, as though offering some helpful advice.

"Could you give a sedative, perhaps?" Alicia broke in to ask.

"He just won't take any medication. Says he wants all his faculties when he's talking to his friend, Jesus. I asked him what was to stop him talking to him in bed."

"Wot did 'e say ter that?" Elsie asked in a tone that implied she could well guess.

"He said he'd never prayed lying down, and wasn't going to start doing it now."

"Aye, well, that's 'im fer ye," Elsie declared as she reseated herself.

"That's all very well," Alicia said, "but he's not doing himself any favours." She turned to Matron. "What does he *do* out of bed?"

"Knocks on resident's doors asking if there's anything on their consciences they want to pray about. Some take exception. They're over ninety, some of them."

"'E's never bin backward in doin' that," Elsie offered to the whole assembly.

"But, grandma, this isn't the time," Alicia said firmly "He's recovering from a severe chill."

"I have to be plain with you. If he doesn't conform, I'll have to get him into the hospital," said Matron, adamantly. "I can't take the responsibility for his welfare."

"Is he in his room, now?" Alicia asked.

"I'm hoping so, but I can't bank on it."

"Can we have a word with him?"

"I wish you would, for his sake."

Matron led the three of them up to his room and knocked on his door. At first there was no answer, but at the second knock, a feeble voice, like that of someone who has just woken up, responded with a "yes?"

"Your family's here to see you. Can we come in?"

"There's on'y the door what's stopping ye," the reply came back.

Matron opened the door, to reveal Fred sitting in his armchair next to the bed. There was a bible on his knees, but it was patently obvious he had just been awakened, for he did not focus on them immediately.

"Mr. Butterworth, I've just explained my position to Mrs. Wainwright, and your granddaughter, and we all agree…"

"…I've ter stay in me bed," Fred completed in a resigned gruff voice.

"Can we see you getting into it right now, please.?" Matron placed her hand under his armpit and assisted him to rise and climb beneath the sheets. Tim observed that, despite his gargoyle expression, he had neither energy nor disposition to resist. He looked at Alicia, who was sharing the same impression that he was, at the same time, restive and enervated. Elsie had also been taken by surprise at his lack of resistance, and stood, looking helpless, while Matron attended to plumping up his pillows and tucking the sheets round him.

When he was finally esconced with his back leant against the pillows, making him look like a depleted Eastern Potentate giving audience to his courtiers,

Matron turned to the three visitors and said curtly, "Well, I'll leave him to you. Perhaps you could drop into my office before you go." Without any formality, she left the room.

Tim got two chairs from the other side of the room and placed them near the bed for Elsie and Alicia, and as soon as he did so, he felt marginalised.

"Would you like me to leave you with him?" he whispered to Alicia.

"No!" she hissed back in obvious distress at the idea. "He'll want to see us all together." She clutched at his arm to show the intensity of her feeling.

"Of course. Sorry."

"What're ye whisperin' 'bout, yeou two?" Fred asked, to ensure they realised he was in possession of his faculties.

"Nothing, Uncle Fred."

"I've never bin afeared o' anythin', but I'm alus afeared o'nothin'. It leads ter t' worst o things."

"All ye've ter worry 'bout is getting' yer 'ealth back," Elsie said, trying to sound severe. "An' ye won't get near ter doin' that, if ye keep climbin' out o' yer bed."

"What've ye got to cheer me, then?" Fred asked, attempting to divert Elsie.

"We've got some good news! Tim's friend has made him a partner and they're going to show my paintings in his Blackbridge High Street shop!" Alicia proclaimed, whereupon Elsie, her eyes as wide as saucers, responded by reaching out to her and patting her arm. "Ee, that's a turn up fer t' book! My girl's goin' ter be famous! What d'ye think, eh, Fred?"

"Gherraway wi' ye. I've know'd that all along!" he retorted. "It were jus' a matter o' getting' 'er 'itched up ter t'right connections." He nodded towards Tim. "I knowed 'e were the one, all along ter make 'er 'appy."

The idea of Fred being Able to prognosticate his role as Alicia's agent made him smile inwardly. Alicia looked possessively at him, sufficient to make his innards revolve with an excitement he could hardly contain. Who was it said the seat of passion is not the heart, it is the entrails? He was right. He smiled modestly to hide his jubilation.

"And so,…" Alicia prefaced, putting on a serious face, and diverting the conversation back to the matter in hand, "..as we were saying, are you going to be sensible and do what Matron tells you?"

He remained silent and looked at the ceiling. Alicia looked at Elsie for support. She pursed her lips and shook her head as if to say miracles might change the habit of a lifetime.

"Nay, but Fred, ye've ter be good fer t' sake o' yer 'ealth." It wasn't admonition this time, but an urgent appeal to good sense and her own feelings. He looked at her for a while as if from a distance, and then relaxed his gaze into one of warm memories.

"I know, Elsie love, ye've alus bin one ter fuss o'er me. I may not a showed gratitude, but I knowed ye meant well. Trouble is, ye've bin contendin' wi' 'abits I've 'ad all mi life." The next minute, he translated back into the Fred they all knew, and said in a business-like manner, "Now afore ye all go, I jus' want ter say as" - and here he spoke as if he were ticking off items on the agend to be covered - ".. I'm pleased ye've come, I'm fair made over wi' yer news, I know as 'ow ye're doin' t' right thing, I 'ope ye don't wait too long ter get 'itched, yeou two, and,.." - turning to Elsie, - "ye've not ter let t'ome fires burn out while I'm away. An' now,.." - appearing satisfied he'd covered everything, - "since ye're so concerned I get mi sleep, I'd be thankful if ye'd give me peace an' quiet."

He did look tired and with silent accord, they nodded and rose. Alicia kissed him on his cheek, Elsie touched the back of his hand and said softly, "It's all fer t'best, Fred, love." He nodded and muttered, "Aye."

Tim stepped forward and took Fred's hand in a firm grip, and, without knowing precisely what he meant, simply said, "Thanks."

Fred looked up at him, as if unable to fathom what there was to be grateful for, then squeezed his hand. "Ye've ter thank 'Im, who'e bin workin' it all out fer us." Tim nodded assent, but was not sure whether it was to please Fred or because he had accepted the truth of it.

When they spoke to Matron, Elsie assured her that he would probably be good from now on, without specifying what the word 'good' meant. Matron raised her eyebrows at the word 'probably, but let it go. Alicia asked her to be sure to ring them if there was anything they could do. She assured her that there would be no need to send him to hospital, and Matron agreed on the understanding that she was not to be made responsible for the consequences of any disobedience. They parted reasonably amicably and believing they had done the best they could, went back to Elsie's.

They sat at the kitchen table, cradling their teacups and going over the day. Elsie pestered Alicia about her paintings, and wanted to know how long it would be before she was famous. Tim made all the right noises and told her in what high esteem Nathan held them, and that it was only a matter of time before first Blackbridge and then the whole art world would show interest. Alicia looked modestly sceptical, throughout, but was incapable of persuading her grandmother of the impossibility of their being hung in the National Gallery. They spoke of how things were in Netherton, and the old days, when things were far harder than they are today, thus turning to the part Fred had taken in their lives. Naturally enough, this brought them back to their visit to him that day, and how, being the character he was, it was hardly to be expected he could change his ways over night. They encouraged each other with optimism and humorous comments on the difficulties the Matron would necessarily have in dealing with such a strong-willed old man. Finally, Elsie started on the delicate subject of whether Alicia and Tim would travel back to her place in the evening or settle for bedding down at Elsie's, when the telephone rang.

They were all a little startled. Elsie's contact with the outside world was restricted to maybe Alf or Bert, ringing in to say they were going to be late from work, or some matter to be resolved by the local council. Elsie went into the hall to receive the call, and Tim and Alicia gave half an ear to her. They became vaguely concerned when Elsie remained silent. Alicia rose and crept to the door to listen, just as Elsie said, "Right ye'are, then," in a dispirited way.

Elsie turned back to the kitchen and met Alicia.

"Is everything all right?"

Elsie gave her a dazed look and clucked her tongue. "'E's at it again. Would ye credit it? They can't even find 'im, now."

"He's got out of bed?"

"We've ter get down there again, 'cos she's rang t' police."

Tim got up from his seat and exchanged a look with Alicia. "I'll get us there straightaway."

"I don't know what ter say," Elsie murmured, all optimism having been swept away.

"Let's hear what *they* have to say, more like," Alicia said, steeling herself to the task of confronting Matron again.

They were at the home within ten minutes, and once again before her daunting presence.

"I'm very sorry," she said, in a tone that expressed irritation rather than sorrow. "I did warn you what the result would be if he got out of bed again."

"P'raps 'e's gone visitin' some other inmate?" Elsie suggested.

"We've looked in every room in the place. If you mean our *'residents', they* haven't seen him," she retorted. "He must have left the premises. My first thought was he might have gone to you."

There is a moment in most people's lives which they recall as having been telepathic, or supernaturally inspired, lateral to their reason, or who knows how what Tim was visited by can be described. It wasn't a notion of what might have happened; it was not a question of surmising, it was that he knew precisiely what had happened. Yet, however sure one might be, one cannot avoid the possibility of the margin of error that prevents one from sharing it with others. He knew, but, like Casssandra in the Greek legend, could not tell. In a strange sense, he also felt that it was privy to him; that it was not meant to be shared. He could feel the distress in the ladyfolk, and the frustration in Matron, and a sense of fate lodged in his mind.

"Well," Matron said adamantly, "I've put you in the picture. It's in the hands of the authorities now. You'd best go back home and be ready to take a call from the police. I've recommended him to be taken into the hospital, so you might get a call from them, as well."

Tim drove the dejected ladies back to the house. As he arrived he had already made up z his mind what to do. He let the ladies out of the car and then, in as firm a voice as he could muster, that brooked no contradiction, said, "You go in. I'm going to drive round and call on the police myself,.. see what I can find out."

"Do you want me to come, too?" Alicia asked.

"You're better staying with Elsie."

Alicia saw Elsie needed her support. She was uncharacteristically quiet, a permanent frown sewn on her forehead and her lips puckered into a wrinkled 'o'. She nodded assent, and Tim left them to lean into each other in a way he could have no part in.

There was no surprise or dread as he entered the park; it felt predictable. The early evening held a stillness, and the mackerel clouds broke the sky up with their chains of thin grey pools. It was like opening a page in a picture book. Fred, dressed in his cap and old mackintosh was sitting on the bench opposite the fishless fishpond under the chestnut tree, whose leaves were just about to turn. No flowers were competing to enliven the railinged beds, but across the field, beyond the bench, faint cries of children could be heard playing out their frivolous game before the light faded.

Tim sauntered over to the bench and sat next to the old man. The vacuous silence bent an eager ear to hear that "aye-oop", full of challenge and cheerful disrespect. Tim looked sideways at his form, slumped slightly forward, his hands resting on his lap, as if dozing in front of the Dragon's Arms' hearth. It was surely the sleep of the blessed, but perhaps of exhaustion, too. What monumental effort had it required for Fred to reach the park from his sick bed? Tim bent forward to rest his elbows on his knees, and inclined his head on to his hands. He was sitting next to a stubborn old fellow born and bred to northern specifications, a simple man, who walked an uncompromising path as straight as an arrow; someone whose name would never resound in the world at large. Yet there was something epic in the moment, like the passing of a Viking. Tragedy is often defined as the destruction of greatness in the eyes of the world. For Tim it was not tragedy, nor pathos, just personal loss. He was aware of the pain that Elsie and Alicia would feel, far greater than his, naturally, but one which would unite them all. His first response was not sadness, but thankfulness; for being put to a test he had never begun to fully understand till now, for having had a door opened that had invited, and maybe forced, him into full manhood. Fred had always seemed to believe in him, and that was the greatest legacy he had left.

"So, this is the end of an era, we might say." Tim sighed.

"What do you mean by that?" asked Jesus.

"I mean,.." - Tim sought for words, impatiently, and came up with, "..an old warrior has passed away, leaving a vacuum.

"What do you mean by that?" said Jesus in the same voice.

"Heavens! I mean we'll miss him! He was a formidable force in my life!"

"Right. But what has passed away?"

"What?.. Why *he* has! His life has passed away!"

"I must disagree with you. He may have passed on. but he's with us all, and will help to define, not only what you do, but who you are."

There was a silence for some moments, while Tim assimilated the thought.

"Incidentally," said Jesus, "Are you still supposing I am a figment of your imagination?"

Tim sighed. "I can't muster the imagination to talk to a figment any more. You've got to be here to make sense of it."

"Can you tell me what clinched it for you?"

"Don't you know?"

"Of course I do. I still want you to tell me."

"I suppose it's a mixture of things. Watching this old man putting his faith into action,... having love brought on a plate by a wonderful woman, who draws me into her world,... loving her enough to want to share her faith in you... and maybe.., yes, maybe, most important, Fred's persistence."

"All these things have their part. But of course, none of it it ends here. You've been handed a baton. There are more doors to open, and you've got people to care about, now."

"Do you know...?" Tim began.

"Don't I always?"

"I'm sure Fred said his goodbyes to us all earlier."

"He managed to avoid all the embarrassing sentimentality."

"Yes," Tim reflected, "he would need to do that."

Tim looked at Fred and he saw in his hunched form an uncharacteristic surrender to death. Asking silent permission from him, he tilted his head back to rest on the bench top, facing up to the sky. Ah! That was so much more defiant, so much more confident of the dance he looked forward to. Tim remembered as clearly as yesterday, what he had asked for all those months ago, as he had sat next to his friend, Tom. The word had gone around and come around.

A small boy had ambled along and came abreast of Tim on his way home, and stood, holding a ball. With the cruel candour of innocent youth, he said, "By 'eck, mister, that fella don't look chirpy. Is 'e all right, then?"

"He's fine", Tim replied in a tired, casual way.

"Was 'e listenin', or is 'e asleep?"

"He's asleep."

"What was ye talkin' ter 'im fer?"

"I wasn't talking to him."

"Yes, ye was. I saw ye."

"It was talking to myself. Better cut along home, hadn't you?"

The boy, not entirely satisfied but recognising that he would learn no more, sloped off. Tim rose and with a last glance at the proud old man, walked down the path, out of the park to take the news to the police station.

Epilogue

A gentle breeze soughed through the leaves of the poplars standing sentinel over the cemetery. Tim, Alicia, with Elsie and her adopted lodgers stood over the grave as Fred's coffin was lowered into the ground. Behind them, stood twenty or more men, in various attempts at formally respectful dress, that Tim had never seen before. They nodded at Elsie, who nodded back almost imperceptibly, hiding her tear-stained cheeks behind her handkerchief. He had been taken aback by so many attending the short service in the chapel or remembrance, for neither Fred nor Elsie had referred to a wide circle of friends or acquaintances, nor any history that would give a clue as to their identity. Elsie knew them and the news of Fred's demise had obviously spread by word of mouth. They carried an air of gratitude that spoke clearly of Fred's involvement in their lives, but hardly resembled your average churchgoer. Tears were silent, and the faces of these men told stories of broken hardness and of hope reinstated. While Alicia leant on Tim's arm from time to time, Elsie was private in her grief and gently shook off his proffered arm, preferring to preserve northern stoicism. Alicia rested a hand on her shoulder from time to time, and she acknowledged this by tilting her head towards her. As Tim looked round under half-closed eyelids, the range of the assembled company's ages spoke of a substantial history. When 'dust to dust' was intoned, they fidgeted and some blew their noses loudly. Monty's sad smile expressed loss tempered by unquestioning faith in Fred's spiritual destination. Alf was seen by all to be quietly sobbing throughout the proceedings, and Bert kept nodding, as if everything depended on his good opinion.

Later, when many dedicated tales had been told over sandwiches and tea, (or light ale for several) in the local memorial hall, a long history of Fred's involvement in men's lives was revealed, which Tim gleaned as an important part of the insight required to put his own experience with Fred in some perspective.

For Tim, a new life began; one is tempted to say 'real life'.

Alf and Bert moved into Tim's old room. Bert took over the work engagements, being the one with persuasive skills, and Alf gladly conceded to the arrangement, since proceeds were equally shared. Elsie kept the 'home fires burning', but she soon lost much of her bounce and cocksure desire to interfere in people's lives, and needed constant news of Alicia and Tim's progress to reassure her of her participation in the world. They both agreed to have her come and live with them, but she would have none of it, saying she felt God's presence closer where Fred had always shared with her.

Tim and Alicia got married in the small church in Netherton, and exchanged vows in the sight of God and the small 'family' assembly, and Tim surrendered his belief to it, because, as Fred's echoing voice reminded him, he wanted to. He resigned from the firm and became a partner in Nathan's shop, where he was stimulated to explore how life, art and the written word are part of the same mystery. He was able to promote Alicia's work, not only in Blackbridge but in London's art world, the success of which belongs to another story. In all this, Tim was sustained by a woman's passionate love and absolutes that the old man had demonstrated throughout his richly woven, outrageous life.